DANGERS KISS

~

SARAH McKERRIGAN

FOREVER

NEW YORK   BOSTON

Copyright © 2008 by Glynnis Campbell
All rights reserved. Except as permitted under the U.S. Copyright Act of 1976, no part of this publication may be reproduced, distributed, or transmitted in any form or by any means, or stored in a database or retrieval system, without the prior written permission of the publisher.

Art direction by Claire Brown
Cover art by Craig White

Forever
Hachette Book Group USA
237 Park Avenue
New York, NY 10017
Visit our Web site at www.HachetteBookGroupUSA.com

Printed in the United States of America

Forever is an imprint of Grand Central Publishing. The Forever name and logo is a trademark of Hachette Book Group USA, Inc.

First Printing: May 2008

10 9 8 7 6 5 4 3 2 1

A WILL OF HER OWN

"Unhand me, sirrah!"

"You're not sleeping in my bed." He started for the door.

"But I was there first!"

"'Tis *my* bed."

"You weren't using it." She actually wedged her limbs in the doorway, trying to prevent his exit.

"Well I'm going to use it now."

"'Tisn't fair!"

He didn't feel like arguing the absurdity of a tiny lass expropriating his huge bed while he lay cramped on a small pallet by the fire.

"The only way you're sleeping in that bed," he whispered wickedly, "is if you're sharing it with me."

~

MAY   2008

ALSO BY SARAH McKERRIGAN

Lady Danger
Captive Heart
Knight's Prize

For my dear friend and fellow author
Lauren Royal—
For offering the best advice
And, when all else fails, her shoulder . . .
For sharing laptop plugs
and tangled plots and Piesporter . . .
And for always knowing exactly what to say.

Acknowledgments

My warmest appreciation for...
"America," Gail Adams, Debi Allen, Kathy Baker,
the Campbell clan—Brynna, Dylan, Richard, and Dick,
Carol Carter, Lucele Coutts, Sue Grimshaw for
letting me borrow her husband's name,
Lynette Gubler, Angelina Jolie, Karen Kay,
Melanie and Frances for their patience,
Adrian Paul, "Silvermane" for sharing his
sleight of hand, and Worf (RIP, little guy);
and my elite sales force—"Sarah's Champions":
Ana Isabel Arconada, Denise C. Asbury, Beth,
Jackie Bishop, Terra Codack, Mariah Kathleen
Crawford, Joelle Deveza, Diane Dunn, Donna Goldberg,
Marguerite Hembree, Carol Kemtes, Tori Longton,
Etta Miller, Lois J. Miller, Heather M. Riley,
Sandra M. Schaeffer, Betty Talken, Earl Talken,
Shirley Talken, Megan Thiele, Leslie Thompson,
Carolyn Todd, and Jodi Villanueva

You can become one of Sarah's "Champions" at
www.sarahmckerrigan.com

DANGER'S
KISS

Chapter 1

February
1250

THE BELLS OF CANTERBURY CATHEDRAL tolled unexpectedly in the distance, startling the traveler who trudged irritably toward the town. The dull ringing, muffled by the snow, still managed to breach the icy silence to deliver a message as chill as the wintry wood.

Desirée stopped in her tracks, squinting through the falling snowflakes. She'd wasted the last several hours, waiting in the harsh cold for a man who'd never arrived, and she was in no mood for surprises. Her skirts were soaked. Her feet were numb. And her mood was ugly.

Suddenly, the rhyme Hubert had recited six years ago, when he'd first taught Desirée the fine art of thievery, sprang to mind.

Bells on the Sabbath are an outlaw's curse,
Bells middle week fill a clever thief's purse.

'Twasn't the Sabbath. The bells could mean only one thing, then...a public execution. And where there was an execution, there was a crowd of distracted onlookers, easy prey for a nimble-fingered thief like Desirée.

Or, she reflected, for a sly old fox like her longtime mentor, Hubert Kabayn.

Desirée frowned. Had Hubert *known* there would be an execution today? Was that why the greedy sot had sent her away? So he could take all the spoils himself?

"Hubert Kabayn, you backstabbing son of a..." Her oath of fury fogged the frigid air like dragon's breath.

She picked up her wet skirts and slogged angrily forward, cursing the conniving old cheat with every step. There certainly was no honor among thieves. She would do well to remember that in future.

Hubert had deliberately ordered her away this morn, sending her on what she now realized was a fool's errand. He'd told her he needed her for an important task. Since he was locked up in the town gaol at the moment, the old thief wanted her to conduct a piece of business for him.

She was to meet a man at the ruined bridge south of town, a man who owed Hubert three shillings. With her accomplice in crime out of commission for the last sennight, coin had grown scarce, and Desirée had been only too eager to comply.

She kicked at the new-fallen snow. How could she have been so gullible?

She'd waited at that cursed bridge for hours. No one had come. And now she realized there'd never been a man at the bridge.

She should have known better. For weeks now, Hubert had been trying to get rid of her, pushing her away like an unwanted pup. He'd growled at her that she was losing her light-fingered touch, that at nineteen, she was too old to be of use to him anymore. He'd snarled at her to quit pestering him, to leave the thieving trade, to seek work as a lady's maid or mayhap trick a wealthy merchant into marrying her.

But this...this was the ultimate betrayal. Hubert had no doubt managed to slip the gaoler's bonds and was circulating among the crowd even now in one of his guises, cutting purses that he had no intention of sharing with her. Forsooth, 'twas likely his plan to give Desirée the slip ere she returned.

She ground her teeth. Hubert might have taught her all the tricks of his trade, but her tenacity was her own. The crafty old bastard wouldn't get rid of her that easily.

By the time she found her way to the town square, a sizable audience had already gathered, huddled against the bitter cold. But for once she wasn't tempted by the dangling purses and gaping pockets. Instead, she scanned the onlookers for signs of a figure making his stealthy way through the crowd. He might resemble a ragged beggar or a distinguished noble or even a withered old crone. But Desirée would recognize the artful trickster anywhere.

Forsooth, so engaged was she in seeking out the traitor, she paid no heed to the poor soul being led to the gallows.

By the time she spared him a glance, 'twas too late.

Across the crowded square, a damsel's scream pierced through the falling snow. "Nay!"

Nicholas flinched. Bloody hell. As the shire-reeve of Kent, 'twas his duty to preside over executions, but it had been so long since the last one, he'd forgotten that sound—the sound of desperate feminine grief. And now he was certain that even the several pints of ale he intended to quaff afterward wouldn't erase it from his memory.

He steadied the shivering old man he was walking to the gallows, who'd faltered at the unearthly wail.

Why did women have to scream at executions? God's bones, all men had to die, whether 'twas by battle or sickness or the hangman's hand. At least this way a condemned man's wife or mother or daughter could pay her respects and pray for his soul. And the lucky bastard wouldn't die alone.

Still, no matter how Nicholas tried to justify the man's execution in his mind, administering death never sat well with him, even when 'twas deserved. And in this instance, he wasn't sure *'twas* deserved. Still, the man had refused to fight the charges, not that it would have done much good. When 'twas a common thief's word against that of the wealthiest noblewoman in Canterbury...

"You son of a whore!" the maid cried over the murmuring crowd. "You'll rot in hell if you hang him!"

Nicholas ignored the threat, grumbling low to the victim, "She's only frightened. But you have no cause to be. Remember what I told you."

Hubert Kabayn, condemned murderer, nodded, taking strength from the reminder that Nicholas had assured him of a swift and painless end.

Death was never the difficult part for his victims. Nicholas saw to that. He used only the most efficient executioners, refusing to let men suffer on the gallows, no matter what the bloodthirsty crowd wished.

But this, the final walk through the village, was the real

torture. And 'twas caused by more than just the inevitable wench screaming in despair.

Something about the spectacle of an execution turned men ugly. Townsfolk who smiled and nodded and exchanged kind words with a fellow one day suddenly became sneering, jeering, heartless wolves the next when that fellow was bound for the gallows.

Nicholas glanced down at Kabayn's feet. They were bare, red from trudging through the bracing snow, but he knew the old man didn't feel the cold. His thin white nightshirt clung almost transparently to his spare frame, and his gray hair grew sodden with the falling snow, but the condemned man was past feeling.

"Let him go, you bastard!" the woman shrieked, her voice shrill above the self-righteous reprimands of law-abiding villagers and the vulgar shouts of craven lads who'd piss their braies were they in the old man's place.

Nicholas clenched his jaw. Did women not realize how cruel their pleas were on a condemned man's ears? How they inspired false hope? Why could they not instead call out softly like welcoming seraphim? Why could they not ease the unfortunate's way from this world?

'Twas what Nicholas always tried to do. He believed in justice, aye, but swift justice. Witness to too many slow stranglings from cruel hangmen, he'd devoted himself to learning the quickest, cleanest, least painful methods of delivering death, and he intervened when 'twas necessary. He saw himself as an angel of mercy, doling out one final gesture of kindness to otherwise God-cursed men.

He'd sat up with Kabayn all night, as was his custom with the men he was about to send to their death. He'd spoken a little, listened a lot, and helped the man come to terms with his inevitable fate.

He'd brought a full bottle of good Spanish wine laced with opium for the prisoner. In his experience, women and death were prettier companions when seen from the bottom of a bottle.

Kabayn had refused the wine. He wanted to face the hangman with a clear head, he'd said. He wondered if the old man regretted that now.

At the bottom of the gallows, Kabayn turned to him. His eyes were rheumy, evidence of the wasting sickness that had kept him coughing all night and would have killed him by spring, anyway. His voice was but a whistle, as faint as the wind through a cracked shutter. "You'll keep your promise?"

Nicholas nodded. He might have been despised by some as the cursed arm of the law, and feared by others as the right hand of the devil, but he was a man of his word.

The chaplain began murmuring the sacrament while the hooded hangman flexed his gloved hands in preparation, and Nicholas took a deep breath, turning to the crowd with a dramatic swirl of his black cloak, preparing for the spectacle. Angel of mercy he might be, but he dared not let the people of Canterbury know that. After all, he had an unyielding, iron-fisted reputation to uphold.

Desirée kicked and struggled and spat curses at the burly man-at-arms who restrained her at the back of the crowd.

This couldn't be happening. They couldn't be hanging Hubert Kabayn. He was far too clever for that.

Aye, he was as black with sin as Lucifer, and he could

be a mean son of a whore to her at times. But he'd always been able to wriggle his way out of the shackles of lawmen, even when he had to resort to sacrificing some of his hard-won silver to do so.

What was the old fool doing? Why wasn't he using that shrewd tongue of his to talk his way out of this? Why was he climbing the gallows ladder so complacently while the ruthless brute of a shire-reeve ordered his death?

'Twas absurd. No one bested Hubert Kabayn. She had to stop this farce at once.

"Leave him be!" she yelled at the shire-reeve. "You black-hearted spawn of the devil!"

The lawman gave no response.

"God-cursed demon!"

Her words fell on deaf ears.

"Murderer!" she cried. "You'll burn in—"

"Silence!" he roared.

The oath stuck in her throat as the lawman whipped his head about, even at this distance picking her out of the crowd with a glare of condemnation. Suddenly she felt as if she'd inhaled a lungful of snow.

He didn't speak. He didn't need to. His thoughts were in the dark menace of his gaze.

Or you'll be next.

Desirée didn't frighten easily. But she wasn't stupid. The shire-reeve was a man of power. And the way he was staring at her from the shadows of his hooded cloak, he seemed more demon than human, as if he might swoop over the crowd and snatch her up in his claws.

She swallowed back a lump of misgiving. 'Twould serve naught for her to be strung up beside her partner in crime.

Her eyes blurred with the cold, and she sniffed back the moisture collecting in her nose as the helplessness of her position became frustratingly clear.

Damn that brutish shire-reeve!

Hubert might be a varlet and a cheat, but he didn't deserve to die like this. He was a decent man. Mayhap not a *good* man. But at least no worse than most men.

To be completely forthright, there was no love lost between herself and the conniving bastard who'd bought her six years ago from her desperate, impoverished parents. Theirs had been a business alliance, no more. Young Desirée had served as a pretty distraction for his thievery, and in exchange, Hubert had seen she didn't go hungry.

He hadn't beaten her—not often, anyway. He'd never forced her to lie with strange men for coin, as some would have. And though he seemed determined to cast her aside of late, for six years, he'd seen she was provided for. 'Twasn't his fault if those provisions came from the only talents he possessed—sleight of hand and theft.

Aye, knave and outlaw he might be, but surely he didn't deserve hanging.

"Hubert Kabayn," the shire-reeve intoned for the benefit of the crowd, "you are charged with the crime of murder."

Desirée's jaw dropped.

Murder? Hubert wasn't a murderer. He'd gone to rob the lord's house, not take a life. The old cheat was about as capable of murder as he was of playing a fair game of dice. There must have been some mistake.

Curse his blighted hide! Why wasn't he fighting the charges? 'Twasn't as if he didn't know how to lie. God's eyes! The two of them had spent years doing just that, separating fools from their coin with false promises of health, prosperity, and a place in heaven. The slippery outlaw had wormed his way out of a hundred gaols.

But he wasn't worming his way out of this. 'Twasn't a game of Fast and Loose. There was no way to slip a hangman's knot.

The stupid old fool! He stood at the top of the ladder now, his spindly legs pale against the blackened wood. The shire-reeve read the sentence while the executioner bound Hubert's wrists behind him and looped the rope about his neck.

As he took up the slack in the noose, Desirée felt her own throat close around a final thin scream of disbelief. "Nay!"

As if he meant it for her ears alone, the shire-reeve turned to the crowd and proclaimed in somber tones, "No one comes between Nicholas Grimshaw and the law!"

The lawman nodded then to the executioner, giving him leave to twist the ladder. Desirée tore her gaze away and squeezed her eyes shut, unable to endure the grisly spectacle.

But though she could blind herself to the sight, there was no turning a deaf ear to the ominous squeaks of the rope as Hubert's body swung from the gallows timbers.

Desirée swayed in stunned silence, unable to move, unable to breathe, vaguely aware of the villagers yelling out around her, some in disappointment, some in morbid glee. When she finally dared to open her eyes, Hubert was already dead.

The shire-reeve, his jaw clenched, held up his hand to quiet the chaotic outcries of the crowd.

"Hear you well!" His voice cracked over the words,

as if he were equally shocked by the brutality of Hubert's death, as if he were somehow not responsible for it. Then he quickly regained his composure, biting out a dire threat. "Let this serve as a warning to you all. So die all murderers in my shire. Do not think you can outrun justice or outwit Nicholas Grimshaw. No man is above the law. And one of you," he said, scanning their faces from the depths of his hooded cloak, "may well be next."

Desirée, reeling with shock, watched as Hubert's lifeless body, no longer of interest to the crowd, swung back and forth from the blackened arm of the gallows. She felt her own bones go limp, and the man-at-arms, sensing she'd be no more trouble, released her. She sank down onto the snow, heedless of the cold.

For a long while she sat frozen, hypnotized by the sway of the rope, while snowflakes gathered on her lashes and dusted her cloaked shoulders.

She might have borne little affection for her partner in crime, who'd all but tossed her aside like garbage. Indeed, on her miserable journey here, she'd thought of a thousand ways to punish him for his betrayal. But never had she wished upon him so cruel an end.

Nicholas Grimshaw must have broken him. There was no other explanation. Hubert had been ill of late, and Grimshaw must have preyed upon his weakness, forcing him to confess to a crime he didn't commit.

What ominous threats the shire-reeve continued to issue to the crowd she didn't know, nor did she measure how long she sat there. But by the time she at last blinked away the film of shock, the square had grown quiet and most of the villagers had dispersed.

The demon in the black cloak remained by the gallows, however, as stark as a raven against the fall of snow, conferring with his constable, the executioner, and a few others. A stout troll of a man dressed in finery approached the others, dug in his purse, then dropped several silver coins into the shire-reeve's palm.

Blood money for hanging a helpless old man.

The sight made rage rise in her like ale stored too long in the keg. Casting about, she snatched up a sharp rock from the ground and, with a hoarse cry of pure fury, hurled it forward with all her might.

To her astonishment, it sailed true, striking the shire-reeve in the face. He staggered back, pressing his hand against his cheek, drawing back bloody fingers.

"Seize her!" the constable cried, drawing his sword.

But the shire-reeve took one look at her and stayed the constable's arm. "'Tis only a child. Leave her be. 'Tisn't the first stone I've caught. Won't be the last."

The constable reluctantly sheathed his sword, but Desirée was already beating a hasty retreat down the lane. She might have been reckless, but she was no fool. Nor was she a child.

Huddled behind the stone wall of a butchery shop, she peered down the long, narrow street. The snow was falling more heavily now, but she could still make out the silhouette of the black-cloaked man striding past the distant gallows, defiling the white landscape, like a crow waiting to feed on the spoils of his kill.

She would wait for him. She knew he was mortal now. He could bleed. She fingered the short dagger cached in her skirts. The blade was cold and sharp and merciless...just like revenge.

Chapter 2

GOD'S HOOKS! 'Tis colder than an old trot's teat," the constable complained.

Nicholas stomped the snow from his boots and nodded toward Hubert Kabayn's still-hanging body. "Go on," he bade the executioner, "cut him down. He's not getting any deader." The sooner he got this business over with, the sooner he could see to the nasty gash on his cheek and the sooner he could drink himself into oblivion by a warm fire. Anything to erase the dreadful image of Kabayn's death.

"The law's the law," said the squat, pig-eyed steward of Torteval, who stood between them, jabbing a scolding finger at the air in front of the constable's nose. "A full hour."

Nicholas ground his teeth. Abiding by the law was one thing. Following it to absurd limits was another.

"You owe it to Lady Philomena," the steward insisted. Then, as if Nicholas were both blind and deaf, the man jerked his thumb toward him and confided in a loud whisper to the constable, "He cheated her."

Nicholas frowned down at the steward, who was small enough to squash with his thumb. "Cheated her? How?"

Like a spooked squirrel, the man trembled at being directly addressed by the shire-reeve. Then he licked his lips and blurted out, "The outlaw didn't suffer in the least."

"The man's dead," Nicholas said.

"But Lady Philomena specifically requested—"

"I don't give a bloody damn what..." Nicholas bit his tongue. He knew better than to get into an argument of ethics with the steward from the richest holding of Canterbury, the household that paid the bulk of his wage.

Emboldened by Nicholas's silence, Lady Philomena's man smirked at the constable. "How do you expect to thwart outlaws if the bloody wretches don't suffer?" He brushed the snow from his shoulder. "Soon there'll be murdering miscreants crawling all over Torteval Hall." He shuddered. "My lady will be displeased, *very* displeased."

As far as Nicholas was concerned, Lady Philomena could kiss his arse. He wasn't her damned servant, for God's sake. He was a servant of the law. The woman hadn't bothered to show up for the hanging, anyway. And as for this mincing Torteval steward...

The constable diplomatically interrupted before Nicholas could finish his silent threat. "Well, the rest of the crowd was most impressed," he told the steward. "One need only whisper 'Nicholas Grimshaw' now to keep the outlaws of Canterbury quiet for weeks."

'Twas what Nicholas hoped. He was far more interested in preventing crime than punishing it.

Apparently, Lady Philomena's man did not agree. He narrowed his beady eyes in anger and, with a flip of his cloak that scattered snowflakes everywhere, stalked off. "An hour, Grimshaw!" he called over his shoulder.

Nicholas cursed under his breath, then glanced at the executioner, who waited for his orders, his beefy arms crossed over his barrel chest. From his earnings, he counted out the five shillings the man was owed. "Go get yourself a pint. I'll put him in the ground."

As the executioner gratefully retired to the nearest inn, the constable, shivering with the cold, tucked his hands beneath his arms, glancing around the nearly empty square. "No kin?"

"He said he had a young granddaughter."

"Living in Canterbury?"

Nicholas shook his head. "They were passing through."

The constable winced. "Not pilgrims, I hope?"

"Nay. The old man wasn't looking for absolution. He was a seasoned outlaw."

The constable nodded, then began pacing back and forth before the gallows, clapping his arms and rubbing his hands together for warmth, glancing up occasionally at Kabayn's body. "Why do you suppose he—?"

"I don't know." 'Twasn't exactly true. He could guess why Kabayn had leaped from the ladder before the executioner had a chance to force him off. He'd spoken to the outlaw long enough to learn that, feeble as he was, Kabayn was a man accustomed to making his own rules and steering his own fate. 'Twas one final act of defiance for him to cheat the hangman.

Not that it mattered that he'd added suicide to his list

of crimes. Kabayn's soul was already cursed by the sin of murder. Nicholas would have to bury his body in unhallowed ground.

"An hour indeed," the constable muttered. "'Tis a stupid law. The man's neck is obviously broken."

Nicholas agreed. The law had been made for victims of simple strangulation, to ensure they were truly dead. He sniffed. "The law says at *least* an hour."

"Aye?"

"If there's no kin to know one way or the other, we'll leave him for the night. No one will steal the body. Not even a carrion crow would brave this cold. I'll cut him down in the morn ere anyone's up and about."

Bidding the thankful constable good afternoon and casting one last glance toward the silent, snow-dusted corpse, Nicholas shouldered his satchel and trudged down the lane toward his lodgings, trembling less from cold than from fatigue.

At the moment, he desperately needed a belly full of ale and a good night's sleep. Early on the morrow, he'd bury Hubert Kabayn and seek out the man's grandchild so he could honor the fellow's last request. It had been a long two days, and dispensing death always weighed heavily on his soul.

Desirée's breath made plumes in the air as she crept on kitten-soft feet through the shallow snow, her footprints dwarfed by the giant who trod the path several score yards before her. He was but a shadow in the distance, disappearing around corners and down winding lanes. But few other souls braved the snow-covered streets of Canterbury now, so she had no trouble following his tracks.

He naturally didn't live in the village proper. Merchants of death like Nicholas Grimshaw lodged outside of town, away from decent folk, in order to thwart the kind of vengeance she was about to take.

Desirée shivered, as much from apprehension as from the cold. She'd never killed anyone before. She wasn't even sure she could do it, despite the icy rage filling her veins. But she knew she'd never find peace until she avenged Hubert's death.

Hubert wouldn't be pleased. A good cheat would never succumb to passion, particularly anger. A good cheat kept a level head, wore a guileless smile, and evened the score in more subtle ways, usually by lightening a man's purse right under his nose.

Perchance Hubert was right. Perchance Desirée wasn't a good cheat, after all. Perchance she should retire from her life of crime.

And perchance she would…right after she paid the ruthless shire-reeve back for his cruelty.

The man wasn't as cautious as he should have been. The stupid fool had no idea someone was following him. He didn't even bother to glance behind him when he arrived home, swinging open the wooden gate in the high stone wall surrounding his demesne at the edge of the forest.

Nonetheless, Desirée waited outside until snowflakes an inch thick covered the top of her boots, giving him time to settle in and drop his guard. Then she lifted the latch and slowly pushed the gate inward.

She expected to find a lair befitting a malevolent savage behind the wall. Perchance a cave dripping with bats. Or a squat, squalid hovel with yellow smoke boiling from the chimney. Or a jagged fortress carved out of gleaming black jet.

What she discovered instead was an ordinary modest house of wattle and daub with a thatched roof. Pale gray smoke drifted up from the chimney through the falling flakes of snow. A pair of bare-limbed fruit trees stood sentinel over the cottage. In the yard were furrowed rows where a summer garden had once grown, and a gruesome vision flashed through her mind of the shire-reeve harvesting cabbages with a great beheading axe.

With an apprehensive gulp, she stole forward along the cobbled path, grateful that his shutters were closed. Upon his doorstep, she drew the dagger, then with painstaking caution forced the door open a crack.

The fire on the hearth cast a golden glow over the interior of the cottage, in stark contrast to the wintry white of the outside world. The pitch pop of burning wood made cheery music in the room, and shadows danced merrily upon the plaster walls.

Desirée hesitated, biting her cheek in indecision. 'Twasn't how she'd envisioned the den of a lawman. This was no dank, dark dungeon. The walls weren't stained with the blood of unfortunates. And the evil Nicholas Grimshaw wasn't stirring a cauldron of boiling oil over the fire.

A long, soft snore issued from the cottage, and Desirée pressed the door open another inch. From here, she could see only the man's long legs stretched out toward the fire and his dangling left arm, the fingers of which loosely gripped an empty clay flagon.

She smiled grimly. The fool was fast asleep.

He snored again, a low rumbling sound, and she pushed the door wide enough to slip her head through the gap.

He half reclined on a bench, pushed up against the interior wall. He'd removed his boots, and his wet, stockinged feet, propped on a three-legged stool, steamed from the heat of the fire. His cloak lay crumpled atop a nearby table, beside a keg of ale, where he'd likely filled his flagon. And his sheathed sword was propped in the corner, a good four paces from where he dozed.

The knife felt heavy in her hand. She wasn't sure she could slay a man in cold blood. But under the circumstances, it certainly seemed an easy task. All she need do was steal up beside him and slit his throat.

No one would suspect charming Desirée of the crime.

Hubert Kabayn would have his vengeance.

And there was likely not a soul who would mourn the death of this beast of a man.

She opened the door wide enough to step through, closing it softly behind her as she dropped her satchel by the entrance and scanned the interior. Naturally, she'd take a few things with her when she left. The sword was likely valuable. And the boots, if she could find anyone with feet that large. He might possess jewelry, plunder confiscated from his victims, or treasures he'd accepted as bribes. And she knew he had coin in his purse, the day's wages.

She crept forward, belatedly wondering if such a man might keep a great mastiff in his home to ward off trespassers. But as she edged closer to the bench, she heard no stirring, only the even sawing of the shire-reeve's breath.

At her next step, the fire gave a sudden loud pop, and the man snorted, dropping his cup. Desirée froze, her heart pounding, as he shifted on the bench and his head lolled toward her. She tightened her grip on the knife, ready to defend herself. He grunted once but thankfully remained asleep.

Now that he faced her, she could see the monster that the hood of the black cloak had concealed, and the closer she drew to him, the more her fingers faltered on the dagger.

He wasn't the slope-headed, heavy-browed, pox-scarred mongrel she'd imagined. And he was much younger than she'd thought, probably not yet thirty years of age. His swarthy cheeks were lean and sturdily boned, his nose slightly aquiline, his mouth generous.

Dark hair fell in unruly locks across his brow and along his neck, and his wide jaw was in need of a shave. A thin white scar ran along his chin, a second marked his forehead, and the fresh cut she'd given him high on his cheekbone was surrounded now by a blackening bruise. But naught could mar the undeniable rugged handsomeness of his face.

She wondered absently if his eyes were as black as they'd seemed in the village square.

From the corner of her vision, Desirée saw something white suddenly streak past the hearth. Startled, she sucked in a loud breath. Too late she realized 'twas only a cat.

Nicholas didn't know what woke him. He'd thought he was in a dead sleep. But what he glimpsed, peering beneath his drowsy lids, made his eyes widen at once.

A maid stood over him with a dagger. Granted, she was distracted at the moment, glaring at the hearth. But there was no mistaking her intent.

Before she could act on that intent, he lifted up his sleep-dead left arm and seized her wrist.

She shrieked in surprise.

He clapped his right hand over the narrow guard of the dagger, intending to pry the weapon loose. But the wily wench twisted in his grip and withdrew the blade, slicing the webbing betwixt his thumb and finger.

He hissed in pain, making a second grab for her with his left hand, catching the folds of her skirt.

She tugged away, and when she couldn't tug loose, she slashed downward with the dagger. He pulled his hand back in time to avoid another slash, and she made a gash in her skirt instead.

Fully awake now, he vaulted to his feet.

She should have fled in fear. He was twice her size. One backward sweep of his arm could knock the scrawny wench unconscious against the wall. But she only stared at him, her gaze as wild and piercing as that of a mother swan protecting her brood from a wolf.

He narrowed his eyes in sudden recognition. "You!" His fingers went involuntarily to the wound she'd inflicted upon him earlier.

To his astonishment, one corner of her lip curled up smugly.

His hand stung like the devil, and blood was dripping down his palm, but he still had one good hand. 'Twas all he required to subdue the spindly damsel.

He seized her by the throat, his fingers wrapping easily around her tiny neck, and picked her up.

Like an indignant kitten, she hissed and squirmed and tried to stab at him. But with his injured hand, he caught her wrist and applied pressure till she dropped the weapon. Then he kicked it, sending the dagger skittering halfway across the room.

She scrabbled furiously at his arm. He wasn't strangling her, not yet, but one squeeze of his fingers would be all it took. Fortunately for the wench, unlike *her,* he wasn't a cold-blooded murderer.

But she didn't need to know that.

"I could snap your neck like kindling, child," he growled.

"You don't scare me!" she choked out with remarkable bravado. "And I'm no child!"

He blinked. 'Twas true. He could see now she was endowed with the ripe curves of a woman full-grown. But what was wrong with the maid? Was she diseased in the head? No one challenged Nicholas Grimshaw. People fled from him in terror. She should have been begging for his mercy, not inciting him with taunts. After all, she was little more than a mouse in his deadly talons.

Nicholas took a moment to study the curious wench. She had lovely features, despite the grimaces and vile oaths distorting them. One would never guess so much bloodlust lurked behind that pretty face. Her brows came together like dark slashes over fiery green eyes with impossibly long lashes. Her chestnut-colored hair, now loosened from its thick braid, hung in strands over beautifully sculpted cheekbones and a stubbornly jutting jaw. Her lips were full and supple and expressive. Indeed, for one brief moment he found himself idly wondering what such lips would taste like pressed against his...

Until the barbarous wench kicked him hard between the legs.

A shock of blinding pain made him sink reflexively to

the floor. Sheer determination alone allowed him to keep a grip on the wicked woman's throat.

He gasped, unable to speak as the dull ache spread inexorably through his loins. Meanwhile, the merciless shrew fought him tooth and nail, shrieking, snarling, pounding and scratching at his arm. But the pain of her attack was naught compared to the misery afflicting his ballocks.

Finally able to talk, he bit out a weak threat. "You'll regret that, wench."

Incredibly, she spat back, "Not if it keeps you from spawning."

Somehow he summoned the strength to stand again. Still holding her by the throat, he looped his free arm around her waist and hefted her sideways, settling her onto his hip, where she could do minimal damage. But he knew she wouldn't be harmless for long. The little imp was as slippery and full of squirm as an eel out of water.

"Let me go, you arse-wisp! Bastard! Unhand me!"

Somewhere he had a pair of iron shackles. Mayhap if he secured her somewhere, he could scare some sense into her. Then he'd release her, she'd run off, properly frightened, and he could nurse his hurts and go back to dozing by the fire.

Desirée screamed in wordless rage. Her voice was hoarse, partly because she was being throttled and partly because she'd worn it out, cursing the shire-reeve with every oath she knew.

He was a fool for not killing her with his bare hands while he had the chance, for now she didn't dare leave his house until his blood drenched the floor and he was staring up at the rafters with glassy, dead eyes.

"Be still, wench!"

He clamped her against his side, so tightly she could scarcely draw breath. She fought him, to little avail, twisting against ribs that were as unyielding as iron bars, scratching ineffectual furrows down his arms with her bitten nails.

With an exasperated growl, he lurched forward, and she struggled even more fiercely as he headed through the passage into the next chamber.

When she glimpsed the huge pallet shoved against one wall, her heart congealed into a lump of ice. God's blood! Did he mean to...

She heard him take something down from the wall, but she was too preoccupied with the implications of the bed to notice anything else.

"Nay!" she shrieked at him, bucking wildly back and forth in an attempt to loosen his grip on her as they neared the pallet.

Suddenly she was flung forcefully down onto the big bed, and before she could scramble away, his knee came down beside her, blocking her way. She would have rolled in the opposite direction, but he snatched her wrist and, ere she could pull free, clamped a shackle around it.

Bloody hell! She was in trouble now.

With her free fist, she struck at him again and again, bruising her knuckles on his hard skull, swishing through air, connecting solidly once with his jaw.

"God's eyes, wench!" He raised his arm to block another punch, meanwhile securing the adjoining shackle to the base of the bed's support.

Panic streaked through Desirée's brain, but she didn't dare succumb to it. There was still a chance she could knock the man out with a well-placed kick.

She twisted, thrashing her feet until they were free of her cloak and heavy wool skirts, then propelled them with the force of a fulling hammer into the man's belly.

To her satisfaction, he let out an "oof" and staggered backward, crashing hard into the wall. For one brief moment, her heart fluttered with hope.

But the cursed giant somehow managed to hold on to his wits and his footing.

Not so his temper. His eyes closed down to angry slits. His nostrils flared. His jaw clenched. He growled. His broad shoulders seemed to expand as he closed his massive hands into menacing fists.

But 'twas not his threatening countenance that widened Desirée's eyes and sent her heart plummeting to the bottom of her stomach.

Behind him, rattling from hooks on the wall, was a vast array of sinister iron implements—pincers, knives, thumbscrews, shackles, flails, brands, saws, shears—whose purposes were too gruesome and grisly to imagine.

She tried to scream, but fear had sucked all the spit from her mouth. Only a thin wisp of sound came out.

꒰

Chapter 3

NICHOLAS WAS HARDLY IN A MOOD to allay the woman's fears. The cursed wench had sliced his cheek, slashed his hand, bruised his ballocks, and ruthlessly kicked him in the gut. He was exhausted and half-drunk, and something sharp was sticking him in the back.

Suddenly, the wench blurted out, "The house is surrounded."

He blinked. "What?"

"The house. It's surrounded." Her eyes glittered. "Did you think I'd come alone?"

He frowned. Surely she was bluffing. She'd seemed alone enough in the village square. If she'd had allies, they hadn't bothered to defend her.

"If I'm not outside in a quarter hour," she assured him, "a half-dozen men will break down the door."

Nicholas studied her face. Years of interrogating prisoners had taught him to spot a lie almost instantly. There were telltale signs—licking the lips, avoiding the eyes, stammering, blinking. The woman exhibited none of those signs. She was staring at him with a gaze as steady as a rock.

God's blood! Was it possible? Could she be telling the truth? Had she brought others with her?

"Go on," she urged. "See for yourself."

His captive was secure enough. He pushed away from the wall and ducked through the doorway. Jesu, he was in no shape to deal with an irate mob. The last time, he'd come away with two broken ribs.

Azrael brushed past his leg, and he scooped the cat up, not wanting him to dart out the door if there were angry men outside.

Slowly, he opened the door a crack, peering out into the yard. The snow had stopped, and the world seemed as still as death. No one appeared to be awaiting the woman's screams.

He cautiously opened the door wider. The only breaks in the white landscape were the gray stones of the wall surrounding his demesne and the black underbones of the snow-laden tree branches.

More confident now, he stepped outside, stroking Azrael's bristled fur as he scanned his property.

The wench was lying. No one lay in wait. Or if they did, they'd long ago frozen over and been covered by snow.

"Come on, Azrael," he whispered, suddenly feeling the cold of the ground beneath his bootless feet. "Mayhap we'll find a scold's bridle to curb the little liar's tongue."

The cat jumped from his arms the moment he reentered the cottage, trotting over to the hearth, obviously wanting no part of whatever dire punishment his master intended.

Nicholas closed the door behind him, calling out to the woman. "It appears your friends have gone a—"

Coming through the doorway, he saw the lass draped halfway off the bed, frantically scrabbling at the shackle lock with her cloak pin.

"What the devil...?" He strode toward her.

She glanced up, gave a little squeak of fright, then resumed wiggling the pin back and forth. The little whelp was trying to pick the lock. Nay, he decided, she *was* picking the lock.

With a metallic click, the shackle sprang open. If he hadn't dived forward, snapping it shut again, she would have freed herself. As 'twas, he earned himself a stab of the cloak pin in his shoulder.

With a yowl of pain worthy of Azrael, he knocked the pin from her grasp and dodged back out of range in case she had any more weapons on her person.

The woman screamed in thwarted fury, rattling the shackles as if she might break them open by pure force of will.

Who was this she-devil?

Hubert Kabayn had claimed to know no one in Canterbury, so Nicholas had assumed the woman shrieking in the square was simply one of those females who couldn't abide bloodshed of any kind.

His bleeding shoulder proved otherwise.

But if she didn't know the victim, and she wasn't averse to blood...

"Who are you?"

She whipped her head around, spitting a strand of

hair from her mouth. "I'm not your whore! That's for certain!"

Sex was the last thing on Nicholas's mind. His ballocks still ached from the kick she'd given him. The woman might be as beautiful as an angel, but she clearly had the devil's temperament. He preferred his lovers gentle. And willing.

"Nor do I intend to be your prisoner for long!" she added, straining at the shackle until her fingers blanched white. "You may have held Hubert, but you'll not hold me!"

He frowned. "Hubert? How do you know Hubert?"

She didn't reply, only struggled all the harder with the shackles.

A sudden and unpleasant possibility occurred to him then, a possibility that sent a frisson of terror up his spine as he slid slowly down the wall onto his hindquarters.

"You aren't...his granddaughter, are you?"

The woman froze midstruggle, confirming his suspicions.

His breath escaped him in a thin, long-suffering sigh. "Shite." He wasn't going to get any more sleep this day, he could see. He rested an elbow on his upraised knee and rubbed hard at the spot between his brows that was beginning to ache. "I thought you'd be...The way the old man talked...I expected a child." He perused her from head to toe from beneath his hand.

She was no child. Hubert Kabayn had omitted the fact that his granddaughter, whom he'd portrayed as a helpless, homeless waif who'd be without a friend in the world after he was dead, was indeed a full-grown wench with a definite will of her own.

Nicholas shook his head. He should have known better than to trust the word of a felon. "Ballocks!"

He'd made Hubert a promise. He was honor-bound to keep it, no matter how it grated on him to do a good deed, not for an innocent child, but for a foul-tongued lass who was obviously poured from the same mold as her outlaw grandfather.

"Let me go, you pox-riddled son of a whoremonger!"

He stared at her, wondering what to do.

"Teat-sucking spawn of the devil!" she spat.

Now that he knew who she was, he couldn't very well toss her out in the snow.

"You hound-swiving," she said, banging the shackle on the bedpost, "nun-beating, shite-eating scourge of the earth!"

He raised his brows. He thought he'd heard every curse known to man. Because of his despised profession, which included collecting taxes, he was constantly barraged by vile oaths. Apparently, there was no sport more gratifying than swearing at a lawman.

For the most part, such words rolled off his back like water off a swan. But this maid showered him with oaths he'd never even thought of, much less heard from the sweet mouth of a woman. Her foolish grandfather must have spared the rod with the child, for she swore like a fishwife.

At last, catching her breath, she snapped, "What are you staring at, murderer? What's churning in that diseased brain of yours?"

"I'm wondering when you're going to run out of curses."

She jerked hard on the shackle, and he saw a bloody

scrape where the iron met her wrist. "As soon as you let me go, you overgrown minion of Lucifer!"

He sighed and came to his feet. The wench was obviously not going to listen to reason anytime soon. She was scared, like a wolf caught in a trap, willing to bite off her paw to gain her freedom.

He couldn't give her that freedom yet. If he let her go and something happened to her—if she was attacked by miscreants, or she froze to death, or grief caught up with her and she tried to kill herself—'twould be on his head. Whether she liked it or not, her grandfather had made Nicholas responsible for her.

The damsel probably had no place to stay for the night, anyway. He'd be doing her a favor by letting her take shelter in his home.

"If you don't let me go," she bit out, "I swear I'll break off this bedpost and shove it so far up your—"

"Cease!"

He had no intention of using a scold's bridle on her— the horrible spiked thing had hung unused on his wall for as long as he could remember—but that didn't mean he wouldn't take other measures to ensure himself a peaceful night's sleep.

He delved into the chest at the foot of his bed and drew out a scrap of linen for a gag. 'Twould serve two purposes. Her cries would be muffled, and he could rest assured she wouldn't be chewing off her paw in the middle of the night.

The moment Desirée saw the gag, she prepared to fight. The secret to overcoming formidable foes, she'd learned from Hubert, was unrelenting aggression.

It worked for cats. She'd once seen a kitten fend off a pack of dogs with naught more than fierce hisses and threatening swipes of its paws.

And it had always worked for Desirée. Men who mistook her for a frail flower, theirs for the plucking, were treated to a spate of flying fists and loud curses that would curdle cream. They couldn't flee fast enough.

But this damned shire-reeve, unmoved and undaunted, came for her as if she *were* but a kitten, a troublesome creature to be subdued.

Even with one hand shackled, she might have been able to fight him off. But the brute sat on her. While she was gasping from the indignity and sheer weight of his bulk atop her writhing legs, he managed to shove the wad of linen into her mouth. Not even pounding his back with her free hand could prevent him from tying the gag around her head. Then he grabbed that wrist, too, completely immobilizing her.

Incensed, she tried to scream, but the cloth muffled the sound to a pathetic whimper. He nodded in satisfaction, infuriating her more.

She might not be able to curse him, but there was more than one way to get her message across. Summoning up all the pain and rage and frustration she felt, she skewered him with a smoldering glare full of hatred.

It had little effect, but then, she supposed a lawman was accustomed to glares of hatred.

Her legs began to tingle from lack of blood, but he only continued to sit there, staring at her as if she were some curious sort of beetle he'd never seen before.

Every instinct told her to look away. But she'd survived on the streets by temerity, not timidity. If there was any hope of enduring this ordeal, 'twould be by fearlessness. So she met him, stare for stare, and tried to think of something, *anything* other than the rack of gruesome instruments on the wall.

Green. The knave's eyes were green. She tried to convince herself they were the color of pond slime and frog warts and snake scales. But in fact, the hue reminded her of fresh summer meadows.

His mouth she expected to be cruel, but there was a surprising softness to it that ill befit a man accustomed to violence. His brows were dark and expressive, and his nose was unbroken, a miracle considering the scars of past injuries to his face. His unruly black hair looked as if he seldom bothered to cut or tend to it. Why, she didn't know. He certainly owned enough sharp blades to do the task.

She gulped against her will. From the edge of her vision, she could still make out the grisly silhouettes of his tools.

"Go to sleep," he said wearily, releasing her wrist and easing off of her legs. "There's a chamberpot beside the bed. We'll talk on the morrow."

As the blood flowed back into her legs, relief coursed through her veins. He didn't intend to torture her, then. At least not this eve.

But she'd seen the vicious way he'd killed Hubert. He was capable of great violence. She dared not forget that.

She watched him walk away, his hand dripping blood where she'd sliced it, his linen shirt askew from the struggle, flecked with crimson at the shoulder where she'd stabbed him with the pin. When he reached the doorway, he hesitated but didn't turn around.

"He didn't suffer long," he muttered. "You should know that. The hangman showed him mercy."

Then he left.

Alone in the dim chamber, Desirée felt tears prickling at the corners of her eyes. She silently cursed them. Damn it all! She wasn't going to cry. Crying was for the weak-hearted. Tears were something Desirée only feigned to loosen men's purses so Hubert could pick them. Hubert would have given her a tongue-lashing for weeping over him.

Was it true, what the lawman said? Had Hubert been shown mercy? She'd never witnessed such a horrible spectacle. Still, she had to admit the old thief's suffering *had* been brief.

She glanced at the wall. Surely the lawman was lying. How could someone who owned such a gruesome array of torturous devices feel a shred of mercy? What would someone capable of inflicting pain without batting an eye know of suffering?

With that whole armory of malicious instruments looming over her, waiting to taste her flesh, and a brute willing to use them only a chamber away, she thought she'd never get to sleep. But she'd had an exhausting day.

She'd sold everything she owned to pay for Hubert's upkeep in gaol, starving herself so he might eat. All morn she'd waited in the freezing snow for a man Hubert had invented, only to discover he'd betrayed her. Between the trauma of watching her old mentor hang from the gallows and her fevered battle with a lawman as strong as an ox, she was overwhelmed with fatigue. Before she'd taken a dozen breaths, the heavy fog of slumber fell over her eyes.

*   *   *

Nicholas woke early, not because he was eager to rise, but because there was a cat licking his chin. He brushed the beast aside, groaning as his backbone popped. Lord, he felt like he'd slept on the rack. A man his size shouldn't have to spend the night perched on a bench. Especially when there was a mite of a wench taking up his whole bed.

He stretched, wincing as his joints complained, then snorted, raked the hair back from his face, and hauled himself to his feet. 'Twas yet dim, perchance not even dawn, but he had one more task to do this morn before he was finished with Hubert Kabayn.

In the kitchen, he poured water into a basin and washed his face, taking care with the gash on his cheek and the tender slice between his thumb and forefinger. Then he carved a hunk off the bacon hanging on the wall, giving Azrael several generous bites. He took down a pair of mismatched wooden flagons and poured ale into them. The maid in his bed would likely have a fierce thirst after her scathing tirade of last eve.

He paused at the doorway to the chamber and peered in. The damsel appeared to be deep in slumber. He crept in quietly, then stood over her, perusing her as she slept.

The woman was absolutely stunning when her features weren't contorted with rage and hatred. Her brows were finely arched, her lashes long and luxurious. Her skin was luminous, even in the dim light, and her hair sprawled across the bed in dark, gentle waves.

Forsooth, with her prominent cheekbones and angular jaw, she looked a bit underfed. But then, her grandfather had been little more than a sack of bones himself. Doubtless their life of traveling from village to village, scraping by on petty thievery, kept them living hand to mouth.

Her fingers were curled under her chin, and he could see the nails were bitten down to the quick. 'Twas fortunate, since she'd run those nails down his arms several times yesterday.

But her most intriguing feature was her mouth. He wished he hadn't needed to gag her, for it seemed a crime to desecrate those sweet lips. For a woman who could spit out curses with all the fury of a heretic spouting proverbs, her mouth was deceptively soft and full, like a ripe peach ready for the tasting. Indeed, if he wasn't sure she'd bite him, 'twould have been tempting to wake her with a kiss.

'Twas an absurd idea, of course. No one kissed the shire-reeve of Kent. He was despised and feared. The only women who offered Nicholas their affections were lawbreakers trying to entice him into leniency, and he refused their bribes.

The lass's temper might have cooled, but she'd still hate him. After all, he'd ordered her grandfather to the gallows. And no matter what heinous crimes a fellow committed, his kin never believed he deserved death.

In this instance, he couldn't be sure the man *did* deserve death. Kabayn seemed to Nicholas more of a fox than a wolf, a conniving cheat, mayhap, but not a ruthless killer. Nicholas had given the old man every opportunity to fight the charges, slim though his chances were against the powerful Lady of Torteval. In the end, Kabayn admitted he'd probably earned a dozen hangings in his life, anyway, and he'd sooner face a quick death upon the gallows than the wasting sickness that currently afflicted him.

Nicholas supposed 'twas useless to let the matter trouble him. After all, the outlaw was gone now, and in a way, his death had been a mercy.

He crouched beside the pallet with the cups of ale and frowned, suddenly realizing he didn't know the wench's name. Kabayn had never mentioned it.

· "My lady," he called softly. "My lady." There was no response. He leaned in closer. "My—"

Her fist flew out so quickly, he almost didn't dodge it in time. She narrowly missed his chin, but her forearm caught the cups, knocking them sideways and spilling ale all over the floor.

"Bloody hell, wench!"

The damsel hadn't been asleep at all. She'd been lying in wait. A good night's rest apparently hadn't tempered her mood in the least.

He scowled. "Two pints of good ale gone to waste!"

Not completely to waste. Azrael was already sauntering through the doorway, eyeing the frothy brew. He had a taste for ale that rivaled his master's.

Nicholas blew out a disgusted breath. "So you're not ready to make peace," he said flatly. "Fine."

He slammed the empty cups down on the table, then snatched up his cloak.

"I'd hoped a good night's rest would make you more malleable," he muttered, whirling the cloak about his shoulders.

By the mutinous smoldering of her gaze, the woman was going to make him drag her, kicking and screaming, to the town square. Nay, he amended, not screaming. He had no intention of removing the gag now. At this early hour, if he hauled a shrieking shrew through the streets, he'd incur the wrath of all of Canterbury.

He opened the low chest beside the wall and pulled out a coil of rope. He'd need to bind her tightly if he wanted to avoid a new barrage of blows.

The task proved harder than holding on to a mud-slick piglet, but he managed, by sitting on her and gathering her knees beneath one arm, to tie her kirtle about her ankles. Then he unlocked the shackle from the bedpost and locked it again around her other wrist, cuffing her hands behind her.

All the while she thrashed and tossed her head until her hair was a tangled mess and the ties of her kirtle came undone. Even when he rolled her onto her belly to lace them again, she fought him, until he had to plant a knee in her back to get her to hold still.

"God's bones, wench! Do you *want* to walk naked through the streets of Canterbury, then?"

~~

Chapter 4

DESIRÉE WENT STILL. The streets of Canterbury? Where were they going?

His knee was crushing her spine, but his fingers were oddly gentle upon the back of her neck as he secured the ties. Still, it took all her resolve not to fight against him.

Lord, but she was thirsty. She regretted spilling that ale. The wad of linen had sapped all the moisture from her mouth. She couldn't have screamed if she wanted to.

He gave the laces one final tug, but no sooner did the weight of his knee lighten upon her than she was scooped up off the bed. The oaf slung her over his shoulder like a sack of barley.

"Fight me and you'll only hurt yourself. 'Tis a great distance to fall," he said, his hand clasping her thigh with far too much familiarity. "We've got a long walk. Don't make it seem longer."

Every instinct told her to fight her way free. But he was right. With her arms shackled behind her and her feet bound, even if she managed to extricate herself from his grip, she wouldn't get far, and she'd only succeed in injuring herself.

Lord, 'twas humiliating. Bent over his shoulder with her backside close enough for him to bite, she was treated to an unwelcome view of the man's buttocks. She wasn't sure whether 'twas dangling upside down from his shoulder or sheer mortification that sent the blood rushing to her cheeks.

He opened the door, and her nose quivered with the first breath of sharp, frosty air. Perchance 'twas a blessing she didn't have to walk, after all. Better the knave should have to soak *his* feet, tramping through the snow.

The squeak of his boots and the flap of his cloak were the only sounds as he moved with long strides down the empty lane. Not a soul roamed the streets to offer her aid. Not that any would. One had to be a fool to tangle with a man of the law. A fool or a wench bent on vengeance.

Where was he taking her? No shops were open at this hour. The bakers were only beginning to fire their ovens. The inns were shuttered tight. Even the patrons of the town harlots hadn't yet begun to stumble home from the brothels.

Mayhap he was carrying her to the main road out of the city to banish her from Canterbury. Or perchance he was conveying her to the cathedral to force her to repent of her sins.

With her limited vision, she didn't at first recognize where they were when he at last stopped in his tracks. But when he upended her and set her carefully on her bound feet, the first thing she saw was the stark black post of the gallows.

Her heart bolted.

God's eyes! He meant to hang her.

The devil meant to hang her beside Hubert.

One glance at Hubert's snow-stiff corpse and panic sluiced through her veins.

With a startled squeak, she broke loose of his hold and tried to escape. After two desperate hops, she staggered and fell sideways, thankfully onto a thick cushion of snow.

"Wench!" he hissed. "What ails you?"

Determined to escape despite the odds, she squirmed and bucked and wriggled along the ground. But alas, she succeeded only in moving a few yards beyond his reach.

He easily closed the distance and hunkered down beside her, studying her with a perplexed gaze. "Where the devil are you going?"

How he expected her to answer, gagged as she was, she didn't know. Ignoring him, she resumed her writhing.

He shook his head, then took her by the shoulders, picked her up, and set her aright again, this time gripping her arm so fiercely in his giant hand that she couldn't jerk free.

When he began drawing her forward toward the gallows, she hung back with all of her might, leaving ruts in the snow.

Lucifer's ballocks! Was this how her life would end? Hanged beside her partner in crime, in a city she didn't know, with nary a witness? For God's sake, she was only nineteen!

She'd hardly tasted life. She didn't have a place to call home. She'd never borne a babe. Jesu, she'd never even lain with a man. 'Twasn't fair!

Nicholas didn't want to shackle the lady to the gallows. But damn it, he had no choice. She wasn't being the least bit cooperative. And to think he'd brought her here as a courtesy.

Forcing her to sit on the edge of the wooden platform, he unlocked one of the shackles and attached it to a support timber at the base of the gallows, flinching as her freed hand began its inevitable pounding at his battered back.

Finished, he stepped back while she rattled the shackle in rage and in vain.

He crossed his arms over his chest and shook his head. "I thought you'd want him cut down by loving hands."

She stopped struggling and looked up at him, her enormous eyes like brilliant green gems set in her pale face. Surprise lit her gaze.

"Why else would I bring you here?" he asked.

Her glance at the gallows crossbar was reply enough. She'd thought he meant to hang her, as well.

He frowned. Why did people always assume he was a harsh, unyielding brute who took great satisfaction in administering justice? Could it be, he thought with grim irony, because he did his best to perpetuate that myth?

"I've no warrant to kill you, wench. I'm a shire-reeve, not a judge. I don't take the law into my own hands. I brought you here to bury your grandfather."

The longer she stared at him, her gaze beautiful and brilliant, yet full of mistrust, the guiltier he began to feel about the way he'd dealt with the maid. She had cause to doubt him. Most lawmen were as crooked as a crone's teeth, using their positions of power to extort coin or favors from hapless victims. He supposed he should be more patient with the lass. After all, she'd just lost a man who may have been her only kin.

"Listen. Swear you won't cry out and I'll take that off," he said, nodding to the gag. Even as he said the words, he thought he must be the greatest fool in all England. The wench was the granddaughter of an outlaw. Certainly her promises were as hollow as dry bones.

Nonetheless, he chose to trust her when she bobbed her head in agreement. She didn't even try to beat him to a bloody pulp this time when he drew near. She sat patiently as he picked the knot and took the wad of linen from her mouth.

She tried to speak, but her voice came out in a croak. Clearing her throat, she made a second attempt. "He's not my grandfather."

Nicholas blinked. "What?"

"He only told you that. We were... traveling companions."

He should have known. He wondered how much else of what Kabayn had "confessed" was invented. But why would the man have made such a claim?

"Your family?"

"Gone."

Nicholas sighed. He'd heard the tale a hundred times. It seemed most of the criminals he dealt with had sorry beginnings. Sometimes they exaggerated their tales of woe, but often they were indeed desperate and turned to a life of crime because they had naught else. This damsel was surely as much an outlaw as Hubert. She'd simply had the good fortune not to get caught.

For a long while she said naught, only staring at the snow at his feet, avoiding looking at the corpse hanging but a few yards away. Her every muscle was taut. She was primed like a cocked bow, ready to fire.

Lord, what was he going to do with her? He'd promised Kabayn he'd see to her welfare, and he intended to keep his vow, despite the man's manipulations. But what was he to do with a full-grown woman?

'Twould have been easy to find a childless couple eager to adopt a homeless little lass to help with chores. But this was no tractable child.

He supposed he might find her a husband. Surely a woman so beautiful should have no trouble making a man fall in love with her. But she didn't strike him as the kind of maid to go willingly into marriage. And the man who married this snapping vixen would have to be made of stern stuff indeed.

The idea of finding suitors for her left a bitter taste in his mouth. What did he know of courting? It had been years since he'd engaged in courtship.

Nay, he'd have to think of another solution. Meanwhile, he had a task to do.

"What's your name, lass?"

She hesitated, as if weighing the consequences of divulging such information. Finally she conceded. "Desirée."

Desirée. *Desire*. That was certainly fitting. "Well, Desirée, I'm sure he wouldn't mind a few kind words spoken over him, grandfather or not."

He propped the ladder against the gallows post, then climbed it, drawing his dagger. With one arm wrapped around the frozen body, he sawed at the rope. With as much reverence as he could manage, he carried Hubert down the ladder and laid him out in the snow.

"You'll come to bury him?" he asked her.

She gazed at the body, stiff and pale upon the ground, then gave an infinitesimal nod.

He unlocked her shackles and stuffed them into his belt, then extended his hand to help her up. "Don't make me chase you down."

She refused his assistance. She might be cooperating, but she was clearly not doing so willingly.

He shook his head, then hefted the body over his shoulder and started out along the main road leading out of Canterbury, expecting her to follow.

She didn't. When he turned around to see what was delaying her, she was frowning.

"Isn't the chapel *that* way?" She gestured in the direction of St. Mildred's.

He frowned beneath the hood of his cloak. Didn't the wench understand? "Lass, your grand-, companion... was a criminal. He cannot be buried in hallowed ground."

For an instant, he thought she might cry. Her chin trembled, and her eyes grew liquid. Then he realized she wasn't bereft. She was vexed.

"Fine!" she snapped, picking up her skirts and stomping through the snow toward him. "Go ahead and bury him in the sinner's graveyard... next to your *mother's* plot."

Desirée kicked at the snowdrifts as they traveled down the road, silently cursing the shire-reeve for ruining her life. If he hadn't hauled Hubert into his gaol, fabricating that charge of murder, things would have been fine.

After all, Hubert and she had lived by the seat of their braies and the edge of their wits for years, drifting like goatsbeard seeds along a stream, never lingering any place long enough to grow roots, staying one step ahead of trouble.

They would have left Canterbury in another day or two, moved on to the next town, cheated a dozen half-wits out of their coin, and lived on their winnings for another sennight, long enough to travel to the next village.

So she told herself. But the truth was, things had changed irrevocably between Hubert and herself long before his arrest. The bitter old man's criticisms had grown harsher and harsher, his aggravation with her more and more apparent. He demeaned her at every turn, constantly threatening to trade her in for a younger, more gifted lass.

Sooner or later he would have left her behind, if not in Canterbury, in some other town. And the selfish old cheat would never have looked back.

Still, it chilled her to recall that when he'd made the deadly mistake of trying to rob Torteval Hall on his own, claiming Desirée had become too much of a liability to include on such delicate missions, she'd crowed over his capture, glad the smug bastard had been caught in the act, thinking 'twas no less than he deserved for his heartless desertion of her.

She'd foolishly hoped a few days in gaol would make him regret his actions and put an end to his talk about replacing her. Never had she imagined 'twould put an end to his life.

Desirée's breath made puffs of mist on the air as she struggled to keep up with the shire-reeve. Despite his heavy burden, he gobbled up the road with his long strides.

Lucifer's ballocks, where were they going?

At last, far from the outermost cottages of Canterbury, the road cut through a thick forest, eventually crossing a narrow lane. 'Twas there he stopped.

"Crossroads," he explained as he carefully lowered Hubert's body to the ground.

Indeed, a wooden cross marked the site. Such places often served as the burial ground for outlaws. 'Twas the next best thing to being interred in hallowed soil.

The spot had been used before. Secreted behind one of the trees was a spade. For a brief, ignoble moment, she wondered if she might wrest the thing away from him, whack him on the back of the head, and bury him in a shallow grave in Hubert's stead.

But he was already digging up the earth in a clearing between two oaks, desecrating the white snow with black soil.

She let her gaze drift to Hubert's body. 'Twas strange to see the old man so still. He'd been quick and sly and adroit in life, his tongue slipping over lies as smoothly as butter melting on pandemain, his wrinkled hands moving with a litheness that deceived all but the keenest eyes.

He'd told her once, before he'd taken to disparaging her skills, that she had that same touch, that grace, that speed. But she'd never believed him. No one was as clever or nimble-fingered as Hubert Kabayn.

"Ready?"

She glanced at the grave with disdain. It couldn't have been more than a yard and a half deep. "I hope the wolves won't dig him up," she grumbled.

He placed Hubert's body in the shallow pit. The man's movements were gentle, almost caring, and Desirée wondered how he could possibly be the same man who'd so viciously broken Hubert's neck.

She neared the grave, looking down at the quiet body. The shire-reeve had crossed Hubert's arms piously over his chest. But Desirée feared 'twould take much more than that for an outlaw like Hubert to broach the gates of heaven. He'd likely have better luck *stealing* his way in.

Now that she stood over him, she didn't know what to say. She'd harbored no great love for the man. Forsooth, he'd been harsh, hardhearted, and oftentimes cruel. In return, she'd given him as good as she got. There were no words to describe the unsentimental nature of their bond.

Besides, Hubert had liked sappy proclamations of false affection about as much as he liked weeping. She couldn't very well extol his virtues, since he had so few. And her prayers would likely do little for him, coming from a sinner like herself.

But as she gazed into the grave, it suddenly struck her that Hubert had shown her one last kindness. He must have known all along that he was going to the gallows. The fool's errand he'd sent her on was his way of keeping her at a safe distance from his execution. 'Twas not an act of betrayal. 'Twas an act of protection.

She felt her throat thicken with emotion as she recognized the truth—Hubert hadn't hated her as much as he pretended. At the very least, he cared enough for her to keep her from harm with his dying breath. As callous as he could be sometimes, he *had* always looked out for her. She supposed she owed him something for six years of watching over her.

His spirit would not be eased by tears or praise or

prayers spoken over his dead body. Only one thing would ensure the quiet repose of his soul.

"I'm going to hunt down the real killer, Hubert," she decided. "You may be dead, but I'll see you rest in peace. I promise. No matter what it takes, I'm going to remove this stain upon your soul."

'Twas the least she could do. Hubert wasn't a murderer. He'd been wrongfully hanged. And she wouldn't rest until his death was avenged.

She could see she'd been wrong to blame Nicholas Grimshaw alone. He might have been the one who ordered Hubert's execution. But the real target of her vengeance was whoever committed the murder and let Hubert face the gallows for it.

She stepped away then and let the shire-reeve fill in the grave. As he tamped down the last of the dirt, then placed a large rock at one end as a crude marker, the truth hit her like a boot in the belly.

Hubert was well and truly gone. The only proof she had that he'd ever existed were the Fast and Loose chain he'd given her, a useless iron key he'd stolen, and a weighted die. She was on her own. She'd used up the last of her coin on food for him in the gaol. Their room at the inn had been let to someone else. And with the weather so bleak, most of the alehouses, where she might take a drunken fool's purse in a game of Three Shells and a Pea, would be empty.

She had nowhere to go.

The shire-reeve must have read her thoughts. "Come back to the cottage. I'll make frumenty," he said, returning the spade to its spot. "You could use some meat on your bones."

Frumenty. It had been a long while since she'd eaten more than maslin bread and ale for breakfast. Indeed, it had been a long while since she'd eaten at all. Forsooth, a bowl of creamy wheat pottage would do much to warm her blood. With her belly full, perchance she'd be better able to consider the future and how she was going to keep her promise to Hubert.

Besides, taking advantage of the shire-reeve's hospitality was almost as satisfying as cutting his purse.

❧

Chapter 5

NICHOLAS STIRRED THE POT over the fire, wary, suspecting that behind him, Desirée was likely contemplating his death or, at the very least, musing over what valuables she might steal from him. What she didn't realize was that he'd hung a polished steel spoon over the hearth and he could watch her every move in its reflection. So far, she hadn't budged from the bench, except to stroke Azrael, who'd taken a curious liking to the wench and who currently brushed back and forth along her damp skirts.

"Take care. He has sharp claws," he called over his shoulder.

She didn't answer him. Instead, she defiantly scratched the cat behind the ears, eliciting a loud purr, then whispered to the beast, "Do you like that, Snowflake?"

Nicholas snorted. "Snowflake? His name is Azrael."

"Azrael? Isn't that the..."

"Angel of Death."

She paused for a moment to think that over. "I'm going to call him Snowflake."

Nicholas shuddered. 'Twas a good thing the cat couldn't speak her language. The proud beast would be highly insulted.

He poured the steaming frumenty into his only bowl and carried it to Desirée. She dropped one spoonful onto the floor for Azrael, who lapped it up as if 'twere the sweetest ambrosia.

"You'll spoil my cat," he chided.

"I won't be here long enough to spoil him."

"Aye, about that." He began pacing before her while she stirred her frumenty to cool it. "You will no doubt be pleased to know that your grand-, Hubert made a final request of me. Since you have no one else, he asked me to look after you."

Her spoon clattered in her bowl, and her eyes darted to his. "You? The shire-reeve of Kent?" After a moment, she gave him a dubious smirk. "Of course he did."

"He might not have been your grandfather, but he was concerned for your welfare."

"If that varlet was concerned for my welfare, he'd not leave me in the hands of a killer."

Nicholas's jaw twitched. "I'm not…" he snapped, then steadied his tone. "I'm not a killer. I'm a lawman. There is a vast difference."

Her bark of laughter was humorless. "Indeed?"

Nicholas clenched his fists reflexively. He hated feeling defensive. Damn it all! He was not a murderer. Aye, he presided over executions, but if *he* didn't, someone with far less pity would have done it in his stead.

"Who lives or dies is not by my will. I'm merely an instrument of the law. Even Hubert understood that."

"Did he? And how would you know that?"

Nicholas scowled. Must the wench challenge him at every turn? "Because I spent his last night with him. That was when he bade me look after you."

She studied him, as if gauging whether he told the truth. "He was ill. He didn't know what he was saying."

"Aye, he *was* ill. But he was sound of mind." He shook his head. "Sound of mind enough to deceive me into thinking you were no more than a helpless child."

The merest trace of a wistful smile touched her lips. "Hubert always had a talent for deception."

She spooned a bite of frumenty into her mouth, then another, then another. He wondered how long it had been since the poor waif had eaten.

It didn't matter, he thought. 'Twasn't his responsibility to watch over every starving creature that came crawling to his door. He'd already taken in Azrael. He didn't need another mouth to feed.

"Listen," he said, crossing his arms over his chest. "I made a vow, and I mean to keep it. I won't throw you out into the streets. But the truth is I can't have you staying with me for long." He resumed pacing before her. "A shire-reeve's life is brutal. I work long days, travel from town to town. And you'd be a target for abuse. 'Tis no kind of life for a young maid, and—"

She began laughing, nearly spewing the last bite of frumenty from her mouth. If she hadn't clearly been laughing *at* him, he would have found the musical sound oddly pleasing.

He uncrossed his arms and frowned. "What?"

When she'd regained her composure, she told him in no uncertain terms, "You needn't worry. I'd sooner rot in a nunnery than live with a man of the law."

"Indeed?" Nicholas testily snatched the empty bowl from her, carrying it to the cutting block and slopping water into it from his pitcher. "Well," he muttered, his ire piqued by her insult, "Hubert obviously considered me a fit guardian."

"On the contrary." She rose to take the bowl from him. "Hubert knew you'd never take me in." She sloshed the bowl vigorously to clean it. "But he saw you were a man of substantial wealth and guilty conscience. He only said what he did to fleece you of your coin."

She crossed to the hearth, tossing the dirty water onto the coals, which sizzled and smoked like a vexed dragon. Then she faced him, holding out the empty vessel and cocking a brow. "That *is* what you're about to do, isn't it? Offer me coin?"

When Nicholas didn't take the bowl from her, she placed it on the cutting block herself.

Nicholas scowled. Indeed, that was exactly what he'd intended. He'd planned to give the maid a sizable purse, enough to keep her alive for several weeks, long enough for her to find employment or a suitable husband.

Had Hubert played him for a fool? He'd seemed so sincere. The old man's plea had been heartfelt, he was sure.

"Don't worry," Desirée said, her lids flattening over sulky eyes. "I won't take your coin. You're right. I'm not a child. I can make my own way." She raked him disdainfully with her gaze. "Besides, your silver has the stench of blood upon it." With that, she whirled about and headed for the door.

Usually such scorn blew past his ears like the Latin spoken at Mass, heard but not absorbed. Not a day passed when someone wasn't spewing insults at him.

Yet for some reason, her words cut him to the quick, as surely as the stone she'd hurled. Damn the wench! He was a good man, an honorable man, and it vexed him that she should think otherwise.

'Twas his own fault, he supposed. He'd cultivated a reputation for harshness. 'Twas what kept him employed.

But the truth was Nicholas didn't have a harsh bone in his body. And the knowledge that the wench thought him a callous murderer rankled him.

He charged past her, blocking her exit. Naught changed the fact that he'd made a vow to Hubert, a vow he intended to honor, even if he had to stuff the coins down the woman's bodice.

He crossed his arms over his chest and spoke in challenge. "You'd refuse my help? You'd deny poor Hubert his dying request? The man who called you granddaughter. The man whose last thoughts were for your welfare. The man who—"

"Ballocks!" She narrowed her eyes to wicked slits. "Don't you understand? You've been cheated. Deceived. Betrayed. He told you that just so he could rob your purse." She smirked. "Not even death could stop a hardened outlaw like Hubert Kabayn from filching just one more farthing."

He uncrossed his arms and began digging in his purse. "It doesn't matter. I won't throw a penniless waif out into the cold."

"You're not throwing me out. I'm leaving of my own accord. *If* you'll get out of my way."

"Not until you accept my coin." He held out a generous handful of silver.

She smacked his hand aside, and the coins spilled across the floor like scuttling beetles, startling Azrael from his hearthside nap.

"I won't be bought," she bit out. "Hubert died unjustly. If you think that handing me a purse full of silver can wipe away the blood on your hands and ease your guilt, you're mistaken. Now stand aside."

He ignored her command. "Where do you think you'll go? What will you do? How will you survive?"

"'Tis not your concern."

"Have you any skills?"

Irritation smoldered in her gaze.

"Any *lawful* skills?" he corrected.

"Are you going to let me pass, or do I have to—"

"I won't turn an outlaw loose in Canterbury."

She arched a brow. "You don't believe I can make an honest living?"

His silence was damning.

"Out of my way!" she hissed.

Behind her, his cursed cat hissed at him, as well, as if taking Desirée's side.

"Bloody hell," he muttered.

He couldn't very well force the lass to take his coin, but he wasn't about to give up on his oath. Damn the lass! Why couldn't she just quail beneath his commands like everyone else?

He stabbed a finger of warning at her. "Listen, you bullheaded wench. I'll let you go now, but I'm not through with you. I've got friends all over Canterbury, and if I hear you've gotten into any sort of—"

"Friends?" She rolled her eyes. "Oh, aye, a regular hero of the people you are. Nicholas Grimshaw, everyone's favorite tax collector. I think I hear the ladies clamoring at the door now."

Her words were like punches pounding him in the gut, for they were more accurate than she knew. The only people who ever spoke to Nicholas Grimshaw at any length were his constable and the unfortunates called up before him on charges. Nobody willingly trafficked with the shire-reeve of Kent.

With his eyes smoldering and his hands fisted, after a long silence, he stepped aside and let her pass.

To her credit, her tone softened as she picked up her satchel and murmured grudgingly, "My thanks for the frumenty." As she pulled the door open and stepped out into the hostile frozen world, she called over her shoulder, "Adieu, Snowflake." Then she closed the door with a hollow finality.

For a long while, Nicholas only stared at the door. Then, out of mindless habit, he walked straight to his keg and dispensed himself a cup of ale. Slumping onto his bench, he downed the brew in a series of deep gulps, slamming the empty cup down beside him.

He belched, and Azrael fled the room with his tail twitching in irritation.

What the lass had said was true. Nobody liked Nicholas Grimshaw. He served a purpose. He was good at his work. The king was grateful for his services, mostly because it kept the royal coffers full and his own hands clean. The folk of Kent had Nicholas to thank for keeping the streets safe. But who could truly appreciate the man who confiscated their earnings and threw their neighbors into the stocks?

Men never looked him in the eyes, and women clutched their children to their skirts when he passed. He inspired violence in young lads, terror in young lasses. Indeed, only innocent babes, too pure of heart to recognize the power he wielded over life and death, ever smiled at him.

It had never bothered him. He'd learned to bear disdain like a monk wearing a hair shirt. At times he'd even encouraged their loathing and fear, for 'twas what kept the population civil.

He'd taken on the mantle of justice, embraced the aloofness of his position, and grown accustomed to seeming more than a mere mortal. He'd elevated and distanced himself from the mob by choice.

But now one nettlesome slip of a wench, with her snapping eyes and fearless tirades, had reminded him that he was, after all, human. That somewhere beneath his menacing black cloak and magisterial chest beat a human heart with human dreams. Dreams of marriage. And babes. And a laughter-filled home.

"Pah!"

He couldn't afford to start thinking like that. Christ's bones! He had two outlaws going in the stocks today and three prisoners to question. He was the damned shire-reeve, for God's sake.

He pushed himself up and poured another cup of ale. For the unpleasant day ahead, he needed all the fortification he could get.

Desirée thought she must be the biggest fool to walk the earth. Slogging through the silent snow, she imagined she could hear Hubert bellowing at her from the grave.

Why hadn't she taken the man's coin? He'd offered it to her willingly. And from the looks of the silver scattered across the floor, 'twas a considerable amount, enough to provide her a room and meals for the rest of the winter.

Stupid pride had gotten in her way. That and the niggling knowledge that she'd already stolen enough from the man. After all, he'd given her a night's lodging, a decent burial for Hubert, and a hearty breakfast without charging her a farthing.

But now, of course, she had naught. She'd be reduced to begging, borrowing, or stealing. Of those three options, stealing was always preferable. But where would she find a gullible target in this foul weather?

Even if she found a target, 'twas nigh impossible to pull off good sleight of hand without an accomplice. When Hubert and she engaged in such games, Desirée had usually been the distraction. She'd be the one clapping her hands with glee, fluttering her lashes, flashing blinding smiles at the players while Hubert slipped the pea under another shell or made the exchange of a weighted die.

She pulled the cloak tighter about her face, peering surreptitiously down alleys and into shops as she sauntered along the streets, searching for opportunity.

A few chill hours later, she began to think on the shire-reeve's cottage with a desperate sort of wistfulness. It hadn't been so bad. The man knew how to build a fire and make frumenty. Despite the fact she'd been chained to it against her will, his bed had been remarkably comfortable and extravagantly large. Aside from the horrible display on the wall, his furnishings had been pleasant enough. And he had a friendly cat to keep the vermin away.

She began to think seriously about swallowing her pride before she froze to death tonight. Indeed, she'd turned her feet in the direction of the shire-reeve's house when two drunkards came stumbling toward her out of an inn, their purses bulging with coin.

'Twas a sign, she decided, abandoning all thoughts of returning to Grimshaw. She greeted the men with a disarming smile that would have made Hubert proud.

Chapter 6

LADY PHILOMENA PEERED from the window of her solar at Torteval Hall, watching the distant spires of Canterbury Cathedral disappear in the waning daylight. Ignoring the pathetic whimpering of the servant groveling behind her, she thumped her fingers casually atop the ledge. Her father-in-law might be a useless dullard, but at least he'd had the wisdom to choose a perfect location for the family demesne. 'Twas sufficiently distant from the town to avoid rubbing elbows with the rabble, yet close enough to wield a powerful influence over the local government.

The constable, the justices, even the priests of Canterbury knew very well 'twas Lord William Torteval who so generously endowed their coffers. And very soon that responsibility would pass to Philomena.

Closing the shutters against spying eyes and prying ears, she wished she could just once get Lord William's dimwitted servants to do her bidding without mucking things up.

She examined the throbbing knuckles of her right hand, resting upon the shutter. Beside her ruby ring, there was a tiny streak of blood. She licked her thumb and rubbed gently at it. Thank God, 'twasn't hers.

'Twas the blood of that simpering pig of a man who held the title of steward of Torteval Hall, the fool who'd once again dared to disappoint her.

She felt no remorse. He deserved her wrath. This was the second time Godfry had disappointed her in two days. Yesterday, he'd failed to ensure that Hubert Kabayn suffered on the gallows, squirming in agonizing death throes. He'd allowed the shire-reeve to show mercy to the murderer.

And today...

"I pray you, my lady," he sobbed obsequiously, cradling his injured nose, "don't send me away."

She curled her lip. If he continued to cower in the corner, blubbering over his bloody nose like a wee lass, she'd show him what a *real* beating was.

Instead, exercising great self-control, she addressed him in a deceptively magnanimous voice. "Don't be silly, Godfry. You're Lord William's oldest, most loyal servant."

She crossed the solar at a leisurely pace, tapping her fingers along the immaculately polished Spanish oak table, plucking the strings of the small gilt harp perched there, pushing the silver chalice half-filled with claret back from the edge, finally stopping to stand over him like a hungry wolf over a wounded lamb.

Despite her best efforts to appear sweet, innocent, and charitable, Godfry trembled as she neared, his red face sweaty with strain.

She crouched so she could look him in his piggish eyes and spoke slowly, as if to a child. "As long as you do as you're told, you'll have a place in my house-, the Torteval household."

He swallowed visibly.

"And what I've told you to do, dear Godfry, is find that key."

"But my lady, I've looked high and low, and—"

She raised her fist again, and he cringed, covering his head with his arms.

Philomena clamped her teeth together hard enough to shatter them, willing her rage to subside. As much as she enjoyed the thrill of power that beating her father-in-law's servants afforded her, 'twould serve little purpose.

Besides, she might break a fingernail.

When her calm was restored, she rose and turned away from him. "Go. Out of my sight." He scrambled to comply with all haste. "And keep looking."

When he was gone, when there was no more need to keep up appearances, dread overwhelmed her again and she half swooned, catching herself on the table's edge.

Lord, what if she couldn't find the key?

She'd been working on this plan for months. If something went awry now, when she was so close to her goal...

Blessed Mary, she needed a drink. She eyed the chalice of wine on the table and almost made the mistake of reaching for it. Withdrawing her hand, she erupted into giggles. That would have been a *grave* mistake indeed, she thought, and her laughter became nigh hysterical.

That chalice was for her father-in-law. She took him claret every night, to help him sleep. At least, 'twas what she told him. But even the soothing effects of the wine couldn't dispel the sickness that gripped his bowels and made him weaker by the day.

When her laughter subsided, she reached again for the chalice, this time with no intention of drinking it. She swirled the liquid around the cup, marveling at what a perfect poison arsenic was. It had no color, no odor, no flavor. Even better, no one questioned her frequent purchases of the powder to kill rats, for she couldn't keep a cat to do the task. Cats were unbearable to Philomena. They made her itch and sneeze and turned her eyes red.

Still, Lord William's demise was taking much longer than she'd anticipated. He'd almost foiled her plans, suddenly summoning his lawyer to alter his will, giving everything to his nephew.

But fortune had smiled on her. The very night the lawyer arrived, a robber broke into Torteval Hall. While the unknowing thief ransacked the place, Philomena stabbed the lawyer to death and pinned the blame on the intruder. After the shire-reeve and his constable dragged the culprit and the corpse away, she'd simply tossed the new will into the fire with no one the wiser.

There remained but one problem. The key. Somehow in the chaos of the murder, it had gone missing.

She dug her fingernails into the waxy rim of the table. Without that key, she wouldn't be able to unlock the cell. If she couldn't unlock the cell...

She let out a shuddering sigh. 'Twould do no good to panic. She hadn't gotten this far in her ambitious twenty-four years by letting her nerves get the best of her.

She patted her sleek auburn hair into place and pinched her cheeks for color, then practiced a frown of compassionate concern as she started toward the door. Her poor father-in-law was growing steadily worse and worse, and there was naught anyone could do.

Thank God.

"Not now, Azrael."

With one hand, Nicholas picked the cat up from his lap and plopped him back down on the floor.

He'd had a miserable day. In sooth, he'd had several miserable days, starting with the day he'd hanged Hubert Kabayn. Since when had the shire become so overrun with criminals?

He'd had to put a boy in the stocks today, a lad as starved and bony as a broomstick. The wretch was fortunate he hadn't been ordered to hang, for his crime was thievery, and in Kent, punishments were severe. The poor lad had managed to wolf down the loaf of bread before the baker caught him, thus destroying the evidence. The stocks were a warning.

Nicholas hated the stocks. 'Twasn't that they were particularly distressing or painful, in and of themselves. But when a victim was thus displayed in the village square, the severity of his punishment was determined by the mercy or brutality of the populace at large. And in Nicholas's experience, people were more likely to be cruel than kind.

He did his best to regulate what transpired by standing guard over the stocks, creating an ominous presence that discouraged more than the usual mischief of yelling insults and hurling garbage.

But he was still haunted by the memories of the times he'd let his guard slip. Once, a pack of three lads had stolen past him to cut off a man's thumb. Another time, a sweet-faced maid had burned her sister's bare feet with a candle. And the stones...

Nicholas ran his thumb over the scar along his jaw. Standing watch over the stocks came with its risks.

No one had thrown anything today, but their taunts had cut the lad in the stocks to the quick, driving him to tears of humiliation.

Nicholas blew out a weighted breath. Some days he despised his position as shire-reeve. He was expected to uphold the law of the land, and he did so as honorably as he could. But there were days when he saw innocents punished while monsters walked free, and it wrenched at his gut that he could do naught about it.

So now he drowned his guilt in ale, wishing he could set aside enough of his earnings to cover the taxes of *all* the starving peasants instead of only the most desperate. 'Twas unconscionable to punish a hungry man for stealing a loaf of bread.

Azrael jumped up on his lap again, and this time he let the beast stay, idly petting his snowy fur while he purred.

"Snowflake," he murmured.

It had been six days since Desirée had left his cottage with a self-assured swish of her skirts. Six days since he'd seen her fiery emerald eyes and luxurious hair and succulent, swearing lips. But it hadn't been six days since he'd imagined her. The enchanting witch seemed to intrude upon his every thought, as distracting as the persistent itch of a bug bite.

Had she found shelter? Food? Employment? Or would she be reduced to stealing bread like the lad he'd just punished?

Azrael growled as Nicholas unwittingly clenched his

fingers in the cat's fur. Nicholas released him, and the cat jumped down, crossing to the hearth with an indignant shiver.

Nicholas eyed the black cloak he'd tossed down beside his keg. Perchance he'd seek out the lass and check on her condition. 'Twas just the thing to get his mind off the bony lad with the tears streaming down his cheeks.

"Torteval Hall?" Desirée repeated as nonchalantly as possible, rubbing the pair of dice between her palms. Villagers pushed and shoved and sidled past her makeshift oak barrel gaming table along the narrow lane as she entertained her current pair of targets.

"Aye," the player said proudly, giving her a wink. "I'm master of the mews there."

"Indeed?" She cast the dice across the circular top of the barrel. Mayhap her luck had just changed. This man might have just the information she needed to learn the truth about the murder.

Five and three.

"Zounds! I did it, Bardolph!" the man cried, elbowing his dour companion, who seemed impatient to leave. "I won again!"

Desirée sighed in feigned disappointment and slid the coins toward him. "Lady Luck is certainly with you today, sir."

He beamed, showing off a gap-toothed row of teeth. "I'll go again. A halfpenny this time, eh?"

She nodded, placing her coin beside his, but the fellow beside him grunted something in disapproval.

"Lady Philomena will wait," the master of the mews said. "You heard what the wench said. Lady Luck is with me. Right?" He grinned at her with gleaming, greedy eyes.

"So 'twould seem," she agreed.

She shook the dice in her cupped hands, surreptitiously exchanging one of them for a weighted die from the purse at her waist.

'Twasn't a perfect system. One of the dice would still be completely unpredictable. But the other would always land on a one. The odds were in Desirée's favor, for she knew that naught higher than a seven could ever be thrown.

She added casually, "I hear Lady Luck was not at Torteval *last* week."

"Mm?"

"Was there not a murder at the place?"

"Oh, aye. Caught the bastard who did it, though, and strung him up. Nicholas Grimshaw himself gave him the final tweak. Did ye see it? Cracked the killer's neck like a twig."

Her grip faltered and she dropped the weighted die, quickly scooping it back up, but not before she earned a mistrustful frown from Bardolph. Her voice was hoarse as she asked, "What number, sir?"

"Eight again."

"Very good. I'll take...five."

The dice clattered across the barrel. One and three.

"Damn!" The coins remained where they were. He squinted at the silver left in his purse. "Another penny?"

Desirée had to be frugal. She'd barely made enough coin in the last six days to pay for her keep, and that was living on one trencher of pottage a day. Still, she didn't have much choice. She needed to keep the man playing if she wanted to find out more about the murder.

"All right. Five again." She placed a halfpenny beside the others, then began shaking the dice in her hands once more. "'Twas a lawyer murdered, aye?"

"Aye. I'll wager seven. 'Twas the lord's own man."

"The lord?"

"Lord William." The man moved closer to confide in a whisper, "He's dyin', ye know. Summoned his lawyer to write up his will."

Bardolph jabbed him with an elbow, then skewered her with a glare. "Just cast the dice."

She shrugged and released the cubes across the barrel. One and four. Thank God.

"Shite!" The man pounded his fist on the edge of the barrel.

Desirée couldn't help the smile that teased at the corners of her mouth. Two pennies. She'd eat again tonight. Though a part of her mourned the loss of her longtime partner in crime, she didn't miss having to turn over the greater portion of her winnings to the old lout. Hubert would have snatched that two-penny pork pasty right out of her mouth.

As she reached out to claim her take, her hand was suddenly covered by a massive paw.

"Leave it there."

She whipped her head about. Who dared interfere in her game?

The master of the mews answered for her, removing his cap and breathing in awe, "Nicholas Grimshaw."

Bardolph poked him, muttering, "I told ye we should've gone."

Desirée wasn't about to let go of her hard-won profit. She glared into the shire-reeve's dark eyes. "What are you doing here?"

"Cleaning up the streets of Canterbury."

The master of the mews twisted his cap in his hands. "We was playin' an honest game o' dice, m'lord. No mischief. I swear."

"No mischief," Bardolph assured him, adding for good measure, "and I wasn't even playin'."

"No mischief?" Nicholas intoned. "Then what's this?"

Before she could stop him with her free hand, he yanked the purse from her waist and upended it over the table. What spilled out were a few farthings, four walnut shells, her silver Fast and Loose chain, a comb, the iron key Hubert had given her, two ribbons, a couple of dried peas, and the condemning unweighted die she'd exchanged, all she owned in the world.

"God's hooks," the master of the mews said in wonder. "'Tis a trick die."

"She was cheatin' us... *ye*," Bardolph told him.

Desirée was more vexed than embarrassed. When you relied upon deception for a living, getting caught now and then was inevitable. A bit of smooth talking, a few coins slipped into the right palm, and a hasty departure usually served to get one out of such scrapes.

But she wasn't ready to leave Canterbury. She had a task to finish. And she had no coin to spare on bribery. Lord, at the moment, she couldn't have left if she wanted to. She couldn't even remove her hand from the shire-reeve's grip.

"How much did you lose to her?" he asked the men.

"Not much. Only the penny there," the master of the mews said.

But Bardolph recognized opportunity when he saw it. "Two shillin's!"

"What?" The first man frowned at him.

"Two shillin's! She took two shillin's from us...him." Desirée gasped. "I did not!"

"Two shillings," the shire-reeve drawled. "Indeed?" He clucked his tongue. "Why, gentlemen, 'tis enough to have her flogged."

$\sim$

Chapter 7

DESIRÉE'S HEART DROPPED to the pit of her stomach. Flogged? He couldn't be serious.

"Bloody hell!" she hissed in disbelief. "'Tis a penny! 'Tisn't as if I snatched a pound from the king's coffers!"

Ignoring her, Nicholas told the men, "I'll summon the constable to take her away."

"Nay!" she cried. The passersby, though giving the shire-reeve a wide berth, turned their heads at her shriek, so she lowered her voice. "'Tis barely coin enough for supper. And 'twas won from willing participants in a game of chance."

Nicholas paid her no heed but began scanning the square. "It shouldn't take too long. I saw the constable a moment ago."

Desirée turned to the men, imploring them, "Tell him. Tell him you were willing participants."

The master of the mews only stared at her, confused.

"Of course," Nicholas continued, "you two will have to stay to give the constable a full report and—"

"What?" Bardolph's eyes widened. "Oh, nay, nay, nay, nay, nay," he said in a rush. "We wouldn't want to delay our progress home." He kicked his cohort.

"Oh!" The master of the mews suddenly realized their humiliating predicament. If Lady Philomena discovered they'd been dawdling at the gaming table... "And we wouldn't want to... trouble our mistress with such trivial matters."

"You're sure?" Nicholas asked.

They both nodded enthusiastically.

Nicholas forced her hand over, and she was too stunned to resist when he collected the coins from her and handed them to the master of the mews.

She was still reeling when the men hastened away from the table. When she could catch her breath, she looked up at the lawman, incredulous. "Sweet Mary, you would've flogged me for a penny?"

"I just put a lad in the stocks for stealing a loaf of bread, wench!"

Nicholas had answered her with more venom than he'd intended, startling even the passersby with his harsh words. But he was still shaken by the sight of Desirée engaging in unlawful wagering in plain view of the citizens of Canterbury. If anyone else had chanced to notice the way she'd slipped that weighted die onto the table...

Jesu! He should never have let her leave his cottage. He should have realized she'd end up resorting to crime. 'Twas likely all she knew.

Calming himself, he tapped on the barrel top. "Is this all the coin you have?"

She pursed her lips defensively. "I would have had more if you hadn't interfered."

"Oh, aye. You could have used it to purchase a fresh whip for your flogging."

She irritably collected her meager belongings from the top of the barrel and stuffed them back into her purse. "I've been doing this since I was a child. No one's ever troubled me about it before."

"Well, your luck is about to change. Where are your things?"

"What things?"

"Your clothing, your bedding, your…things."

"You're looking at all I own," she sneered. "I had to sell everything to keep Hubert fed in your stinking gaol."

That made up his mind.

Nicholas had thought long and hard about Desirée as he'd searched the streets of Canterbury. Punishing a poor, desperate lad without enough to eat had convinced him he couldn't let the lass suffer a similar fate. So he'd come to a decision. If the damsel didn't have a decent occupation, if she hadn't found herself a position or a husband by now, he'd take matters into his own hands.

'Twouldn't be a permanent arrangement, of course. But hopefully, 'twouldn't take too long to set the wayward wench on a more virtuous path.

He took her elbow and dragged her forward.

She instantly tried to pull out of his grip. "What do you think you're doing?"

"I'm retiring you from your life of crime." He tugged her away from the barrel.

She tugged back. "You can't tell me what to do!"

"Whether you like it or not, I'm responsible for you. I made a promise."

"To hell with your promise!"

They were drawing the attention of passersby, who were doubtless intrigued by the sight of someone actually daring to defy the formidable Nicholas Grimshaw. 'Twas just the sort of spectacle he didn't need.

He lowered his voice. "I have a proposition for you."

She arched a skeptical brow. "What kind of proposition?"

Perchance one day Desirée would recognize him as her savior and be grateful. But today wasn't that day.

"You'll come work for me, and I won't haul you in for your thievery."

"What?"

"I require three meals a day, two if I've got a full work day. Laundry once a week. Floors swept daily. Furnishings waxed once every—"

"What!"

Now they had the attention of the entire lane. Even the constable, patrolling the shops at the opposite side of the square, paused to see why a crowd was gathering.

"You'll have room and board," he murmured, "and I'll pay you a shilling a week."

"I told you before," she said, yanking her arm hard out of his grasp, "I will not live under the roof of a lawman."

He gathered the nape of her gown in a viselike fist and waved across the square. "Constable!"

She gasped. "You're not serious."

"Here, constable!"

The constable crossed the square as casually as he

could, considering the stir caused by the sound of a summons from Nicholas Grimshaw.

"You wouldn't," Desirée breathed.

He motioned the constable toward him.

"I don't even have the coin!" she protested. "You have no proof!"

"You might get off with a day in the stocks," he admitted.

"Damn you, Nicholas Grimshaw," she said between her teeth, wary now of arousing the constable's suspicions.

"Just say the word and we'll be on our way."

"Bastard!" she hissed.

"That's not the word."

The constable was but ten yards away when she finally conceded.

"All right, you bloody knave, I'll clean your damned hovel."

"And cook?"

"Fine."

He released her.

"Constable," he said by way of greeting as the man approached. "Come meet my new maidservant, Desirée. Desirée, my constable."

The last thing Nicholas expected was Desirée's brilliant smile and extended hand. "Constable, my pleasure," she gushed.

And damned if the constable, caught off guard by her disarming greeting, didn't absently press a kiss to the back of her hand as if she were some titled lady instead of a lowly maid.

"Well," the constable said, blinking in confusion.

"You're a...a brave lass. Not every maid would take up residence with a...with a...with Nicholas Grimshaw."

To his astonishment, Desirée laughed and gave Nicholas's cheek a patronizing pat. "He's a kitten, really. Wouldn't hurt a flea. Isn't that right, Nicky?"

Shite! This was *definitely* not the sort of attention he needed. The conniving wench was going to ruin his fearsome reputation.

He nodded briefly to the astounded constable. "We'll be going now." He quickly ushered her away, adding loudly for the villagers' benefit, "Have to show her how to oil my thumbscrews."

Desirée grinned in satisfaction. She might not have won the battle, but she wasn't going down without a fight. She wasn't about to let the lout believe he could snap his fingers and summon her to his side like a trained hound.

As he took long strides across the square, making her scramble to keep up, he muttered, "Don't call me that."

"Call you what?"

She could hear him growling behind his teeth. "Nicky."

She smiled again. Of course, now she'd call him Nicky at every opportunity. If she proved irritating enough, perchance her forced residence at the house of the unpleasant Nicholas Grimshaw might be cut short.

As they wound through the streets, she asked sweetly, "How's Snowflake?"

His annoyed silence was reward enough.

Nicholas Grimshaw might have extorted housekeeping services out of her, but in exchange, she could make his household miserable.

Scarcely had she dropped her satchel onto the floor of the cottage when her new slave master began listing her duties for the evening. Biting the inside of her cheek to stifle her simmering temper, she remained silent while he dictated his supper requirements and pointed out the various kitchen utensils.

But it didn't take long, after Nicholas had drawn himself a draught of ale and retired to his bedchamber, for Desirée to begin stirring up mischief to pay the knave back for his extortion.

Several moments later, he emerged again with his face freshly scrubbed, raking back his damp hair and wrinkling his nose. "What's that smell?"

"What smell?" Desirée looked up innocently from her place at the chopping block in the kitchen, where she was slicing bacon for the evening stew.

Nicholas glowered at the hearth. Smoke was rising from the pot on the fire. "*That* smell."

She glanced at the smoking pot, then shrugged. "Supper."

"'Tis burning."

"Is it?"

She could almost see smoke pouring from his ears, as well, as he scowled at the pot of burning neeps and cabbage. A few meals like this and surely he'd be glad to release her from her servitude.

He said naught, returning to his bedchamber.

She smiled in satisfaction as she dropped the bacon into the smoldering pot, where it snapped and sizzled. As soon as it began to blacken sufficiently, she'd add water, stirring the vile mess into a noxious stew.

Nicholas emerged again, this time clad in his cloak. "I'm going out."

"But supper's on the hearth."

"*Your* supper's on the hearth," he said, cocking an amused brow. "I'm going to find something edible in town. And don't even think of running away. I'll only hunt you down again."

Her jaw dropped. Before she could come up with a scathing retort, he was gone. In a burst of pique, she took off her shoe and threw it at the closed door.

Sighing, she stared down at the burned mixture. *She* wasn't about to try to choke it down. Wrapping a bundle of rags around her hand, she took the pot off the fire.

"Kitty-kitty-kitty. Here, Snowflake."

Even the cat turned up his nose. She ended up tossing the mixture out into the back yard. Perchance some animal with less discriminating tastes would make a feast of it.

Meanwhile, she was reduced to sharing a cold slab of bacon, a stale bannock, and a cup of ale with the cat while she dreamed up other ways to provoke her gaoler.

"Snowflake, my precious," she said, digging in her purse, "how would you like a pretty ribbon?" She pulled out a frayed rose-colored strip of velvet she used to tie back her hair. While the cat finished off his dish of minced bacon, she tied the ribbon about his neck, perching the bow at a jaunty angle above his left ear.

Satisfied with her handiwork, she tapped her fingers on the table, wondering what other subtle havoc she might wreak.

She'd learned that a man's nature could be quickly judged by his possessions, and that once one knew a man's nature, 'twas a simple thing to prey upon his weaknesses. With Nicholas gone, the cottage was hers to explore. Perchance she could find some clue to the man's frailties.

She started in his bedchamber. The requisite chest of clothing squatted at the foot of his great bed. Most of his garb was dark and plain, as befitted the solemn nature of his office. The few white linen shirts bore faint stains that might or might not have been blood. The sight chilled her, drawing her gaze to the instruments hanging on the wall. Swiftly shoving the garments back into the chest, she let the lid drop.

A half-dozen spears of various size leaned against the corner of the wall, and Desirée spied a small, carved wooden box tucked behind them. Moving the spears carefully aside, she opened the box. To her amazement, 'twas full to the brim with silver coins. 'Twas a veritable treasury, and she wondered, if he had so much wealth, why he lived so modestly. Surely he could have afforded a stately manor house with that coin. Desirée could have survived for several years on such an amount.

The temptation to take it was strong. But if Nicholas had intended to flog her for stealing two shillings, what would he do to her for robbing him of his fortune?

She bit the corner of her lip. She *could* slip a few coins from the box each day, diminishing his riches a penny at a time. But something told her he was the sort of man who kept a careful watch on his possessions. 'Twouldn't surprise her to discover he counted his coins every night.

Nay, 'twas too big a risk. Later, mayhap, when she'd finished her business in Canterbury and intended to flee, she'd consider absconding with his treasure in one bold parting gesture. But for now 'twould have to remain an unrequited possibility in the back of her mind.

She closed the lid, moved the box back, and replaced the spears.

Atop his table, beside the usual comb and razor and bowl of soap, were a bottle of ink, parchment, and a quill. What would a shire-reeve have to record? Purchases of hanging rope? Laundry charges for bloodstain removal? A tally of lopped-off body parts?

Desirée knew how to read and write, though 'twas a rare skill among women. Indeed, the only reason she'd learned was that Hubert had been convinced 'twould profit them. He'd managed to extort lessons for her from a priest who couldn't pay off his wagering debts. Once she'd mastered the skill, Desirée forged letters of introduction to gain access to wealthy households, which, of course, they'd subsequently rob.

Curious, she opened another chest beside the table and found dozens of rolls of parchment, bound with leather ties. She plucked one out and unrolled it.

Her eyes flattened as she read the words. 'Twas a warrant of death, charging Nicholas Grimshaw with the execution of one Walter atte Redehulle. Nicholas's bold mark was made at the bottom, beside those of the town constable and the executioner. With a shudder of revulsion, she rolled it back up and glanced at the others in the chest. No doubt one of them had Hubert Kabayn's name on it.

She slammed the lid.

She perused the chamber, looking for other clues as to his possible weaknesses. She'd hoped to find something more interesting, more incriminating among his effects.

Perchance a favorite book of perverse illuminations. Or a collection of love letters to some lost sweetheart.

But despite his store of wealth, he had only enough possessions to afford himself the most spartan of existences. Nicholas Grimshaw was apparently a man of thrift.

And that, she decided with a calculating grin, was the key to how she'd provoke him. Nicholas didn't own half the things Desirée would require if she were going to be his cook and housemaid.

Her brain whirring, she sat at his table, drew a piece of parchment out, dipped the quill into the bottle of ink, and began compiling a list of necessities, *expensive* necessities.

Beeswax candles. Saffron. Galingale. Cinnamon. Cloves. Good Spanish wine. A linen apron. A low stool. A plunger churn. Lavender for the bath.

She tapped the quill feather against her lip. 'Twas enough for now, she supposed. 'Twould take a good lot of the coin he kept in that box to purchase the goods. With any luck, he'd decide his servant was too expensive to keep.

For a long while, she waited for him to return, relishing the look of displeasure on his face when he beheld her list. But after several hours, she decided he must have stopped by an alehouse on the way home. An alehouse or a whorehouse. Despite his comely face and brawny form, a man of his villainous reputation likely paid for companionship.

Soon the fire died down, and Snowflake started on his hunting rounds. Before long, as she sat in front of the dwindling flames, Desirée's eyelids began to droop.

She wasn't about to make her bed on the hard wooden

bench or the stone floor. If 'twas Nicholas's decision to be out until the small hours of the night, then *he* could scrounge for a place to sleep. That was, if he wasn't already dozing betwixt some harlot's legs. As for Desirée, she was going to take that enormous down-filled pallet. 'Twould serve him right for tricking her into slavery.

Chapter 8

THE TREK HOME TOOK LONGER than Nicholas expected. He supposed he shouldn't have been so demanding about the pallet he was buying for his new servant, but it didn't sit well with him to luxuriate on a great downy mattress while Desirée shivered in the straw. Even if the irksome wench *had* intentionally burned his supper.

After all, what the constable had blurted out was true. Not every maid would take up residence with a shire-reeve. The least he could do was give her a decent place to sleep.

So after a savory meal of two pork tartees and a cup of mulled perry, he'd stopped by the pallet merchant. None of the straw-stuffed pallets had seemed soft enough to him, but he wasn't about to splurge on goose down. In the end, he compromised on chicken feathers and had to wait while the grumbling merchant hand-stuffed the mattress to his specifications.

'Twas dark by the time he paid the merchant, hefted the mattress on one shoulder, and headed for home.

Shuffling awkwardly through the cottage door with his burden, he saw that no candles were lit and the fire had gone out. He wondered if Desirée had actually eaten the slop she'd cooked for supper. He felt half sorry for the scrawny wench. She could ill afford to do without a meal. But she'd only brought the punishment upon herself. In the morn, he'd make certain she ate a generous bowl of frumenty.

Where was the lass, anyway? Surely she'd not been so foolish as to run away.

He slipped the pallet off his shoulder, shoving it alongside the hearth, and removed his cloak. He peered around the shadowy room. There was something on the table, a piece of parchment. Opening the shutter, he held the page up to the moonlight.

'Twas a list. Apparently, Desirée could read and write, which surprised him immensely. 'Twas a rare talent among women, even rarer among peasants. As he scanned the items, he smirked and shook his head. She also knew how to spend coin. Extravagantly.

He replaced the parchment, then crept toward his bed-chamber. Perchance the maid had taken her responsibilities to heart and was already hard at work, polishing his furnishings.

Aye, he thought, and perchance Mary Magdalene was a virgin.

He spotted Desirée at once, by the light of a moonbeam filtering through the shutters. She was asleep, luxuriously sprawled across the coverlet like a cat with a belly full of cream, commandeering his pallet as if her spindly frame required every inch of it.

"Oh, nay, you don't," he murmured. He might feel

sorry for the orphaned lass, but he wasn't about to let her usurp his bed. "Desirée," he called.

She didn't move.

"Desirée."

Still no reply.

He drew closer, not close enough that she could swing out with a stray fist and clip him on the jaw, but close enough to be heard.

"Desirée."

She still didn't stir, but Azrael, tucked behind one of her knees, lifted his head.

Nicholas frowned. There was something tied around the cat's neck. Something distinctly feminine.

"God's eyes! What have you done to my cat?"

That woke her. She rose on her elbows, her eyes glazed, her mouth making sleepy smacks. "What?"

"What did you do to Azrael?"

She glanced down at the cat, as if trying to recall. Then her lips curved up in a smile that was pure mischief. "He thinks it's pretty," she said, crooning, "doesn't he, Snowflake?"

Nicholas seized Azrael, who yowled once in complaint, and immediately untied the silly bow, dropping it atop the coverlet.

Desirée shrugged off his actions and snuggled back down under the blankets. "Did you get my list?" she murmured.

He gave Azrael a consoling pat and set him down again on the pallet. "Your list? You mean that nonsense about lavender and beeswax candles? Do you know how much saffron costs?"

"Come, Nicky, you can't expect me to keep your house properly if I don't have the required supplies."

"I seem to have done fine before without them. And stop calling me Nicky."

"What would you prefer? Your Majesty?"

Nicholas exhaled on a growl, trying to recall why he'd felt sorry for the pesky imp. "I've bought another pallet. I've placed it beside the fire."

"Mm, good," she purred. "I'd hate to think of you getting cold in the night."

He blinked. The audacity of the naughty wench was amazing. Unable to think of a fitting verbal response, he decided to let his actions speak for him. He threw back the covers and, ignoring her indignant shrieks, scooped her up into his arms.

"Unhand me, sirrah!"

"You're not sleeping in my bed." He started toward the door.

"But I was there first!"

"'Tis *my* bed."

"You weren't using it." She actually wedged her limbs in the doorway, trying to prevent his exit.

"Well, I'm going to use it now."

"'Tisn't fair!"

He didn't feel like arguing the absurdity of a tiny lass expropriating his huge bed while he lay cramped on a small pallet by the fire.

"The only way you're sleeping in that bed," he whispered wickedly, "is if you're sharing it with me."

With a gasp of disgust, she tucked in her arms and legs so he could carry her through the doorway.

But when they reached the hearth, she eyed the pallet, muttering, "I'll wager it's hard as a rock and full of burrs."

His patience at an end, he abruptly dropped her onto the mattress, eliciting from her a squeak of shock. Then he shrugged. "Seems soft enough." While she sputtered in outrage, he gave her a smirk and a gentlemanly salute. "Good night."

The pallet was more comfortable than Desirée expected. Indeed, aside from his own goose-down mattress, 'twas more comfortable than anything she'd slept on her entire life. She fell soundly asleep in moments, and when she woke the next morn, she was startled to realize she'd slept through Nicholas's departure.

She wondered where he'd gone. Probably off to a neighboring village to torture some unfortunate soul. She hoped he'd remember to purchase the things on her list before he returned. Since she didn't intend to burn her own supper again, she'd need a few spices to make the fare palatable.

But when she sat up and glanced at the table, she saw he'd left the parchment there. And when she rose with a frown to retrieve it, she discovered he'd scrawled a list of his own on the back side.

"Feed cat. Dust away cobwebs. Launder and dry clothing and linens. Sweep floor. Scrub walls. Cook supper. Home late."

Ire simmered in her veins. How dare the brute issue commands as if she were his lowly maidservant!

She pursed her lips. Damn it all, she *was* his maidservant.

"Piss!"

She crumpled the parchment in her fist and dropped it onto the floor. Snowflake trotted over to sniff at it, then looked up expectantly, as if alerting her to the "feed cat" on the list.

"Aye. Aye. I will."

She ignored his nagging meows long enough to wash her face and weave her hair into a braid, then sliced off a bit of bacon for the cat and slathered butter on a bit of bread to break her own fast.

And then she sat, drumming her idle fingers on the tabletop. Nicholas Grimshaw might have blackmailed her into becoming his servant, but that didn't mean she had to be an *obedient* servant. She smiled grimly. She wasn't about to let His Majesty's list dictate her life.

In Desirée's usual line of work, every hour of daylight presented an opportunity to wheedle coin out of some fool's purse. Her food and lodging depended upon not wasting a single moment. But now, free of Hubert's demands, with a roof over her head, a pallet by the fire, and food in the cupboard, all urgency was gone. 'Twas a curious feeling to experience leisure for once in her life, and she had every intention of enjoying it to the hilt.

The first hour was pleasant. She watched the cat eat, gazed into the flickering fire, peered through the shutters at the cold world outside. She yawned with her mouth wide, stretched her arms over her head, ran a fingertip back and forth over a bump in the worn wood of the table. When she tired of sitting, she ambled about the room, examining in detail the stones of the hearth, the wood grain of the cutting block, the cracks in the plaster wall.

But by her fifth circuit, she was beginning to be bothered by the dense spiderweb woven between the keg of ale and the wall. 'Twas interfering with her sense of peace. Snatching up a linen rag, she swiped away the tangled mess. With a nod of approval, she sauntered toward the hearth. Another web draped two stones a few feet from the ceiling. She wiped that away, as well. Indeed, she realized that in her circling of the room, she'd memorized the location of several spiderwebs. 'Twas the work of a few moments to sweep them all away.

Then she could sit back down at the bench and enjoy her leisure.

That lasted another few moments. Until she realized how grimy the walls were. Those near the fire were the worst, blackened by soot. But there were other stains on the plaster, splashes of oil or ale or God knew what else. She supposed she could scrub them away, since there seemed to be naught else of interest to do in the cottage.

Soon she found herself scouring the plaster and sweeping the floors, and when she picked up the crumpled list to move it out of the broom's path, she gave it a casual glance to see what other things she might do to occupy her time.

Leisure, she quickly discovered, was more desirable in theory than in practice. For a woman accustomed to the rapid pace of picking pockets, outwitting fools, and dodging authorities, sitting alone in a cottage with a cat was deadly dull. As much as doing chores went against her intent to antagonize her captor, she supposed she owed him something for the night's lodging.

Besides, she thought, arching a sly brow, just because she was doing his will didn't mean she couldn't take the opportunity to add her own personal touches to the chores.

*   *   *

It never occurred to Nicholas as he trudged home from his day in the Canterbury gaol that his new maidservant might not obey his commands. After all, no one dared gainsay Nicholas Grimshaw. Indeed, when he swung open the door to his cottage, pausing to stomp his muddy boots on the step, he saw what he expected to see. The walls were scrubbed clean, the floors were swept, and damp laundry was draped over ropes and poles placed strategically near the crackling fire.

What he didn't anticipate was the horrible stench. The steam rising off of the shirts and braies and stockings perfumed the air with the cloying scent of roses. As he stepped through the door, the heavy perfume irritated his nose and he let out a great sneeze, startling Azrael into a hasty retreat to the bedchamber.

"What the devil?"

"Good even, Nicky."

He winced. She was stirring something over the fire for supper, but all he could smell were overwhelming floral fumes. She glanced up at his arrival, using her forearm to sweep the stray tendrils from her brow. She would have looked like the perfect portrait of a hard-working servant, but there was a glint of mischief in her pretty green eyes that gave her away.

"God's blood. What have you done?" he demanded, shrugging the cloak from his shoulders.

"What do you mean?"

"Why does my cottage smell like a brothel?" He left the door open, hoping to disperse the noxious odor, but it didn't prevent him from sneezing again.

"Bless you!" She wrinkled her brow in false concern. "Sweet Mary, are you getting a murrain?"

"What is that infernal stench?"

"'Tis only the laundry." She left the hearth to cross to the table. "You commanded me to do it." She put a distinct edge on the word "command," then picked up the parchment he'd left, which had somehow become crumpled. "Aye, here 'tis," she read. "Launder and dry clothing and linens."

"In what did you launder them? Goat piss?"

"Rosewater."

"Rose..." He ran a weary hand over his face. Surely the maid knew better. A shire-reeve couldn't wear clothes reeking of roses. He grumbled under his breath.

"But if you like," she added with coy innocence, "I could use goat piss next time."

He ground his teeth. God's eyes. He hadn't even known he *owned* rosewater. Of course, he probably didn't any-more. No doubt she'd used the entire bottle to perfume his clothing.

"Next time use the lye and fuller's earth in the cup-board," he bit out.

She shrugged and went to fetch a pair of clay flagons.

He set aside his heavy satchel of tools and unbelted his surcoat. His garments were soaked. He'd stood watch over the stocks for an hour today in the pouring rain. Out of habit, he pulled the sodden surcoat over his head and draped it over the bench, following it with his long linen shirt.

Desirée glanced up. Her face blanched, and she lost her grip on the flagons. They fell to the floor, shattering on the stones.

Bloody hell. He'd forgotten. He was accustomed to living alone, where a man could walk about half-naked with no one to offend but the cat.

He swept up his surcoat again, bunching it before him. "Sorry," he mumbled. "I—"

"Nay," she said awkwardly, fixing her gaze elsewhere. "'Tis my fault."

"I should have—"

"'Tis your house, after all, and—"

"I'll just..." With forced offhandedness, he tossed the surcoat aside again.

He moved toward her, with the intent of sidling past her to snag the first dry shirt he found. But the lass didn't move out of his way. Indeed, she seemed rooted to the spot, her gaze fixed upon him, as if she'd never seen a man's chest before.

Desirée could feel the color creeping into her cheeks, and there wasn't a blessed thing she could do about it. Nor could she seem to tear her gaze away.

'Twasn't as if she'd never seen a man's bare chest. She'd lived in close quarters with Hubert, and the old man hadn't possessed an ounce of modesty. But then, Hubert hadn't possessed an ounce of muscle, either. Now, looking upon Nicholas Grimshaw, she realized 'twas as if the two men were completely different animals.

Nicholas's shoulders were broad, his chest massive, and his exposed arms bulged with muscle. His narrow abdomen was sculpted into smooth bands beneath his ribs. A sparse dusting of black hair connected his flat nipples and dipped to his recessed navel and below.

"If you'll kindly..." he murmured.

Only then did she realize she was staring. Not that it stopped her from continuing to stare. But she managed to step aside to let him pass.

His back, too, as he reached for a clean garment, was a thing of beauty. Powerful muscles rippled outward from his spine and over his ribs as he lifted first one shirt, then another.

"Oh!" she suddenly realized. "They're not dry. I've just hung them up."

He turned back, and she gulped hard as his arm flexed with the motion. Sweet saints! Was that the massive shoulder atop which she'd ridden to the town square a week ago?

For an awkward moment, he looked as uncomfortable as she felt. He glanced at the hanging laundry. "That's all of them, isn't it?"

She nodded.

He made a frown of distaste. "I could put the wet shirt back on."

"Nay! Nay." She couldn't ask him to do that. On the other hand, if she was forced to stare at his naked torso...

As if reading her mind, he crossed one arm over his chest to grip the opposite shoulder in a gesture that was curiously self-conscious. "I didn't mean to...distract you."

She met his gaze then and saw the smug glimmer forming in his eyes. The lout! He knew very well what effect he was having on her, and he was thoroughly enjoying her discomfiture.

She couldn't have that.

"Don't blush on my account," she said nonchalantly,

crouching to pick up the shards of pottery, a perfect excuse
to avert her gaze and recover her wits. "You've naught I
haven't seen before."

'Twas an outright lie. She'd never seen a body so flaw-
lessly sculpted. Apparently, administering floggings and
dragging dishonest bakers through the street worked up a
considerable set of muscles.

"Ah," he said, though she could tell by his knowing grin
that he didn't believe her. "Well, if that's so..." He took
her at her word, and the way he casually strode through
the room after that, dodging the maze of laundry to make
his way to the keg of ale, she got the impression that, living alone, he prowled his house shirtless all the time.

Somehow she managed to keep her composure while
she finished cooking the herring pottage, but 'twasn't
easy. Nicholas kept... doing things. Like tossing his head
back to finish his ale. And bending down to pet the cat.
And bringing in a load of wood to add to the fire. Every
movement he made displayed his sinewy perfection.

By the time Desirée brought supper to the table, her
skin felt afire, and 'twas not from working beside the
hearth.

While he settled onto the bench, she picked up his cloak
and draped it over the stones by the fire to dry. Then, taking a seat across from him at the table, she trained her
gaze upon her trencher, using all her willpower to resist
looking at his far too kindly endowed torso.

When the silence became too uncomfortable, Desirée
mumbled, "How's the pottage?"

"Tastes a bit... floral."

Desirée hadn't put rosewater in the stew, though

'twould have been a clever idea. But the odor permeating the cottage had definitely infused the pottage.

"Smoke," he added.

"Smoke?"

"Smoke." He rose partway off the bench.

She sniffed at her pottage. It didn't smell particularly smoky to her. Then she noticed he was glaring at something over her head.

She turned to look. Something was smoldering on the hearth. By the time she got to her feet, he'd made his way around the table. The instant she realized 'twas one of his garments, she shot forward.

Flames flared up as she reached the hearth, and she thrust her hand forward, intending to snatch the garment from the fire.

"Nay!" he roared, batting her hand out of the way with a bruising blow.

Seizing the poker, he retrieved the cloth, dropped it on the stones, and stomped out the flames with his boot. When he lifted the singed cloth with a frown, she realized 'twas the charred edge of his black cloak.

She bit the inside of her cheek.

He sighed. "'Tisn't *completely* ruined, I suppose."

His tone irritated Desirée. Or mayhap 'twas the scent of roses making her head throb. 'Twasn't her fault if she'd been distracted and dropped the cloak too near the fire. She rubbed pointedly at her aching forearm.

"Did I hurt you?" He wrapped large fingers around her tender wrist.

She shrugged and pulled away. "I suppose I'll grow accustomed to it. After all, *most* masters beat their servants."

He gave her a withering glare. "I wasn't beating you, wench. I was keeping you from burning yourself."

"I wasn't going to burn myself."

He gave her a look that said he knew better.

"I *wasn't*," she insisted. But the truth was she'd been so distracted that she hadn't even given it a second thought. Jesu, what was wrong with her? She was no better than one of her targets, blinded by a comely face into bad judgment.

Embarrassed and vexed with herself, she wheeled about and stormed back to the table.

"I'm sorry if I hurt you," he murmured, passing by her to return to his bench.

She glanced up at him in disbelief. An apology for inflicting pain from a man who tortured prisoners for a living?

She blew on a hot spoonful of pottage, changing the conversation to a safer subject. "Did you happen to purchase the items I requested today?"

"Some of them."

She was surprised. She'd assumed, since he hadn't even bothered to take the list, that he didn't intend to fulfill any of her wishes. She waited for him to elaborate.

He shrugged. "Cinnamon. Cloves. Wine, but it's French, not Spanish. An apron."

They were the least expensive things on the list, but she was impressed that he'd bought anything at all. "And when will you be buying the balance of the list?"

He took a bite of pottage, swallowed, then told her, "Next week, when the king grants me my barony."

That took her aback. She stopped midbite.

Then he arched a sardonic brow at her. The knave was jesting.

"Of course, I could always take the purchases out of your wages," he offered.

Her frown deepened. If he did that, she'd be debt-bound to him forever and she'd never leave Canterbury.

He gave her a chiding smile. "I'm sure you'll manage fine without beeswax candles and saffron." He finished off his ale, then leaned forward to murmur, "And after what you've done to my laundry today, I'm not about to supply you with lavender."

He waggled his empty flagon. Flashing him an insincere grin, she snatched the cup and rose to refill it. Curse the varlet! Her strategy to drain his purse and irk him into releasing her wasn't working as effectively as she'd hoped. She'd have to increase her efforts on the morrow.

She filled his flagon and made her way back to the table, narrowly dodging Snowflake, who darted in front of her on his flight to his master's feet.

But as she leaned forward to set the cup before Nicholas, she made the mistake of glancing into his eyes. His gaze had drifted to her bosom, and the smoky glaze that rippled through his eyes and the slight flare of his nostrils betrayed his thoughts all too clearly.

Her breath caught, and the tiny sound startled him into lifting his gaze to hers. He quickly tempered the desire in his eyes, but not before she spied the heady, smoldering hunger there. Forsooth, so caught off guard was she by its intensity, she completely missed the table when she set down his drink. The cup caught the edge, splashing ale all over his magnificent chest, then spilling into his lap, drenching him.

Chapter 9

NICHOLAS HAD NEVER HAD HIS ARDOR cooled quite so literally. He gasped as the cold ale seeped into his braies, effectively dousing the fevered beast that had been roused beneath. On reflex, he half rose from the bench, but Desirée was already trying to repair the damage.

"Shite!" she hissed. "What the devil—"

"Never mind. 'Twas an accident." Aye, an accident, just like Nicholas being momentarily distracted by her breasts—her creamy, rounded, perfect breasts—had been an accident.

But when she grabbed her linen napkin and began dabbing away at the spill, oblivious to where she was touching him, 'twas one accident too many.

His heart leaped into his throat, and he snatched her wrist, gently but firmly, to make her cease. "I'll...I'll do that."

Her eyes and her mouth grew round as she realized what she was doing. If his body hadn't begun eagerly responding to the uninvited but welcome attention, he would have found the situation comical.

"Oh. Oh." She surrendered the napkin and staggered back onto her bench, her cheeks reddening, her glance averted.

There was an uncomfortable silence then, broken only by Azrael's hungry meow and the crackling of the fire.

"I don't suppose any of my braies are dry?" he asked.

She shook her head.

He sighed.

Then panic widened her eyes. "Don't even think of it," she muttered breathlessly.

"I wasn't." He might be at ease without his shirt, but the last thing he wanted to do was swagger about before her without his braies. "Mayhap I'll just retire for the night."

She nodded.

He eased from the table, keeping the napkin bunched over the wet place that now clearly proclaimed him a man. Sidling between the dripping laundry, he made it to the refuge of his chamber and began stripping off his boots and braies.

After he was completely nude, she called him from the next room. "Oh, um, Nicky?"

God's eyes, the maid was asking for trouble. "What?"

"On the morrow. Will you be gone all day?"

He sighed. She wasn't asking because she'd miss him. Nay, the little imp likely wanted to know how much time she had to wreak havoc on his household.

Desirée wasn't fooling him for an instant. The woman was far too clever to accidentally burn his supper and dress his cat like a beribboned gentlewoman and wash his shirts in rosewater. She was trying to earn his wrath so he'd release her from their contract.

But she had a lot to learn about Nicholas Grimshaw. Despite his pretense of violence and volatility when he performed his duties as shire-reeve of Kent, in sooth he had the patience of a monk. He'd made a promise, and he wasn't about to let a slip of a wench confound his good intentions. Desirée had a long battle ahead of her if she thought she could wear him down anytime soon.

"I'll be in town," he told her carefully. "I'm not sure when I'll return."

He could tell by her silence that his answer displeased her. But at least he'd rest easy on the morrow. After all, what mischief could she possibly make in half a day?

The next morn, after he'd gone, Desirée gathered the dry clothes from around the room, pensively biting her lip. What mischief could she make in half a day?

Nicholas had left her a list again, but she could tell by perusing it that the tasks would take less than a few hours to complete. Then she'd be bored again. If she happened to come up with her own deviously creative undertaking, she reasoned, 'twould be half his fault for not giving her enough to keep her occupied.

Mayhap she'd use charcoal to decorate the newly clean white plaster walls with a lovely mural. Kittens frolicking in a field of daisies. Or butterflies flitting over gillyflowers and hollyhocks. Or a horned demon in a black hood with the face of the shire-reeve of Kent.

She sighed. Shirts draped across her arm, she stepped to the window and cracked the shutters. 'Twas gloomy and overcast again, but there was no rain or snow. Though she'd been ensconced in the executioner's cottage less than two days, already she felt like a prisoner. While she languished in this isolated cell, opportunities for profit were wasting away out there, and she was losing precious time in her quest to discover the real culprit in the Torteval murder. Indeed, the killer might be halfway to Scotland by now.

She was restless. She needed some excuse to leave the cottage, to go into town, some reason to mingle with the villagers and seek out valuable information.

As she folded the shirts, Snowflake trotted across the kitchen to sniff at something on the floor. He gobbled it up at once. Desirée suspected 'twas a piece of bacon she'd dropped earlier, which gave her an idea.

Abandoning the shirts, she crossed the room to where the bacon hung on a hook above the counter.

"Did you like that?" she asked Snowflake. "Would you like more?"

She'd hoped 'twould take but the casual flick of her wrist to dislodge the hook from the meat, that she could make it appear like an accident. But she struggled for a long while with the thing, cursing it by every name she knew, before the bacon finally surrendered and dropped heavily to the counter.

With a casual whistle, she nudged it to the edge and pushed it over. It landed on the floor at Snowflake's feet. Desirée shook her head sadly. "How unfortunate."

The cat wasted no time. Licking his whiskers and giving her one cautious glance, he dove in.

She clucked her tongue. "I suppose I'll have to buy another. Can't very well make bacon pottage without bacon."

She'd have to use the shire-reeve's coin, of course, which meant acknowledging she knew about his cache.

But surely he'd realize, leaving her home alone for two days, she was bound to discover his secret treasury.

Nicholas had left but an hour ago, so if she departed at once, she could probably be back before he returned.

She plucked out four pence from the little wooden chest and dropped it into her satchel.

"Of course, one can never be sure of the cost of bacon in a town like Canterbury," she murmured, adding two more. The silver gleamed up at her. "Nor what other necessities one might stumble upon." She quickly tucked two more coins into her purse, then a seventh. And an eighth.

Then, before she could get completely swept away by greed, she slammed the lid, donned her cloak, and set out for town.

The air was crisp and cold as she hurried along the streets of Canterbury, past bakeries and spice shops, alehouses and brothels, until she reached the lane of butcheries. Unfortunately, the village seemed to be deserted today, giving her little opportunity to cross paths with anyone, let alone anyone from Torteval.

She purchased a slab of bacon from the first butcher, inquiring with wide-eyed awe if he'd ever sold his goods to anyone of the noble class, perchance the Lord of Torteval?

He hadn't, but her flattering admiration earned her a discount on her purchase. Tucking the threepence bacon under one arm, she stepped out onto the street and frowned at the crowd gathering at the bottom of the lane.

Her thieving instincts were roused immediately. Where there was a crowd, there were purses to be picked. But without an accomplice and burdened by a slab of meat, she lacked the stealth to carry off any sleight of hand.

Still, she wondered what all the fuss was.

She narrowed her eyes and couldn't help but shudder as her gaze caught on the distant stark timbers of the gallows, empty now, but still menacing. Had it been only a sennight since Hubert had been hanged there?

A trio of young lads scurried past her toward the town square, and she snagged one of them by the sleeve. "What's going on?"

"A floggin'," he replied, his eyes alight.

With a sigh of disgust, she let him go, and he skipped after his companions. Why people were so fascinated with public punishments she didn't know. But she and Hubert had always managed to profit the most when cutting the purses of fools transfixed by some disciplinary spectacle.

Shaking her head, she turned to go back to the cottage, against the flow of the herd.

Then she froze.

If there was to be a flogging...

God's blood! 'Twould be Nicholas wielding the whip.

She spun back around, frowning down the lane, and before she realized it, she found herself swept along with the rest of the onlookers.

He *was* there, and for one stunning moment, her breath caught, and she blinked at the nearly unrecognizable figure prowling the village square. 'Twas hard to believe the menacing official rolling his shoulders as he paced before the gallows was the same gentleman she'd supped with last night.

As he walked along, he let a whip slither through his gloved hand like a rogue snake, dragging it along the ground, then snapping it forward suddenly, as if testing its bite.

A fishmonger in the crowd raised his fist and roared, "Who steals from the fishmongers of Canterbury steals from Nicholas Grimshaw!"

His fellows cheered wildly, and Desirée glowered at them. The poor wretch tied to the whipping post was nearly as thin as the post. If he'd stolen from a fishmonger, 'twas likely only to fill his empty belly.

Nicholas cracked the whip in the air above his head to silence the crowd. The villagers gasped at the loud snap, then giggled nervously. *Stupid townsfolk*, Desirée thought, half hoping someone *was* weaving through the crowd, cutting their purses.

"Eight pounds of fish," Nicholas charged when the crowd was quiet. "Eight lashes."

The victim sagged against the post, but the crowd had a mixed response to the sentence. A few cried out in satisfaction, but more grumbled, and the fishmongers voiced loud disapproval, demanding a harsher sentence.

Nicholas turned on them, snapping the whip against the stones of the square, demanding, "Think you 'tis not enough?"

The crowd shrank back.

The constable assured them, "Eight lashes from Nicholas Grimshaw is like eight *hundred* from any other man!"

The villagers crowed their approval then, and Nicholas sauntered before them, taking his time, stroking the whip, until he stood directly behind his victim.

Desirée's blood began to simmer with a mixture of disgust and anger and nausea. How could she have ever believed the shire-reeve had an ounce of mercy in him? 'Twas clear he was as cruel and heartless as Lucifer.

She didn't intend to stay for the flogging, but it began before she could turn away. Nicholas's powerful shoulder raised the whip high and came down with a vengeance, as if he meant to drive a stake through rock.

Gasps rose around her, and the victim yelped in surprise as the lash landed. Desirée felt sickened by the blow, more so when she heard people around her calling for more.

Obliging them, Nicholas shook out his arm, then raised the whip from the other direction, slashing it in a backhanded motion.

Desirée bit the inside of her cheek. The townspeople around her were now transfixed by the performance. But she'd had enough. She wrenched herself away, but the close crowd wouldn't let her move.

She elbowed the man beside her. His face aglow with fascination at the debacle before him, he hardly noticed the jab.

"Stand aside!" she barked.

Still no one made room for her, though they silenced at the third crack of the lash.

Now was her chance. "Get the bloody hell out of my way!"

The crowd finally parted, and she elbowed her way through the tangle, grumbling her disgust with every step.

She supposed she should have been afraid. After all, she was living under the same roof as that merciless minion of the devil. Worse, she was guilty of far more serious crimes than the man being flogged in the square.

But mostly what she felt was rage.

And suddenly she felt no remorse at all about filching eight pence for a threepence bacon.

Nicholas's arm stuttered as he drew back the whip for the fourth lash. That voice...

From beneath his scowling brow, he scoured the breathless mob. There she was, his waif of a maidservant, shoving her way through the villagers, her hips twitching with anger.

Jesu! What the devil was Desirée doing here?

His grip faltered on the lash, and undeserved guilt threatened to rear its ugly head. He felt like a toothless hound caught in a coop full of dead hens.

But he couldn't afford to let his control of the situation slip, to let down his guard, for one instant. He was Nicholas Grimshaw, for God's sake, fearsome shire-reeve of Kent, right hand and strong arm of the law. Besides, since his clothes reeked of roses, he had to make doubly certain no one mistook him for a softhearted fool.

So instead of dissolving into a pool of shame, which would do no one any good, he steeled his spine to finish the task ahead.

Thankfully, the crowd quickly reminded him of just who he was. They began chanting for blood. Nicholas walked in a slow arc past them, caressing the whip, using the time to steady his nerves.

The cursed lass. What was she doing in the town square, anyway? He hadn't given her permission to leave his demesne.

He cocked his head hard to the left, cracking his neck as he faced his victim once again. Between the deceptively loud snap of the lash and the cunningly violent movement of Nicholas's arm, no one but the man at the whipping post could tell that the blows were feather light. 'Twas all about the *appearance* of severity. His methods had always been more bark than bite. But Desirée didn't know that.

Shite. Now he'd lost count. The damned wench had thrown him off his stride.

It didn't matter. Raucous lads in the crowd inevitably called out the lashes.

He rolled his shoulder back, preparing to lay on another stripe. This time, as the lash kissed the victim's back, Nicholas let out a loud bellow. The startled man jerked in response, rousing the crowd to a hearty cheer.

"Four!" someone shouted.

Only four more, then. The thief could survive four more. So could Nicholas. And then his victim would be free to rush into the tender arms of his weeping wife, who stood at the edge of the crowd, her face buried in her hands.

He took his time reclaiming the whip, letting it slide along the ground like a lazy eel, giving his victim time to recover and brace for the next blow.

'Twasn't *his* fault that Desirée had stuck her nose where it didn't belong. Bloody hell. If the lass hadn't the stomach for a flogging, then, by God, she shouldn't have come to the town square.

The day seemed to last an eternity. After the flogging was over, Nicholas had to elicit confessions from a pair of dishonest millers in the gaol. Once he separated the two, one of the millers was easily convinced by the mere menacing lift of Nicholas's brow to admit his guilt. The other required a glimpse of Nicholas's shirt, strategically stained with pig blood, and his instruments of torture, along with a fabricated but thorough description of what hideous persuasions Nicholas had employed upon his partner.

'Twas late afternoon when Nicholas packed up his unused instruments in his oversized satchel. He strode with dark menace through the streets of Canterbury, frightening away any daring lads stupid enough to consider throwing stones, and headed for home, eager to drown his fatigue in a cup of ale.

After, he amended, *after* he scolded his maidservant soundly for leaving the cottage.

It still rankled him that she'd come to the flogging. But it troubled him more that she'd stalked away from it in fury. Even if he'd given the man a sound whipping instead of merciful strokes that left no mark, Desirée had no right to condemn him for his livelihood, especially considering what *she* did for a living, the little cheat. His labor put a roof over her head and paid her wage. How dared she stand in judgment over him?

By the time he arrived home, bursting through the cottage door, tearing the singed cloak from his shoulders, and tossing it down on the table where Desirée sat, slicing a loaf of bread, he no longer felt shame for what she'd caught him doing. He was primed for a fight.

"You know, 'twasn't half as bad as it looked!" he blurted out. "The lash didn't even leave a mark."

Then he scowled. Why the devil had he said that? 'Twas a completely defensive statement and not at all what he'd meant to say. Bloody hell. He couldn't tell her the truth.

If she found out he wasn't as fierce as he pretended to be, 'twould be the ruin of his reputation.

"Indeed?" she replied coolly, proceeding to cut a thick slice from the crusty maslin. She shrugged, but her voice was heavy with sarcasm. "Well, perchance you can strengthen your arm, so next time the crowd can enjoy his screams."

"Damn it, wench!" he barked, dropping his heavy satchel to the ground. "That's not what I meant."

What *did* he mean? Why was he trying to excuse his behavior? He owed her no explanation. What did he care that she might think him a villain? Everyone else did.

"You know what I think?" she bit out nastily, sawing more vigorously at the bread. "I think you relish every moment of it. The blood. The shrieks. The applau—"

"You know naught!" he bellowed, his frustration flaring like straw on the fire.

The woman should have recoiled in terror. His roar left grown men quaking in their boots. But the maid only pierced him with her narrowed green eyes, her fist clenched pointedly around the knife.

He had to admire her. She was fearless. But 'twas a dangerous thing for Nicholas. Fear had always been his method of control. If he couldn't inspire fear in his own maidservant...

"What were you doing in town?" he growled.

She smirked. "Why? Am I a prisoner here?"

"I gave you chores to do."

"Which I've done."

"And so you came into town for what? To spy upon me?"

She frowned and stabbed the knife hard into the remains of the bread. "Spy upon you? Why would I need to spy upon you? 'Twas a public spectacle. You were *performing* for all to see."

The way she said "performing" grated on his ears.

"If you can't abide the sight of blood," he bit out, "then you should stay away from my workplace."

She arched a sardonic brow. "And how will I do that? Isn't your workplace all of Kent?" She rose and moved to the hearth, where something savory bubbled in a pot.

"I told you I'd be in Canterbury today."

"Ah. Then perchance on the morrow I may venture out?" she said with false deference. Wrapping a heavy cloth around the bail, she lifted the pot off the fire. "Unless you conduct your gruesome little displays on the Sabbath, as well."

Displeasure flared in him. "Why must you venture out at all?" he demanded, regretting his rash words as soon as he voiced them. After all, he didn't intend to make her a prisoner, no matter what she thought. She could come and go as she pleased...

As long as she returned to fulfill her household obligations.

And as long as she let him know where she was.

And as long as she didn't get herself into trouble.

Jesu, 'twas a challenging task, watching over a woman with a will of her own.

She set the heavy pot on the counter. "*Someone* has to keep the larder full."

"The larder *is* full."

Desirée nodded toward the corner of the kitchen. Azrael perched guiltily atop the grisly remains of the fortnight-old bacon that had hung in the kitchen. The cat's belly bulged grotesquely, and he licked his chops with unadulterated pleasure.

Nicholas didn't want to know how his cat had managed to climb up to unhook an entire haunch of meat.

Nor did he want to know how Desirée had paid for the new bacon sitting atop the counter.

He was weary.

His head hurt.

And he wanted a drink.

Chapter 10

DESIRÉE SKEWERED NICHOLAS with a hate-filled stare as he headed for his keg of ale. She was furious with him—*furious!* She detested him for hanging Hubert. She despised the way he made a cruel spectacle out of a flogging. And she hated how he pretended to be merciful when 'twas obvious he didn't have a morsel of compassion in him.

But damn it all! Even as she glared at the nefarious brute whom she'd cursed all the way home, the moment he slumped down guiltily onto the bench—his shoulders hunched, his head lowered, his brow furrowed—she felt her ire start to fade into grudging pity.

Despite her cross words, Desirée had always had a strange capacity for understanding the very worst of humanity. Perchance 'twas because she'd lived among thieves and learned to forgive their foibles and failings. Indeed, by strict moral standards, she herself was part of the dregs of society.

It must be wretched work, this occupation of his that drove him to drink and lie about the severity of his punishments just to ease his guilty conscience. She supposed if *she* spent her days applying thumbscrews and scold's bridles and stocks to outlaws, she'd work up a thirst for oblivion, as well.

She studied him as he moped over his ale. How could she stay angry with him, when he kept looking so irresistibly miserable?

Even with shadowed eyes, furrowed brows, and a grim frown, he was handsome, in a pathetic sort of way. Forsooth, 'twas a pity he was a lawman. If 'twere not for his hateful profession, he'd likely have the ladies swarming after him like bees after honey.

Mayhap then he wouldn't be so melancholy.

But while her heart softened fractionally toward him, she couldn't turn off her calculating mind. She realized she might be able to play upon his guilt to get something she wanted. As she'd learned from Hubert, one had to look after one's own interests, because nobody else would.

Sensing she'd have better success with honey than verjuice, Desirée waited till he was on his fourth cup of ale, then filled the trencher of maslin with bacon pottage and set it on the table before him.

Still staring into his cup, he murmured, "I'm a lawman, Desirée. I do what I have to do. If you can't—"

"I know."

She casually swept Snowflake up from where he was licking his paws—no easy feat, since he seemed to have gained several pounds. She cradled the purring beast in her arms. Surely Nicholas wouldn't bellow at her now, not while she was holding his beloved pet.

"Nicky," she ventured softly, then corrected herself. "Nicholas. I'm...sorry. I didn't come to the town square to spy upon you. I had no idea there was a flogging today. I came to purchase a new slab of bacon. That's all. But...there's something I'd like to discuss with you."

He sniffed and stared into his ale.

She began sauntering back and forth before him, scratching Snowflake behind the ears. "You see, I haven't lived in a proper house for years. I'm not accustomed to being closed up behind walls. I've always come and gone as I pleased."

'Twasn't precisely true. She'd usually come and gone as *Hubert* pleased.

"Perchance you're right," she continued. "Perchance Hubert *did* ask you to see to my welfare because he...he cared about me." She pretended to wipe away a tear with the edge of her thumb. "But I'm certain he didn't mean for me to be kept like a slave."

"A slave?" Nicholas scowled.

She shook her head sadly. "I might as well be chained to the hearth."

His eyes closed down to smoldering slits. He clearly wasn't moved to pity by her speech. But he was at least listening. "What is it you want?"

She gave Snowflake one last pet, then lowered him to the floor. "I want to go out. I want to go into town. I can do the shopping." She sat down across from him and continued enthusiastically. "Surely after a long day of..." Flogging thieves? Torturing prisoners? Cutting off thumbs? "Work," she decided, "the last thing you want to do is shop for provender."

She could see by the pensive twist of his mouth that he was considering her offer.

"I can go while you're out," she said, "keep the shelves stocked, learn the latest gossip, breathe a little fresh air—"

"Play a few games of chance?" He stirred idly at his pottage.

She frowned. "Certainly not!"

Forsooth, the idea *had* occurred to her briefly. She could make double her maidservant's wage in a few hours at Fast and Loose. But watching the thief suffer under Nicholas's whip hand today had convinced her to lie low and make an honest living for a while.

He swirled the contents of his cup. "How do I know you won't take my coin and leave Canterbury?"

She shrugged. "You'll just have to trust me."

He chuckled humorlessly into his ale. "A lot of men have made *that* mistake, I'd wager."

He was right. Nonetheless, she chided him with a frown.

"Very well, then," she proposed, "make it worth my while to return."

He stopped middrink, peering up at her over the lip of his flagon. "Worth your while?" A hint of smoke entered his eyes. "What did you have in mind?"

What Desirée had in mind completely flew out of her head when his gaze slipped lower, touching her lips, her throat, her bosom with subtle speculation.

She should clout him for his straying eyes. Desirée never suffered the leering of lechers. Unless, of course, there was profit to be gained.

But Nicholas's attention engendered a different response in her altogether. Her breath caught, her skin tingled where his gaze alit, and suddenly the air grew uncomfortably warm.

At her continued silence, he lowered his cup, running his thumb slowly back and forth across the lip. She wondered how 'twould feel brushing over her own lip.

Then she gave her head a shake. God's blood! What was wrong with her? Was she mad? This was the man who'd hanged Hubert. A man who flogged people for a living and flaunted his power before bloodthirsty crowds.

It didn't matter that he had a handsome face.

And sad eyes.

Unruly hair.

And the body of a god.

Flustered and angry with herself, she snatched the cup from him and marched over to the keg to refill it.

By the time she returned with the brimming flagon, she'd regained most of her composure. 'Twas time for real bartering. She might despise what Nicholas Grimshaw did for a living, but it had its uses.

"There *is* something that will make it worth my while to return." She took and released a deep breath. "I'd like your assistance with my investigation."

His eyes flattened. 'Twas clearly not the exchange he'd had in mind.

"Your investigation?" He took the cup from her. "What investigation?"

"The murder at Torteval Hall. Hubert didn't do it. I *know* he didn't. I intend to find the one who did."

"Ah." His tone was predictably patronizing. "And what do you want from me?"

"I want you to help me question witnesses."

"By help, you mean..."

She avoided his eyes, running a finger casually along the edge of the table. "Coerce them to talk. Persuade them to—"

"You mean torture them?"

She shrugged. "If need be."

He sniffed, then blew on a spoonful of pottage. He took a bite, then nodded. "This is good."

She bit her lip in impatience. Of course 'twas good. She knew how to cook. 'Twas only evil intent that had made her burn the first supper. "So will you?"

He rested the spoon in the trencher. "You're wasting your time."

"'Tis mine to waste."

"According to the law, a man has already been hanged for the crime. Justice has been served."

"Justice!" she burst out more vehemently than she intended. 'Twould do her cause no good to engage Nicholas in an argument. She forced her voice to calm. "I only wish to discover the truth for myself, to put Hubert's soul to rest."

But he wasn't easily gulled. "And perchance exact a bit of personal vengeance?"

She didn't know how to answer him. 'Twould be hard to convince him she *wasn't* seeking retribution, particularly since that first day, she'd come after Nicholas with a dagger.

He chuckled.

Vexed, she turned her back on him and walked away, tempted to dump the remainder of his pottage over his head.

His mouth half-full, he said, "I'll make a bargain with you."

Steeling herself, she faced him again.

He pointed to his trencher. "You make supper this delicious every night, stay away from my work, and stop calling me Nicky, and I'll question your witnesses."

Nicholas wasn't overly concerned about keeping up his end of the bargain. Desirée had no authority to summon witnesses. And 'twas unlikely she'd find anyone foolhardy enough to follow her to the house of the shire-reeve. If she showed up at the gates of Torteval Hall, Lady Philomena would simply throw her out.

But he wasn't about to tell her that. Not if it meant he could leverage her cooperation with a harmless promise.

"Done," she agreed.

The way her eyes lit up, he couldn't help but give the wench a grudging smile.

'Twas a strange thing, but for all the broken crockery, burned supper, ruined clothing, destroyed bacon, and general havoc she'd caused, coming home to Desirée somehow seemed like the bright moment in an otherwise bleak day.

He'd never noticed before how cheerless his existence was. Perchance 'twas all the years armoring his heart in impermeable chain mail and drowning his pain in drink. But now that he shared his cottage with a beautiful woman who stood up to him as an equal instead of screaming in terror or spitting at him in derision, something inside him was softening. He began to think he might miss the lass when she was gone.

As for the lust that kept bubbling to the surface when

he set eyes on Desirée's inviting lips and full breasts and swaying hips, he tried to pay it no heed. 'Twould serve only to frustrate him. He couldn't recall the last time he'd slept with a woman, and he'd be a fool to imagine there was any chance of it happening in the near future, not so long as he wore the mantle of the shire-reeve of Kent.

He finished his pottage, then let Azrael scramble up on his lap, stroking the overfed cat while Desirée cleaned up the kitchen.

Soon, between the several ales he'd consumed, the pleasure of a purring cat on his lap, his sated appetite, the soft crackle of the fire, and the strangely calming comfort of a woman moving about the cottage, a veil of contentment descended over him. So easy was his mood that his eyelids drifted closed, and he was gradually lulled to sleep.

The next thing he knew, Desirée was standing over him, jostling him awake.

The memory of their first encounter flashed through his muddled brain, and he instinctively grabbed her wrist.

"Nicholas!" she scolded, trying to pry loose.

He blinked the grogginess from his eyes. This time, she wielded no dagger. But he was amazed that he'd let down his guard so completely. He must have been relaxed indeed.

He released her. "Sorry."

She clucked her tongue. "You should get into bed."

He nodded. Then he smiled. Usually 'twas Azrael who nagged him to bed when he was passed out on the bench, brushing up against his legs till he roused.

Sleepily, he murmured, "Want to curl up at the foot of my pallet?"

"Certainly not."

His grin widened. "I was talking to the cat."

"Hmph." She scooped Azrael off of his lap so Nicholas could get to his feet. "Do you think it wise to sleep with him? He seems the kind to steal the coverlet."

"Azrael? He wouldn't dare."

She gave him a sly glance, cradling the beast against her breast. "*I* was talking to the cat."

When Nicholas woke the next morn, he lay abed for a long while, staring at the timbers of the ceiling. Azrael, who despite Desirée's predictions had been left plenty of the coverlet in which to burrow, slept blissfully on. But Nicholas was restless.

Today was the Sabbath.

Nicholas had never been comfortable in church. He knew the last thing the people of Canterbury wanted to see looming over their shoulders in the sanctuary was the shire-reeve of Kent, the enforcer of attendance at church. The congregation always cut him a wide berth, at the same time catching his eye to ensure they were counted among the adherents.

What they didn't suspect was that Nicholas wasn't the least bit interested in punishing that sort of sin. After all, whether a man attended or didn't attend church did no harm to anyone save himself. Nicholas preferred to reserve his powers for far more serious crimes.

He wondered what the people of Canterbury would think if the enforcer of church attendance didn't attend church this Sabbath. He sighed, throwing back the coverlet. 'Twas what he wondered *every* Sabbath.

Desirée was probably already up and about, preparing

for Mass, washing her face, combing her hair, smoothing the wrinkles from her surcoat. Nobody would look upon the lovely young Desirée with fear or disdain, even if the wicked lass cut their purses while they said their prayers.

Tying up his braies and slipping into a clean linen shirt, he crept into the adjoining room to find Desirée still dozing by the banked fire. The air was chill, and he was tempted to stoke the fire, but he didn't have the heart to wake the lass, even for the Sabbath.

Loath to make any noise that might disturb her, he tried to sneak back into his bedchamber. But Azrael shot past him, and though Nicholas made a grab for him, the beast slipped through his fingers and headed straight for the sleeping beauty.

While Nicholas cursed the cat under his breath, Azrael brushed up against the peacefully slumbering maid, waking her with a rude sweep of his tail full in her face.

Nicholas winced as she sputtered to consciousness.

She seemed to forgive the cat for his transgression at once, stroking him affectionately. "Good morn, Snowflake." Her voice came out on an endearing croak, and she looked at the cat with her one open eye.

Nicholas cleared his throat to announce his presence.

She blinked her second eye open, then rose up on one elbow. "What's wrong?"

"Wrong? Naught's wrong." He strode to the hearth to prod the ashes to life.

Desirée sat up with a yawn, rubbing at her eyes to clear the cobwebs. "You're up early."

"'Tis the Sabbath."

*   *   *

The Sabbath. Shite. Desirée felt a lump of dread drop into her belly.

She hadn't been to church since her parents had sold her to Hubert. The last thing a pair of sinning thieves wanted to do was set foot in a holy sanctuary, where God would be most tempted to strike them with a bolt of lightning.

She didn't regret avoiding Mass all these years. Desirée knew what she was. She knew she didn't belong among the penitents. After all, she wasn't sorry for what she did. 'Twas a living. She figured 'twas a man's own fault if he allowed himself to be cheated out of his silver.

And 'twasn't that she was godless. She believed in heaven and hell, and she expected she'd be joining Hubert in the latter one day. But she didn't need a priest reminding her once a sennight that she had no place among the angels.

The one concession she and Hubert had always made was that they never took coin on a holy day. 'Twas an admirable sacrifice on their part. Crowds in their finery, their purses fat with silver, gathered at the churches every Sabbath. 'Twould have been easy profit. But she'd resisted the urge, and that small gesture had become the sum total of her offering to the Lord.

Ballocks.

She didn't want to go to Mass, especially not in that imposing cathedral that loomed over Canterbury like the fortress of God Himself. Besides, it had been so long, she doubted she could even remember the Latin.

"St. Mildred's is the closest church," Nicholas said, adding a new log to the smoldering coals, "though if you've never seen the cathedral, 'tis worth the walk."

She bit her lip. "Actually...I'm not feeling well."

He shot her a surprised glance. "Indeed?"

She nodded weakly, pressing fingers to her temple, re-inforcing her claim with a soft moan. She sank back onto her elbows. "I think I had better stay abed."

His brow furrowed slightly, as if he doubted her. "'Tis that serious?" It might have been her imagination, but she swore a hint of amusement flickered behind his eyes.

"Mm." She tried to look as miserable as possible. "Per-chance," she suggested, peering at him from under droop-ing eyelids, "you would be so kind as to say a prayer for me at church."

"If you're that ill…"

She sniffled.

"Mayhap I should stay home to nurse you back to health."

"Oh." She hadn't counted on that. "Oh, nay, I couldn't ask that of you. 'Tis only a…a passing ailment, I'm cer-tain. You go to Mass without me. I'll be fine."

"Nonsense. I promised Hubert I would take care of you. 'Tis what I intend to do."

She opened her mouth to protest but could think of naught to say. He'd caught her in her own deception. Now, instead of playing a penitent for the priest, she'd be playing an invalid for Nicholas.

She slumped back down onto the pallet with a little cough.

Chapter 11

NICHOLAS STIFLED A GRIN. 'Twas the most pathetic pretense of sickness he'd heard in a long while. Desirée was no more ill this morn than he was. But he wasn't about to expose her piece of trickery.

He should have realized an outlaw like herself would rather not be reminded of her sins. As for Nicholas, he'd rather entertain himself this Sabbath morn, tending to the dissembling lass, than police the poor souls in the cathedral to ensure they didn't curse or scratch or fall asleep.

He trained his brows into a frown of concern and hunkered down beside her. "Are you fevered?"

"I . . . I'm not sure."

He laid his palm upon her forehead and she stiffened in surprise. His breath caught, as well, at the unexpected current that seemed to flow between them where they touched. Her skin was warm, though not overly so, and softer than he expected.

Their glances met for an instant, then darted apart. He

cleared his throat, then let his fingers trail down the side of her face, ostensibly checking for fever while secretly enjoying the silken texture of her skin.

Lord, it had been too long since he'd touched a woman in this way, tenderly and at his leisure. 'Twas causing his blood to stir. He swallowed hard, then murmured, "You feel a bit...warm."

Her voice came out on a cracked whisper. "Do I?"

His fingers dipped into the soft tresses behind her ear as he cradled her jaw. "Mayhap I should mop your brow," he croaked. His thumb brushed past the inviting corner of her mouth, and she parted her lips in reply.

"Aye?" she breathed.

The delicate shell of her ear was irresistible. He traced it slowly with his fingertip. Her eyes glazed in response beneath dipped lids, igniting his desire, and her warm sigh sent shivers along his skin. Holding her face within that gentle grasp, he took a shuddering breath and lowered his gaze to her mouth, open and delectable and tempting, and felt a sudden mad desire to kiss her.

"Would you like that?" he whispered.

She fixed her eyes upon his mouth, knowing full well what he was asking, and let her lids close in anticipation.

Then, just as he would have closed the distance to press his lips to hers, his devil of a cat sprang between them. Nicholas ended up with a mouth full of fur.

"Azrael!" he sputtered. "You son of a—"

His oath was drowned beneath Desirée's outburst of laughter. At his look of consternation, she judiciously turned her giggles into a string of faux coughs.

The mood was broken, but 'twas just as well.

What had he been thinking? He *hadn't* been thinking.

That was the problem. He'd let his desires get the best of him. He was supposed to be protecting Desirée, not seducing her.

He should have realized that living in close proximity to a woman would be taxing to a man unused to female company, a matter complicated by the fact that this particular woman had the face of an angel, the body of a goddess, and the spirit of a wild child. She was a dangerously desirable wench, and he'd best guard against her feminine charms.

Bearing that in mind, he rose to dampen a rag, but instead of sitting with Desirée's head in his lap as he'd imagined, murmuring soothing words and attentively cooling her fevered brow, he wisely plopped the wet rag into her palm for her to use, leaving her to make breakfast.

As he poured thickened milk into a pot of soaked wheat, he asked over his shoulder, "Do you feel well enough to eat?"

She answered carefully. "I suppose I could try a few bites." She coughed lightly, pressing the cloth to her throat.

Nicholas smiled. The artful lass was certainly playing her role to the hilt.

He spoon-fed her the frumenty while she half-reclined on her pallet, and though at first she ate tentatively, her appetite quickly recovered. By the time she finished off a second bowl, she seemed to have forgotten her ailment altogether.

"Better?" he asked, taking away the empty vessel.

She withered slightly, letting out a weak sigh. "A little."

"Perchance you'd like more sleep?"

"Sleep?" She feigned a yawn and blinked heavily, but not before he spied a glimmer of mischief enter her eyes, a glimmer that told him he was about to be beguiled. "Are you offering me your big bed?" she asked, her gaze wide and grateful. "How kind."

A scowl crossed his brow, but before he could protest, she flashed him a brilliant smile of appreciation. There was naught he could do but chuckle at her wit and bow to her clever manipulation. "As you wish," he said, gesturing to his chamber in grudging welcome.

As it turned out, Desirée had locked herself in a prison of her own making. While Nicholas performed his morning ablutions and tended to the fire and honed his knives in the next room, he could hear the ropes of his mattress squeaking as she tossed and turned, climbing in and out of the bed, as restless as a trapped wolf.

He supposed he'd have to rescue her sooner or later.

For the twelfth time, Desirée flopped down onto her back on the giant pallet. Heaving a vexed sigh, she swung her feet back and forth over the edge.

What was wrong with her? She should be enjoying the fruits of her deception, now that she'd tricked Nicholas out of his luxurious bed. But no matter how comfortable his mattress or cozy his coverlet, she couldn't force herself to doze when she was . . . agitated.

She tried to convince herself 'twas her itching feet. She wasn't accustomed to staying in one place so long. Hubert and she were always on the move. Since they refused to steal on the Sabbath, 'twas usually their day of travel. They'd flee while everyone was at Mass and there was less chance of pursuit. The restlessness she felt was simply her natural instinct to move on.

But as she lay studying the beams of the ceiling and gathering the coverlet in her fists, she realized 'twas more than that.

Nicholas had thrown her off her guard this morn. He'd almost kissed her. Worse, she'd almost let him. And that was something to which she was completely unaccustomed.

'Twasn't that she never kissed men. Strategic flirtation was a tool of her trade. With a flutter of her lashes, she could wrap a target around her little finger. But she'd learned to always, *always* maintain the upper hand.

Something had happened when Nicholas touched her. 'Twas as if his fingers had melted the resistance inside her and set her nerves on fire.

Then their glances met, and she saw in his eyes the faint gleam of a long-slumbering hunger. His dark gaze had sent a dangerous thrill through her bones.

Another instant, and she would have fallen into the web of his desire. If not for Azrael, she would have drunk willingly from the fount of his lips.

'Twas disgusting.

And yet...

"Feeling better?" Nicholas called out suddenly from the doorway.

Her heart leaped into her mouth, and she sat bolt upright, her face as guilty as a novice cheat's. Shite! How long had he been standing there?

"Your ailment?" he reminded her, his eyes shining with amusement.

"Oh." She tried one unconvincing cough. "Aye. A bit."

"I don't suppose you feel up to playing draughts?"

"Draughts?" Desirée hesitated.

"You do play?"

Of course she played draughts. Quite well, in fact. *Too* well for him. Hiding the speculative gleam in her eyes, she murmured, "A little."

"If you'd rather rest..."

"Nay!" She was tired of resting.

"You still look a little pale."

"I'm fine."

He shook his head. "I'd hate to make your condition worse by—"

"I'm actually feeling much, much better. See?" She sprang to her feet and twirled about. "Forsooth, I believe I'm completely cured."

He gave her a wry grin. "Thanks to my medicinal bed?"

She smiled sweetly back. "No doubt."

"Then you accept my challenge?"

She shrugged. "Why not?"

It might be a sin to steal silver on the Sabbath, but she'd gladly rob Nicholas of his pride. She welcomed the chance to regain the upper hand. While she made her way casually into the next room, preparing to thoroughly outfox him, he fetched a gaming box from his bedchamber.

'Twas a beautiful thing, varnished, hinged with iron, decked with scarlet and black squares on the outside, painted for backgammon on the inside. She wondered where he kept it hidden, for in all her ransacking of his room, she hadn't seen it before.

Desirée could have made good use of such a box. Hubert and she had owned only a painted linen cloth with pieces of bone for draughts.

"Where did you get this?" she asked.

"My father." He laid out two dozen dark and light wooden disks inlaid with silver on alternating squares. "'Twas a gift to him from the king."

"The king?" she asked, her voice dripping with doubt. He nodded.

"Your father had the king's favor?" Desirée frowned. "You're jesting. How could a man beloved of the king have a son who's..." Too late, she realized her insult.

"A lawman?" Nicholas drawled, rapping one of the black pieces on the board.

She bit her lip.

"I'm a bastard," he explained. "After my father died, I received a share of his wealth and a few trinkets like this."

'Twas more than a trinket. 'Twas a treasure. If she'd seen it that first day, the day she'd planned to murder him, she definitely would have taken it with her. 'Twas still in the realm of possibility. Perchance she'd pilfer it, stuffed with his silver, when she left Canterbury.

With his flagon in one hand and the other poised on the tap, she offered, "Ale?" 'Twas always easier to conquer an opponent who was deep in his cups.

"Nay."

Hiding her disappointment, she settled across from him at the table where the dark pieces were arranged.

"Would you prefer white?" he asked.

"Nay, black is fine," she said with feigned nonchalance. Forsooth, 'twas best if *he* had white. 'Twould be easier to palm his light-colored pieces in her fair hands when the time came.

"Very well. After you, my lady."

At first she played without artifice. 'Twas the best way to earn an opponent's trust. She made predictably careless moves and let him claim a few of her pieces.

"Sweet Mary," she sighed as his light piece jumped over her dark one, "why did I not see that?"

As he triumphantly took her piece from the board, she surreptitiously removed one of his light pieces from the outer edge where 'twouldn't be missed.

"So tell me about yourself," he said, waiting for her next move.

"What do you want to know?"

"Anything. Everything."

She moved her piece diagonally forward, simultaneously nudging the piece behind it in tandem with the heel of her hand.

"There's not much to tell," she said. "I was born and raised in London."

Nicholas examined the board, then slid a piece forward. "Your parents?"

She glanced at the arrangement of the pieces. "They were very poor. My father was a rat catcher. My mother was an invalid. Six years ago, they sold me to Hubert, and ever since—"

"Sold you?"

"They needed the coin," she explained.

"*Sold* you?"

She tapped an impatient finger on the table. "'Tis not as bad as it sounds." Forsooth, it had been horrifying and traumatic at the time, but she'd long ago come to terms with it.

"Bloody hell, Desirée," he said, incredulous.

Desirée shrugged.

"Bloody *hell!*" he repeated.

Desirée raised her brows. Nicholas was truly upset over an incident she'd all but forgotten.

"Your parents, are they still alive?" he bit out, sounding as if he intended to remedy that.

"I don't know."

He frowned and shook his head. "How could you not...how could your own mother...Jesu, Desirée..."

She stared in awe. His outrage was flattering. No one had ever been vexed on her behalf before. 'Twas rather pleasant, even if 'twas misplaced.

She glanced down at the board again, slipping two of her pieces forward with one movement.

"What about Hubert?" he demanded. "What kind of a man would—"

She waved away his concern. "For Hubert, 'twas only a matter of enterprise. He gave me food and lodging while I served as a foil for his targets."

"A foil?"

Nicholas was thoroughly engaged in her story now, which had definite benefits. Beating him at draughts would be as easy as stealing sweetmeats from a child. She suddenly wished she were playing for coin.

"Are you going to move?" she asked.

He furrowed his brow, haphazardly sliding another piece behind his first line. "What do you mean, a foil for his targets?"

"His targets, the men he planned to gull at dice or Fast

and Loose." She studied the board. "When I was young, I was his beloved little 'granddaughter.' I helped to lend him an air of innocence."

She sacrificed one of her pieces but had to point it out to inattentive Nicholas before he claimed it.

"And later?" he asked.

"Later I was a distraction."

He narrowed his eyes. "Distraction?"

"Aye."

"What do you mean, distraction?"

He'd asked for it. With a devilish lift of her brow, she leaned forward over the board until her kirtle gapped, giving him a clear view of the upper curve of her breasts. Then she dipped her eyes in sultry invitation and flashed him a blinding smile.

While the fool's jaw slackened in amazement, she nudged one of his pieces off the board with her elbow.

Chapter 12

NICHOLAS, UNABLE TO FORM WORDS, merely wheezed.

Lord, the lass was beautiful. Seductive. Breathtaking. And the little vixen knew exactly what she was doing. He had to admit, Hubert had been clever indeed to enlist her services.

For a moment, his body seemed absolutely convinced he was about to indulge in an afternoon of sensual pleasure.

Then Desirée straightened with a smirk, hitching her kirtle back up over her shoulders, and he realized it had been naught more than a well-executed ruse.

Meanwhile, Desirée, completely oblivious to the blood sizzling in his veins and the sweat forming above his lip, casually scanned the board, discovering a move. "Aha!" She jumped over his piece and took it out of the game.

Nicholas stared at the black and white pieces, unable to make sense of them. Real or feigned, Desirée's flirtation had utterly rattled him. No woman had looked at him like that since... since he'd become a lawman.

When women had the courage to look at him at all, 'twas with terror or loathing or tearful supplication. He'd forgotten what 'twas like to be the object of a woman's flirtation.

Apparently, he'd also forgotten how to play draughts. He moved a piece incautiously forward, directly into her path.

"See?" she said, claiming it at once. "Distraction."

He shook his head at his own folly. It might have been a long while since he'd been seduced by a wench, but at one time his female admirers had been as commonplace as daisies. All the lasses had adored the butcher's youngest son. Indeed, before Nicholas had taken on the mantle of the law, he'd been quite the seducer himself.

"What about you?" she asked. "Tell me about your childhood."

He avoided her gaze and studied the board, determined not to make another mistake. "After I was born, my mother wed a butcher with two sons. I worked with them in his shop as a lad."

"What about your real father?"

He rested his fingers tentatively atop one of his pieces, considering his next move. "He hoped I'd become a mercenary. He secretly paid to have me trained in warfare."

"Indeed? Then why did you become a lawman?"

Startled by her question, he knocked the piece askew, then returned it to its place. No one had ever asked Nicholas that before. Most people believed he was born to violence, the way a wolf is born to killing.

He'd told no one the ugly truth, that when he was

five-and-ten, his stepfather had been hanged for selling tainted meat to a lord. After all these years, the gruesome image still haunted him, the horrible kicking and thrashing and gagging as his stepfather slowly strangled to death. But the worst part was that it should have been Nicholas on the gallows. He was the one who'd sold the meat. His stepfather had gone to the gallows for him.

From that day forward, riddled by unbearable guilt, Nicholas had sworn to do everything in his power to make certain no innocent suffered on the gallows like that again. He'd taken on the unenviable position of reeve of the shire to ensure that merciful justice was upheld.

But he wasn't about to tell Desirée that. He had a ruthless reputation to preserve.

"It paid well," he lied.

He slid a disk forward, then narrowed his eyes suspiciously at the board. Bloody hell, how had he lost so many pieces?

Desirée wasted no time in deliberation, slipping one of her dark pieces closer to his side of the board. "And your mother?"

"She died years ago."

He scowled. Something was definitely not right. How had Desirée advanced so far across the board in so few moves? He nudged a piece closer to the middle.

She pushed her piece to counter his move. "So where did you get the scars on your face?"

He quirked up a corner of his mouth. "Angry women throwing rocks at me."

He glanced up, and she guiltily averted her eyes.

"Which scar do you want to know about?" he asked, reluctantly making a sacrifice of one of his pieces.

She picked up his disk and nodded to his forehead. "The one there, on your brow."

"Dover. Angry crowd. Thought my victim didn't suffer enough in the noose."

"What about that one?" She gestured with his disk toward his cheek.

"A pack of lads ambushed me on a dare in Tenterden." He smiled grimly at the memory. "I nabbed one of them and took him back to the inn, showed him my instruments of torture. Never had trouble in Tenterden again."

"And this?" She reached out to touch his jaw, and for a moment he was taken aback. She touched him so fearlessly. 'Twas another thing to which he was unaccustomed.

"That was from a woman I put in the stocks in Folkestone."

"A woman?" Desirée pushed a dark piece across the board.

"She fought me like a wildcat," he said, rubbing a thumb over the scar, "afraid to be left in the stocks, terrified she might be violated in the night."

"And was she?"

He smirked. "Nay."

Desirée arched a dubious brow.

He confessed, "I...watched over her all night."

Her knowing smile was irritating. And when he looked down at the board again, he would have sworn his pieces weren't where he'd left them. "Whose turn is it?"

"Mine." She reached his side with her next move. "King me."

Grumbling, he crowned her piece, then made a quick count of his own pieces, committing the number to memory. He pushed one of his disks against the edge.

She studied the board. "So how many executions have you ordered?"

He gave her a withering glare. "I think 'tis my turn to ask *you* a question."

"But I've already told you everything about—"

"What's your favorite color?" He sat back against the wall, folding his arms over his chest. He suspected she was cheating, and if she was, two could play at that game.

She picked up one of her pieces, prepared to move it. "Why would you want to know that?"

"No reason. Just curiosity."

She took a moment to decide. "Blue. Nay, green."

"What kind of green?"

"What do you mean?"

She moved her piece to a new square, and he saw her casually nudge one of his pieces off the board and into her lap. He pretended not to notice.

"Emerald green or pine green?" he asked her. "Moss green? Meadow green?"

A tiny crease furrowed her brow. Obviously, no one had asked her such a thing before. "I don't..."

"Or," he said, leaning forward to take her hand and gazing into her eyes with purposeful, sultry seduction, "mayhap you prefer the smoky green of my eyes."

She looked startled and aroused all at once. Her hand tensed in his grip, but she didn't pull away. "I...I..."

"Aye, my little cheat?" he purred.

She blinked. "What?"

"King me," he whispered.

"What?"

"King me." He nodded to the board.

She followed his gaze and frowned. While she was

floundering under his attentions, he'd used his forearm to slide four of his pieces to her edge.

"How did you . . . ?"

He ran his thumb over the back of her hand and gave her a sly grin. "Distraction."

"Bloody hell," she muttered, slipping her hand from his and reluctantly crowning his pieces.

He laughed. "'Tis a foolhardy lass who'd try to cheat a lawman."

"'Tis a foolhardy man who'd invite a cheat to play in the first place."

"True."

And yet Nicholas willingly made that mistake again.

And again.

And again, challenging Desirée to new games of draughts until the morn became afternoon. Rather than stop their play for supper, they nibbled on cold bacon and stale bread and shriveled apples. When afternoon became evening, and the candles began to gutter out one by one, still they played. Finally Azrael started on his nightly rounds, prowling the cottage for mice, but only after Desirée's third yawn in a row did Nicholas reluctantly bid her good night, leaving the gaming box on the table and retiring to his bedchamber.

Never had he spent a more enjoyable Sabbath. What a delight the wicked lass had turned out to be. For her, it seemed the challenge of the game was not the game itself, but her ability to cheat at it without being caught. As for Nicholas, he couldn't have cared less about the draughts. He simply enjoyed her company.

Desirée was a bright, charming, desirable woman, one

of those rare creatures whose wit was as startling as her beauty.

God help him, he didn't want her to leave. Not yet.

As she snuggled closer to the banked fire, Desirée smiled. She hadn't had so much fun since the time she'd won three shillings off of a drunken lord in one afternoon of Three Shells and a Pea. Today she'd wagered naught and won naught. But because of the pleasant company, the hours had flown by at a delirious pace.

Forsooth, 'twas not such a bad existence, staying in one spot, spending cold morns making frumenty in a warm cottage instead of slogging down muddy roads with a tough crust of horsebread, sleeping on a feather-stuffed pallet rather than flea-infested straw. Having a partner for draughts and a friendly cat to weave through her legs while she did simple chores for a decent wage was far from a miserable life.

'Twasn't as much coin as she would have made at Fast and Loose, of course, but 'twas honest work. She never had to look over her shoulder, go hungry two days in a row, or wonder where her next lodgings would be.

Hubert had always said that outlaws could ill afford to let the grass grow beneath their feet. But even he would have to agree this was a rather lucrative situation for her. In fact, 'twas exactly the kind of situation he'd been pushing her toward for weeks.

And indeed, the fact that her benefactor was a shire-reeve might not be the liability it seemed. What woman wouldn't want the protection of the most feared brute in town?

The only problem was Nicholas himself. He'd made it

perfectly clear this was to be only a temporary arrangement. Somehow she'd have to convince him otherwise.

She grinned at the glowing coals. That shouldn't be too difficult. The other thing Hubert always said was that Desirée could charm the braies off a monk.

Lady Philomena was wrenched from sleep with a hoarse cry. Her pulse pounded in her breast. The terrifying nightmare had left her shivering in a cold sweat.

Someone had *stolen* the key!

Seized by sheer, unmitigated panic, she threw back the covers, whimpering as she became entangled in the bed curtains. Tearing the silk aside, she frantically dressed in the dark, throwing on her underdress and surcoat with uncharacteristic carelessness.

For days now she'd scoured the hall for that infernal key. But neither her own meticulous searching nor charging the flinching steward with its recovery had borne fruit.

At first, she'd been convinced 'twas only misplaced. It must have fallen from its hiding place atop the display of crossed swords in the great room and gotten kicked under the cupboard or behind the wall hanging or wedged in a crack of the stone floor. She'd forbidden the servants to sweep out the old rushes, for fear the key might be lost among them.

But after hours of forcing Godfry to root among the rushes in the hall like the pig he so resembled, to no avail, she'd come to the conclusion that the thing must have been found by someone, probably a naughty kitchen lad who didn't know what 'twas, a child who'd thought it a comely prize.

In that instance, she had only to apply pressure through the steward to extract the necessary information and convince the culprit to surrender what he'd pocketed. So far, that pursuit had yielded no results.

But now her horrifying dream raised a third possibility.

Perchance someone knew exactly what the key fit.

Someone in the Torteval household.

Someone with keen ears. Watchful eyes. And, she decided, a wish for death.

Worse, they might even now be foiling her perfectly laid plans.

She had to assure herself 'twas not the situation. She had to be certain naught had been compromised. And she had to do it now.

Time was of the essence, forcing her to take matters into her own hands, which struck terror into her soul. Her plans, after all, required that she remain aloof, discreet, unconnected to anything even remotely nefarious. 'Twas risky enough that she was slowly poisoning her own father-in-law. What she was about to do was as treacherous and foolhardy as a fox waving its tail under the noses of a pack of hounds.

Still, what other choice did she have? She could trust no one else with the task.

Quickly, before anyone could question her purpose, she swirled her maidservant's drab brown cloak about her shoulders, pulling the hood far forward over her face. As dawn began to lighten the sky from black to iron gray, she passed through the gates of Torteval, making her way toward the village proper and the dank, foul, hellish place she'd glimpsed only once, half a year ago.

For Nicholas, the day passed in a blur. After the pleasure of Desirée's company yesterday, he could hardly keep his mind on his work. All he could think about was getting home to her as soon as possible.

But at twilight, when Nicholas hurried home and swung open the garden gate, his smile of anticipation faded and his heart lurched with misgiving.

No smoke rose from his chimney.

No welcoming glow emanated from the cottage.

The shutters were tightly closed.

Had Desirée betrayed him? Had she shown her true colors and turned on him? Had she run off with the coin he'd given her to go to the market this morn?

'Twas his own fault. He knew better than to trust a woman who trafficked in deceit. Still, he couldn't help but feel a sharp pang of disappointment. Curse the wench, in only a few days he'd grown accustomed to coming home to the sight of her pretty face and the smell of something burning on the fire.

There was no question. The damned imp had definitely stolen a piece of his heart.

Sighing, he closed the gate behind him. He slipped off the hood of his cloak and raked back his hair, then plodded toward the cottage. He wondered what else she'd stolen.

The moment he opened the door, he knew he'd been mistaken. Desirée *was* there. Her womanly scent lingered in the air, and in the dim light of the cottage, he saw a plucked chicken sitting on the counter, a full sack of flour on the shelf, and new flagons by his keg of ale.

"Nicholas?" she called from his bedchamber. "I'm in here!"

As ridiculous as 'twas, his heart actually fluttered at the sound of her voice. She hadn't betrayed him, after all.

And as he closed the door behind him, an even more wondrous thought crossed his mind, a thought that fired his blood and roused his loins. Why was she calling him from his bedchamber? Was she waiting for him there? In his *bed*?

Irrational hope quickened his pulse as he stepped into the dark room. "Desirée?"

A flint sparked as she lit the candle beside his pallet.

She wasn't in his bed.

But someone *else* was.

♋

Chapter 13

NICHOLAS'S LARGE SATCHEL OF TOOLS hit the floor with a heavy thud. "What the..."

"'Tis the master of the mews from Torteval Hall," she proudly announced.

Indeed, sprawled across Nicholas's huge pallet, his arms and legs bound with rope, his mouth gagged, his eyes rolling in fear as he glimpsed first Nicholas and then the wall of torture instruments, was the man Desirée had cheated at dice.

"Lucifer's ballocks, wench! Are you mad?"

She frowned, irked by his question. "Mad?"

"What the devil is he doing here?"

"I brought him here."

"How?"

She shrugged. "I may have said something about letting him take a peek under my skirts."

"What!"

"Well, I didn't *let* him."

Nicholas shook his head. He glanced again at the man bound to the bed. Desirée couldn't have overpowered him. The fool must have willingly let her tie him up.

"*Why* did you bring him here?"

"He's a witness. I told you, he's from Torteval. He likely knows something about the mur—"

"Don't!" He glanced at the master of the mews, who was listening with far too much interest. "Don't say another word."

She crossed her arms and skewered him with a glare. "You aren't going to try to slither out of this, are you? We had a bargain. You promised me you'd—"

"God's wounds! I didn't think you'd actually—"

"What? You didn't think I'd find any witnesses?" She narrowed her eyes to slits, then shook her head in slow comprehension. "You son of a...You never intended to hold up your end of the bargain, did you...*Nicky?*"

He straightened to his full height, highly offended, and stabbed a finger toward her nose. "Listen, you impertinent wench, whatever else you may think of me, I am a man of my word."

She studied him with a sulky gaze. Behind her, Azrael twitched his tail, as if mirroring her irritation.

Certainly the damsel had no cause to disbelieve him. He'd kept his word to Hubert Kabayn, after all.

At long last she let out a sigh of reluctant trust. "You'll do it, then? You'll torture him?"

A muffled squeal came from the pallet as the panicked prisoner tried to thrash free.

Nicholas caught Desirée's elbow to steer her out of the hearing of the poor wretch tied to the bed. "I'll question him," he whispered. "I never agreed to torture."

She scowled in disappointment and hissed, "I thought you were a cold-blooded lawman."

"And I thought you were a sweet-natured lass."

She let the remark pass. "How do you expect to get the truth out of a man like that if you don't torture it out of him?"

He frowned. "You have a lot to learn about interrogation."

Instead of taking umbrage at his remark, she picked up the three-legged stool perched against the wall and strode to the middle of the room, planting it at a safe distance from the bed. "Teach me," she said, taking a seat.

Nicholas thought he'd never met a more dauntless woman. But here, she was over her head in perilous waters. She might be able to cheat men out of their silver without blinking an eyelash, but squeezing information out of them was another matter.

"Have you ever seen a man tortured?" he asked.

She shrugged. "Nay, but—"

"I thought not." He jerked his thumb toward the doorway. "Go."

"I have a strong stomach. I can—"

"Now."

The wretch on the bed began struggling hysterically against his bonds, flapping his arms like a hen cornered by a fox.

"See?" Nicholas said. "He wants you to stay. Do you know why? Because he knows there are certain vile things I can do to him that I won't undertake in the presence of a lady."

Nicholas rubbed his hands together, as if relishing the torment to come.

"If you leave," he continued silkily, "he fears my violence will know no bounds." He turned to the man. "Isn't that right? You want her to stay, do you not?"

The man, blinking in confusion, rapidly nodded.

Desirée sighed. 'Twasn't that she was bloodthirsty. On the contrary, she was rather averse to violence. The only reason she'd ever attended public floggings and executions was to cut the purses of distracted onlookers.

But she wanted to make sure Nicholas questioned the man thoroughly. She needed to get as much information out of him as possible. After all, she could hardly lure a different servant home each day without arousing suspicion.

Still, Nicholas was probably right. With her looking on, he'd likely stay his hand. She glanced at the sinister tools on the wall. Mayhap she didn't want to watch him, after all.

"Very well."

The master of the mews wagged his head frantically back and forth, telling her nay, but she rose to go.

Before she left, she caught Nicholas by the sleeve and murmured, "Ask him what the murderer looked like." She turned to leave, then thought of something else. "And find out what weapon was used." She took a step away, then back. "And try to—"

"Wench, do not tell me how to do my work."

She furrowed her brows at him, then stalked from the room. "Come on, Snowflake." The cat dutifully followed her.

She set about preparing supper, trying to pretend naught unseemly was happening in the next room. She started a fire on the hearth. She poured a small dish of cream for the cat. She began chopping greens for pottage, all the while listening for telltale sounds that Nicholas had broken the witness.

All she could hear was the low, indistinguishable rumble of Nicholas's murmuring. She hoped he knew what he was doing.

At the first horrible shriek, Desirée almost chopped off the ends of her fingers. The knife clattered on the cutting block, and her heart leaped into her throat. Dear God, what was Nicholas doing to the man?

"Nay!" came a scream.

Murmur, murmur.

"Nay! For the love of God, nay!"

Murmur, murmur, murmur.

"Please, my lord, not that!"

Murmur.

Desirée's stomach wasn't quite as strong as she'd thought. She gripped the counter, feeling sick.

"Nay-nay-nay-NAY-NAY!" he cried in increasing panic.

Bloody hell! What vile instrument was Nicholas employing?

The man screamed again, a long scream that turned Desirée's knees to custard. She clapped her hands over her ears and squeezed her eyes shut.

After a moment, there was only silence. She cautiously opened her eyes.

God's wounds, had he killed the man?

She carefully peeled her fingers away from her ears.

Nay, Nicholas was still talking to him, in words too quiet to discern. The man had stopped screaming, and he seemed to be gasping out something.

Desirée wanted to know what he was saying, but she dared not move from the spot. She didn't want to hear that scream again at close range.

With trembling fingers, she resumed chopping the cabbage, then leeks, then onions. But when she reached for the chicken, she heard a scuffling at the doorway.

What she saw almost made her drop the knife. Nicholas was escorting the master of the mews, looking none the worse for his ordeal, toward the door, and the lawman's arm was wrapped around the smaller man's shoulders, as if they were old companions.

While she stood agape, Nicholas opened the door for him, issuing a good-natured warning. "Remember what I said, Odger. I know where you dwell. 'Twill go badly if you cross me."

"Aye, my lord." The master of the mews nodded without hesitation, then scurried out the door.

"What was that all about?" Desirée demanded when the door closed. "Where is he going?"

Nicholas pulled a draught of ale into one of the new flagons. "Home."

"You let him go?"

"Why?" he said with a smirk. "Did you want to keep him?"

She pursed her lips. "Did he tell you anything? Did he confess?"

"There was naught to confess."

"What do you mean?"

"He didn't see anything." He took a sip of ale.

She clenched her teeth in frustration. Surely the man knew something. He was a servant, after all. Weren't they always poking their noses into their masters' affairs? "Mayhap you didn't press him hard enough."

Nicholas wiped the foam from his lip. "Did you *hear* the screams?"

She worried her lip between her teeth, then ran a finger along the edge of the chopping block. "What did you...do to him?"

He smiled coyly before he took another swig from his cup. Then he let out a long sigh of satisfaction. "Naught."

Desirée blinked. "Naught?"

"Naught."

She gave him a cursory glance from head to toe. There was not a drop of blood on him. Indeed, she couldn't remember seeing any blood on the master of the mews, either. "But...How...I heard..."

"'Twasn't what I did to him. 'Twas what he *thought* I was going to do to him."

Nicholas chuckled at the endearing frown of confusion on her face.

"We're a pair, you and I," he said, raising his ale in a mock salute. "You fool people into thinking you're an innocent, and I make them believe I'm a monster."

Nicholas was good at his work, renowned for his success at eliciting confessions. But nobody understood how he managed to get them so cleanly or so quickly.

He relied upon reason. Failing that, he tried guilt. If that didn't work, he used fear. Rarely did he need to resort to violence, and even then, the kind of violence he inflicted was far more bark than bite.

One would never guess it to examine his wall of instruments—forge-blackened iron twisted into shapes designed to pinch and prod and torment delicate human flesh—hung in full view of any soul luckless enough to intrude upon the shire-reeve's chambers.

"You didn't torture him?"

He smiled and shook his head.

But instead of admiring his finesse, she let out a breath of disgust. "Why not?" She jabbed the knife in the air, punctuating her words. "If you didn't torture him, how do you know he was telling the truth?"

"Torture doesn't give you the truth. Men will say anything to stop torture."

"Then how do you know—"

"Logic. He's the master of the mews, Desirée. He sleeps with the falcons. He wasn't anywhere near the hall when Hubert murdered—"

"Hubert didn't murder anyone!" she cried.

He set down his ale and raised his palms in apology. "Listen, Desirée…"

"He didn't, damn you!"

He reached out to take her arms, and the knife she was holding swung dangerously close to his chin. Worse, she seemed in no hurry to lower it.

"Put that away."

She glared at him. He glared back. She thinned her lips, but his cold stare won out, and she dropped the knife.

"Listen." He took a bracing breath. "I should have told you this long ago. You know I spent that last night with Hubert in the gaol."

She gave him a dubious nod.

"Condemned men often wish to…unburden their souls before they die." He smiled gently. "Hubert had a long list of sins. He said he'd always managed to stay one step behind the devil and—"

"One step ahead of the law," she finished.

He nodded. "He told me he was gravely ill. He knew he was going to die soon."

Desirée's eyes grew unexpectedly misty, and Nicholas suddenly felt the mad urge to wrap comforting arms around her.

Instead, he continued. "He said he had wanted to carry out one last great robbery before he died, one profitable enough to make certain his granddaughter was provided for." He gave her arms a tender squeeze. "Unfortunately, things went wrong. A man was killed. Hubert was caught. He told me when they dragged him away, 'twas almost a relief."

Her brow creased in bewilderment.

"He was dying. Slowly. Painfully." He added softly, "Don't you see? A charge of murder ensured him a quick death."

She gasped in shock and tried to extricate herself from his grip.

But he held on. 'Twas important that she hear everything. "I don't know if the murder was intentional or an accident. He never said. But he refused to fight the charges. So I promised him a swift and easy end."

Her moist eyes narrowed as she spat, "Easy! Easy? You forget, I was there! There was naught easy about—" She choked off her words, trying to break free again. He wouldn't let her.

"What I did was a mercy."

"Mercy?" she cried. Then she reared back her foot and gave him a hard kick in the shin.

He released her immediately, sucking a breath of pain between his teeth. "Aye," he gasped, rubbing at his aching leg. "Don't you understand, wench? He preferred to hang rather than die slowly from illness."

Desirée never wept. Not in earnest. Hubert hadn't allowed tears. Unless, of course, they were used as co-ercion, to inspire pity in men with bulging purses. Other-wise, crying was a sign of weakness.

So she'd learned to armor her heart against those strength-draining emotions. She turned hurt into rage, sorrow into fury. Rather than weep, she cursed.

But for the first time since the awful day she'd been sold by her parents, she felt her armor give, yielding be-neath the sharp lance of the painful truth. Without Hubert near to scold her, a lump lodged in her throat and the sting of imminent tears burned behind her eyes.

Was it true? Had Nicholas shown Hubert mercy in his final moments? But how could that be? Everyone knew the shire-reeve was pitiless. She'd seen the evidence with her own eyes.

"What about the thief you flogged?" she choked out. "Were you showing him mercy, as well?"

His shoulders sank. "Aye."

She blinked in surprise.

"You may as well know." He scowled, admitting, "'Tis a trick of the whip, all noise, no contact. I didn't leave a mark on the man."

Desirée's chin quivered. Was that possible? Was it all farce? He'd said before that Desirée, too, knew how to playact for an audience, knew how to manipulate men's emotions for her own gains. Was Nicholas only *pretending* to have a heart of iron?

A wayward tear slipped from the corner of her eye, and she felt a long-forgotten tightness in her chest. She glanced at Nicholas, who was still grimacing from the pain of her kick, and his image blurred as tears filled her vision.

Then, to her horror, uncontrollable spasms began to wrack her body and ragged gasps were wrenched from her throat. She staggered back, covering her face in her hands, wishing she could hide somewhere.

"Oh, lass," Nicholas said on a sigh full of pity.

She didn't want his pity. She didn't want him to see her. Crying left her too vulnerable.

He started toward her, and she spun away from him, looking for somewhere to run in the small cottage.

"Come, little one, 'tis all right."

'Twas *not* all right. She was weeping like the child who'd been sold now, tears streaming down her cheeks, her face twisted in grief, wretched sobs coming from deep inside her.

She stumbled toward the wall.

He followed her.

"Weep all you want, lass."

"I'm not weep—" she hiccoughed, then realized 'twas a pathetic lie.

When she reached the cold stone of the wall, there was nowhere else to go.

His voice came from directly behind her. "Let it out. 'Twill help the pain pass."

His words and his proximity triggered her defenses. Suddenly she felt trapped, physically and emotionally. She whirled toward him and, without even realizing she was going to do it, slapped him hard across the face.

The blow startled him for only an instant. He immediately seized her offending hand and grabbed the other for good measure.

There was no anger in his eyes, no condemnation, only patience. And the silent understanding in his gaze was what prevented her from striking out again.

No one had ever looked at her like that, with acceptance and compassion. And in that moment, she realized what he'd said must be true. Though the shire-reeve wielded his authority over the crowd like a black-hearted demon, beneath his fearsome dark cloak, he was an angel of mercy.

To her dismay, the thought only increased the flow of tears.

Rather than scolding her as Hubert would have, Nicholas released her wrists and gathered her in his arms.

She fought him at first. Experience had taught her that men who grabbed her like that wanted only one thing. But he made no further assault on her. He only hushed her gently, holding her close against his chest, cupping the back of her head. And after a few halfhearted struggles, she succumbed to his comfort, sobbing softly into his shirt.

'Twas a curious feeling, letting down her guard, relinquishing control over her tears, and not being reprimanded for it. Such surrender was against all her instincts. For the first time since she'd left her mother and father, she felt free to be vulnerable.

Nicholas neither mocked nor judged her. He only held

her. And all the while, it seemed as if he absorbed her sorrow into himself.

His arms felt secure and capable around her. His voice was warm and kind and reassuring. As he cradled her head against his chest, she could hear his heartbeat, strong and steady, and she began to wonder idly what 'twould be like to fall asleep to that pleasant sound.

After a while, she couldn't even recall what she was crying about. It seemed she was weeping out all the tears she'd collected over the years. And still Nicholas had the patience to say naught, letting her drench the front of his shirt while he stroked her hair with the same fondness he used to pet his cat.

At long last, she ran out of tears. As she rested her head upon the lawman's comforting chest, an amazing peace settled over her, as if she'd run a long way across a rocky field and now lay fatigued upon a grassy, sun-drenched knoll.

'Twas a dangerous place to be—exposed, vulnerable, open to attack—and yet she felt no fear in his arms. Instead, a welcoming warmth suffused her blood and quickened her pulse as he continued to hold her close. And part of her never wanted that feeling to end.

Chapter 14

NICHOLAS'S SHOULDER HAD BEEN SOAKED with tears more times than he could count. Shown the smallest sign of compassion, the men he interrogated wept like children. Nicholas never made them feel weak or foolish for their sobs. God's wounds, Nicholas himself often broke down over a cup of ale after an execution.

But Desirée's tears were different. Each hot drop seemed to burn his skin, searing guilt into his soul. *He* was the cause of her weeping. And even though he knew he was not to blame—he'd not determined the sentence, he'd only carried it out—still he bore the burden of her grief.

He held her until her tears dried, until the hitching of her ribs calmed, and still she didn't move away. He closed his eyes, relishing the rare pleasure of a woman in his embrace.

Women never touched him. Most wouldn't even meet his gaze. Since he'd become a lawman, even harlots wouldn't traffic with him, fearing to incur his wrath.

He hadn't realized it until this moment, but he was lonely.

A terrible isolation came with his position.

And a part of him, a part he usually kept under lock and key, hungered for intimacy, some human contact that lasted beyond the single night he spent with the condemned.

Holding Desirée in his arms made him realize he was weary of his life. Which was absurd, considering he was three years short of thirty.

Yet what did he have to show for it? Dozens of outlaw graves, scars from stonings, and an enviable collection of torturing implements as unsullied as the day they were forged.

What he didn't have was a single friend.

Desirée gave a shuddering sigh against his chest, and he instinctively leaned down to kiss the top of her head. Her hair was soft and fragrant. He couldn't remember the last time he'd run his fingers through a woman's tresses.

After a moment, he began to wonder if she'd fallen asleep. She didn't struggle out of his arms or push him away. She remained in his embrace, as if 'twas the most natural thing in the world.

But for Nicholas, 'twas not natural at all. Indeed, while her soft breath ruffled his shirt and her hands curled upon his chest, while her hair tickled beneath his chin and her breasts pressed warmly against his ribs, a breathless chaos of sensations assaulted him.

A fierce protectiveness gripped him, a need to guard Desirée from harm. Yet simultaneously, he felt an overwhelming urge to take advantage of her vulnerability, to kiss her face, to caress her, to sweep her up and carry her into his bedchamber, to have his way with her.

Unaccustomed desire flared his nostrils and heated his blood. His breath grew rapid. His face grew hot. Lust buzzed inside his head. And within his braies, pressed against her warm womanhood, a sleeping dragon awoke.

Somewhere deep inside her haze of contented half-awareness, Desirée realized 'twas a mistake of the worst kind for a woman to let down her defenses. But she couldn't pull herself away from the comfortable haven of his arms. So she floated for nigh an hour in oblivion, unwilling to speak or move or think, for fear 'twould shatter the serenity of the moment.

All grief, all care, all shame melted away until she no longer felt anything but comfort. His arms felt heavenly around her, like the safe cocoon of a snug fur coverlet. His fingers weaved through her hair with such tenderness, 'twas hard to remember his formidable strength. His chest was solid yet supple, a perfect pillow for her head. And the warmth of his body, pressed close to hers...

Her eyes slipped open. She felt a stirring against her belly, evidence of his lust, swelling and growing rigid. The breath caught in her throat.

She should have been outraged, offended, scandalized. But those emotions warred with feelings of sweet satisfaction. To her surprise, a font of answering desire immediately flooded her veins, and she shivered with its astonishing power.

'Twas but a shiver, yet it startled Nicholas from his attentions. To her dismay or relief, she wasn't sure which, he extricated himself from the embrace and set her at arm's length.

As she stood before him, she didn't dare lower her eyes, where the manifestation of his desire intruded between them like a lance primed for battle.

But there was no mistaking the naked craving in his

eyes, dark now with smoldering fire, and she wondered if her own gaze burned with the same wanton flame.

He cleared his throat, but his voice was still ragged. "I could use a drink. How about you?"

She licked her lips, salty from tears, and nodded.

But the instant he broke away, she felt his loss. As ludicrous as 'twas, she wanted him to hold her again.

Just as quickly, she silently chided herself for her foolishness. She was as pathetic as his cat, she thought, brushing up against his leg in hopes of a scratch.

She watched him from the corner of her eye as he filled his cup, tossed it back, furrowed his brow, then filled it again before bringing her ale.

She took her flagon, murmuring, "You drink too much."

"Do I?" He dragged a stool close to the fire for her, then sat himself on the floor.

"Aye." She settled onto the stool, and they gazed into the fire.

"Eases the pain." He tapped his flagon lightly against hers, then took a nip.

"The pain?" She furrowed her brow.

A rueful smile curved his lips.

Desirée's cheeks grew warm. "Oh."

He took another sip. "Don't fret," he murmured, staring into the flames. "'Tis a pain to which I've grown accustomed."

She smirked. "Right." Accustomed indeed. With his store of coin, he could afford a different harlot every night of the week to ease his pain.

He sniffed and gave a shrug.

She stared at him doubtfully. "Wait. Are you saying you don't...?"

He continued to watch the fire in silence.

"Ever?" she pressed.

He frowned into the flames.

She didn't know what to say. She'd never heard of a man outside of the church who didn't...

By the saints, even shriveled old Hubert stole off to the stews every Saturday.

'Twas hard to believe. Suddenly, her own cares seemed inconsequential and far less interesting. "When was the last time you—?"

His eyes widened. "I don't think that's any of your business."

She gasped. "God's blood! You're a virgin, aren't you?"

"What? Nay, I'm not a virgin." He turned on her with a disconcerted scowl.

"Then why—?"

"For God's sake, Desirée, I'm the bloody shire-reeve of Kent."

"And?"

"Come, lass, who would want to lie in the arms of the law?"

She opened her mouth in shock, then closed it. 'Twas the saddest thing she'd heard in a long while, not to mention an appalling waste of manhood. True, Desirée was a virgin, but then, she was a woman, she was only nineteen, and she'd had an eagle-eyed guardian watching over her for the past six years.

A man as handsome and virile as Nicholas shouldn't be condemned to chastity simply by virtue of his profession. God's eyes! Even her father, the rat catcher, had found himself a willing wife.

But even as she was moved to pity by his plight, the

devious part of her brain was plotting ways to use this bit of information to her advantage. Knowing his weakness, she might exploit it to secure a more permanent position for herself in the lawman's household. 'Twas a significant dent in the armor of Nicholas Grimshaw. And if she could tap away at it long enough...

Hubert had once said Desirée could wrap a man around her heart with the mere wink of an eye. She'd find out tonight if that was true.

"Well," she said, polishing off her ale, "it seems a terrible waste if you ask me."

Nicholas drew his brows together as she rose to finish cooking supper. He wondered if she meant that. He wondered if she was right.

Seven years. That was how long he'd been a lawman, how long it had been since he'd lain with a woman. Jesu, he might as *well* be a virgin.

There was a time in his impetuous youth when he'd crawled into a different wench's bed every night. But now...

Most of the time, he was too busy to think about women. When he wasn't busy, he was too weary or drunk to care. But having Desirée in his house...

She aroused things in him that had been missing for a long while, not only lust, but tenderness and companionship and laughter.

Perchance he *was* wasting away beneath his occupation. But there wasn't much he could do about it. Desirée was the only woman brave enough to peer beneath his cloak of authority and look him in the eyes.

As he gazed into the flames, sipping at his ale, he almost regretted having told her the truth about Hubert. Now that she realized there was no vengeance to be had for his death, there was no excuse for her to stay in Canterbury.

Perchance 'twas a selfish regret, but there was no telling when he'd get to be this close to a woman again. Mayhap never. 'Twas a rare wench who didn't run screaming at the sight of Nicholas Grimshaw, the shire-reeve of Kent. And he was reluctant to give up that pleasure.

Of course the day would come when she'd leave. That had always been his intention. And her wish. But he'd begun to hope 'twould be later rather than sooner.

Meanwhile, though he might not be able to quench his bittersweet thirst for Desirée, at least he could enjoy a few sustaining sips of her loveliness.

While Desirée finished filling the pot, he rose to stoke the fire. Before long, the cottage was filled with the hearty aroma of chicken pottage bubbling over the hearth.

This was contentment, he decided an hour later as he finished off his supper—a full belly, the slight buzz of ale in his head, Azrael licking his paws by the fire, and a beautiful lass across the table.

He saluted her with his cup of ale. "You're a very good cook."

She shrugged. "'Tis sleight of hand. Forsooth, I made the pottage from sticks and stones."

He chuckled. A beautiful, *amusing* lass. "Well, you fooled me."

She smirked. "You're *easy* to fool."

"Me?"

"Oh, aye. A prime target." She ran an idle finger around the top of her cup. "I could rob you blind at Fast and Loose."

"That sounds like a challenge."

She answered him with an arched brow and a smug smile.

"Fine," he said, pushing what remained of his trencher out of the way. "Give it your best, wench."

"Where's your coin?"

"No coin. Let's play for honor."

"Honor," she scoffed, shaking her head. "You mean with that box of treasure you've squirreled away, you're not willing to part with a single farthing?"

"That? Nay, that's to be spent elsewhere."

"Indeed? On what? Saffron? Lavender? That plunger churn I want?" She wiggled her brows.

"'Tis for taxes."

"Taxes?" She leered at him, incredulous. "By the saints, how much tax do you owe?"

"Not *my* taxes," he said with a chuckle.

"Then whose?"

He shrugged. "Some of the townsfolk can't afford to pay, so..."

Desirée was struck speechless.

Nicholas, squirming under her amazed regard, replied to her silent question. "'Tis the least I can do."

She narrowed her eyes. "You're not half the brute you seem, are you?"

"Shh," he bade her. "Don't tell anyone." He gave her a wink. "So what say you? Will you play for honor?"

"Honor? I'm afraid I have no honor to wager, sir."

"Indeed?" he said with a thoughtful frown. "All right, then. Let's play for...cleaning up supper."

She smiled. "Done." She rose to get the Fast and Loose chain from her satchel.

She let him inspect it. It appeared to be a normal chain

of silver links. She placed the chain on the table, making a double loop in the middle and coiling outward to leave one end at the right and one at the left. Then she looked at him askance.

He chose the left loop, planting his finger in its midst.

"Are you certain?" she asked.

Nay, he wasn't certain. How could one be certain? 'Twas a game of risk, wasn't it?

She goaded him. "That's the loop that will hold fast to your finger, then?"

He narrowed his eyes at her. The sly vixen was trying to get him to change his mind. "Aye, that's it."

She drew the ends of the chain apart, and they slithered out of the coil, leaving his finger loose.

"Shite."

She giggled.

"Do it again," he grumbled.

"You want to try it again?" She obliged him, winding the chain out carefully while he studied her movements.

It appeared she'd laid out the chain exactly as before, so he reasonably assumed the right-hand loop was the proper choice. He placed his finger there.

"You're sure?" she asked.

He nodded. He wasn't going to let her plant uncertainty in his brain.

"'Tisn't too late to change your mind," she teased.

"I'm not changing my mind."

He should have changed his mind. The links slipped out and away from his finger, leaving it free.

"Bloody...How did you do that?"

She wound the chain around her fingers with a shrug. "Luck."

He didn't believe that for an instant. The wench was up to something. "One more time. Slowly."

She grinned, coiling the chain with exaggerated care as he watched her every move. When she was finished, it appeared the same as before.

This time, instead of studying the chain, he studied her eyes for clues, but she looked at him with absolute aplomb.

He stuck his finger in the right-hand coil.

She gave him a skeptical frown. "Are you—"

"Aye, I'm sure."

"Hmm," she said thoughtfully. "Fast? Or loose?"

So she was giving him an option now, making him think he might have chosen wrong. Or perchance the chain *never* came up fast.

"Loose," he decided.

But when she pulled the chain, it wound in a perfect circle, enclosing his finger.

He growled and banged his free fist on the table.

She leaned forward, still holding his finger fast in the chain, and arched a brow. "Go once more and I'll divine your future for you." She arranged the chain upon the tabletop again. "Loose, and you'll remain free. Fast, and you'll wed within the year."

"Pah!" He crossed his arms.

"Come on," she goaded him.

"I'm a lawman, Desirée."

"And?"

He leveled an irritated glare at her. She knew very well what he meant.

"Fast or Loose?" she asked, all innocence.

He unfolded one of his arms to stab a finger carelessly into one of the coils, challenging her with a stare. "Loose."

She clucked her tongue as she slowly pulled the ends apart, leaving the chain neatly wrapped around his fingertip. "Fast."

He yanked his finger out of the loop. "'Tis nonsense."

"Oh, but you can't argue with fate, Nicholas." She wound the chain around her hand. "You'll be saddled with a wife come next winter."

Nicholas grumbled, but in sooth, the absurd idea secretly pleased him. Especially if his wife turned out as charming and witty as Desirée.

"Perchance you'd like to try Three Shells and a Pea," she suggested.

"Why?" he said with a smirk. "Will that tell me how many children I'll have?"

"Oh, nay," she said with a laugh, putting away her chain. "I don't have enough peas for that."

She dodged his swat, then proved just as handy at Three Shells and a Pea, and by the end of the evening, he owed her not only supper clearing, but his enormous, comfortable bed all to herself for the night.

Yet despite his muttering and grousing the entire time he was scrubbing at the cookpot and cleaning up vegetable scraps, he hadn't been so cleverly entertained in a long while. And though he punched her pallet in irritation when he discovered his feet hung off the end of the puny thing, a part of him knew he'd gladly sacrifice some of his creature comforts in exchange for more of her warm company.

Desirée might have been teasing him with her fortune-telling games, but tonight she'd played Fast and Loose with his heart.

Chapter 15

Lady Philomena prided herself on her keen eyes and ears. Not a servant sniffled without her knowing. She knew all about the stable lad and his midnight trysts with the kitchen maid. She knew the household priest imbibed too freely of the sacramental wine. She knew that the milkmaid was with child, that the cook sometimes slipped bits of meat to the hounds, that the physician who came to cure her father of his dread disease had no idea what he was doing.

And tonight Philomena could tell by the master of the mews's odd behavior that something had happened to him in the town.

Perchance 'twas naught. Perchance he'd been turned down by a whore who thought she was too good for a mewskeeper. Perchance he'd gotten some bad meat at an inn. Or perchance he'd met up with an old friend to whom he owed coin. Whatever 'twas, Odger was less than his usual jabbering self, and she wanted to know why, which meant she'd need to swallow her distaste and pay a visit to the mews.

Lord, why was it she'd been forced of late to go to the most despicable of places? This morn it had been that horrid tomb of a gaol.

Thank God her nightmare had proved to be only that, a nightmare. No one had used the key. Everything had been as she'd left it, and no one but the gaoler had witnessed her arrival and departure.

But now she had to visit the mews.

She despised the mews. In fact, if falconry hadn't been one of the required pastimes of proper ladies, she would have butchered all the birds for supper long ago and turned the coop into something more useful. A slaughtering shed, perhaps. Or a place to confine disobedient servants.

But 'twas not to be. At least not yet. Not until she commanded enough respect far and wide to dictate fashion. Then she'd declare falconry a distasteful avocation, and ladies all across England would follow her lead, abandoning the messy diversion once and for all.

Until then, she'd pinch her nose and pick her way through the dropping-strewn rushes to confront Odger.

'Twas past midnight when she threw open the door of the mews, flooding the interior with light from her candle. Odger shrieked, and from their perches around him, the startled falcons screeched in echo and flapped their wings, stirring up the feathers and dust that made a fetid carpet at her feet.

"Oh!" Odger cried, scrambling to his feet, snatching the nightcap from his head and holding it over his heart. "'Tis *ye*, m'lady."

She narrowed her eyes and stepped reluctantly into the

mews, shutting the door before his precious birds could escape. "Whom were you expecting?"

"No one, m'lady." She could see by the sideways slip of his gaze that he was lying.

"A withered old trot come to hike her skirts for you?" she guessed. "Or mayhap a brute with a cudgel, collecting on a wager?"

He gulped. "Neither, m'lady."

"Indeed." She didn't believe him, not for one instant. There had been terror in his eyes. She was sure of it.

She ambled about the mews, pretending to inspect the hooded falcons, holding the candle flame dangerously close to their feathered breasts. From the corner of her eye, she saw Odger grimace and clench his fists.

"M'lady, if ye please..."

"Have you ever set a falcon on fire?"

He gasped.

"Do you think it goes up in a blaze all at once," she mused, "never knowing what's happened? Or does it scream in agony, flapping wildly and setting the rest of the mews aflame?"

"M'lady, these falcons were bred by Father Thomas himself. They're worth—"

"Pah! I know how much they're worth!" she snapped. She moved her candle just under the talons of the most valuable bird. It shuffled along the perch, trying to escape the heat.

"M'lady, please," he begged.

"I'd wager the whole mews would catch fire in a matter of moments. Poof!" She turned to him. "And you? You'd no longer be master of the mews then, would you?"

He gave her a confused frown. She could see he was

too dim-witted to understand what she was driving at. She supposed she'd have to clarify.

"I want to know, dear Odger, what has you jumping at shadows this eve."

He averted his eyes and worried the cap in his hands.

"And believe me when I tell you," she added, "that whatever you dread, my punishment will be far worse if your answer displeases me."

At his hesitation, she swung the candle toward his favorite falcon, sending the bird into a fluttering panic.

"Nay!" Odger cried. "I'll tell ye! I'll tell ye!"

She withdrew the candle, and he complied.

"I was in town today, and there I met a lass of...of willin' ways, if ye know what I mean."

"You met a wench who was willing to overlook the stench of the mews upon you?"

He frowned in shame. "Aye."

"Go on."

"I went with her back to her cottage, she took me into her bedchamber, and there she...she..."

Philomena didn't relish listening to the tawdry details of his afternoon swiving. "What?" she snipped. "Did she drag out your skinny little worm and pump it dry?"

"Nay! She...tied me up."

"Tied you up?"

"Aye." His mouth worked in embarrassment. "She told me we were goin' to have some fun."

Philomena thought she was beginning to understand. She laughed. "Did the little thief cut your purse, then? Did she steal all your pennies and go on her merry way?"

"Nay."

"Nay?"

He swallowed hard at the memory. "'Twasn't her cottage at all. 'Twas the cottage of...of Nicholas Grimshaw."

Philomena blinked in surprise. "The shire-reeve?"

He nodded. "He wanted to...to torture me."

"Torture you?" For a long while, she stared at him, mulling over his claim. "Why?"

"He wanted to know about the murder."

"The murder?" Philomena's hand tightened on the candleholder.

"Of course, I didn't know naught, so I didn't say a word." At her glower, he added, "I swear. I only—"

She silenced him with her upraised hand. She needed quiet to think. Why the devil would the shire-reeve be looking into the lawyer's murder? A man had already been hanged for the crime. It made no sense.

"Who was the wench?" She couldn't imagine any woman keeping the company of Nicholas Grimshaw.

He shrugged.

"You swear you told him naught?"

"Not a word, m'lady. I know naught. I was out here, sleepin' with my falcons."

She believed him. He was wholly devoted to the foul-feathered flock. Forsooth, she'd no doubt if she were to set the mews afire, he'd willingly burn right along with his precious birds.

But at the moment, she required his dedication to *her*.

She couldn't very well intimidate Nicholas Grimshaw. He was twice anyone's size, with ice in his veins and a penchant for violence.

But his female companion...

"Odger," she said, modifying her voice to a less strident tone, "I have a very important task I need done." She glanced carefully about the mews, then whispered, "A task for which I can trust no one but you."

Her flattery worked. He puffed out his chest like a pigeon. "I'm at your service, m'lady."

She flashed him a grateful smile, while inside she was thinking how much she despised her father's gullible servants. The only thing she could depend upon where they were concerned was their undying loyalty, earned under threat of dismissal. She certainly couldn't rely upon their brains. When she took over the household, she decided, she'd do away with the lot of the whimpering, obsequious cowards.

Desirée picked up a ripe pomegranate from the vendor's cart, sniffed it, and, while the man's gaze followed a saucy young lass mincing down the lane, stuffed it into her satchel. She had enough coin to pay for the fruit, but old habits were hard to break.

There was that feeling again, the feeling she was being watched.

She gathered her wool cloak tighter about her throat and continued along the lane. All the while, as she strode from shop to shop in the light rain, purchasing a partridge here, a loaf of pandemain there, a pinch of saffron, a jug of wine, a sack of neeps, she felt eyes upon her back.

She swung her head around, searching the crowd for a spy, but she saw no one.

Perchance 'twas only habit after so many years of running from the law. Mayhap she simply couldn't accustom herself to living a life without looking over her shoulder.

'Twould be a huge adjustment. Yet Desirée thought she might like it once she grew accustomed to it. Perchance 'twould not be so bad to make a living the honorable way, without relying upon sleight of hand and lying lips to provide her supper and a place to sleep.

Especially if that place to sleep was in Nicholas Grimshaw's comfortable cottage.

Mayhap Hubert had known what he was doing, after all, when he'd tricked the shire-reeve into taking her in, for Nicholas Grimshaw was not the somber, menacing figure everyone imagined. He was a man of quiet authority and great wit and deep compassion. Forsooth, she was still astounded to discover he used his own earnings to pay others' taxes. If a man like Nicholas had been shire-reeve when she was a girl, 'twas likely her parents wouldn't have needed to sell her.

The most astonishing thing was she found herself actually looking forward to his arrival this evening. Charming him was as easy and pleasurable as deceiving him at Fast and Loose. And tonight she planned to surprise him with what he'd confided was his favorite supper—roast partridge with mashed neeps and onions, and a golden custard afterward.

If his full belly didn't convince him that she was worth keeping, she'd simply have to dazzle him with seductive charm.

She glanced over her shoulder one last time before she left the square and thought she saw the flicker of a face staring in her direction. But the man pulled a cap down over his eyes and swiftly disappeared into the crowd.

She started the trek toward the cottage, but not without keeping a firm grip on the dagger she wore upon her belt. She might give up her outlaw ways, but she'd never lose her instinct for danger. If someone pursued her, she'd be well prepared to defend herself.

She'd been walking along the wet lanes for but a few hundred yards when the hairs at the back of her neck began to rise again. Now that she was out of the throng, the sensation of a presence following her was more pronounced.

She didn't want to lead anyone to the lawman's cottage. While 'twas no great secret where Nicholas Grimshaw made his home to someone intent on finding out, 'twas not a discovery he invited, with good reason. 'Twas better kept a vague mystery.

Shifting her purchases to leave her dagger hand free, she caressed the hilt, ready to draw the blade, and slowed her pace.

Mayhap fifty yards behind her, she heard the scrape of a boot. Testing whether the man was in sooth following her, she diverted down a side street. The sagging buildings leaned together overhead like gossiping old trots, and Desirée wondered if she'd made a wise choice in going down the dark and narrow passage. She walked with a light step, listening for sounds of pursuit.

Within moments, she heard faint footfalls behind her in the lane. Someone *was* following her.

A lifetime of evading the law lent her calm when another woman might have panicked. Keeping her gaze fixed on the lane ahead, she strode purposefully to the end and turned right, onto another narrow passage.

Ducking out of sight around the corner, she dropped her packages, drew her dagger, and waited for him to arrive.

The hooded cloak that came swirling past obscured the

man's face, but she saw the silver flash of a dagger within the folds and reacted instantly.

She sprang forward with her own weapon and grazed the man's arm. He shrieked in alarm and staggered backward, dislodging his hood.

"You!"

'Twas Odger, the master of the mews. What the devil was he doing following her? Hadn't Nicholas put the fear of death into the man yesterday?

Now that Odger was discovered, he quickly lost his love of the chase. Scrabbling the hood back over his head as if he could obliterate his face from her memory, he skipped back and fled down the lane.

A less intrepid lass might have let him go, counting herself lucky to escape with her life. But Desirée wasn't a woman to be daunted by danger. She wasn't finished with the miserable master of the mews. Abandoning her purchases, she tore after him, dagger in hand.

"Stop! Stop it, damn you!"

Her words only fueled his fear, accelerating his flight.

"You cursed son of the devil! Come back here!"

He sped away on legs much longer than hers. 'Twas obvious he didn't intend to stop anytime soon. So she halted in her tracks, took aim, and hurled her dagger forward.

The blade stuck in his shoulder, and he yelped. But it hadn't gone deep. As she bolted forward, he yanked the blade out and dropped it on the ground, casting one last fearful glance at her, then fleeing as if death itself nipped at his heels.

"Ballocks!"

She'd lost him.

Her heart still throbbing with the excitement of the

chase, she strode forward to reclaim her weapon. She rinsed the blood from it in a puddle of rain, sheathed it, then returned slowly down the lane to retrieve her purchases.

Unfortunately, when she rounded the corner, vultures had already descended upon her goods. A half-dozen beggar children were digging through her things.

"Shoo!"

They scattered at her shout. But one of them had already made off with her neeps. Two more hefted the jug of wine between them, staggering down the lane.

"Bloody buzzards!"

She supposed she could have given chase. If she weren't already winded from chasing Odger, she might have caught up with the little robbers.

But she was suddenly assailed with the image of poor Nicholas forced to flog the starving waifs for thievery.

She didn't have the heart to turn them in. After all, they needed the sustenance more than she did. She'd been such a waif once, hungry and desperate. And now that she knew how kind Nicholas was to such wretches, she could hardly be less charitable.

Still, losing half of Nicholas's supper did naught to improve her mood. She'd spent her own wages on that cursed partridge. Now she had no more coin and not even the heart to steal what she couldn't purchase. She'd have to make do with what she had.

Arriving at the cottage in a foul temper, she kicked open the door and slammed down the packages, frightening the cat into a mad scurry for the bedchamber.

Heaving a guilty sigh, she set to work building a fire and preparing supper. She hoped Nicholas wouldn't be too late. He'd traveled to the neighboring village of Chartham for the day.

She cleaned the partridge and set aside the offal for Snowflake, in the event he ever emerged from hiding again. Then she searched for a spit upon which to roast the fowl.

She looked through all the cupboards, beside the hearth, even at the back of the cottage, where a shovel and ax were perched against the wall. But he seemed to have no spit.

Then she remembered. On his wall was a selection of iron tools. Surely she could use one of them.

Indeed, she found an instrument that looked like a curious cross between a short spear and a poker. She threaded the partridge onto the makeshift spit and hung it over the fire, smiling in satisfaction.

Beneath it, instead of Nicholas's favorite mashed neeps, she'd place a pot of cabbage and onions to catch the drippings, making a savory accompaniment to the fowl.

While the partridge cooked, she prepared a custard, breaking eggs into a pot of warm milk and adding the precious thread of saffron. She'd drizzle melted butter and honey atop the custard when 'twas set.

But she needed a second pot in which to nest the first, for the custard should steam over a bath of simmering water. Again, his shelves yielded naught, but 'twas not surprising. After all, a man living alone had little use for more than two pots.

Once more she ventured into his chamber to view his work tools, and her gaze alit on a strange instrument pushed up against the corner of the wall. 'Twas made up of a wooden frame with an enormous metal screw going down the middle. The screw was attached to an iron bowl, just the perfect size to hold a water bath for the custard. All she had to do was remove the bolts of the iron strapping that held the bowl in place.

'Twas not as easy as it appeared. The bolts seemed to be rusted on, as if the thing hadn't been used in a long while. She had to use a pair of ominous-looking pincers from the wall to pry them loose.

Snowflake watched her from a dark corner of the room, his eyes glowing with curiosity and mistrust.

Finally she wrested the bowl free. It proved a satisfactory vessel, once she perched it on an improvised rack made of long steel rasps she discovered among his tools.

With supper sizzling successfully on the hearth, she took a moment to sit on the bench, reflecting on what had transpired at the market.

Odger must have come after her for revenge. She'd hurt his pride, luring him to the shire-reeve's house the way she did, and he yearned to pay her back.

'Twas not an unfamiliar situation for Desirée.

Most of the time the men she gulled at dice or Three Shells and a Pea or any of the numerous games Hubert had taught her took their losses in stride. They sheepishly gave up their coin, realizing they'd fallen prey to wittier minds and quicker fingers.

But once in a while, some men took the game too seriously. They stung more from the loss of their honor than the loss of their silver, and they itched to exorcize their humiliation. Usually with violence.

'Twas the reason Desirée slept with a dagger close at hand. 'Twas why she looked over her shoulder when she traveled. One never knew, Hubert had taught her, when a target would come to reclaim his losses in flesh.

But Odger was a coward at heart. Even if he'd caught up with her today, she doubted he would have had the ballocks to actually stab her. If he *had* stabbed her, didn't he realize he'd have to answer to the shire-reeve? Desirée had heard Nicholas warn the master of the mews that he knew where he resided, that he'd come for him if there were trouble. Surely, after catching the sharp end of her dagger today, he wouldn't be bothering her anytime soon.

Of course, Desirée didn't plan to tell Nicholas anything. There was no need to involve him. 'Twas her affair. Besides, she was trying to barter her way into a permanent place in his household. The last thing she wanted was for him to believe she was the kind of person who attracted trouble.

Gradually, the soft crackle of the fire, the sumptuous scent of roasting partridge, and the warmth that seeped into her rain-soaked bones combined to lull Desirée into a half doze.

When the door suddenly scraped open, it startled her so, she leaped out of sleep and off the bench, every muscle primed, her heart pounding.

"'Tis only me, lass," Nicholas said with a chuckle, pulling off his hood and shaking out his messy locks. "Were you dreaming the Grim Reaper had come to the door?"

Desirée didn't know what she'd been dreaming—probably that Odger had come back for her, after all. She clapped a hand to her racing heart.

He set a large bundle down next to his keg and sniffed the air. "Mmmm." He glanced toward the hearth. "What have you got—" Then he narrowed his eyes in disapproval at the fire. "Is that...is that the bowl from my brain crusher?"

"Your what?"

"My brain crusher. That bowl sitting atop..." His frown deepened, and he moved closer to the hearth. "Atop my...my rasps. Bloody hell, wench, those aren't cooking implements!"

Unintimidated by his bark, she shrugged. "Well, you don't seem to use them for anything else."

He opened his mouth to argue, then froze. There was no argument. He *didn't* use them. He settled for grumbling, "Well, I can't use them now, can I?"

She grinned. "And see?" she said, pointing to the spit. "'Tis the perfect size for the hearth."

His face went suddenly white. For an instant, she thought his heart might have stopped.

"What is it?" she asked. "What's wrong?"

He'd dropped his satchel of tools and was staring in horror at the partridge, which was browning nicely over the fire.

"Where's Azrael?"

❧

Chapter 16

Nicholas felt sick.

Broken crockery, burned supper, and scorched clothing were one thing, but this...

He was further confounded when Desirée abruptly burst into laughter. "God's eyes!" she cried. "You don't think..."

He didn't know what to think.

Desirée crossed her arms and shook her head, frowning in mock disgust. "Lucifer's arse! I spent my own good coin on your favorite partridge when I could have simply roasted up your cat."

"Partridge?"

She nodded, then called out, "Snowflake! Come out, lad. Your master fears I've made minced meat out of you."

The cat came trotting obediently out of his bedchamber, not a whisker out of place, and Nicholas felt like a fool. He bent to scoop the furry beast up and gave him a scratch under the chin.

"Roast cat indeed," Desirée said with a smirk, going to the hearth to stir the pot hanging below the carcass.

It suddenly occurred to Nicholas what she'd said. She was roasting partridge, his favorite, and she'd spent her own silver to purchase it.

Desirée continued to grumble as she turned the partridge on its makeshift spit. "After that remark, I'm inclined to eat it all myself."

"Nay!"

"Well, perchance I'll share a bit with Snowflake."

He set Azrael down on the floor again and approached the hearth, his mouth watering at the sight of the partridge, golden and gleaming and dripping with luscious juices. "Is there naught I can do to regain your favor?" He rubbed at his chin. "I'd do nigh anything for a bite of that partridge."

She arched a brow and gazed up at him. "Anything?"

He nodded. After all, what could she ask of him that he wouldn't gladly give? He'd already provided her a roof over her head, honest employment, and, as of today, a new kirtle he'd picked out himself, one in her favorite color.

Desirée grinned. "I'd never realized the bargaining power of partridges before."

"Oh, aye," he said with mock gravity. "Men will lay down their lives for a partridge."

A chuckle escaped her. "I don't think I shall ask you to lay down your life."

"What then, my lady? Shall I slay a dragon for you? Bring you the Holy Grail? Capture the moon and the stars for your crown?"

She giggled. "All that for a partridge?"

He glanced at the fire. "As long as 'tisn't burned."

She gave him the sultry gaze of a temptress, murmuring, "Don't fret. 'Twill be roasted to perfection."

"In that case, name your price, my lady."

"Hmm." She crossed her arms, considering her options. "Ah," she decided. "Let me cut your hair."

"My hair?"

"Aye."

"What's wrong with my hair?" He pinched a lock between his fingers.

"'Tis ragged, and it hangs upon your shoulders. When was the last time you cut it?"

He shrugged.

She smirked. "'Tisn't as if you've a shortage of scissors."

He arched a chiding brow. "Those scissors aren't meant for cutting hair."

"Well, they might as well serve *some* useful purpose."

"All right," he conceded with a grumble. "But see you don't forget what you're about and lop off my head."

Desirée grinned, turning the spit while Nicholas sharpened the carving knife on a whetstone.

"So how was your day, my lady?"

"Uneventful. Just the usual haggling with shopkeepers and dodging raindrops. And yours?"

"Put a woman in the stocks for an hour."

"For?"

"Cursing in church."

"Ah. She should do as I do and stay out of churches."

Nicholas smiled. They understood each other now. An outlaw was as unwelcome in church as the lawman who enforced attendance.

She stirred the vegetables. "I'm afraid you'll have to

settle for cabbage and onions. On the way home, I tossed the neeps to some starving children."

He shook his head. "Poor souls. England's full of them. And full of unscrupulous merchants, as well. I marched a baker through the streets of Chartham today with one of his short-weight loaves about his neck."

She clucked her tongue.

What a curious conversation, Desirée thought. Though their tone was familiar and nonchalant, she was lying through her teeth about an attack that might have killed her, and he was speaking casually about his occupation of inflicting punishments. They were an odd pair indeed.

Snowflake hovered close, licking his whiskers, and Desirée took mercy on him, setting the bowl of partridge offal on the floor for him before serving up supper.

Nicholas ate with as much relish as his cat, smacking his lips and lapping at his fingers, and Desirée decided her coin had been well spent indeed, even if she'd had to make do without the neeps and wine.

"Divine," he told her around his last bite of partridge.

She smiled as she rose from the table. "I hope you've left room for custard."

"Custard?" His eyes lit up like a child's.

She lifted the pot from its water bath, setting it on the counter, then topping it with a thick slab of butter, which began to melt at once atop the warm custard.

"You'll spoil me, wench," he told her.

"Are you complaining?" she asked, drizzling honey over the top of the melting butter to make a sweet, golden glaze.

"Indeed," he told her. "I shall grow accustomed to playing draughts and eating partridge and having company by the fire." She glanced at him. He was staring into his ale. "How will I manage without you?"

"Without me?"

Her heart stuttered in her breast. She'd prayed he might have forgotten about her leaving.

Aye, he'd specifically said theirs was a temporary arrangement. Aye, he'd hired her only out of pity and honor in the first place. And aye, since her business in Canterbury was concluded, he'd expect her to move on.

But she'd hoped all that had slipped his mind.

She bit at her lip, watching the honey pool atop the custard, sweet and warm and tempting.

Damn it all, *she* could be sweet and warm and tempting. She wasn't going to give up that easily. She'd change his mind, if it took every last ounce of her charm. In fact, she'd have him *begging* her to stay. Forcing a bright smile to her face, she carried the custard to the table.

"God's eyes!" she said. "Quit sobbing in your ale. You shall be glad to be rid of me, and you know it."

"Glad?"

"Aye." She gave him a wink. "You'll tire of me constantly outwitting you at Fast and Loose."

Nicholas gave her a rueful smile that didn't quite reach his eyes. By the saints, he'd gladly let the lass win every game if only she were there to play him each night.

'Twasn't fair, of course. Desirée had come into his household out of desperation, not choice. Given the choice, she'd certainly never have picked a lawman for company.

Besides, she had a promising future ahead of her. She

was young and beautiful, charming and witty. What bachelor of honorable means wouldn't pursue her like a hound after a vixen?

Nay, she *would* leave him. Mayhap not this week, if he were lucky, but soon. Still, she was right. There was no point in sobbing in his ale. He might as well enjoy her company while she was here.

'Twas pleasant company indeed.

The saucy maid raised an enticing brow and dipped a spoon into the custard. She lifted it to his lips, and he took a bite, closing his eyes to savor the taste.

"Mmm."

'Twas rich and sweet, as smooth as velvet. He opened his eyes to tell her so, but the words caught in his throat. Desirée was staring at his mouth, and there was unmistakable hunger in her eyes. He lowered his gaze to her lips, which were parted in a smile, and for a wicked moment, he wondered if they tasted as sweet as the custard.

Before he could do something he might regret, he took the spoon from her and scooped out a generous portion of custard for her, slipping it between her lips.

'Twas too large a bite, and she laughed as it oozed out between her teeth. But the taste made her moan softly with pleasure, and that sound, as innocent as 'twas, sent a rush of desire into his loins.

With a scheming grin, she grabbed the spoon and dished out an enormous bite. He shook his head, but she advanced anyway. "Open wide," she teased.

Unable to resist her wicked challenge, he complied, and she shoved the overloaded spoon into his mouth. Custard seeped out the sides of his mouth and dribbled down his chin.

She laughed and leaned toward him to scoop the spill from his chin with her finger. Then she popped her finger in her mouth, sucking off the custard.

He nearly groaned aloud. Did the naughty lass know what she was doing? Or was he so starved for a woman's attentions that he'd melt at the slightest provocation? He swallowed down the custard, licking a bit of honey from the corner of his mouth.

She must have glimpsed the lust in his gaze, for she suddenly froze with her fingertip still at her lips.

They were so close, inches apart. He could see the candlelight dancing in her green eyes, smell the subtle fragrance of the rain on her hair, feel her soft breath. He need only ease forward a little to capture her lips with his own.

'Twas such a temptation. Her mouth would be yielding, he knew, and she would taste of honey. It had been so long since he'd felt the sweet pressure of a woman's kiss.

But, God help him, he didn't dare.

Desirée stared at the stray drop of honey on his lower lip. She felt the most wicked urge, and she'd had just enough ale to bolster her courage. With a mischievous giggle, she inclined her head toward his and lapped up the drop with her tongue.

His soft groan did something delicious to her insides, and she suddenly felt reckless and playful and impulsive. Instead of pulling away, she licked his lip again. And again.

"Mmm," she purred, rubbing her mouth over his, "you taste like—"

He cut off her words, suddenly seizing the back of her head and slanting his mouth over hers, kissing her with a fierce longing that was both tender and powerful.

She gasped in surprise. For a moment, panic gripped her, as if she'd dived into waters far deeper than she'd expected. After the first breathless moment, as he continued demanding kisses from her yielding mouth, the panic faded, only to be replaced by an even more dangerous sensation.

Desire.

In Desirée's line of work, she'd learned early that kissing was one of the most effective forms of distraction. She'd kissed hundreds of men in the name of profit.

None of them had made her feel like this.

His breath blew hot upon her skin, igniting her senses. His lips closed over hers as if claiming her, devouring her, and she shivered with the yearning to respond in kind. Liquid lust filled her veins and made her heart throb like an ocean wave pounding the shore.

She tangled her hands in his shirt, dragging him closer, deepening the kiss, never wanting it to end.

But with a growl of frustration, he tore his lips from hers and pushed her gently away. Reeling in surprise, she plopped with bone-jarring force back onto her bench. Her elbow caught the pot of custard, and it tumbled upside down into her lap.

"Oh!" She shot to her feet again, watching in horror as the sticky mess oozed down her kirtle.

Nicholas reached across the table to offer his napkin. "Oh, hell. I'm sorry. 'Tis my fault."

She glanced up. His eyes were still glazed with yearning, the same yearning she felt in her breast. God help her, but she wanted to forget the custard and kiss him again.

"I should never have—" he started.

"Nay. 'Tis my—"

"I had no right to—"

"You didn't—"

Their eyes met one last time, uncomfortably, then they both looked away. Whatever current had passed between them had dimmed, and they were left with only embarrassment and awkward silence.

"Damn," she said to break the tension as she dabbed at her sticky skirts. "I just did the laundry."

"Wait." Nicholas scraped his bench back and started toward the door. "I forgot. I brought you something from Chartham. A gift."

"A gift?"

He unwrapped the bundle he had left by the keg and held up the gift. 'Twas a kirtle of smoky green, the most beautiful shade Desirée had ever seen, and for a moment, she could only stare in wonder.

"For me?" she asked.

He nodded. "Your favorite color, aye?"

"Aye." She was overwhelmed. Preparing a savory meal for him was naught compared to the purchase of a new kirtle. Surely he didn't mean to simply give it to her. "How much do I owe you?"

"Naught. 'Tis a gift." He glanced down at her soiled clothing. "And a timely one, 'twould appear."

She advanced slowly, taking the garment carefully from him, then rubbing the soft fabric against her cheek. It had been so long since she'd had a new kirtle. She couldn't believe Nicholas had been so thoughtful.

Then she froze. A sudden, horrible thought crossed her mind, morbid enough to make her blanch.

"What is it?" he asked. "You don't like it?"

She held the garment away from her now. "Where did you get this?"

"In Chartham. I told you."

She bit her lip. She couldn't think of any polite way to ask. "Did you get this off the woman in the stocks?"

Chapter 17

NICHOLAS'S EYELIDS FLATTENED. Of course, Desirée had every right to expect he'd extorted the kirtle from a helpless woman. He was a fool to think otherwise. Just as he'd been a fool to kiss her. For a moment, he'd forgotten who he was.

"I don't steal from my victims," he said tightly. "Nor do I accept bribes."

"Oh." She blushed. "I'm sorry. Of course you don't. 'Tis only—"

"I know. I'm a shire-reeve. They're a corrupt lot. Naturally, you'd assume—"

"Nay! Nay. I should have known better." She gave him a sheepish smile. "You're not an ordinary shire-reeve."

"I assure you," he told her solemnly, "I purchased this with my own coin. If, however, it offends you to wear garments bought with a lawman's wage..." He reached out to take the kirtle back.

She gasped, pulling it out of his reach and holding it

defensively against her breast. "I...didn't say that. Not at all. Forsooth...I think I'll put it on now." She hurried toward the bedchamber, afraid that if she hesitated, he might take the kirtle away.

While she undressed in the next room, Nicholas sat and stared into the flames of the hearth, trying not to think about her undressing in the next room.

"'Tis a beautiful color," she called to him.

"It matches your eyes." He winced. He shouldn't have said that. Did he really want her to know he'd memorized every feature of her face?

"I haven't had a new kirtle in two years."

Mayhap he'd done something right, after all. "This one should last as long, if you don't make a habit of dousing it in custard."

"Oh, shite!"

"What?"

"I just snagged my underskirt on one of your cursed...torture...things."

He opened his mouth to reply, but he couldn't get the vision of her in her underskirt out of his mind. He wondered if the sheer linen clung to her curves, pulling taut across her breasts, draping seductively betwixt her thighs.

"*That's* how you interrogate women, isn't it?" she called. "You threaten to shred their favorite garments with these...these hooks and knives...and they sing like sparrows."

He chuckled. She wasn't that far from the truth. "Usually I threaten to cut their hair. Women hate that."

"I can see why, once they glimpse what you've done to your own."

He frowned.

"Speaking of which," she said, "you promised you'd let me trim your hair after supper."

"That I did." He stared over at the cat, who took a moment from his fat-bellied dozing to lift his head. "What do you think, Azrael? Am I putting my life at risk?"

Desirée emerged from the bedchamber with a brilliant, dimpled smile, holding aloft two pairs of shears, snicking them like a crab as she twirled in her new kirtle.

Lord, she was adorable. The gown fit her perfectly. The soft fabric settled low upon her creamy shoulders, hugging her breasts and narrowing at her waist, then flaring over her hips in graceful folds that brushed the floor.

"What do you think?" she asked.

What he thought was that he'd like to strip the kirtle back off of her. "You look like a queen."

"Queen of the Shears," she announced, dancing playfully toward the table.

'Twas a curiously disturbing sight, the lovely lass spinning about in sparkle-eyed innocence while she wielded scissors designed to lop off ears and noses. Not that he'd tell her that, of course.

"Come close to the fire," she beckoned, pulling the stool to the hearth.

"You're sure you know what you're doing?" he said, eyeing the oversized shears.

She grinned. "I've got stanch-weed nearby so you won't bleed to death."

He shook his head at her grim humor. "You're a wicked lass." He rose to take a seat by the fire anyway, never imagining how truly hazardous a position he was putting himself in.

From the moment Desirée ruffled her fingers through his lush hair, she knew the task would be naught like cutting Hubert's sparse wisps. Despite Nicholas's savage appearance, his thick locks were deceptively soft and silky, and the loose curls wound seductively around her fingers.

"Most women would kill for hair like this," she murmured.

He frowned dubiously up at her. "Not a thing to say when you've shears in your hand, lass."

"You *are* at my mercy now, aren't you?" She taunted him with teasing snips of the scissors.

He sighed, admitting, "For partridge that tasty, you can clip me bald as a pilgrim."

She chuckled. She'd do no such thing. His mane, though unruly, was luxurious. In fact, 'twas tempting to save up all the snipped locks and make a pillow out of them.

She started behind him, judiciously trimming away only the longest strands that straggled down his back, so his hair still curled sinuously at the nape of his neck. Humming softly, she worked her way up, each snip of the scissors adding buoyancy as she cut the weight off his hair.

"What's that?" he asked.

"What's what?"

"That song."

"Oh." She'd hardly realized she was singing. She thought for a moment. *"Tempus es iocundum."*

"Indeed?" His voice cracked over the word.

Suddenly she realized she'd chosen a bawdy song proclaiming that she was burning with lust. "'Tis a song

about...ducks, I believe," she lied. "I heard it from
a...duck herder."

"A duck herder."

She could tell by his voice and the twitching of a grin
at his lip that he recognized the song. And he knew 'twas
not about ducks. "Or so I was told," she hedged.

She continued trimming, this time in silence, cutting
carefully over the tops of his ears, leaving a short piece
in front of each to accentuate the hollows of his cheeks.
As she worked on the sides, she glanced occasionally at
his face. There was a slight furrow between his brows,
and when she slid the hair through her fingers, his eyelids
dipped and his nostrils flared.

She was in a powerful position, she realized, for Nicholas was a man unaccustomed to touch. No one embraced
a lawman or held his hand, caressed his cheek or cut his
hair. That made him exceptionally vulnerable. With the
right touches, she thought, she could easily make him
melt like butter in the palm of her hand.

'Twas a wicked game, one Desirée had played a thousand times in order to soften up targets for Hubert's
fleecing.

But with Nicholas, she quickly discovered 'twas an entirely different matter. The emotional distance she always
maintained between herself and the targets was absent. As
she slipped her fingers through his tresses, the mere sight
of Nicholas's lusty expression ignited her own sensual
fires. She licked her lips, recalling his kiss. Her breath
quickened, and her breasts began to tingle with longing.

That desire only worsened when she moved before
him to cut the front of his hair. He averted his eyes, lest he

stare directly at her breasts, but she could tell, by the rapid rise and fall of his chest, 'twas a strain for him.

The knowledge that she could make a man want her had always given her a certain heady pleasure. But the knowledge that Nicholas wanted her left her perilously giddy.

She should have recognized the danger. 'Twas foolish to lose control. She'd already come close. Yet even her own swiftly rising desires couldn't stop her from playing with her newfound power over the formidable Nicholas Grimshaw.

Dipping her eyes in sultry invitation, she murmured, "Spread your legs."

"What?" he croaked.

She gave him a coy smile. "I can't get close enough to reach your brow."

Clenching his jaw, he reluctantly did as she bade him, and she slipped between his knees.

Heat seemed to roll off of him as she stood in that intimate position, and she felt an intoxicating sheen of sweat rise upon her own skin.

His eyes were squeezed shut now, and when she raked her fingers back through his hair, she saw his brow was set in a deep scowl.

She took her time trimming the front, weaving her fingers through his locks, gently blowing away snippets of hair when they fell upon his face, bending close to make sure her cuts were even. When she glanced down, she saw the white knuckles of his fists resting on his spread thighs, as if he fought some silent internal battle.

The sight made the breath catch in her breast. She suddenly felt like a tasty mouse, recklessly teasing the cat between whose paws she played.

Yet she couldn't stop herself. She craved the thrill of danger, the risky possibility that something untoward might happen, that Nicholas might impulsively kiss her again.

His eyes were still tightly closed, so she could inspect him at her leisure. With the weight gone from his hair, sensual waves framed his face, accentuating its lean planes. His nostrils flared again, as if to catch her scent, while his lips compressed with increasing unease.

Deliberately taunting him, she stepped forward another inch, brushing the insides of his thighs with her own, placing a finger under his chin to tip his head back, ostensibly to gain better access to his hair.

His frown intensified as he clenched his fists even tighter, and she felt as if she grew drunk on his sweet torment, drinking deep an intoxicating brew of command and lust. 'Twas cruel, she knew, to tempt him so, but she couldn't seem to stop herself.

She let her gaze drift down over his massive shoulders, his heaving chest, his muscular thighs, and then she saw a slight movement below his hips. She caught her lip beneath her teeth. He might be able to hide his desires with a clenched jaw and fisted hands. But there was no denying the lusty beast roaring between his legs.

She wickedly wondered what would happen if she nudged forward just a few more inches, let her knee come into contact with...

Suddenly his knees clamped together, trapping her. She gasped, glancing up into his narrowed eyes.

"Don't even think of it, wench," he whispered.

She opened her mouth to issue an indignant denial, but none would come out.

"Are you finished?" he asked.

She reluctantly nodded.

He rose, picking her up by the waist and setting her away from him, then shaking his head vigorously to dislodge the loose cuttings.

"And they call *me* a master of torture," he muttered.

❧

Chapter 18

NICHOLAS HAD GOTTEN VERY LITTLE SLEEP. Between the physical torment of his unquenched desire and the mental anguish of knowing his time with the tempting lass was limited, he'd thrashed between lust and loss all night.

Yet already Azrael nagged at him to rise, meowing relentlessly beside the pallet.

"Hush, cat."

Surely 'twasn't morn yet. 'Twas too early.

Azrael disagreed. He resumed his persistent meows until Nicholas opened one eye to scowl at him.

Then he opened the other eye. "What in the—?"

Azrael had brought him a gift.

Once every few months, the cat, an expert mouser, having eaten his fill of rodents, left a tribute for Nicholas.

Nicholas grimaced. At least the thing was fully dead this time.

"Aye, thank you," he told the cat, "but I think I'll save it for later."

Sitting up, he rubbed his eyes, wondering how morn

had arrived so quickly. He raked a hand back through his hair and for a moment was startled by its abbreviated length. Then he remembered the wench who'd cut it short, the same wicked wench who'd lengthened another part of him, he was certain, quite deliberately.

The lass was dangerous. She was far too beautiful and tempting for her own good. She invited trouble with her coy glances and sly smiles. If she weren't careful, she'd seduce her way into a situation beyond the realm of play, a situation beyond her control. Perchance beyond his.

Though Nicholas prided himself on his self-restraint when it came to violence—'twas a necessary skill when one applied physical coercions—he was out of practice at tempering his lust.

The sooner he got her out of his household, the safer 'twould be for the both of them. Yet the thought of her going away left a hollow spot in his heart. Life would be lonely without her.

He glanced again at Azrael marching proudly beside the dead mouse. Mayhap he'd get a second cat. Or a hound. Or that wife she'd predicted for him.

He frowned. No maid, no matter how desperate, would agree to live with the shire-reeve of Kent. No maid but intrepid Desirée.

With a heavy sigh, he rose, skirting around Azrael's offering. The lass was likely still abed. He'd have to remove the carcass before she woke and discovered the grisly thing.

He pulled on his braies and selected the eye gouger from the wall to scoop up the limp rodent. Carrying the spoon carefully so as not to spill its burden, he crept toward the cottage door. Opening the door a crack, he reversed the spoon and catapulted the dead beast across the yard, hoping 'twould serve as carrion for the crows.

When he closed the door again, he saw Desirée, perched on her elbows in her pallet, looking at him, her hair messy from sleep, her eyes half-lidded.

"What are you doing?" she mumbled.

Lord, she looked adorable. No longer a calculating vixen, she seemed childlike, vulnerable, innocent, harmless.

"Shh. Go back to sleep."

She yawned and scrubbed at one eye with her fist, and 'twas all Nicholas could do to resist crossing the room to sweep her up and carry her into his own still-warm bed.

He dared not stand before her long, clad only in his braies, for already his loins stirred with yearning. Soon he'd display his lust for all the world to see.

"Are you leaving now?" she murmured.

One corner of his mouth drifted up. "I'm not dressed yet."

She blinked to clear her vision. "Oh."

An awkward span of silence passed while they stared at each other. Desirée's gaze roamed over his half-naked body, and he felt it like the touch of flame. There was no hiding his desire now. His cock strained with blatant need at his linen braies.

"Go back to sleep," he croaked.

"I'm awake," she said, rubbing sleepily at her cheek. "I should make you some breakfast."

"Don't trouble yourself. I have to be on my way." He ducked into his bedchamber, calling out, "I'll pick up a cocket in town."

"Where are you going?"

Safe in his bedchamber, he adjusted his braies to better accommodate his state of arousal. "Sturry." He took his tunic off its hook and shook out the wrinkles. "Someone absconded with the miller's daughter yesterday. I have to find out where she is."

"When will you be home?" Her voice came from the doorway this time, startling him.

He swiftly thrust his arms through the shirt and pulled it over his head. 'Twas one thing for Desirée to gaze at him from her spot at the hearth, across the room, another for her to watch him dress in his own bedchamber. Even more disconcerting, she was standing there, clad in naught more than a fur coverlet.

She looked at him expectantly.

Suddenly he couldn't remember her question. "What?"

"When will you be home?"

"I'm not sure." He turned away from her to buckle his belt. "It depends on how long the abductor holds out."

She crossed the room in front of him, and he caught the scent of sleep and flowers and spice coming off of her, a tantalizing scent unique to Desirée. She picked up his boots and returned, handing them to him.

"I hope you're home in time for supper." She gave him a seductive smile, wriggling her brows. "I'm making pike with galentyne."

Sweet saints. Did the lass not know *she* was far more tempting than anything she could whip up over the hearth? If Nicholas came home early, 'twould be for her, not for pike with galentyne. "I'll do my best."

She thankfully left him alone then, so he could concentrate on which tools to pack.

Most he tossed into the bag for their menace value, instruments with jagged teeth and rust-stained edges. Victims might not be able to guess their purpose. Indeed, Nicholas wasn't always sure himself. But their gruesome appearance alone served as an effective tongue loosener.

Just for good measure, he threw in rope and shackles and the eye gouger he'd just used to catapult the mouse, mostly so Desirée wouldn't try to use the thing to stir supper. By the time he emerged to wash his face, the lass was snoring softly by the hearth again. Finishing his ablutions quietly, he donned his hood and cloak. He shouldered the large satchel of clanking tools and crept out the door, closing it softly behind him.

Sturry was but a few miles away. Thankfully, the road wasn't the muddy mire it had been in the last two days. There was no rain this morn, only a thick fog that softened the stark silhouettes of the bare trees. With any luck, he'd have the abductor singing like a sparrow before noon, rescue the victim, and be on his way home to Desirée in plenty of time for supper...and draughts...and whatever other pleasantries the evening held.

A gray shroud of mist still draped Canterbury a few hours later, dampening spirits and giving the streets a gloomy cast. Still Desirée couldn't help but smile as she made her way through the somber crowd. She felt beautiful in her new kirtle, even if 'twas mostly covered by her old cloak. And the vision of Nicholas this morn, standing by the door in next to naught, his formidable chest deliciously bare and his nether parts straining at his braies, remained clear in her mind's eye, keeping her at the edge of yearning all day.

She stopped first at the fishmonger's stall for the pike she'd promised him. While she was inspecting the fish to see if the eyes were clear or cloudy, a sumptuously dressed woman sidled up, clad in enough layers of clothing to give her face a livid red cast, despite the chill.

"Is the lamprey fresh?" she demanded of the fishmonger.

"O' course, m'lady. Caught only this morn."

Desirée glanced down. The woman's purse sagged open, and several silver coins winked from within it.

"What about the oysters?"

"Right here, m'lady," he said, pointing to a basket, "fresh from Hyrnan Bay."

Desirée bit the corner of her lip. The woman was wearing so many layers of wool, she'd hardly feel a person bumping into her. And if Desirée distracted her, she'd scarcely notice the loss of a few coins from her purse.

"And bream? Have you bream?"

"Caught last night, just brought in, m'lady."

Desirée picked up a grayling and sniffed at it. Then she pretended to lose hold of the slippery fish.

"Oh!" She let it slither from her grasp, and it slid across the row of pikes toward the woman. Making a wild grab for it with one hand while the woman jumped back in surprise, Desirée delved with her other hand into the woman's purse, snatching up a handful of silver.

The woman swatted at Desirée as if she were a pesky fly, and Desirée, carefully concealing the coins, returned the fish to its place.

"I'm sorry, my lady, it slipped from my—"

"Oh!" the woman said with an exasperated shiver. "Just get your fishy hands away from me."

"Aye, my lady." Glancing carefully about for witnesses, Desirée dropped the coins surreptitiously into her own purse and resumed inspecting the pike.

As the woman continued to question the fishmonger, blissfully unaware of the theft, Desirée began to feel a curious discomfort with what she'd done.

A fortnight ago, Hubert would have congratulated Desirée on her cleverness. They would have celebrated with a cup of ale and laughed over the target's stupidity.

But today, she was haunted by thoughts of Nicholas. He would hardly praise her actions. In fact, the more she thought about the shire-reeve and his unexpected generosity—the roof he'd put over her head, the stipend he was paying her, the taxes he paid for the poor, the new kirtle he'd bought for her—the heavier the stolen coins in her purse seemed to grow.

Desirée had to face the truth. She wasn't a thief anymore. She didn't need to steal to survive. 'Twas only a nasty habit now. Even if the target was rich and haughty and rude, 'twas no reason to take what rightfully belonged to her.

Desirée sighed, picking up a pike and staring into its eyes as if to question it. Now what was she going to do? Her purse felt like an enormous lead ball against her hip.

The woman seemed to have made her decision at last and began fumbling with her purse.

Desirée put the pike down. Sneaking coin back into a purse was harder than fishing it out. The woman was alerted to her, and she was keeping her distance. So Desirée opened her own purse and picked out the coins she'd stolen. Then, when the woman finished counting out payment to the fishmonger, Desirée dropped the coins into the dirt beside her.

"My lady," she said, "I believe you dropped your silver."

"What?" The woman's eyes widened when she saw the coins. "Oh." She bent to pick them up without a word of gratitude.

Still, Desirée felt much better having returned what she'd stolen. The burden of guilt fell from her shoulders. After the woman left, she picked out a pike as long as her arm and paid for it... with her own coin.

As she continued down the lane, the parchment-wrapped fish tucked under one arm, she couldn't help but feel a lightness in her step.

Twice more, the opportunity arose for her to dip her fingers into gaping purses—once from the affluent patron of an arkwright and once outside of an inn, where two drunkards staggered into each other, their coins rattling around as loosely as their wits.

Yet she resisted the urge to steal from them. And by the time she finished up at the pie maker's shop, purchasing a freshly baked pear pie that steamed when she carried it into the cold outdoors, she felt quite proud of herself.

A fortnight ago, she would have seized the opportunity for easy profit. Now, each time she fought off the instinct to steal, she felt her willpower grow stronger. By John the Baptist's beard, she believed Nicholas Grimshaw was turning her into an honest woman.

Exhausted, Nicholas turned away in frustration from the dismal young man chained to the three-legged stool. He'd tried everything. He'd spent hours laboring in this suffocating smokehouse, since the town of Sturry had no gaol, and he'd gotten nowhere.

He'd reasoned with the lad. He'd explained that the miller was only worried for the safety of his daughter, who was plump with child and due to give birth any day. Nicholas had assured the abductor that all would be forgiven if he'd only return the maid and leave Sturry.

But the stubborn lad had refused to talk.

Nicholas had tried shame. He'd scolded the lad for making a father fret over his only daughter. Then, guessing there might be a personal motive for the abduction, since the young man had demanded no ransom, he'd tried to convince him that the maid would think him a coward for kidnapping her.

But the lad had only sat glumly silent.

Then Nicholas had resorted to fear. He'd begun dragging out his implements of torture, sighting along the blades, running a thumb over edges to gauge their sharpness, testing them in the flesh of the carcasses suspended on hooks within the smokehouse. He talked silkily of the various uses of the tools, some of them real, some invented.

But the man had given absolutely no response. And Nicholas feared for the welfare of the lass and her babe if he didn't discover her whereabouts soon.

Thus, having tried every other option, he was reduced to using real violence. Steeling himself for the encounter, he cracked his knuckles once, then turned toward the lad. With no word of warning, he backhanded him, hard enough to knock the lad over, stool and all.

The lad's face flushed red from the blow as he groaned in pain on the ground. Nicholas came to stand over him, sickened by the sight of what he'd wrought, rubbing his bruised knuckles.

Then the poor wretch began to cry. Not soft whimpers of pain or fear, but gut-wrenching sobs of pure anguish.

Nicholas bit back a natural urge to comfort the lad, instead pressing his advantage, crouching beside him and demanding, "Where is she?"

The lad pinned him with intensely baleful eyes and cried, "She is no more!"

Nicholas's heart jerked as if he'd been stabbed. 'Twas his worst fear. He bit out, "You killed her?"

The man rolled his head back and forth in the straw, wailing in misery.

"What did you do to her?" Nicholas barked.

"Naught," he sobbed. "Naught."

"Where is she?"

The man's chin quivered. "At the bottom of the cliff at Hyrnan." He wailed, "Oh, God."

Nicholas's heart went cold. If the lad had killed an innocent lass, one with child…

He choked back rage, asking with false calm, "And how did she come to be at the bottom of the cliff?"

"I begged her not to do it. I begged her. I told her I would take her away. I don't have much coin, but I'd see she had food and shelter."

Nicholas swallowed hard, and his fury dissolved into despair. Now he understood. "She leaped from the cliff?"

The man nodded, then his face crumpled with grief.

Nicholas's shoulders sank. He knew the lad was telling the truth. He hadn't been reluctant to speak before. He'd only been in shock. "Why?"

"He'll kill me now, won't he?" the lad blubbered. "He'll say I did it, and then he'll string me up."

"Why did she kill herself?"

The man's sobs subsided, and a burning anger slowly replaced the sorrow in his eyes. "'Twas *his* babe."

"Whose?"

The young man looked at him with all the searing hatred he felt. "The miller's," he bit out. "Her own father's."

Nicholas felt a chill blade slice across his soul. "Bloody hell."

He knew men were capable of unspeakable acts. He'd dealt with the worst of humankind. But this was among the lowest. To think that the miller would get his own daughter with child and then accuse an innocent man, a merciful man, of abducting her...

'Twas beyond reprehensible.

'Twas diabolical.

Yet what the lad said was true. The accusation might be false, but there were no witnesses to say 'twas not murder. 'Twas only the word of a stable lad against that of the village miller. The townsfolk cared not if a lowly servant swung from the gallows, as long as they still had a place to grind their grain.

'Twas unjust. But naught could save the wretch. The evidence against the lad was overwhelming. Once the maid's body was found, he'd be accused of the crime. Once accused, he'd be quickly convicted and sentenced. Forsooth, Nicholas might be called upon to summon the executioner before nightfall.

"Why did you return here?" he muttered. "Why did you not run when you had the chance?"

The lad's eyes turned as cold and gray as an approaching storm. "I came back to kill him."

Nicholas nodded. He understood perfectly. His own fists itched to beat the miller to a bloody carcass.

But no man could serve two masters. Because he was a servant of justice, he had to take the side of the law. Revenge was not the prerogative of a shire-reeve.

He rose slowly and hung his head. At times like these, he wished he'd become a mercenary, like his father wanted. Or an armorer. Or a fishmonger. Anything but a lawman.

"Shite!" He turned, punching the nearest haunch of pork in frustration. Was there naught he could do?

He glanced down at the helpless young man weeping on the floor of the smokehouse. Aye, there was one thing he could do. He could make certain the lad's final moments were swift and painless, get him senselessly drunk, help him make peace with his death.

His mind suddenly swerved, as if someone else had jerked away the reins of his thoughts. While he stood over the doomed lad, staring at the pork roast he'd just punched, a most insidious idea began to brew and curdle and twist into possibility. And that possibility ripened into a plan before he recognized who 'twas exerting such an influence over his brain.

Desirée.

The devious wench's ways must have been rubbing off on him. Her "distractions" and her weighted dice and her sleight of hand were perverting his morality. Yet for the first time since he'd donned the cloak of the shire-reeve, he felt a thrill of hope.

"Listen to me, lad. Here's what we're going to do."

❧

Chapter 19

"Ye want some help carryin' that?"

Desirée should have known better than to stop. But she *was* juggling an enormous pike, a pie, and a jug of wine, and 'twas no easy task. Accustomed to enlisting the aid of men with the mere flutter of lashes, she whipped around at the inquiry, smiling brightly at the pair of lads trailing her like worshipful pups.

Any other day, she might have gauged them with a more cynical eye. But today, resplendent in her new kirtle and having thrice resisted thievery's call, she felt saintly and generous of spirit, and she wasn't thinking properly. Surely the lads only meant to offer assistance and perchance earn a kind word for their efforts. And she could use the help.

"You are too kind, gentlemen," she replied.

One lad took the pike. "I'm John."

The other took the pie. "I'm John, as well."

"Indeed? Good morn, John and John-as-well."

"And what's your name, m'lady?"

"I'm Desirée."

"Desirée," the first John repeated carefully, as if he meant to memorize it.

"Do ye live nearby?" the second John asked. "I haven't seen ye in Canterbury before. Have ye, John?"

"Nay, haven't seen her before."

"Me neither. How long have ye been here?"

"Not long," she replied, "a fortnight."

"What business do ye have in Canterbury?" the first John asked gruffly.

The second John scowled at him. "Ye're goin' too fast."

"Sorry."

Desirée furrowed her brow. Going too fast? What did he mean by that?

"'Tis a lovely day, isn't it?" the second John asked.

Desirée glanced about the streets, still gloomy with fog. "Is it?"

"But then, any day would be lovely, walkin' beside a maid such as yourself."

Desirée resisted the urge to smirk.

"I'm surprised ye don't have an escort," he said. "Is there no one who's—"

"Have ye got a husband?" The first John apparently disliked mincing words.

"John!" The second reached around her to shove the first.

"What? Isn't that what ye want to know?"

"Pardon my friend," John the second said. "He's got no manners."

"You're pardoned," she said. But she didn't answer his

question. In fact, she became suddenly wary of their interest. Before, she'd always had Hubert to intercede if men took too much of an interest in her. Now she was on her own.

She stopped in the lane. "Perchance I should continue on myself." She reached for the pike.

He pulled it away. "Nay, m'lady. John didn't mean no harm. Besides, ye don't want to walk these streets alone. They're dangerous. All manner of thieves and scoundrels roam about, ready to pounce on a lady all by herself."

An inner alarm warned Desirée the Johns shouldn't be trusted. After all, only yesterday, Odger and a pack of urchins had cost her the greater part of a savory meal. She didn't want it to happen again.

"Give us another chance," he urged. "John won't say another word, will ye, John?"

"I s'pose not," he said unhappily.

"See? And we'll take ye home, safe and sound...to your husband." He hesitated, obviously waiting for her to confirm or deny his statement.

She refused to take the bait. Perchance if they suspected she had a husband, they'd leave off their pursuit. "Very well." She resumed walking.

"I *told* ye she was wed," the supposed-to-be-silent John said.

"And I told ye to be quiet! Besides, she didn't say if she was or wasn't." He winked at Desirée. "Mayhap she prefers to...leave her options open."

Desirée smiled, wondering what the lads would say if she told them she was maidservant to the shire-reeve of Kent.

As they traveled on through the fog, straying farther

and farther from the crowded center of town, she realized, of course, that she would have to mislead the lads. She didn't want them to know where Nicholas lived. So as John the second continued on with his prattle, asking her questions that she answered as vaguely as possible, she picked out a walled demesne along a side street and stopped before it, indicating 'twas her home.

John the silent scratched his head. "Here? The shire-reeve lives here?"

"Fool!" John the not-so-silent cuffed him.

Desirée glanced between the two men. They glanced back, their eyes alarmed and guilty. Now on high alert, she clenched her hands around the jug of wine, ready to use the thing as a weapon, if need be.

"What did you say?" she asked.

John the second tried to laugh off the situation. "He didn't say nothin'. He's just addled in the head."

She wasn't fooled for an instant. "What did you say about the shire-reeve?"

The first John sputtered an unintelligible response, then his eyes went wild with panic. He dropped the pie and lunged forward, seizing her around the waist.

Desirée clung to the claret. She wasn't about to lose a second jug of wine.

"John! What are ye...?" the second John spat, glancing about to see if there were any witnesses. "Stop it! What the bloody hell..."

But John the first wasn't about to let go, and Desirée was having a hard time fighting him off, since she was desperate to hang on to the claret. "Let go of me, you son of a—"

John number two clapped a hand over her mouth. "Shh, lass. It'll be all right. I promise."

She bit down hard on his fingers.

"Ow!" He yanked his hand back, but as soon as she took a breath to scream, he dropped the fish and attacked her from behind, locking his arm around her throat.

Desirée had no choice but to sacrifice the wine. She gave the first John a swift knee to the groin. While he sank to the ground with a bloodless face, she swung the jug up over her shoulder and bashed John the second in the head.

To her delight, the jug didn't break, and her assailant was rendered dizzy by the blow.

The first John looked up from where he was doubled over in pain. "Ye're not the shire-reeve's wife, then, are ye?" he wheezed. "Ye're his whore. Right?"

Desirée gasped in outrage, then drew back her fist and punched him hard in the nose. He staggered backward, moaning, one hand cupping his crotch, the other cradling his nose.

"Ye fool," the second John groaned, holding his cracked brow. "This isn't her demesne. She just said that to get rid of us."

The first John's words were muffled by his hand. "Then she *does* live with him."

Desirée had had enough. Her knuckles ached, and her supper lay in disarray upon the ground. Confounded by their questions and incensed by their assault, she tossed her head and shouted, "Aye, I live with the shire-reeve!" She narrowed her eyes at John the first and gave him a nasty smile. "And when he hears that you attacked me...John..."

His eyes grew round with fear. With a sound that was half-gasp, half-squeak, he lurched off down the lane, still shielding his injured parts.

"John! Come back here!" his companion called. "Coward!"

Desirée turned on the remaining John, advancing on him with her jug raised until he was backed against the wall of the demesne. "Who sent you?"

He gulped. "Nobody." He blinked nervously. "John didn't hurt ye, did he? If he did, I swear I'll—"

"Who. Sent. You?"

He lifted his palms in a defensive gesture, clearly afraid to lay a finger on her, lest the shire-reeve come after him. But neither did he want to answer her.

He needed more incentive. Unwilling to risk breaking the jug, she quickly set it down, simultaneously scooping up the pike from the ground. Then she hauled back and slapped him full across the face with the fish.

He sputtered in shock, reeling from the blow.

"Who sent you?" she repeated.

He shook his head. "I told ye, no—"

She smacked him with the pike on the other cheek.

"Ah, God." He made a moue of disgust. "Prithee, m'lady, don't—"

Smack!

"Oh!" This time the odor of the fish hit him full force.

"Tell me," she warned.

"All right," he choked out. "All right. Just don't hit me with that foul thing again."

"Well?"

"'Twas Odger, master of the mews at Torteval."

"Odger?" Desirée lowered the fish. "What did he want?"

"He wanted to know what the shire-reeve was to ye."

"Why?"

He shrugged. "Perchance he wanted to court ye?"

"I doubt that. I showed him the sharp side of a blade yesterday."

He looked at her in horror. Apparently, Odger had omitted that fact when he'd enlisted these men to do his work.

Now that she had him cornered, she figured she might as well question him. "You live at Torteval?"

He clamped his lips shut.

She raised the fish.

He winced.

She repeated, "You live at Torteval?"

"Aye."

"Where were you at the time of the murder?"

His brows shot up. "The murder? Ye mean the lawyer?"

"Aye."

"I was sleepin' with the hounds. I'm the houndskeeper."

"And did you see anything?"

He shook his head.

"What about the other John?"

"I didn't see him neither."

"Nay. Did *he* see anything?"

"He sleeps in the stables."

Desirée pensively bit her lip. Why she bothered to pursue the incident, she didn't know. After all, Hubert was dead. According to Nicholas, he'd *wanted* to be hanged for the murder.

But something wasn't right about the whole thing. She still didn't believe her old companion was capable of killing, not even accidental killing.

"Why do ye want to know about the murder?" John asked.

She pierced him with eyes of frost. "My grandfather was hanged for it."

John froze, and his eyes slowly widened. "Bloody hell. Ye mean, ye're the granddaughter of a...of a..."

With a desperate lurch, he shoved her out of the way. Then he tore from the wall and hurtled down the lane as fast as his legs could carry him, never looking back.

For a moment, Desirée stared pensively after the man as he disappeared into the fog.

Something curious was going on at Torteval. What was Odger up to? He'd clearly sent someone else to do what he hadn't the courage to do himself. But why should he care about her relationship with Nicholas?

Unless, she mused, he wanted to get rid of her permanently and needed to make sure he wouldn't incur the wrath of the shire-reeve for doing so.

She shivered, suddenly wishing she'd told them Nicholas was her lover, her very *possessive* lover. Then again, the three assassins she'd met thus far had proved to be clumsy, cowardly, and dim-witted. She supposed she hadn't much to fear from them.

Brushing off her new skirts, hoping she hadn't ruined them in the altercation, she scanned the ground. The jug of wine was intact, but the pie had landed upside down.

"Piss."

The pike had come halfway out of its wrapping, and though it looked decent enough despite its bout with

John, she needed to tuck it back in its package to carry it. Otherwise, she'd arrive home smelling like a fishwife.

Unwilling to give up the pear pie, she shoved the re-wrapped pike under one arm and carefully scooped up the linen-covered pastry. 'Twasn't soiled. 'Twas only smashed. And she'd be damned if she was going to have another supper ruined.

Nicholas hadn't felt this good in a long while. He strode home in the fog, a lightness in his step, a faint smile upon his lips.

He knew what he'd done wasn't right. But 'twas just. And the satisfaction he felt as he left the town of Sturry was well worth the loss of his fee.

He wondered what his little cheat of a maidservant would have said about his deviation from the law. He shook his head. Desirée was definitely a bad influence on him.

The deception had been easy to pull off. Desirée was right. Distraction was a useful tool.

He'd unhooked the freshest carcass in the smokehouse and dressed it in the young man's clothing. Then, together with the lad, he'd beat it to a pulp with the tools he'd brought. The careful cut he made in the lad's hand provided a bit of fresh blood to make the scene believable.

He'd made the lad hide in the straw while he ruefully explained to the authorities that once he'd learned the lass and her babe had been brutally murdered, he'd lost his mind and…

When he revealed the bloody mess on the smokehouse floor, no one questioned his actions. Nicholas Grimshaw, after all, was known to be a vicious individual with a ruthless temper. Who could blame him for taking out his rage on the lad?

The miller couldn't complain. As far as he knew, Nicholas had only expedited the lad's inevitable execution. And the town had been saved paying an executioner's fee.

Naturally, Nicholas had given the lad a stern warning. No matter how unjust it seemed, no matter how tempting 'twas to mete out punishment to the miller, 'twould serve no purpose. Naught would bring back the lass and her babe. He was to forget about vengeance, leave Sturry at nightfall, and never return. By the time he finished speaking with the lad, Nicholas was confident the grateful boy would take his advice.

However, now that Nicholas had taken the law into his own hands, to good effect, 'twould be a terrible temptation to do it again. 'Twas far more satisfying to right a wrong than to carry out unfair justice.

He saw now how difficult it must be for Desirée to resist the urge to lift a purse here or roll a weighted die there when the winnings were lifted off of scoundrels who probably deserved to lose their coin. Still, he didn't plan to make a habit of bending the law. And he had no intention of letting Desirée know what he'd done.

By the time he pushed through the garden gate, 'twas late afternoon. Smoke wafted from the chimney, and even from the yard, he could detect the pleasant smell of roasting fish. His mouth watered, and he realized he hadn't eaten since wolfing down the cocket and ruayn cheese this morn.

Desirée was fast spoiling him. He was growing accustomed to coming home to a warm supper. Not since he was a lad had anyone cooked for him. Most evenings, too tired to cook for himself, he dined on a slab of smoked meat, a stale hunk of bread, and several cups of ale. 'Twas hard to think about returning to that kind of existence again.

So he decided *not* to think about it. On the morrow, he'd begin to plan for Desirée's inevitable departure. But tonight, he intended to celebrate...his newfound sense of justice, Desirée's delicious supper, the cat's successful capture of a mouse, all their victories, big and small.

The moment he stepped through the doorway to the pungent smells of galentyne sauce and peppered pike, Desirée whirled toward him. "You're home!"

Her look of pure pleasure he'd hold dear to him long after she was gone, he knew. That one memory alone could serve to warm him for weeks.

She clucked her tongue. "I suppose I'll have to give Snowflake the bad news."

He'd scarcely pulled back his hood when she came up to unfasten his cloak. "Bad news?"

"It looks as if he won't get your share, after—" She stopped abruptly, staring at the middle of his chest.

He glanced down. Bloodstains marred his shirt. He'd forgotten.

He quickly clenched the fabric in one hand, as if he could cover the evidence. But 'twas too late. An unmistakable shiver of revulsion went through her.

"'Tis not what it seems," he tried to explain.

She averted her gaze then, but though she attempted to maintain her smile, it grew brittle before his eyes.

He made a second try. "'Tis only—"

"Perchance you could change your shirt before supper," she said lightly, but her gait was stiff as she turned to walk toward the hearth.

His shoulders sagged. He should have known better. Though this once he'd done the right thing, his reputation as shire-reeve had been a part of his life for too long to erase it with one good deed. He couldn't expect Desirée to overlook years of being an enforcer. He was no better than Azrael, bringing in a dead mouse, thinking to impress him.

Discouraged, he ducked into his bedchamber, hauling in his bag of tools. Thankfully, he'd stopped to wash them before making the journey home. At least she'd be spared the sight of gore-covered blades.

The hard truth was that his existence was too harsh for a maid. Not only was his life on the road grueling, but as much as he managed to avoid violence, he did traffic in meting out punishments. He had no right even imagining he could share such a life with a woman, *any* woman.

He took off his shirt and crumpled it into a ball, stuffing it behind his pallet, out of sight. He'd launder it later himself. He wished he could discard it, toss it into the yard for the crows, the way he had the mouse.

Desirée knew she should say something. The silence between them was thickening like overcooked frumenty, and if she didn't say something soon, they'd never be able to slog through a conversation.

"I bought us a jug of wine," she called gaily from the next room, trying to pretend she'd forgotten all about his bloody shirt.

"Ah."

Curse it all! She hadn't meant to act so repulsed. 'Twas

only that for a moment, she'd forgotten what he did for a living. To have the evidence of the violence he'd perpetrated today displayed so vividly caught her off guard.

She knew 'twas part of his work. Forsooth, Nicholas coming home with a bloodstained shirt was no different than a dyer coming home with woad-stained hands. Still, she couldn't help but wonder what spilling all that blood did to a man's soul.

Perchance she could make amends for her response and distract him from his burdens by telling him about *her* adventures today. At least *part* of her adventures.

She poured him a cup of wine. "Nicholas, you'll never guess what I..." She turned at his entrance and promptly forgot what she was going to say.

Nicholas hadn't bothered to tie his shirt. It hung loosely about his throat, exposing a delicious triangle of skin and imparting an air of danger to his appearance. But 'twas an intriguing sort of danger, one that made her want to tangle her fingers in the garment and tear it asunder to get to the tempting man beneath.

"Aye?" he asked.

"I...I...like that shirt," she finished lamely.

"This?" He furrowed his brow.

She felt like a half-wit. 'Twas only a linen shirt, after all, just like all his *other* linen shirts. 'Twasn't the shirt so much as what was *in* it. Flustered, she crossed the room and shoved the cup of wine at him. To her horror, it sloshed over the edge and would have spilled onto him if he hadn't stepped backward.

She gasped. God's eyes, what was wrong with her? "I'm sorry. I don't know what—"

He caught her wrist in one hand and carefully took the

cup from her with the other, setting it down on the table. Mistaking her distraction for fright, he spoke in soothing tones. "Listen, lass. You needn't fear me. I've changed my shirt. I'm no longer the shire-reeve, just Nicholas."

She blinked in surprise. "I'm not afraid of you."

"You're not?"

She smirked. "Hardly." Even if he *had* shed blood today—and she didn't intend to ask him about it—she was sure it had been only as a last resort. He'd already proved to her he was a man of kindness, patience, and mercy. "How could I be afraid of someone I can beat at draughts?"

His face bloomed slowly into a relieved smile. "Is that a challenge?"

Lord, his eyes sparkled like jewels when he looked at her like that. "Indeed." Afraid that if she lingered she might succumb to the wild desire to run her fingers beneath the laces of his shirt, she returned to the hearth to tend to supper.

"What is it you wished to tell me?" he said, hefting up the cup of wine and taking a sip.

It took her a moment to recall. "Oh. 'Twas the most wondrous thing. While I was shopping for the pike at the market today, I lifted coins from a woman's purse."

He nearly choked on the wine. "What?"

"Oh, I gave them back," she assured him, adding in a mutter, "though I didn't get so much as a nod of thanks from the old trot." She ladled galentyne sauce over the platter of fish. "Then I saw the fellow in front of the ark-wright's shop. His silver was practically begging to be stolen."

"You didn't."

"Nay, I didn't," she said proudly. "And then, as if Lucifer himself placed them in my path, two drunken dullards came strolling by, coins jangling from their belts, perfect targets, ripe to be robbed."

"And did you rob them?"

She turned to him, her brow creased. "Nay. Don't you see? That's my point. I didn't."

"Thank God."

"And 'twas not even the Sabbath. I believe, Nicholas Grimshaw, your decency is rubbing off on me. You may make an honest wench of me yet."

Desirée expected some word of praise or congratulations for her triumphs. She did *not* expect the slow laughter that began to bubble out of him.

She frowned. "What?"

He shook his head in rueful amusement. "I fear, my lady, you're making a *dis*honest man out of *me*."

Chapter 20

INDEED? YOU? The right arm of the law?" Desirée's voice was laced with sarcasm as she brought supper to the table. But at his silence, she realized he was serious. She set the platter down and cocked a suspicious eye at him. "Nicholas, what have you done?"

He couldn't tell her. Not when she'd just been boasting about her own reformation. He shrugged. "'Tis naught, really."

She leaned forward conspiratorially and whispered, "You didn't steal something, did you?"

He frowned. "Nay."

"Did you cheat at a gaming table?"

"Nay!"

The pesky lass wasn't going to give up. She skewered him with a glare. "I'll find out sooner or later, Nicholas. You know I will."

"'Tisn't proper conversation for the supper table."

She sank down onto the bench, her eyes wide. "You

didn't...murder someone, did you? I mean...other than the usual..."

He scowled. "Nay." He lifted his dagger, intending to slice off a generous portion of pike. "Not exactly."

She suddenly pulled the platter out of his reach. "Not exactly? What does that mean?"

Against his will, his mouth twitched with amusement as he recalled his clever ruse.

She arched a warning brow at him. "You're not getting any supper until you tell me. Everything."

More hungry than remorseful, he acquiesced. As he related the details, her eyes twinkled with mischief, amusement, and—God save both their sinful souls— admiration.

"Let me get this aright," she said. "You pummeled a pork roast to death?"

"Aye."

"And told them 'twas the lad?"

"Aye."

"And they believed you?"

"Aye."

"But that's brilliant!" she crowed, moving the platter back to the middle of the table.

"'Tis unlawful," he argued, shaking his head in self-reproof, though he was sure the pleased glint in his own eyes sent a completely different message.

"'Tis *just*," she countered, laughing in delight. "Admit it. Didn't the deception give you the tiniest bit of pleasure?"

He shrugged, helping himself to pike.

She leaned close. "Come on. Confess it."

"Perchance," he allowed.

She grinned. "You outwitted a villain and saved the life of an innocent lad."

"But one can't ride about taking the law into one's own hands, even if 'tis for good."

"Why not?"

"'Tis..." He frowned. "Wrong."

She arched a brow. "You said yourself, 'twas the right thing to do."

He sighed. Desirée was confounding his thoughts, not only by the way she twisted his words, but by the way she was looking at him, her eyes all a-sparkle, her smile delightfully wicked. "You *are* a bad influence on me."

She gave him a sly grin, whispering, "I'll make an outlaw out of you yet."

He scowled. 'Twas just what he feared.

"Let's have our supper," she suggested. "Then if you like, I'll teach you the finer points of picking pockets."

"I do *not* wish to learn how to rob men of their coin."

"What about gluttonous arse-wisps of barons who've plucked that coin out of the hands of their starving crofters?"

He growled at her.

She looked at him, all innocence. "For instance."

He wanted to tell her that she was an evil wench, that she'd been raised with flawed morals and she was going to wager her way into hell with that line of reasoning. But the truth was, she had a point. What was justice, after all? Was it what the crown claimed was right? Or what God decreed was fair and merciful?

He gave her a grudging smile. "'*Twas* rather satisfying, seeing the look of shock on the miller's face."

She slipped a few bites of pike to Azrael, who was

pacing at her feet. "You fret too much over the letter of the law. Your heart knows what is right. Just as I knew 'twasn't right to take that silver today."

Nicholas nodded, then chuckled in self-mockery. Was he actually listening to the advice of a thief? *Reformed* thief, he corrected.

Still, he couldn't completely trust his heart. After all, his heart had told him some crackbrained things lately. Things like he should settle down. Take a wife. Raise a family.

'Twas all Desirée's fault. Having her in his household showed him clearly what had been missing from it. The irreverent vixen was a perfect companion for him. Her bright spark countered his black smolder. Her laughter countered his scowl. She brought candlelight into his darkness, life into his domain of death.

How would he ever let her go?

Yet how could he hold her prisoner in his grim world?

Desirée jiggled the frayed ribbon above Snowflake's head as she and Nicholas sat cross-legged before the fire. The cat took a few lazy swipes at it, then collapsed onto his side, too stuffed from supper to play.

She laughed. "He's tired of being a cat." She swept the ribbon behind her neck to tie up her hair. "What about you, Nicholas? Are you tired of being a lawman?"

"What do you mean?" He reached out to scratch Snowflake's belly.

"I mean, you don't truly enjoy your work, do you?"

He frowned. "'Tis not meant to be enjoyed."

"Well, then," she said, finishing off the bow, "why not let someone *else* not enjoy it?"

"'Tis not that simple." Snowflake took a swipe at his hand. "Ow!"

"Oh, aye, 'tis. I've done it. I've changed. In the span of a fortnight, I've gone from vagabond outlaw to invaluable maidservant." She winked at him.

He shook his head. "You don't understand."

"What don't I understand?"

He sighed. "I have a reputation. I'm Nicholas Grimshaw, the shire-reeve of Kent."

She snorted. "Snowflake doesn't know you're shire-reeve. He thinks you're the king of cats." As if to prove his devotion, the cat rolled onto his feet and padded over to Nicholas to rub against his thigh. "I don't think of you as the shire-reeve, either. I think of you as...the man I beat at draughts every night."

"The man you *cheat* at draughts every night."

She scooted closer to him until they were almost knee to knee. "You know, if you changed your profession," she said, reaching forward with the intent of tying up his loose shirt laces, "you might get that wife fate promised you."

He threw up a defensive hand, blocking her.

She scolded him with a glare, batting his hand away. But as she lifted the ties to make a bow, a completely different idea came into her head. She'd been tempted by that delicious triangle of skin all night long. Instead of crossing the ties, she pulled them apart, baring his chest.

She glanced down just long enough for a shiver of desire to course through her. But when she looked into his eyes again, something powerful and dangerous burned there, something as potent as hot coals waiting for the nudge of a poker to be stirred to life.

Nicholas wanted her.

That knowledge shot a pang of longing into her breast, like an arrow piercing her heart, a longing that spread as rapidly as a field fire through her body, sizzling in her ears, searing her nipples, burning betwixt her thighs.

She should have been afraid. He stared at her as if he might brand her with his eyes. 'Twas doubtless the same kind of silent, threatening glare he made to force confessions from outlaws.

But instead of fear, she felt a curious exhilaration. Her heart quickened, and a queer tingling began in the pit of her stomach.

Nicholas wanted her. And, by all the saints, she wanted him.

She released one of the ties to rest her hand flat upon his chest. His skin was even more warmly seductive than she'd imagined, and she could feel his trembling breath beneath her palm. His nostrils flared as if in anger, and a muscle flexed in his jaw.

But she wasn't afraid. She was excited.

Holding his gaze, she slipped her hand slowly but brazenly inside his shirt.

His eyes widened, but she continued, sliding her palm over the smooth, supple expanse. Holding her breath, she brushed her fingers over his nipple, and his eyes darkened in response. She emitted a soft moan as it stiffened beneath her touch.

He sucked a breath through his teeth and seized her trespassing wrist.

'Twas a warning. But Desirée seldom heeded warnings.

Her heart pounding at her own boldness, she slowly drew her captured wrist back, bringing his hand along. She pried his grip loose, then opened his palm.

He glowered at her, choking out, "You shouldn't…"

She returned his intense stare with a gaze of unabashed lust. "I know."

Then she turned his palm and lay it flat upon her own bosom.

A sound came from him, almost like a grunt of pain, and he glared at his hand, as if he couldn't quite understand how it had come to be there.

After one delicious moment, he tried to pull back, but she wouldn't allow it. She covered his hand with both her own. A woman bent on having her way, she stared boldly into his eyes and slowly forced his hand farther and farther under the neckline of her kirtle, until he fully cupped her breast.

He exhaled forcefully, prisoner to her will, and his breath sent hot shivers over her skin.

Her eyelids grew heavy as she reveled in the warmth of his palm. His fingers perfectly cradled the curve of her breast as she clasped his hand close to her heart. Naught had ever felt so divine.

Then he began to caress her of his own free will.

With a tenderness she'd never expected, he moved his thumb lightly across her skin. He squeezed her breast ever so gently, and she gasped at the gentle friction of his callused fingers as they grazed her nipple. Yet despite the subtlety of his touch, her body responded with breathtaking haste.

Every nerve seemed to come alive at once. Lust set fire to her flesh and flooded her veins with molten need. She moaned as desire washed over her like a burning wave.

She could summon neither the resolve nor the strength

to stop him. His touch did more than slake the curious thirst within her. It increased her longing.

With a ragged sigh of need, she leaned toward him, breaching the gap between them to press hungry lips to his.

She'd tasted desperation before. Men often stole kisses from her with frantic haste, sure they'd be punished in the next moment for their trespass. And they always were.

But this... this was more than desperation. This was aching need, deep-seated desire, a perilous emotion far too powerful to fight. 'Twas like being pulled into a whirlpool.

Yet she had no desire to resist. 'Twas a current in which she'd gladly drown.

He kissed her with commanding fervency, parting her lips with his, nudging her jaw open, delving within the most intimate hollows of her mouth.

When his tongue brushed hers, 'twas as if a whip cracked and slithered down her body, for she felt its electric lash sizzle along every fiber. Her ears thrummed. Her nipples stung. Her heart throbbed. And a spark of need flared betwixt her thighs.

She wanted...

Bloody hell, she didn't know what she wanted.

Breathless with kissing, yet hungry for more, Desirée knelt within the circle of his legs, combing her fingers through his hair, slanting his head to better access his mouth. Their tongues tangled, and she groaned against his lips. Sweet Mary, she'd never tasted a sweeter ambrosia.

Now his hands roamed over her breasts, squeezing, stroking, plucking at her nipples until she gasped with longing. In answer, she let her hands drift down to spread across his wide shoulders, where a light film of sweat glistened.

"Oh, God, Desirée."

He eased her down until she sat across his thigh, then slid his hand purposefully down the outside of her bodice to her waist. He turned his hand so his fingers pointed downward and continued on, and Desirée held her breath as he drew closer and closer to the place where she ached the most.

She had never let a man touch her there, though many had tried. It had become instinctive for her to clap her legs shut at the first sign of such intent. This time, however, beneath the onslaught of Nicholas's fierce kisses and arousing caresses, her muscles grew mutinous, and her thighs fell open in welcome.

When he delved between her legs, she arched toward his palm, and it seemed her body exploded with fever. She pressed hard against him, desperate to relieve the throbbing there.

He rubbed slowly up and down, and she angled her hips to accommodate him, while they gasped against each other's mouths.

Gradually, he drew the fabric of her dress up, baring her legs, and she could no more prevent him than she could prevent drifting clouds from exposing the face of the moon.

When his fingers contacted her naked flesh, a wave of fresh heat swept through her, flushing her cheeks, snatching her breath, searing her loins. She cried out with the shock of it, and for one awful instant, he drew back his hand.

* * *

Nicholas ground his teeth. He knew he'd gone too far. Hell, he'd gone too far when he'd kissed her that first time. He should never have let her touch him. But she'd been impossible to resist. It had been too long since he'd had a woman. And he'd never had a woman so beautiful. And willing. And hot-blooded.

But now he'd come too far... too far to stop. Already she was gasping in complaint, her brow furrowed with yearning. In another moment, she'd be seizing him by his shirt and demanding he continue. He couldn't leave her unsatisfied. He had to finish what he'd started. He only hoped he remembered how.

He licked his first two fingers, instantly aroused by the womanly taste upon them, while she regarded him in heavy-lidded wonder. Then he slipped his hand back into the sweet folds guarding her womb, sliding gently along her most sensitive parts.

With a cry of wonder, she collapsed against his shoulder. He cradled her head with his free hand, resting his cheek against her silky hair while he continued to rub tenderly betwixt her thighs. He squeezed his eyes shut, whispering soft encouragement, listening to her wordless syllables of passion as she rocked her hips back and forth in response to his touch.

She moaned faintly beneath his caress, as if he tortured her, and he could tell she'd not long endure his excruciating ministrations before she surrendered.

Yet 'twas a kind of torture that tormented him, as well. Her every gasp seemed to draw breath from his lungs. Every squeeze of her fingers awakened his flesh. Each sigh she spent against his ear sent a shiver of longing through his bones. God help him, he hoped she'd finish quickly, for his braies were nigh to bursting, and he didn't know how long he could languish on this rack of lust.

Nor how much ale 'twould be required to kill his pain.

Another moment, he thought, as she tensed upon his thigh, and 'twould be over. Another moment, and he'd be free.

But he didn't count on Desirée's penchant for mischief. By the time she reached down between his legs, brazenly caressing his cock, 'twas too late for him to rein in the unruly beast.

Desirée didn't know what drove her to such boldness. But Nicholas's groan of pleasurable pain as she stroked his swollen staff sent her over the edge.

She'd never felt such a strong surge of sensation. 'Twas as startling as a dip in a midwinter pond, rendering her breathless. And yet in the next moment, it seemed she was immersed in the most warm and wonderful bath. She shuddered with the power of release, crying out in amazement.

For a long while, there was no sound in the room but the crackling of the fire and the mingled rasping of their breath as she recovered from her lust and fed his.

'Twas strangely empowering, holding a fearsome, powerful lawman literally by the ballocks. Yet she felt only a keen desire to return his favor, to give him such pleasure as he'd afforded her.

She knew what to do. She'd watched harlots in alleyways. 'Twas a simple thing.

Reluctantly moving away from his cradling hand, she

urged him gently backward until he leaned against the wall, then knelt before him.

While he looked on with a clenched jaw and a furrowed brow, she gave him a sultry smile and began to unlace his braies. His head fell back, hitting the wall with a soft thud, as he let her have her way with him.

He watched her through his lashes as she carefully freed his cock. For all its size, 'twas much more delicate than she'd imagined. It emerged from a lush nest of black curls, its skin warm and smooth and vibrant. When she ran her thumb over his length, it responded with a gentle lunge.

Mimicking his earlier gesture, she ran her tongue slowly over her fingers to moisten them, then took him tenderly within her palm.

Nicholas groaned in helpless pleasure as she sheathed him in her hand. He felt both strong and vulnerable within her palm, and she savored his pulsing length for a moment. Then she began to slide tenderly over his flesh. His hips thrust upward, guiding her movements, and she quickly learned the rhythm of his desire. Soon his fingers clawed at the floor, and his head rolled from side to side.

'Twas a heady thrill, arousing him to such a state. Indeed, watching him writhe in the sweet torment of passion was heating her own blood. Again. Like a glutton getting up from one feast only to demand another, her body craved him once more.

For one wild and mindless moment, she wondered what he would do if she tossed aside all caution, threw herself at him, and took him into her aching womb right then and there.

Fortunately, she wasn't given another instant to consider it. With a primal cry, he stiffened, arching into her hand again and again, spilling forth his seed.

He finally collapsed against the wall, huffing like a winded stallion.

As Desirée gazed upon his damp brow, his flaring nostrils, his heaving chest, she felt an inexplicable wave of happiness. She'd done it. She'd given pleasure to the shire-reeve of Kent.

She smiled, as content as a kitten with a bowl of cream, and her voice was throatier than she expected when she murmured, "This is far more entertaining than draughts."

Nicholas couldn't help but chuckle at her remark, but he knew he'd made a horrible mistake. He never should have taken such liberties. Nor allowed such from her.

For Desirée, he was likely one in a long line of men who'd accepted her favors.

But for Nicholas, who couldn't remember the last time he'd pleasured a woman in his arms nor the last time a woman had pleasured him, 'twould be an eternity before he'd forget the sweet throes of her release and the thundering power of his.

She might consider the evening's frolic merely an entertaining diversion, but Nicholas could not. One day, Desirée would walk out of his cottage and out of his life, without a regret. But as for Nicholas, God curse his foolish heart, he'd never forget her. Somehow he'd fallen hopelessly in love with the wench.

~~

Chapter 21

THE MIDNIGHT MOON SPIED upon Philomena through a rip in the clouds as she reclined in the steaming rose-scented bath. Though she'd endured twice-daily baths of scalding water, laced with assorted oils and spices, trying to wash away the horrible stench of the gaol, they weren't working. Her visit two days ago had left an odor of excrement and filth in her nostrils that she couldn't completely get rid of, no matter how hard she scrubbed.

And her frustration had only mounted with each passing hour that the cursed key remained missing.

No doubt the four men trapped in the solar with her were grateful she was presently soaking in a tub. Otherwise, she'd have the lot of them hanging from meat hooks on the wall.

Godfry she'd leave alone for now. The split-lipped steward had already done his duty, rounding up the master of the mews and his two accomplices.

"Odger," she crooned.

"Aye, my lady." Odger trembled, fidgeting with the hat in his hands, looking as out of place in her chamber as one of his birds.

"You betrayed my trust."

"I didn't mean to."

His gaze kept dropping to her breasts, as if he'd never seen a naked woman before. She half smiled. He'd probably never seen one as lovely as she.

"And yet you did."

"The wench stabbed me, my lady," he said, yanking down his shirt to show her the wound in his shoulder. "I thought 'twas best to send someone she didn't know."

"Well, aren't you clever?" She lifted the rag out of her bath, closed her eyes, and squeezed it, letting the hot water rain down upon her bosom. "Except that the men you enlisted are bumbling fools with the combined wit of a flea."

As if to verify her reference, one of the Johns slapped at his own neck, making Odger jump.

She perused the men through slit eyes. What a sorry bunch they were. Godfry looked as if he might burst into tears at any moment. Odger's nerves were as strained as a primed bow. One of the Johns kept voraciously licking his lips as he stared at her, and the other glared fixedly at the wall.

"Nonetheless," she allowed, "they've brought me a valuable piece of information. And now, since you've mustered them into your legion, I think 'tis only fitting they finish the battle."

None of the half-wits appreciated her clever analogy. She sighed and dropped the rag into the water. She supposed she'd have to be straightforward.

"I want that wench. I don't care how you get her. Just bring her back to Torteval by the morrow."

"But she's livin' with Nicholas Grimshaw," Odger said.

"The shire-reeve," one of the Johns clarified.

"And she's the granddaughter of a murderer," the other John whispered.

The calming qualities of a bath were only so effective. Her temper at its limit, Philomena wadded up the wet rag and threw it at Odger. It landed with a smack in the middle of his chest, making him yelp.

"I don't care if she's the mistress of Lucifer himself!" she shrieked. "Bring her to me!"

For a moment the men were too petrified to move. Then, like beetles scurrying from a candle, they rushed from the solar all at once, muttering unintelligible assurances that they would do her bidding.

Once she was alone, she shut her eyes and sank back into the scalding water.

How the dullards would manage to pull off an abduction she didn't know, but among the four of them, they should be able to subdue one scrawny wench.

Meanwhile, she'd make plans for the woman's interrogation.

The more she thought about it, the more sense it made that the wench knew the whereabouts of the key. Hubert Kabayn had come to Torteval not as a murderer, but as a thief. He'd had time to skulk through the hall and rifle through her things. He'd probably found the key, assumed it opened a chest of valuables, and tucked it onto his person.

Before Kabayn was hanged, the shire-reeve would

have confiscated all of his possessions, including that key. 'Twould explain why the granddaughter was working in league with Nicholas Grimshaw. She suspected that learning the whereabouts of Hubert Kabayn at the time of the murder would lead her to the location of the treasure the key unlocked.

She tipped her head back and let out a throaty chuckle. She was almost inclined to let the silly wench sneak into Torteval to search fruitlessly for the elusive prize. But Philomena didn't have the luxury of time for such amusements. She'd already spent far more time on this nonsense than she intended, and her treasure wouldn't last forever.

Desirée swept a loose tendril back from her forehead and surveyed her work so far this morn. The counters gleamed, the cupboards shone softly, and the stool by the hearth looked new again, thanks to a soft ball of beeswax and a determined right elbow.

Nicholas couldn't possibly send her away now, not after last night. After all, if he sent her away, he'd have no one to keep his house in order, no one to cook him supper, no one to feed his cat, and no one to...She grinned. Polish his dagger. He'd be alone and miserable the rest of his life.

As for Desirée, it didn't matter to her that lawmen lived apart from polite society. She'd never really belonged to society. Eventually, if she got very ambitious, she'd persuade Nicholas to give up his role as shire-reeve, since he didn't much like his work, anyway.

In the meantime, she could do far worse than Nicholas Grimshaw for company. Indeed, she thought as a warm blush rose to her cheeks, she *loved* his company...his arms around her...his lips pressed to hers...his hot, velvety...

Snowflake brushed against her leg, startling her from her thoughts, almost making her drop the ball of beeswax.

"*You* won't mind if I stay, will you, Snowflake? I'll feed you scraps from the table every night, and scratch you behind the ears, and you can have my nice pallet by the fire all for yourself."

As if in answer, the cat swept past her leg again, his tail quivering.

Desirée resumed rubbing wax on the table, buffing it with the rag till it shone like a moonlit pond.

Nicholas had left early this morn for Faversham, but she couldn't forget the wistful look on his face as he bade her farewell. Nor the pleased surprise in his eyes when she rose on tiptoe to give him a quick kiss.

That kiss had turned into something far less innocuous, a deep, soulful joining of their lips that made her pulse race, her heart sing, and her body crave more.

But any more would have delayed him on his journey. And so he'd left with a final, searching look of regret that sent warm shivers along her skin.

Even now, the memory made her glow.

Softly singing *Tempus es iocundum*, this time fully embracing the lusty lyrics of burning love, she finished polishing the furniture and added another log to the fire.

Just as she was settling down to a cup of watered wine, Snowflake came trotting out from the bedchamber, his teeth clamped around a dead mouse.

"Oh!" She winced in disgust but knew better than to discourage the cat's useful hunting instincts. "Good cat.

Why don't you sit by the fire, way over there, and have yourself a nice feast?"

Unfortunately, it seemed this prize he'd caught for *her*. He proudly dropped the limp gray carcass at her feet.

"Oh."

He sniffed at it as if to make sure 'twas dead, then strutted proudly off.

"How kind."

She couldn't just leave it there, as much as she didn't want to touch the grisly thing. The last thing Nicholas needed in his cottage was a grim reminder of death. She had to dispose of it before he got home.

So swilling the cup of wine all at once to steel her nerves, she used the polishing rag to pick up the tiny beast by the tip of its tail. With a moue of disgust, she crept across the room, intending to fling the carcass into the yard.

Holding the mouse aloft, she swung open the door.

And almost tossed the rodent into the ruddy face of a piggish little man.

She gasped.

He recoiled.

She recovered before he did. "Who are you? What do you want?"

Eyeing the mouse mistrustfully, he ignored her questions. "Is Grimshaw at home?"

She frowned. The man looked like he'd had some kind of altercation recently. His lip was split, his brow was bruised, and there were scratches on his cheek. She didn't trust him. And she didn't like his imperious tone.

"He's not here, is he?" the man guessed, a telltale gleam of hope in his beady eyes.

She stepped through the doorway, dangling the mouse closer to him, forcing him to retreat. As far as she knew, the man might be one of Nicholas's disgruntled victims. "He's sleeping. Shall I wake him?"

He squinted, studying her face. "You're lying. But you're very good at it." With a sudden jerk of his arm, a reflex he must have earned from dodging blows, he knocked the mouse out of her grip, sending it flying into the garden. "The truth is, we saw him leave an hour ago."

We? An alarm sounded at once in her head. She retreated into the cottage and slammed the door. But just before it met the jamb, he shoved it inward. She pushed with all her might, sure she could outmuscle the little man. But suddenly the door moved toward her with greater force.

When she was shoved back into the room, not one, but *four* men burst into the cottage. The piggish man. Odger. John. And John.

Nicholas was in no mood to interrogate anyone today, which was terrible for his reputation. But he couldn't seem to muster the strength of will to inflict pain on any of the three suspected thieves chained to the wall of the Faversham gaol.

Not only had his heart gone soft, but even his muscles felt weak. All he could think about was the tantalizing beauty waiting at home for him, the maid who'd wrapped his soul around her finger and would one day leave him with nary a backward glance. God's bones, he thought, pacing across the dank mud floor of the gaol, he was as sick with love as a wide-eyed virgin.

Damn it all! Somehow he had to pull himself together to question the ragged trio before him. He tugged on his gloves and punched a menacing fist into his palm, making one of the lads jump in trepidation.

"Well, lads, you can make this simple or complicated," he told them, continuing to walk back and forth before them. "You can give me a quick answer, the correct answer, and I won't have to break anyone's bones. Or," he said, pausing to grind his fist into his palm, making the leather squeak ominously, "I can beat the truth out of you."

To his astonishment, his threat loosened their tongues at once, and they began chattering simultaneously. He had to hold up his hands to silence them.

"One at a time. You." He pointed to the first, a thin, pale lad with soulful eyes. "What's your name?"

The lad gulped. "Byron."

"Talk to me, Byron."

Despite his obvious fear, the lad straightened with all the nobility of a titled baron. "I did it."

Nicholas blinked in surprise. "Well. That wasn't so difficult, was—"

"Nay!" the second cried. "'Twas me! Harry! I was the one!"

Nicholas scowled at the round-faced lad with the earnest gaze.

"'Tisn't true!" the third protested, tossing his dark locks with stormy passion. "I snatched up those pearls. And I'm glad. And I'd do it again."

Nicholas let out a growling sigh as they all started arguing again. Here was something he'd never had before, too many suspects for the same crime.

"Silence!" he barked.

They became silent. He looked from one to the other.

These weren't seasoned outlaws. They could scarcely grow beards. But they'd definitely worked in concert to pull off some kind of mischief.

"So it took all three of you to steal one strand of pearls?"

The lads glanced at each other in solemn accord, then all three nodded.

Nicholas ambled over to his satchel of tools. Their commitment was admirable. But he didn't think they fully understood the consequences of false confession. He dug in his bag and pulled out an enormous chopping knife, sighting along its edge.

"So I should cut off all three of your hands?"

Their gasps were audible, but they made no other reply. From beneath lowered brows, he peered at the lads. Byron had gone even paler, Harry looked as if he might cry, and the third's face seemed made of stone. But none of them spoke.

'Twas curious. They were willing to lose their hands, all three of them, rather than name the guilty one. Such loyalty was rare. Such loyalty was absent in the world of outlaws. Dedicated thieves would betray their own mothers to avoid losing a limb.

What could have made the lads so self-sacrificing?

He resumed pacing before them, casually swinging the knife. "There's something you're not telling me."

"Nay, there's not," Harry blurted out.

Byron said, "We took the pearls. We told you already."

The stony lad bit out, "If you're going to cut off our hands, just get on with it!"

Nicholas hunkered down before them and chopped the knife hard into the dirt between his knees.

"Pearls," he murmured. "What would three lads want with pearls?"

"Mayhap we were thinking to sell them," the third lad said in challenge.

Byron added, "They could bring a fine price, pearls."

Harry, who Nicholas had ascertained was less clever than his fellows, chimed in, "I *like* pearls." At the frowns of disapproval from the other two, he muttered defensively, "I do."

"So where are your precious pearls now?" Nicholas asked.

No one replied.

Nicholas rose and ambled up to the third lad. "What's your name?"

The lad glared at him with burning hatred, refusing to answer.

"'Twould be a pity to break that jaw," Nicholas told him. "Then you'd not be able to speak at all."

"For God's sake, Campbell," Harry pleaded, "tell him."

"Harry!" Byron chided.

"Sorry," Harry mumbled.

"Campbell, is it?" Nicholas drew close, close enough to see his own grim reflection in the lad's smoldering eyes. "What have you done with the pearls?"

Campbell clenched his jaw and stared stonily ahead.

Nicholas could have shattered his jaw with a single blow, but there were better ways to get what he wanted. He backed away from the lad and strolled past the other two.

"You see, if we could *find* the missing item, the punishment might be less severe."

"Less severe?" Byron said.

"Oh, aye," Nicholas assured him. "Perchance a finger instead of the whole hand."

"Forsooth?" Harry asked hopefully.

"Don't listen to him," Campbell hissed. "'Tis trickery."

"'Tis no trickery," Nicholas said. "The jeweler only wants his goods back."

"If we find the pearls..." Byron said.

"Nay!" Campbell snapped.

"But Campbell..." Harry whimpered.

"Nay!"

"'Tis up to you," Nicholas said with a shrug. "Which is worth more, the pearls or your hands?"

"Jesu!" Harry sobbed.

Byron gulped. "'Twould be only a finger if we—"

"Nay!" Campbell bellowed. "Don't! You bastards!"

"But she's not worth it!" Harry cried. "Not our hands, Campbell!"

"Aye, Campbell," Byron agreed. "What woman would want a man with one hand?"

"*She* would!" Campbell said fiercely.

"Nay, she wouldn't," Byron said.

"She *would!*"

"Well, I'm not losing my hand for her!" Harry decided.

"Then you don't love her as much as I do!" Campbell raged.

Nicholas shook his head as they continued to pummel each other with words. He should have known a woman was involved. Only a wench could induce such madness in men. No doubt if he unchained the lads, they'd engage in a full-out brawl that would leave them bloody and broken-boned. And *then* what woman would have them?

He let them continue on for a while longer, then bellowed, "Quiet!"

They complied.

"So you stole the pearls for a woman?"

Harry furrowed his brow. "We didn't steal the pearls. *She* stole the pearls."

At this startling confession, the other two snarled and railed at him like tethered wild dogs until the poor lad was sobbing in misery.

Nicholas let out a sigh and scratched the back of his head. This was a coil indeed. The lads were innocent. They were protecting the real thief. With whom they were all apparently in love.

Now what was he going to do?

He couldn't punish the lads, knowing they weren't guilty of any crime. But neither did it sit well with him to chop off the hand of a woman, one who was apparently so prized by the three lads before him that they'd willingly sacrifice their limbs for her.

While the lads continued their battle of words, Nicholas began to consider the alternatives, and once again, he felt Desirée's wicked influence weaving its way through his brain.

There might be another way.

"Lads!"

They hushed.

"How good are you at playacting?"

Chapter 22

Desirée backed into the room, casting about for something, *anything,* she could use for a weapon. It didn't take a brilliant mind to determine that the four men who'd burst through the door were not here for a friendly visit.

If she'd had one more instant to think, she would have retreated to the bedchamber. After all, Nicholas kept a veritable arsenal on the wall.

But the first thing she could lay her hands on was the bowl that had come from what Nicholas had called his brain crusher.

She picked it up and swung it in a blind arc, clipping the piggish man on the side of the head with a loud clang.

He staggered back, dazed, but before she could rear back for another swing, the two Johns advanced on her. Each seized an arm.

She immediately began fighting them, trying to wrench loose.

"Hold her tight," Odger warned. "She's a slippery—"

Before he could finish his sentence, Desirée flung her leg forward, booting him hard in the shin.

He yelped and hopped backward, tripping over Snowflake, who let out a yowl and shot into the bedchamber.

Desirée had done a lot of fighting on the streets of London as a child, and she'd learned some nasty tricks. She kicked at one of the Johns' kneecaps, then dragged her foot down his shin and stomped on the top of his foot.

He bellowed in pain, releasing her.

Then, grabbing the wrist of her captured hand, she pulled it away from the second John, before suddenly reversing to drive her elbow back, catching him on the chin. Stunned by the blow, he sailed backward, thumping his head on the plaster wall.

For one fleeting moment, victory seemed in her grasp.

But as she spun around, wondering what had become of the piggish man, something solid hit the back of her head. Bright sparks exploded outward, then faded like stars disappearing before the dawn, and she sank into dark oblivion.

Sibil, the troublesome lass who'd stolen the pearls and caused the three lads so much grief, wasn't hard for Nicholas to find. They'd given him detailed instructions on the well-worn route to her cottage.

To his surprise, she was no beauty. Forsooth, she was a bit plump and pox-scarred. But he supposed there was naught more attractive to lads of that age than a lass who would tell them aye, and that was likely her charm.

She wrung her hands at the dire appearance of the shire-reeve at her door, but naturally she had no choice but to go with him.

Nicholas didn't speak to her until they entered the gaol. When she saw the lads chained to the wall, she gave a small cry of despair.

The lads, as they'd been instructed, looked appropriately miserable.

"I've asked you here, lass," Nicholas said, "to name me the thief from among these lads. I'm told you know each of them well, their natures, their habits." He bent to retrieve his huge chopping knife from the ground, smacking the handle on his palm to dislodge the dirt. "Which one is the thief?"

Her lower lip trembled as she eyed the blade. "What are ye goin' to do?"

"My duty," he said. "Cut off the hand of the thief."

She whimpered. "But...but..."

"Don't fret, Sibil. 'Tis only a hand," Byron said, his face a perfect portrait of noble sacrifice. "My heart will remain intact."

Campbell looked at her with naked adoration. "I'm not afraid, my lady, not as long as I can gaze into your loving eyes."

Even Harry managed to carry off his piece. "Don't worry, my dear Sibil." Then he added in a whisper, "The important parts will still be in working order."

She looked at Nicholas in horror. "But ye can't mean to...They're not thieves...How can ye cut off a man's hand for...for such a small..."

"Well," Nicholas admitted, "if the item they'd stolen had been recovered, 'twould be only a finger. But—"

"Wait!" She shoved her hand down the front of her bodice, scrabbling until she found a string of pearls, which she presented to Nicholas. "Here. The lads never meant no harm. They only wanted me to have a love token. Prithee don't cut anythin' off 'em!"

"A love token?" Nicholas asked the lads.

They nodded.

"From all three of you?"

"Sibil's my heart's desire," Byron affirmed.

"And mine," Harry agreed.

Campbell added, "I'd gladly sacrifice a hand for her."

Nicholas shook his head. "And what have you to say, Sibil, to these lads who would risk the loss of limb for your favors?"

"I love 'em," she gushed, "and I never meant to hurt 'em."

"All three?"

"Oh, aye." She gazed fondly upon them. "Byron, with his lovely speeches. Harry, with his sweet kisses. And Campbell, with his lusty touch."

Nicholas frowned beneath his hood. Could none of them see the ugly problem looming ahead? "And what will you do when you have to choose one of them?"

"Choose?" she asked.

"Aye, when you have to pick one to be your husband."

"Oh, I don't mean to marry 'em."

Nicholas blinked. "What?"

Sibil explained. "Well, I couldn't possibly marry all three, could I? But I can't bear the thought of livin' without 'em. So I'll love 'em for as long as I can."

Nicholas expected an outburst of outrage from the lads, but they seemed to be well aware of Sibil's intentions.

Byron intoned, *"Carpe diem, quam minimum credula postero."*

"Horace?" Nicholas recognized the phrase.

"Seize the day," Byron translated, "trusting little in the future."

"Aye," Campbell agreed, "live for the moment."

Nicholas shook his head at the naïveté of youth. But to his annoyance, the phrase haunted him as he began unchaining the lads.

Seize the day. He wondered if he should take that advice himself. After all, there was a lovely, willing maid waiting at home for him.

Aye, she might be gone on the morrow. She might break his heart. And he might never find a woman like her again.

But that was no reason to temper his passions.

Perchance he *should* seize the day.

With renewed purpose and a sudden urge to hie homeward as fast as his legs could carry him, he scolded the four youths soundly for their theft and issued a dire warning that he'd not be so merciful next time. Then, with a lie that rolled a little too easily off his tongue, he reported to the local constable that upon investigation, he'd found a string of pearls just outside the jeweler's shop, that they'd obviously not been stolen, but dropped there by the jeweler himself.

Once again, the satisfaction of administering fair justice offset his guilt at breaking the law. When he departed Faversham, 'twas with a contented heart. In fact, as soon as he was out of range of the villagers, for whom he had to keep up the appearance of the grimly silent shire-reeve, he began humming a merry tune under his breath.

He didn't even realize he'd been singing the lusty verses of *Tempus es iocundum* until, by late afternoon, he pushed happily through the door of his cottage.

What he discovered made the song falter upon his lips.

The house was as cold and still as death. No candle glowed in welcome. No supper simmered upon the hearth. No fire burned at all. His gaming box was missing from the table. And Azrael was nowhere in sight.

The satchel dropped from Nicholas's limp fingers, hitting the ground with a thud, a thud as hollow as the beating of his heart.

She'd left him. Desirée had left him.

Instinctively drawn to his keg of ale, Nicholas pulled a draught for himself with trembling fingers.

Then, lifting the cup in a bitter salute, he gave a humorless bark of laughter. "Seize the day."

❧

Chapter 23

DESIRÉE WOKE TO AN ICY SLAP OF WATER. She sputtered and blinked away the cold drops, peering through the wet strands of her hair, trying to recall where she was.

"Desirée," a strange woman crooned. "That's your name, isn't it?"

She squinted up toward the voice but couldn't make out the features of the woman haloed by the stark morning sun.

Suddenly the events of yesterday came rushing back. The four Torteval servants had kidnapped her. She'd been gagged, bound, blindfolded, and dumped in the back of a cart for a long ride.

Awake part of the way, she'd heard bits and pieces of conversation. Odger had been worried that the shirereeve would suspect him, that he would come and hunt him down. But the piggish man had only chortled at that, informing him 'twas the reason they'd taken the gaming box. Grimshaw would never suspect she'd been kidnapped. He'd assume she'd robbed him and run away.

Then the brutes had delivered her to this deserted mill, removing her gag and blindfold and forcing her down upon the plank floor, where they secured her to a splintered pillar that supported what remained of the rotting timbers.

She'd been left alone here until now.

"Desirée? The granddaughter of Hubert Kabayn?" the woman asked. She dropped the half-full bucket of water onto the floor with a thud.

Desirée licked the droplets from her lips. 'Twas the only drink she'd been given since they'd abandoned her. Her belly growled with hunger. Her chafed wrists stung from struggling against her rope bonds. And her voice was hoarse from yelling for help.

Without warning, the woman stepped forward and gave her a jolting slap across the cheek. "I asked you a question."

Desirée fought back the urge to spit in the woman's face. But though she was a stubborn lass, she wasn't stupid. With her legs bound together and her arms tied tightly behind her, she was nigh helpless. Clenching her jaw, she nodded.

"Well, Desirée, I'm Lady Philomena. Of Torteval?" the lady continued silkily, bracing one hand on the broken grinding stone as she hunkered down to look her in the eye. "You seem like an intelligent woman. I think you can guess why you're here."

By the light flooding in through the torn sheepskin window, Desirée could see the woman clearly now. She was coldly beautiful, clad in skirts of gold-embroidered blood-red silk that currently swept through the mouse droppings strewn across the floor. She had sleek auburn hair, alabaster skin, and a shapely mouth. But when she leered as she did now, her dark lips looked like a bloody slash across her pale face, and what Desirée detected in the glittering depths of Philomena's gaze chilled her to the bone.

'Twasn't madness exactly. 'Twas more akin to icy, reptilian hunger. And if there was one thing Hubert had taught her, 'twas to not rile those with the eyes of a snake.

Desirée carefully shook her head.

The woman clucked her tongue. "Think, poppet, think," she urged, her honey voice at odds with her intense gaze.

Desirée croaked, "I don't know what you—"

"Forsooth?" The lady reached out a finger to lift Desirée's chin, studying her face carefully. "And I'd have thought a day without food or water would jar your memory."

Then, without even a blink to signal her intent, the woman scraped her nail suddenly sideways across Desirée's throat, leaving a searing gash that made Desirée gasp in pain.

Philomena's beautiful face was suddenly disfigured by a sneer of impatience. "Where is it, you filthy whelp?"

Desirée's mind raced, but she couldn't figure out what the woman was talking about. "Where is what?"

Her question earned her another vicious slap, and Desirée kept her head lowered this time, stifling an oath as her fingers twitched with the urge to return the blow.

"Don't pretend you don't know, wench," Philomena snarled. "I want my key, and I want it now."

"What?"

"My key!"

Suddenly Desirée remembered something she'd put to the back of her thoughts, it had seemed so insignificant at the time. When she'd first visited Hubert in the Canterbury gaol, he'd boasted that he hadn't left Torteval completely empty-handed. Then he'd slipped her a useless old iron key, the only thing he'd managed to hide on his person. He'd jested with her, saying 'twas likely the key to some noblewoman's chastity belt. She'd laughed and tucked it into her purse without another thought.

Now she wondered if it did indeed belong to something important. Perchance 'twas the key to the Torteval treasury. Mayhap it unlocked a chest of gold coins or deeds to estates or valuable jewels.

Whatever the key opened, 'twas vital enough to warrant the risky abduction of a woman from the home of a notorious lawman.

Desirée made up her mind then and there. No matter what coercions the Lady of Torteval intended, she was not going to surrender.

Indeed, using that key might be her way to exact one final bit of vengeance upon Torteval for the unjust death of Hubert, just one robbery to put her old friend's soul to rest before she abandoned her life of crime forever. 'Twas too tempting an opportunity to pass up.

But first she had to escape her captor.

"I don't know what you're talking about," she told Philomena. "What key?"

The next blow came from her closed fist, bruising Desirée's jaw and knocking her sideways, and she had to shake her head to clear the ringing in her ears.

"I know you have it, wench," Philomena hissed. "Your grandfather took it when he murdered the lawyer."

Desirée instinctively blurted out, "He didn't murder anyone."

"Don't be a crackpate. Of course he did." She allowed a cruel smile to blossom on her face. "Forsooth, 'twas your good friend Nicholas Grimshaw who dispatched him to hell for the crime, wasn't it?"

Desirée bit back a curse. 'Twould be unwise to speak her mind while she was at the mercy of a madwoman.

"That's why you're living with him now, isn't it?" she guessed. "Because he has the key."

Philomena seized her by her throbbing jaw, demanding her gaze. More angry than afraid, 'twas all Desirée could do not to whip her head around to bite the woman's fingers.

"Give me what I want," Philomena purred, "and perchance I won't leave you with scars."

"I don't know what you want," Desirée insisted.

"The key!" Philomena shrieked. This time she caught Desirée completely off guard, kicking her in the belly and robbing her of breath. "The key!"

Desirée couldn't suck in even a wisp of air, let alone speak. Her stomach ached with a dull throbbing, and her lungs seemed to have collapsed against her spine. She wondered if she'd overestimated her capacity to endure Philomena's abuse.

"Don't be stupid!" Philomena cried, pacing back and forth before Desirée in the small space between the moss-covered wall and the millstone. She gave a mirthless chuckle. "You don't even know what it goes to. 'Twill do you no good."

Desirée finally managed to rasp in a painful breath. "I don't have . . . your bloody key."

Philomena's eyes narrowed to fuming slits, and she suddenly turned on Desirée like a wild beast, seizing her by the hair. Desirée gasped as the woman's fists coiled tightly in her tresses, threatening to tear the hair from her scalp.

"You're lying, you filthy harlot!" Philomena spat, twisting her fingers mercilessly.

The pain triggered Desirée's street-fighting instincts, and on impulse, she swept her bound legs violently sideways, catching the front of Philomena's shins.

Desirée lost a few strands of hair as the woman careened, grasping for purchase, but 'twas well worth the price to see her stumble and hit the planks on one knee.

Of course, Desirée's triumph was short-lived. The fall only agitated Philomena all the more. As she struggled to her feet, rage turned her fair skin ruddy, and a lock of auburn hair fell like the tail of a dead rat over one vexed eye.

Desirée bent her knees up under her chin, like a crossbow primed to fire. She might be engaged in an uneven fight, but she meant to leave bruises of her own.

Suddenly, a slice of blinding light fell between them, and both pairs of eyes were drawn to the door. It had creaked open, and lurking in the doorway, as unexpected as snow in summer, was Nicholas's cat.

Desirée frowned. What was he doing here? Had Philomena's men abducted him, as well? Or, she thought with a thrill of hope, did Snowflake's appearance mean Nicholas had somehow tracked her to this mill?

Philomena suddenly screamed in violent outrage, startling Desirée. With a determined swish of her scarlet skirts, she marched toward the door, intent on doing the cat some harm.

"Nay!" Desirée cried. "Don't hurt him!"

Her words stopped Philomena in her tracks a mere yard from Snowflake, who had unwisely held his ground.

Philomena swung her head around, narrowing her eyes at Desirée. "You know this beast?"

Desirée hesitated.

If Philomena didn't recognize Snowflake, then she hadn't ordered the cat's abduction. But Snowflake hadn't brought Nicholas, either, for the lawman would have instantly burst in the door at the sound of a woman's scream. Nay, Snowflake must have come on his own.

"Do you?" Philomena hissed, rearing back her foot, preparing to kick the hapless cat.

"Nay! Aye!" Jesu, she couldn't let the woman hurt Snowflake.

"Well, which is it?"

"Aye, I know him. But there's no need to hurt him. He's only a harmless..."

Philomena sneezed all at once. Normally such a loud sound would send the skittish cat fleeing, but for once the stubborn creature lingered in the doorway.

"Shoo!" Desirée shouted, to no avail. "Go away, Snowflake! Go! Shoo!"

Philomena snatched a flour sack from a hook on the wall and approached the cat furtively. "Come along, Snowflake." She sniffled. "Climb into this nice sack," she said with false sweetness, "and I'll drown you in the well."

"Nay!"

Desirée's cry distracted the cat for only an instant, but 'twas long enough for Philomena to throw the sack over him, effectively trapping him within.

Philomena sneezed again but managed to hold the sack down while the cat snarled and flailed inside.

Wise or not, Desirée could no longer bottle her temper. "Leave him alone, you bloody witch!"

Philomena only laughed and scooped up the sack, holding her thrashing prize up in triumph. "Mayhap now you remember where the key is."

Desirée trembled with rage and frustration, fatigue and thirst. She couldn't let the woman hurt Snowflake. Revenge wasn't worth it. The promise of riches wasn't worth it. Even clearing Hubert's soul of murder wasn't worth seeing the expression on Nicholas's face when he learned his precious cat had been harmed.

Her shoulders sank, and she nodded.

Philomena smirked. "I thought so." She twirled the sack to seal it, making Snowflake mew piteously, then plopped it roughly onto the floor and made a knot in the top.

"If you touch one whisker on that cat," Desirée bit out, "I'll bury the key where you'll never find it."

"Believe me," Philomena said, picking up the sack and holding it at arm's length, "I have no desire to touch the wretched beast."

She sneezed again, then shuddered, hanging the knotted sack back on its hook. Her eyes were swelling rapidly, turning red, and Desirée realized she must be one of those people who couldn't abide cats. She suddenly wished Snowflake had come with all his feline brethren to torment the lady.

Philomena held out her palm. "Now hand over the key."

Desirée swallowed. "I don't have it."

"What!" Philomena doubled her palm into a fist.

Desirée flinched, assuring her quickly, "But I can get it. Let me go. Give me till the morrow, and I'll bring it to you."

Desirée could almost see steam huffing from the lady's ears as she clenched and unclenched her fist. "Let you go? Are you addled?"

"'Tis the only way. 'Tis hidden in the shire-reeve's cottage."

"I'll send someone else to fetch it."

Desirée grimaced, remembering how clumsy Philomena's servants were. "'Tis a task requiring stealth, not force."

Displeasure curled Philomena's lip as she mulled over Desirée's words, but she knew Desirée was right. No one forced the formidable Nicholas Grimshaw to do anything. He'd never allow a stranger to ransack his home.

She narrowed her eyes and bit out a warning. "Heed me well, wench. You'll slip into the house, get the key, and return it to me at Torteval. Do you understand? No trickery. Otherwise, I shall be delighted to kill your cat."

As if in answer, Snowflake yowled pitifully from inside his cloth prison. With a peeved growl, Philomena hoisted the half-full bucket at her feet and doused the poor, bagged, scrambling cat with the rest of the water.

Desirée wanted naught more than to lunge at the barbarous wench and tear her eyes out.

Philomena gave her a nasty sneer. "And remember, your Nicholas Grimshaw may like to tussle with the likes of you betwixt the sheets, but he knows well who pays his wage. If you breathe a word of any of this to him, I'll see that he's stripped of his position and reduced to carting dung for a living."

჻

Chapter 24

DESIRÉE DECIDED THAT WHILE Lady Philomena might be soulless, she wasn't stupid. After seeing that Desirée was fed and cleaned up, she had her gagged and blindfolded for the trek home, so she wouldn't know the whereabouts of the ruined mill and her hostage pet. She'd directed the men to drop Desirée at the outskirts of Canterbury so they'd not be spotted. And she'd ordered Desirée to come alone on the morrow to Torteval, where they would arrange the exchange.

The journey to town had taken a long while, and Desirée suspected the men had circled the cart over the same ground again and again to confuse her. By the time they released her at the edge of the wood, 'twas late afternoon.

The spires of Canterbury Cathedral, rising high above the trees, helped her get her bearings as she trudged toward the shire-reeve's cottage, all the while wondering what tale she'd have to invent to explain her absence.

She couldn't let Nicholas get entangled in this dangerous web, particularly when his livelihood was at stake. 'Twas her own mess to clean up. If she'd listened to him instead of stubbornly insisting on clearing Hubert's name, none of this would have happened. Lady Philomena would never have known she was tied to the man they'd hanged for the murder, would never have suspected Desirée had her precious key, would never have abducted her and held Nicholas's poor cat hostage.

Now, for his sake, Desirée would set aside her need for justice, surrender what belonged to the woman, and break her vow to exonerate Hubert Kabayn.

If she could carry off this one final deception, Nicholas need never know the peril she'd brought to his house. She'd never endanger him again, never give him cause to send her away.

She steeled herself as she latched the garden gate behind her and headed up the walkway.

She was prepared for his anger.

She was prepared for an icy welcome.

But naught could prepare her for what she saw when she nudged open the cottage door.

By the single sputtering candle upon the hearth, she could make out the silhouette of Nicholas, lying asleep on her pallet beside his toppled flagon, curled up like a babe, his arms wrapped possessively around her cloak.

Her heart melted at once. Her eyes grew wet with unshed tears. And instantly she knew she was doing the right thing.

The lonely lawman needed her. And he needed his cat. And she'd make sure he got both before the sun set on the morrow, no matter what distractions or trickery she had to employ to keep him out of harm's way till then.

Bracing herself for the painful deceit ahead, she shut the door with more force than was necessary, fluttering the candle flame and waking Nicholas. *Half* waking him. As he struggled up on his elbows and swung his head toward her, his eyes drooped in drunken oblivion.

"Y'came home," he sighed in pleased surprise.

"Did I?" she snapped, feigning anger, striking the flint hung on the wall to try to light another candle. "Or have I stumbled into an alehouse?"

He was oblivious to her ire. His features relaxed with sheer relief. "Y'came back. Y'robbed me. But y'came back t'me."

She frowned, and her fingers trembled on the flint, finally getting a spark to catch the wick. "That damned gaming box wasn't worth as much as I thought."

He seemed not to hear her. His face broke out in a thankful grin as he slurred, "Ah, God, Des'ree, y'came back." A tear slipped from his eye, and he wiped it away with the heel of his hand. "I feared y'd lef' me. I feared y'd lef' me f'rev'r."

At his gushing confession and the pure gratitude in his eyes, her heart careened dangerously. She felt a lump forming in her throat. Sweet saints, Nicholas didn't even care about his gaming box. All he cared about was her.

She swallowed back the knot of emotion before it could choke her, then crouched beside him to help him sit up. "Left you?" she scoffed. "Why would I do that?"

"I thought...I thought..." One corner of his mouth rose in a sheepish smile as he swayed against her. "I thought y'were gone f'r good."

Lord, the sorrow in his eyes brought tears to her own, but she sniffed them back. "Pah! You'll not get rid of me that easily," she said, wrapping his arm about her shoulder to help him to his feet. "Stand up now. We've got to get you into bed."

'Twas no easy feat getting a drunken man twice her size into a pallet. He leaned heavily upon her, shuffling along, tripping over his own feet.

Halfway there, he stopped abruptly with a frown. "Did y'take Azr'l?"

She stiffened. "Nay."

"He's gone."

Guilt burdened her words. "He's probably off prowling somewhere for a ladylove. I'm sure he'll come back."

He grunted and took two more steps, then halted again, blinking at her. "Y've been gone two days."

"Mm."

He nodded, apparently satisfied with his calculations, but after a few more steps, halted again. "Where'd y'go?"

"Nowhere."

He narrowed his eyes at her, his perception just keen enough to take note of her bedraggled condition. "What happened t'you?"

"Come on, Nicholas," she urged. "Just a few more steps, and you can sleep in your nice, soft—"

He jerked away from her and nearly toppled over. "Did someone try t'hurt you?"

She gulped. "Don't be silly. Who would try to hurt me?"

"Anyone. Everyone." A cloud of melancholy fell over his face. "They all hate Nich'las Gr'mshaw."

His mind was straying, but 'twas to her advantage. She sidled up to him again, grabbing the lit candle as she passed and guiding him toward the bed. "*I* don't hate Nicholas Grimshaw."

"Y'don't, d'you?" He gave her a sloppy smile. "Y'r the only one, Des'ree."

His words caught at her heart, but she couldn't let herself be manipulated by the ravings of a drunk man. She managed to maneuver him next to the pallet and found a perch for the candle. He fell back onto the bed, and for a moment, as she tugged off his boots, she thought he'd passed out again.

Then he mumbled something. It sounded foreign.

"What?" she asked, leaning closer.

"*Carpe. Diem.*"

"What's that?"

For answer, he reached for her, enclosing her in his arms and pulling her gracelessly down on top of him. A hopeless sigh escaped her. Instinct told her to squirm her way loose, but she was too weary to fight him. Forsooth, after her harrowing ordeal, 'twas rather pleasant being held against his massive chest, hearing the steady beat of his heart, feeling his protective arms enveloping her.

"Seize th'day," he murmured against her hair.

She had no idea what he was talking about. 'Twas likely he didn't, either. But the longer he held her, the more comfortable she grew in his embrace. It seemed the most natural thing in the world to lie atop him, snuggling into the crook of his shoulder, draping her arms around his neck.

There was really no point in getting up just now. Soon, she knew, he'd drift off to sleep, and then she could tuck him under the coverlet and stretch out on her pallet by the hearth. He'd likely not even remember how he'd made it to his bed.

But though he was definitely in his cups, he seemed disinclined to fall asleep anytime soon. Indeed, by the obvious hardening against her belly, at least part of him seemed quite alert.

"Stay," he breathed.

She'd thought herself too shaken and exhausted by the adventures of the past two days to do more than collapse into slumber. But she was wrong. His was the voice of lust, murmuring an incantation in her ear that magically dissolved her fatigue, leaving every nerve in her body curiously awake.

Stay? Perchance she would. She shifted her hips, unknowingly rousing him. He emitted a throaty growl as her abdomen pressed against his erection. The bestial sound sent a hot shiver up her spine. The second time she brushed him with her belly, 'twas intentional.

With a chiding grunt, he lowered his hands until they clutched her buttocks, and he hauled her up hard against him. She gasped as her loins responded to the direct contact.

He gave a low chuckle, then lifted his head to capture her lips with his own.

His breath was heavy with ale, but 'twas not an unpleasant taste. His lips were warm, yielding and demanding all at once. He feasted languorously upon her, licking and nipping and making delicious sounds, as if he could not eat his fill.

Her hands drifted of their own will, rambling across his shoulders, up his corded neck, cupping his bristled jaw as she savored his playful, intoxicating kisses.

He laughed and squeezed her against him again, and she moaned at the sensation.

Suddenly her clothing felt too cumbersome. She longed to tear it away, to feel her skin against his.

As if he divined her thoughts, his hands stole up the back of her kirtle, loosening the laces. Never breaking from the kiss, he dragged the shoulders of the gown slowly down until her breasts eased free.

With a chuckle of victory, he released her mouth. Reaching under her arms, he lifted her up until her breasts were suspended above his face.

She held her breath as he gazed up at her, his wicked intentions clear in his sultry eyes.

With a gentleness she didn't expect, he raised his head to lap at her nipple. She bit her lip as it stiffened to a sensitive peak.

"Mmm." With a smile of approval, he moved his head to sample her other breast with a tender brush of his tongue, as well.

She sucked a hard breath between her teeth. Her loins felt afire, and her flesh burned with longing. And shock. And pleasure. All at once.

"S'sweet." His breath across her wet nipples made her shiver. But he remedied that at once, capturing her breast fully in his open mouth, warming her flesh with his swirling tongue.

Lord, it seemed he sucked the very will from her, leaving her dizzy. She sighed as pleasure flooded her veins, weakening her muscles and her resolve.

When he ventured to her other breast, paying it equal devotion, her head fell forward in limp ecstasy. The warmth of his mouth surrounding her radiated outward, heating her whole body.

When he released her, lowering her back to his chest, her sensual appetite had only been whetted. He might have been playing with her, taunting her flesh, teasing her desires. But for her, suddenly 'twas no game. Her lust was a voracious beast, intent on feeding.

With a feminine snarl, she swooped down upon him, savaging his mouth with ravenous kisses. To her surprise, he began to answer her with the same desperate haste, knotting his fingers in her hair to angle her head for deeper penetration, while the fingers of his other hand pressed into the flesh of her hip.

She scrabbled at the laces of his shirt, tearing them open, then left a trail of kisses upon his exposed skin. With a triumphant chuckle, he threw his head back, allowing her access, and she bathed him thoroughly with her tongue.

All the while, Nicholas was stealthily gathering the fabric of her skirts beneath his fingers, hiking them higher and higher. When his fingertip contacted the bare skin of her thigh, she gasped at his daring. He fondled the crease below her buttock, and she squirmed beneath his touch, unintentionally grinding against his loins.

He sucked in a harsh breath, and she suddenly felt a surge of strength, knowing she could overpower him with the mere shift of her hips.

She thrust toward him again, and he groaned, half in pain, half in pleasure. But she wanted more. Gathering her knees beneath her, she lifted off of him enough to untie his braies.

"Oh, aye," he sighed.

Meanwhile, he used both of his hands, caressing the flesh of her buttocks, massaging them, spreading them gently to slip his fingers between, closer and closer to the center of her desire.

He groaned as she freed his straining cock. For a wondrous moment, she held the vibrant staff, glorying at its velvety strength in the palm of her hand.

At the same moment, he parted her nether lips with a delicate touch, stroking the flesh that burned for him. She jerked in response and tightened her grip on him, squeezing a drop of glistening dew from his eager staff.

Suddenly a deeper yearning obsessed her, a profound ache within her that demanded more than the taunting play of his fingers.

Perchance 'twas a sort of catharsis after her joust with danger. Perchance 'twas that she was so grateful to be in his arms again. Or perchance 'twas the fact that one of them was too drunk to say her nay. Whatever the cause, a curious, impulsive madness came over her.

She wanted Nicholas. All of him. Now.

And she didn't want to hear any arguments. From her conscience or Hubert's ghost or the voice of reason.

Swiftly, while the iron was hot, she made her choice, edging toward him with bold intent.

She hesitated just once, as the tip of his cock pressed like an invader at the gates of her womb, demanding entry. After all, once she eased forward, there was no going back.

Then she looked into his beautiful face.

Lord, no one had ever gazed at her like that before.

'Twas not lust, not exactly. She knew the face of lust.

Men had been staring at her with craving in their eyes since she first budded breasts.

Nay, 'twas almost adoration, adoration and need. Not just for her body, but for her being, for her acceptance, for her love. He might be besotted on ale, but there was no hiding the fact that he was equally besotted on her.

For Desirée, there was naught more intoxicating. Her heart melted under his gaze like a pool of butter. Bracing herself with a deep breath, she surged forward.

If she'd known 'twould sting so much, Desirée might have been less anxious to impale herself. It felt like her flesh had been torn by a dull blade, and now he filled her so completely, she feared she'd never dislodge him. Still, it had been her idea. 'Twas not Nicholas's fault that he was as big as an ox.

Nicholas, lost in a ragged gasp of astonished pleasure as he lay fully sheathed within her, seemed oblivious to her pain.

'Twas just as well. Pride would never let Desirée admit that she'd made a mistake, that she might have acted too hastily.

But at his next movement, she couldn't prevent a quick gasp of pain, and he stopped, glancing at her askance and then in realization.

"Y'r a v'rgin."

She swallowed hard. "Not anymore." She gave him a weak smile.

Then his arms came around her in a tender embrace. Speechless, he stared at her, gazing into her face with a sort of amazement, as if she were the most precious angel in heaven.

Instantly, her heart softened, and all the pain in the

world couldn't make her regret what she'd surrendered to him.

She leaned forward, burrowing her head in his shoulder to hide her winces of pain. Then she initiated the motion of lovemaking she'd learned from stealing peeks down alleyways and into shadowy stables.

To her relief, after several slow thrusts, the pain eased, and tingling warmth took its place. A sensual haze began to swirl around her like mist on a marsh, moving her to curious languor, suffusing her with primal desires. Instinct drove her, stealing her will and directing her in the rhythm of passion's dance.

Beneath her, Nicholas gasped in wonder, clinging to her like a man about to drown. His quiet desperation fueled hers, and she turned her head toward him, her breath soughing against his ear. He shivered, growling softly, thrusting upward with his hips to answer her motion.

'Twas a different sensation from before, when he'd brought her to a quick crest. This was a deep, slow-burning, all-encompassing passion that touched every fiber of her body, every thread of her thoughts.

As she rocked gently back and forth, the pleasurable fullness increased. Where they joined, her flesh grew moist and receptive, and her heart seemed to open to him, as well. 'Twas a sweet and wanton feeling, a thirst for power, yet a desire to please, all in the same moment.

He continued to return her thrusts at a gradually increasing pace. With each assuaging stroke, she was spurred to even greater yearning. Now 'twas she who hastened toward the elusive target, for it seemed every thrust that brought her nearer satisfaction also brought her more intense need.

It must have been the same for him. He strove against her, yielding more, demanding more. And now he clasped her to him, one hand holding the back of her head, one grasping her buttock, guiding her with ever-increasing urgency.

Soon her mind had no room for thought, for 'twas too filled with sensation. Her wits deserted her, and she bucked as recklessly as a wild mare, straining at its tether.

An incredible tension commanded all her focus, increasing with each gasp of breath, until she was certain she could bear no more.

Then, with a great lunge, he bellowed beneath her, his arms squeezing her tightly as he drove upward in the throes of violent release. Suddenly the reins on her own passions snapped, and she broke loose, a colt cantering off across a sunlit field, reveling in freedom, buffeted by strong, warm winds of pleasure.

For a long while they held each other in silence, too overwhelmed to move, too weary for words. And long moments later, Desirée shuddered off the last vestiges of lust. But naught could dissipate the lingering sweetness of her union with Nicholas. She'd expected the bone-rattling, skin-tingling climax she'd experienced before. She'd never anticipated this.

She didn't want to stir. Ever again. She'd die happy if she could only lie in Nicholas's arms forever.

Not only were their bodies joined. Their hearts beat in tandem, making joyful music. And her soul felt inextricably intertwined with his, as if they'd been struck by a lightning bolt that had forged them into one.

Desirée felt simultaneously gentled and empowered, vulnerable yet strong. This merging of their bodies and hearts and spirits seemed to have created one being of all the best of both.

Tenderness overwhelmed her. She snuggled against his neck, listening to his breathing slow into the faint snores of sleep. Her last thought as she drifted off to contented slumber was that she was helplessly in love with Nicholas Grimshaw.

Chapter 25

'Twas morn, and Nicholas's head felt like 'twas in a brain crusher. The last time he'd drunk so much in one night was after his first hanging. And then he'd had three days to recover.

He vaguely remembered that he had to travel to Chilham this morn, a journey of a few hours, but his thoughts were so scrambled from whatever he'd done last night that he'd be lucky if he could find his way there.

He hadn't even opened his eyes when he realized he wasn't alone in the bed. Someone was nestled intimately against him, and 'twasn't Azrael.

Cautiously, he lifted one eyelid.

Desirée. She was facing away from him, and her hair cascaded over her shoulders and his hand.

In a sobering rush, he remembered.

Desirée had come back to him. And Jesu! He'd swived the lass. Forsooth, the dear damsel had surrendered her maidenhood to him.

He racked his brain, trying to recall every precious detail. But he'd been drunk, curse it all, and much of his memory was a blur.

Still, 'twas clear enough to make him forget his aching head. And at the moment, the way her bottom was caressing his loins in warm invitation brought a lusty swell to his cock and a hopeful smile to his lips.

Loath to wake her, but unable to resist all the feminine delights so close at hand, he nuzzled the nape of her neck, inhaling her woodsy fragrance, rubbing a silky strand of her hair between his fingers. He let his palm slide lightly over her bare shoulder, where her gown had slipped down, then traced the loose laces of her kirtle along her back, gliding forward over the sinuous narrowing of her waist, spanning her ribs so his thumb rested just below the curve of her breast.

Encouraged by her lack of resistance, he let his hand drift downward over her skirts. Even through the wool, he felt the slight mound of her womanhood, and he imagined the soft curls there, the sweet petals that had parted for him last night. Gently, he slipped his hand farther between her legs, where she was even hotter.

God, he wanted her. He wanted to seize the day once more, make love to her while she lay warm and willing and close at hand, while he was fully awake and aware and sober, while he could ravish her properly, make her so contented she'd never leave him again.

She moaned softly in her sleep as he gathered her skirts in his fingers, dragging them up to bare her thighs, and when he slid his palm over the warm flesh of her womanhood, she woke with a tiny gasp.

"Good morn," he murmured.

At first, her hand closed defensively atop his, as if to yank it away, but when he coaxed a finger gently betwixt her nether lips, she sighed, pressing him closer instead.

She rolled toward him onto her back, allowing him better access, and he eased up on one elbow, enchanted by her beautiful, smoldering green eyes.

"Good morn," she whispered.

His gaze lowered to her mouth, and a furrow creased his brow. There was a tiny cut at the corner of her lip, and the flesh along her jaw seemed bruised. God's wounds. Had he done that? "I hope I didn't hurt you last night."

A sly smile curved her lips. "I hope I didn't hurt *you.* You bellowed like a sick bull."

Giving her a sheepish grin of relief, he lifted the fingers of his free hand to tuck her hair behind her ear. "A *love*sick bull." With the back of his knuckle, he lightly traced the vein pulsing down the side of her neck. Then he noticed a thin red scratch running across her throat. He frowned again. Jesu, what had he done to her?

At his scowl, her hand flew defensively to her throat. After a moment, her eyes widened. "Shite!" She lifted her head to glance toward the shuttered window. "What hour is it?"

The hand cupping her fell away as she hastily scrambled to the edge of the bed.

He scowled. Light filtered in through the cracks of the shutters. "I'm not sure. Past dawn." What ailed the lass?

"Past dawn?" She stumbled from the pallet and began smoothing her skirts, clearly unnerved about something.

"What's wrong?"

She froze. "Wrong?" She licked her lip, and he knew instantly she was about to lie to him. "I'm...I'm only concerned that you might be late for your work." She seemed to take a sudden interest in finding his boots. "Where is it you're off to today?"

As she reached for one cast-off boot, her sleeve slipped up and he glimpsed her wrist. The flesh was raw there, red with abrasions.

He narrowed his eyes. That he knew he hadn't done. Those kinds of marks came from rope.

Their gazes met, and for an instant, guilt flashed through her eyes. Then she averted her glance, pulling her sleeve down over the mark and dropping his boot beside the bed.

God's hooks! Something had happened to her, and the little imp was trying to hide it. She might be a skillful liar and a gifted cheat, but there was no concealing physical evidence like that.

Desirée had been missing for two days, yet she'd given him no plausible explanation for where she'd gone or what she'd done, aside from some nonsense about trying to sell his gaming box. She'd clearly gotten herself into some kind of trouble. And she wasn't going to divulge what 'twas. Not willingly, anyway.

But Nicholas knew how to loosen tongues. 'Twas his trade. He could have her singing like a sparrow within the hour.

He reached out and caught her elbow, gently but firmly tugging her toward him again. "Chilham."

"What?"

"I'm going to Chilham today."

"Chilham? But isn't that a long way?" She resisted his pull, but he had the advantage of strength, and he forced her to sit on the edge of the pallet.

He wrapped an arm about her waist then, anchoring her there, and gave her a sultry grin. "Not that far. I can spare an hour."

"An hour!" she exclaimed, trying to spring to her feet. But he held her fast.

"Or two."

"Oh, nay!" This time she managed to weasel out of his grip, and she surged toward the foot of the bed, where she flung open his wooden chest and began pulling out garments. "I'll not be the ruin of your reputation. If Chilham needs Nicholas Grimshaw, then Nicholas Grimshaw they shall have."

While she burrowed through his clothing, he crept toward her atop the coverlet. When she slammed down the lid, he picked her up by the waist and hefted her back onto the bed.

"At the moment," he purred, "I can think of a certain lusty lass who needs Nicholas Grimshaw more."

By the rood! Did Nicholas have to look at her like that, his eyes flickering like stars through smoke, full of promise?

Despite Desirée's keen desperation to finish her business with Lady Philomena, when he gazed at her that way, she found him nigh impossible to resist.

Her body remembered too well the ecstasy of the night before, the searing passion, the exhilarating flight, and the quiet joy afterward.

But she didn't dare delay. There was no telling what obstacles she might encounter on her trek to Torteval today. And when she thought of Snowflake, hanging helpless in that flour sack, his life at the mercy of a woman who despised cats...

"Nicholas!" she chided, batting away the arm that had somehow found its way beneath her skirts. "You have to get dressed, and I—" She hesitated.

"You what?" His eyes narrowed, as if he was keenly interested in her answer.

"I...have things to do." She managed to wriggle free of several of his attempts to snatch her and finally fled into the next room. Quickly scanning the chamber, she spied the satchel just where she'd left it, beside his keg. She grabbed it up and began digging through the contents, praying the key was still there. Aye, there 'twas. "After all," she called out, "I've been gone for two days. I'm sure we're out of milk and eggs, and—"

His sudden appearance in the doorway startled her, making her drop the key. They both frowned down at the black iron object. Desirée gulped.

If ever there was a time for distraction, 'twas now. Desirée stepped close to him, blocking his view, letting her gaze drift up to his bare chest. She only had to half feign the desire that coursed through her veins as she let her eyes graze the perfectly sculpted muscles and flat planes of his torso.

"On the other hand," she breathed, outlining her lips with the tip of her tongue, "mayhap I *can* spare an hour before I..." She dipped her eyelids. "...get on with my..." She stared longingly at his mouth. "...duties."

She slipped her hand into his and led him back to the bedchamber. 'Twas doubtless a sin of the worst kind, using swiving as a distraction. But she truly did care for Nicholas. Enough to deceive him in order to protect him.

Enough to have given him her virginity, for the love of Mary. And truth be told, a part of her yearned to relive their passionate coupling as much as he did.

"This time 'twill be much better," he vowed softly, bending down to scoop her up in his arms and carry her to the bed. "You'll have no regrets."

She hoped he was right. She hoped this indulgence wouldn't delay her too long. Most of all, she hoped their lovemaking would erase all thoughts of that cursed key from his mind.

Nicholas settled Desirée gently atop the coverlet. He sighed. This interrogation was going to be torture for him as much as 'twas for her. Already his loins ached with longing.

But 'twas the only way to wring the truth from her. And now that he'd had a good look at the key she kept in her satchel, 'twas even more urgent that he discover what secrets she concealed.

Desirée knew him too well to fear the usual warnings of violence he employed when questioning prisoners. She'd laugh in his face if he threatened to skewer her with the tool she'd turned into a cooking spit.

Nay, the lass would be won with passion, not pain.

Though his skills of seduction were rusty, in his youth he'd made many a maid tremble with longing and sigh with desire. He could do so again.

He stretched out beside her, drawing the neckline of her gown down just far enough to place innocent kisses along her collarbone. He nuzzled her neck and sent a soft breath up along her throat. It curled into the shell of her ear, making her shiver.

"Tell me, Desirée," he breathed, slinging his leg over her thighs in sweet possession.

"Aye?" she murmured. She smiled and reached up a hand to caress his hair, but he caught her fingers, turning them to kiss her knuckles.

"Where have you been the past two days?"

He glimpsed alarm in her eyes before she quickly lowered her lids. When she looked up again, she'd reined in her panic to stare lustily at his mouth. "Does it matter?" she asked coyly. "I'm here now."

He chuckled softly. She was good. *Very* good.

She tried to extract her fingers from his grasp, but he held them fast, gently stroking her knuckles.

With the fingertip of his other hand, he traced a sinuous path over her bosom, teasing the cloth of her gown lower and lower with painful sloth, until her nipple languished but an inch from freedom. Lord, her skin was as soft as down, and he bit the inside of his cheek, resisting his own lustful urges as her bosom rose and fell, straining at the gown.

Steeling himself against the desire to suckle at her sweet breast, he instead lifted just the edge of her neckline to peek at the treasure within. "You stole my gaming box," he murmured, his voice smooth despite the harsh words. Then he blew a hot breath into the gap, stirring her nipple to life.

"Nay!" she gasped.

"Nay?"

"I mean, aye." Desirée squeezed her eyes shut, clearly distracted.

"Why?"

She clasped his invading hand in her own, subtly guiding it away from her. "I . . . I thought 'twould bring a good price."

"And did it?" Undeterred, he turned both their hands to delve beneath her neckline, brushing brazenly across her nipple with his thumb.

She bit her lip, and her fingers tightened in his, but she didn't answer.

He gave her nipple a quick pinch that was at once punishing and arousing. She gasped, and he instantly muted the sound, swooping to close his mouth over hers in a deep and lingering kiss of apology while he soothed her breast with the flat of his hand.

She moaned against his lips, a sweet, compelling sound, and he wondered again how he'd ever endure such torment. Already his head buzzed with yearning and his cock strained at his braies.

But Nicholas was a man of control. If he could command the subtle nuances of pain, he could certainly master the exquisite shades of pleasure.

Swallowing down a groan, he nipped softly at her lips. "Ah, Desirée," he murmured hoarsely, "to whom did you sell it?"

"Hmm?"

"The gaming box," he said patiently. "Who purchased it?"

She frowned in mild irritation. She obviously didn't want to answer his questions. She had more pressing interests.

So did he. But this was a matter of grave consequence.

"Desirée."

"Mm."

"Desirée." He withdrew his hands from her, finally garnering her attention.

"What?"

"Who bought the gaming box?"

She shrugged, but an evasive glint marred her innocent gaze. "I don't know. I don't remember."

He brushed a stray tendril from her brow, then delved his fingers into her hair. He cupped her cheek, staring at her lush, inviting lips. Apparently, she needed more convincing. "Perchance I can stir your memory."

He lowered his head to breathe softly upon her cheek, running the tip of his nose alongside hers, drawing out the sultry suspense until her mouth parted hungrily and her nostrils flared with anticipation.

Only then did he consummate the kiss, deeply and completely. He massaged her lips with his own until her jaw fell open in surrender and she moaned with pleasure. Her arms crept up to wrap around his neck, and she arched toward him in invitation. He swirled his tongue within, tasting her need, savoring her passion, and 'twas an intoxicating brew indeed.

For a dangerous moment, he almost lost himself in his own desires.

Then his fingers traced over the mysterious slash on her throat, and he remembered the marks on her body. Someone had hurt Desirée. And he needed to know who. Now.

Never breaking the kiss, he reached behind his neck to clasp both her hands in one of his own. She made no resistance when he raised them up and over his head, nor did she fight him when he pressed them onto the pillow above her.

Holding her thus pinned, he moved his free hand down over her skirts and began easing up the fabric. She moaned once in halfhearted protest. But once she lay exposed and he began to caress the soft inner flesh of her thigh with the back of his hand, slipping higher and higher, closer and closer to the center of her need, her protest became at first beckoning and then insistent.

Now, he thought. Now he had her at his mercy.

He combed his fingers through the silky curls bordering her sweet feminine flower, then broke from the kiss long enough to whisper against her lips. "Now, my sweet, you're going to tell me everything."

He felt her stiffen beneath him. But just as quickly, she calmed, gazing up at him in coy innocence. "But Nicholas, I don't know what you—"

His fingers delved swiftly and expertly betwixt her nether lips to alight like a butterfly upon the swollen bud nestled there, effectively silencing her lie.

Desirée sucked a sharp breath through her teeth. His fingertip seared her like lightning between her thighs, instantly incinerating her thoughts, her wits, and her control.

"Oh, I think you do, my love," he murmured against her hair.

He withdrew his fingers slightly, and in that moment of respite, the truth rushed in on Desirée with startling clarity.

She'd been gulled. Nicholas had tricked her. No better than one of her foolish targets, she'd let herself be blinded by her own desires. Now she was as helpless as a fly caught in a spider's web. Worse, she was at the mercy of a lawman who was an expert at eliciting confessions.

She struggled to free her hands from his grip, but he held them fast. Her legs, too, were anchored by his heavy thigh. The bloody brute knew exactly what he was doing.

"Now why don't you tell me," he purred, "who bought the gaming box?"

Desirée resisted giving him any response. Vexed at him and furious with herself for falling prey to his deception, she clenched her teeth and refused to answer.

But when he slid his finger down to caress her intimately again, she couldn't help herself. Though she managed to limit her verbal reply to stifled groans, her body acted of its own will, tensing in answer to his seductive caress.

"Tell me, Desirée." He stroked her again, and she arched up, welcoming the sweet pressure.

"No one!" she gasped. "No one bought it."

"Then where is it?"

"I don't know."

He nuzzled her ear, making her shiver. "Are you certain?"

His fingers tormented her again, caressing and stretching and tickling her delicate flesh until it seemed she would burst with yearning.

Then his movements slowed and stopped, and she experienced a new agony as her hips thrust upward, straining for more.

"Are you certain?" he repeated. "You have no idea where 'tis?"

Frustration made her voice rough and demanding. "Bloody hell! Nay!"

At long last he resumed pleasuring her, but 'twas as welcome a relief as a double-edged sword. She languished in a perverse sea of ecstasy and self-loathing as her traitorous body succumbed to his seduction.

Then he murmured another question in her ear. "The key you dropped, where did you get it?"

Her heart skipped a beat. Normally, Desirée could concoct a lie as deftly as tucking a pea under a shell. But her brain was muddled by desire, and she only stared at him blankly.

At her stunned silence, Nicholas removed his hand from her, which left her squirming in discomfort, if slightly more clear-headed.

"Where did you get the key?" he repeated.

She could tell him the truth, that Hubert had given her the key. But now that she could think straight, another possibility occurred to her, a more convenient explanation, one that might hasten Nicholas's lovemaking, get him to stop asking her probing questions, and provide an excuse for her to venture out.

"It goes to a room," she lied, "a room at the inn."

"What inn?"

"The one I stayed in the other night." She slid her gaze sideways. "The gaming box is there. I didn't want anyone to steal it, so I locked the door. I mean to go there this morn, to collect—"

He clucked his tongue and shook his head. "Such a rotten lie, and from such sweet lips."

She frowned. "A lie? But I'm not—"

He captured her fiction in his mouth this time, punishing her lying lips with a kiss of plunder while ravaging her nether lips with merciless caresses.

Lost in a raging torrent of conflicting emotions—anger and lust, shame and rapture, love and hate—Desirée felt reason slip away, and soon all that remained was pure sensation. Her skin grew hot, every inch tingling with current, until she felt as if she were about to be struck by lightning.

Nicholas abruptly tore his lips from hers, and she felt his gasps against her cheek. "Where...did you get...the key?"

He drew his hand away just as suddenly, in the midst of her rising passion, and she arched up in protest, crying out with need.

"Answer me," he commanded.

She moaned, thrashing her head back and forth, aching for his touch.

"Answer me," he wheezed, "and I'll give you what you want."

"Hubert!" she cried in desperation. "Hubert gave it to me. He found it at Torteval."

"What does it unlock?"

She shook her head and sobbed, "I don't know."

She met his eyes, and for one awful moment, she thought he'd break his word. But he finally nodded, accepting her answer. His fingers resumed their amazing dance upon her, and when he surged suddenly forward, sheathing his cock deep within her womb, her passions rose with such haste, she could hardly catch her breath.

With a lunge of ecstasy and a shrill cry, she strove against him, and his release followed soon after. Wave after wave of pleasure coursed through her as he finally gave her the ambrosia that would slake her thirst.

When her shudders ceased, he loosed her hands to cradle her in his arms. As she lay panting against his shoulder, her eyes half closed, her body slick with sweat, her limbs as limp as custard, she tried to summon up fury. What Nicholas had done was unforgivable. He'd used her own desires against her, interrogating her under the most insidious form of persuasion.

But the most she could manage was a punch at his shoulder and a halfhearted scolding. "You're a wicked man for torturing me," she muttered.

"You're a wicked lass for lying to me."

She sighed, unable to feel more than blissful relief and a subtle humiliation, the kind her targets probably felt when she outwitted them. "Then I suppose we deserve each other."

After a long moment of catching his breath, Nicholas lifted up on one elbow to look at her. With a casual sniff, he said, "You make it sound as if you intend to stay." But his gaze was anything but casual. Behind the forced cynicism in his eyes, Desirée saw a flicker of hope.

Her throat thickened. Lord, he *did* want her to stay.

Pursing her lips, she gave his chest a chiding punch. "Varlet. Do you think I'd surrender my maidenhood to just *any* shire-reeve who came along?"

The pure adoration in his gaze was almost too much for her to bear, especially knowing she had to deceive him yet again. She looked away and attempted to restore her gown to some semblance of order.

"By the way," she asked, "how did you know?"

"Know?"

"How did you know I was lying about the key?" She frowned. "Did I blink? Twitch? Bite my lip?"

He grinned and shook his head. "Are you afraid you've lost your touch?"

She shrugged. "I just wondered."

And then he said something that stopped her world.

"I knew you were lying because I know what that key goes to."

Chapter 26

FOR AN INSTANT, DESIRÉE COULDN'T BREATHE. She stared at him, speechless. How could Nicholas possibly know what the key went to?

"I know it doesn't go to any room at an inn," he said.

Desirée's heart was beating like a tabor. This changed everything. If Nicholas knew what the key went to, what was to stop her from using it to relieve Lady Philomena of her treasure, after all?

God help her, she knew she shouldn't pursue vengeance. She should be content to return the key and get Snowflake back unharmed. But damn it all, there was still enough of the thief in her that she couldn't resist such easy profit. Besides, she dearly longed to kick Philomena's arse.

Her brain sizzled with possibilities, but she carefully concealed her excitement. Instead, she traced a lazy pattern on Nicholas's stomach and asked nonchalantly, "What *does* the key go to?"

He caught her straying finger and shook his head. "That I'm not going to tell you."

She frowned. "Why?"

"I know you too well." He reached out his fingertip and swiped at the end of her nose. "I know what you'll do."

She thrust out her chin in challenge. "What? What will I do?"

He arched a brow. "Have you ever heard of Pandora?"

She narrowed her eyes in irritation. "I'm not Pandora."

He laughed.

She shoved him. "I'm *not.*"

"Let me see." He counted on his fingers. "You rifled through my clothing, my chest of documents, my box of coins..."

She opened her mouth to deliver a stinging retort but, unable to think of a single thing to say in her defense, closed it again with a disgruntled sigh.

He clucked his tongue. "Pandora." Sliding her aside, he climbed out of bed, stretched, then began to rummage through his chest of clothing.

She sat up. "What if I promise I won't use the key?"

He peered at her over the lid of the chest. "Is this anything like you promising not to cheat at draughts?"

She bit her lip. Damn it! That was the problem with using the same target over and over again. Nicholas had learned not to trust her. How was she going to get the information from him?

"I know." She slipped from the bed and passed by him to retrieve the key from the next room. "I'll give the key to you," she said, offering it to him. "That way I won't be *able* to use it."

He cocked a brow at her. "Why do you so badly want to know?"

She cocked a brow back at him. "Why do you so badly not want to tell me?"

He chuckled and held his hand out for the key. She pressed it into his palm.

He closed the key in his hand. "It goes to a gaol cell."

A chill shiver went up her spine. "A gaol cell?"

"Aye." He chose a linen shirt from the chest.

"What gaol cell?"

"The *old* Canterbury gaol. 'Tis in ruins now." He pulled the shirt over his head and let it shiver down over his shoulders. "So you see, if I'd given you the key, you'd have gone on some wild treasure hunt and wound up locked in a crumbling cell all day."

As Nicholas set out for Chilham, he was glad there were no executions planned today, for he was hardly in the mood to oversee a hanging. Frankly, he didn't even feel up to throwing a good punch. The morning's love-making and Desirée's farewell kiss had leached the will out of him.

He grinned weakly, wishing he could climb back into bed and while away the afternoon with his hot-blooded mistress instead of plodding through the chill fog.

But Chilham needed the shire-reeve. So, closing the garden gate reluctantly behind him, he shifted his satchel of tools to the other shoulder and trudged away from his cottage, away from the mischievous temptress who'd drained the strength from his body and tied his heart in knots with the promise of an evening of continued pleasure.

Fortunately, he was seldom called upon to do anything dire in Chilham. When the local constable knew Nicholas was in residence at Canterbury, he paid him a handsome fee to administer whatever minor punishments the villagers had accrued since his last visit, which usually amounted to putting a wayward lad in the stocks for the day, parading a dishonest merchant through the streets, and perchance stripping a shrewish wench to her shift in the square. He always performed these punishments of shame with exceptional drama. Indeed, the mere presence of the menacing Nicholas Grimshaw in Chilham was enough to allay most crime there for several months.

Nicholas secretly hoped, of course, there was *no one* to chastise today. The sooner he could leave Chilham, the sooner he could get home to his Desirée.

His Desirée. He liked the sound of that. He'd never imagined 'twas possible a woman could learn to love him. He was, after all, Nicholas Grimshaw, fearsome shire-reeve of Kent, lord of shackles, right hand of the devil.

But Desirée had somehow seen past his menacing mask to the merciful man beneath. She'd stripped away his brutality and uncovered his soft heart. God help him, Nicholas couldn't imagine life without her.

He liked the idea of coming home every night to her smiling face and warm supper, a round of draughts and a tryst betwixt the linens. And now, confident that she was safe for the moment, he could look forward to that homecoming this very eve.

He smugly patted his satchel as he walked along the well-worn road. Desirée might have wheedled information about that iron key out of him, but he'd tucked it safely in with his tools, so there was no worry that she'd get herself into mischief today, dreaming about some hidden riches Hubert might have left for her.

There were still too many things the lass had neglected to tell him—where exactly she'd been the last two days, what she'd done with his gaming box, how she'd gotten those scratches and bruises. But he knew her well enough by now that he'd figured out what had happened.

She'd likely made the mistake of agreeing to meet the buyer of the gaming box in secret. He'd roughed her up and stolen the box, then left her tied up. She'd managed to free herself, but now, too proud to admit she'd been outwitted, she wouldn't tell Nicholas what had happened.

Which was probably wise. If Nicholas ever discovered who'd laid hands on Desirée, he'd make minced meat of the brute, without the courtesy of a trial.

Aye, Desirée had betrayed Nicholas in one way, stealing his gaming box and trying to sell it. But he supposed a lifelong habit of crime was difficult to break. 'Twould take more than a fortnight to mend an outlaw's ways. He'd see she paid for the box eventually, one way or another. If 'twere up to him, he thought with a grin, 'twould take her a very long time.

At least she'd come back to him. She might have betrayed his trust, but she hadn't betrayed his heart.

Desirée tucked the iron key into the bodice of her gown and glanced through the crack of the shutters, watching Nicholas leave. She shook her head. The poor man wasn't half as devious as she was. But then, he hadn't been practicing deceit for half his life.

He thought he'd been clever, caching the key in his

satchel. But she was cleverer. She'd retrieved it again when she'd given him that lingering kiss of farewell.

'Twas probably for naught. The key might not even go to the old gaol, as Nicholas had said. Still, 'twas worth a try. Perchance Lady Philomena did keep treasure hidden in one of the cells. If the key didn't fit the lock, she'd simply continue on her journey, give the lady what she wanted, rescue poor Snowflake, and return to the cottage with Nicholas none the wiser.

After a reasonable wait, Desirée donned her cloak and ventured out into the fog, directly to the main square of Canterbury to find the constable. After the exchange of a few friendly words, she inquired casually about several prominent buildings in the town, among them the old Canterbury gaol.

According to the constable, a few years ago, the ground upon which the gaol was erected had sunk several feet in a heavy rain, submerging a good part of the stone structure beneath the mud, rendering it useless.

He further advised her to stay away from the site, as 'twas dangerous. She assured him she had no intention of going there, adding a shiver of revulsion at the thought. Then, smiling sweetly and bidding him good day, she immediately headed off in the direction of the place.

As the constable had indicated, the moss-covered gaol slouched in the midst of a deserted boggy patch at the edge of town. One of the stone walls had crumbled, and long vines of ivy climbed over the top and reached into the sunken doorway. A wattle fence surrounded the area, preventing children and livestock from wandering too near and perchance falling into the ruins.

Desirée skirted the fence in the mist, looking for a

good place to make entry. Halfway 'round, she found a low spot in the wattle crossbars and, beyond that, a path of hardened ground leading to the gaol.

She frowned. Someone had been using this trail regularly, for the grass was worn away in the middle and bent flat at the edges.

Glancing quickly about for witnesses, she hoisted up her gown and climbed over the fence. Then she retrieved the key from her bodice and crept toward the gaol, hoping a family of wolves hadn't decided to take up residence in the sunken den.

Sweeping aside the ivy curtaining the entrance, she peered in. 'Twas as black as coal inside, and she hesitated, worrying the iron key between her thumb and finger, wondering if the treasure was worth the possibility that wild animals or unsavory men might lurk in the dark.

As her eyes adjusted to the lack of light, she noticed a set of wooden steps had been placed at the entrance, leading from the ground above to the submerged floor below. At least she'd not have to clamber down to the lower level.

Gripping the key, she carefully stepped down the five stairs and onto a stone floor, slick with mud. 'Twas still as dark as night, but to her right, the wall began to grow less and less dim, until she saw the widening flicker of reflected flame illuminating the stones.

Someone was coming! Her heart tripped at the sound of footfalls scraping from within the gaol. She swung around, ready to mount the steps and flee.

"Is that you, m'lady?" a gruff voice called from within the passageway.

Desirée froze.

She heard the man grumble as the pool of light grew larger upon the wall.

"Lady Philomena?" he asked, rounding the corner.

Desirée glanced down at the key in her hand. Perchance this *was* where Philomena kept her treasure. Improvising quickly, she whirled back toward the man's voice and straightened with authority.

"Ye're not..." the man growled, coming to an abrupt halt. "Who are ye?"

Desirée lifted her nose. "I'm Lady Philomena's maidservant."

The man looked like a burly old bear, stirred from his winter's sleep. But then, Desirée supposed, dwelling in this crypt of a gaol, *anyone* would be filthy and irritable.

He studied her twice from head to toe, then muttered, "She sent ye?"

"Aye."

"I s'pose ye've got the key?"

She dangled it before her.

"Come along, then," he said on a sigh, hobbling back around the corner.

She followed him into what was more like a tunnel than a hallway. Moisture seeped in at the low ceiling and narrow walls, and the dank odor of earth and rotting food and rat droppings swirled around her in a fetid cloud.

Stopping at a heavy iron door on the right, he waved his torch close, indicating the lock.

"'E's in there."

He? Misgiving fluttered in Desirée's breast. She'd expected the locked cell to contain a cask of gems or stacks of coins or some other form of wealth. She hadn't expected a "he." What...or who...waited behind the door?

She had to find out. 'Twas too late to change her mind. She thrust the key into the lock. It fit perfectly.

"May I?" she said, indicating the torch.

He frowned but surrendered it to her. At her nod of dismissal, he retreated to his well-stocked lair at the end of the passageway, where he slumped down onto a three-legged stool, picked up a foaming flagon, and took a bite of something he'd left on the small table beside him.

Desirée turned the key carefully, ready with the torch should the occupant of the chamber be less than hospitable. The door made a dreadful creak as she pushed it slowly inward, and there was a scuffling within as someone or something sensed her presence.

Leaving one hand on the door, she swept the torch forward, illuminating the small cell.

"'Mena?" someone croaked.

She gasped. In the corner stood a man, or what was left of a man. Though his clothing was that of a noble—a surcoat of richly embroidered tawny wool with a fine linen shirt beneath—'twas filthy and shredded to dirty rags. His hair was matted, and he had a beard that reached to the middle of his chest. There were holes in the pointed toes of his leather shoes, and his face and hands looked as if he'd not seen a bath in months.

"You're not Philomena," he said, shielding his eyes from the unaccustomed light. "Who are you, my lady?"

Desirée doubted she had much to fear from the man. Despite his unkempt appearance, he possessed the attire and manner of a gentleman. But of what value to Lady Philomena was he?

She stepped into the room and closed the door behind her.

"Did my wife send you?" he asked tightly.

Wife? Was Lady Philomena this man's wife? Desirée answered with caution. "Aye."

He raked her once with a glare, then bit the words out between his teeth. "You can tell her I won't be persuaded, no matter what form of temptation she dangles before me."

Desirée had learned that sometimes the best strategy was the truth. "I don't know what you mean."

"I'm not interested in your...charms."

"Ah." The man thought her a hired harlot.

"And I won't be a party to murder."

Desirée blinked. "Murder?"

He emitted a dry, bitter bark. "She didn't tell you? My dear Philomena didn't tell you why she locked her husband in this godforsaken tomb?"

Though his voice was full of hatred, she noted that he staggered slightly on his feet, catching his balance against a wall. For all his show of determination, the poor wretch was as weak as a runt pup. He probably hadn't eaten a decent meal in weeks.

She needed to know more, and the best way to get a man to talk was to convince him she was his ally.

"Are you hungry?"

He swallowed reflexively.

She retreated to the door and opened it a crack. "Gaoler! Come here! And bring me what's left of your supper. This man is half-starved."

"What?" the gaoler whined. "He ate only yesterday. I slipped him a crust under the door. This is mine. I'm not goin' to—"

"Shall I tell my lady," Desirée said, curling her lip, "you've been mistreating her husband?"

"Mistreatin'?" With a loud sigh of exasperation, he did as he was bid, but he grumbled all the way to the cell.

When Desirée confiscated the half-eaten pork tartee and closed the door again, the man eyed the food with keen hunger. Only his nobility prevented him from snatching it from her.

She stepped closer, reeling from the stench of him. "What's your name, my lord?" she murmured, handing him the pastry.

He sank to the floor and fell upon the food with such grateful haste that he couldn't answer immediately. When he'd swallowed a bite, he murmured, "George."

"George. Well, George," she said carefully, "'tis true your wife sent me here to try to change your mind. But now that I see how you're suffering..." She bit her lip.

He forced down a half-chewed bite of tartee. "Aye?"

"I want to help you."

"Help me?" He looked up at her mistrustfully. "You would do that?"

She nodded. Then, ignoring the odor of neglect wafting off of him, she crouched beside George, propping the torch upon the floor. "Tell me everything."

Chapter 27

PHILOMENA DIDN'T LIKE THE SMUG EXPRESSION on the Kabayn whelp's face today. The wench was up to something. She should never have let the woman return to Nicholas Grimshaw's cottage with only her miserable pet and the lawman's livelihood for leverage. Despite Philomena's threats, that menacing shire-reeve might be tracking them even now.

But Philomena had no other choice. She desperately needed that key. 'Twas the only way to unlock the gaol cell where she'd cached her husband. If she lost it, if her husband was *not* miraculously returned to Torteval after his father's death, she risked losing their entire inheritance. And she'd labored far too long and hard at this scheme to do that.

So as she traipsed through the tall weeds of the fallow field behind Torteval toward the old mill, her slender dagger jabbing at the small of the woman's back, she scanned the fog-shrouded woods and wondered if the sinister shire-reeve lurked in the shadows.

When she at last shoved Desirée through the mill door, slamming it shut behind them, the wench surprised her by whipping around and stepping back a pace, out of dagger's reach.

Philomena would have advanced on her, but her nose began to twitch from the presence of that infernal cat, and she was suddenly overcome by the impending urge to sneeze.

She saw through watery eyes that Desirée was retrieving the bagged beast from the hook on the wall. For one horrible moment as the wench lowered it to the floor and loosened the top of the sack, Philomena suspected the wench might use the beast as a weapon, throwing the wretched thing in her face. She cocked back her dagger and fired it forward toward the animal, simultaneously emitting a rib-jolting sneeze.

The dagger stuck in the floor, missing the cat, which streaked off to a shadowy corner of the mill. Only then did Philomena grasp the consequences of her impulsive throw.

The Kabayn woman, realizing her sudden advantage, wrenched the blade loose and, with a grim smile of victory, flashed it before her.

"I believe my terms have changed," she said, tossing the knife in a casual but threatening manner, back and forth between her hands.

Philomena began to tremble with rage and frustration. Why did everything have to be so complicated? Was it too much to ask that people die when they were supposed to, that servants follow her commands without question, that there be no negotiating or nasty surprises...or cats?

"Don't be a fool!" she snapped. "You've got your bloody cat. All I want is that key. If you make trouble—"

"I want the gaming box, as well."

"The what?"

"Nicholas Grimshaw's gaming box. Your men stole it."

Philomena narrowed her eyes. She remembered that gaming box. The servants had been playing draughts on it in the great hall. She'd taken it away from them, because it had been distracting them from their work. Afterward, she'd decided to keep it herself, for the craftsmanship was too fine for their grimy paws.

She chewed the corner of her lip. If 'twere any other circumstance, she'd have told the maid nay, found some way to kill her on the spot, and pried the key from her cold, dead fingers. But she couldn't afford to make any more mistakes at this point.

Things had already gone awry. Too many people knew. She'd had to kill the damned lawyer with her own hands, for God's sake. Now, not only did she have to finish off her father-in-law, but she had to find a way to get rid of the witnesses. And there was already too much blood on her hands.

Perchance if she ceded this once, if she gave the wench her wretched gaming box, she'd go away.

"Very well," she bit out. "You'll have your stupid trinket. But you'll have to come back to the hall to get it, and if you try any trickery, I swear I'll put *you* in a sack and throw you into the river." She punctuated her threat with a brain-rattling sneeze that at last sent the cat bolting across the mill and squirming out under the door, hopefully fleeing as far away as possible.

Things went smoothly enough on the return to the hall.

The woman tried no tricks, and the shire-reeve didn't burst out from the woods. When they entered the solar, Philomena had begun to think she'd overestimated the wench's wiles. Perchance she *did* simply want what was stolen from her.

Then she closed the door, and everything changed.

As Philomena proffered the gaming box with an insincere smile and at last felt the precious key drop into her palm, she was treated to an unwelcome warning.

"I'd use that key very soon if I were you."

She smirked. "You don't even know what 'tis for."

"*I* didn't," she admitted. "But Nicholas Grimshaw did."

For an instant, the smug smile stretched tightly on Philomena's face, and the air seemed to freeze in her throat. Dread pounded in her heart like a lump of lead. "I see," she managed to croak.

"After the shire-reeve left for work this morn, I had a visit with your husband."

Philomena's mouth went dry.

"He told me everything," she continued. "How you feigned his kidnapping and imprisoned him because he didn't have the stomach to go along with your plans to poison his father. How Lord William, believing his son was dead, summoned his lawyer to rewrite his will, naming not *you*, but his nephew as heir, and how 'twas you, not Hubert Kabayn, who murdered the lawyer and destroyed that will. How, after his father is gone, you plan to stage George's miraculous return to claim his inheritance, which you expect he'll share generously with you if he knows what's best for him."

Philomena began to tremble again as her plans unrav-

eled before her eyes. She glanced down at the knife, still
held firmly in the wench's hand. Could she overpower
the woman, recover her dagger, and silence the meddling
bitch forever?

"Don't even think of it," Desirée said, tucking the gaming box under her arm and brandishing the knife. "If I
don't return, the shire-reeve will know whom to blame.
And I don't think you'll be able to strip him of his title
when the hangman's noose is about your neck."

Philomena felt sick. All her plans...all her patience...all her devotion...were they for naught?

Despite the panic writhing in her spine, she couldn't
lose control in front of her nemesis. Nor could she allow
fear to paralyze her. But she needed time to think.

"The wise cheat knows when the game's over," the
wench added. "You've lost. Give up your scheme. Free
your husband. The fool still cares for you. Perchance he'll
forgive you." Then she bit out between clenched teeth:
"But know this. If you continue this butchery, I'll see you
hang from the very gallows where Hubert Kabayn took
his last breath."

With that dire promise and a curt nod, the woman departed, leaving Philomena breathless and shaken. But
shock was soon replaced by rage, and once the wench
was out of hearing, Philomena vented her frustration upon
the room, knocking over the floor candles, shredding the
bolsters on the chairs, smashing the crockery against the
plaster walls.

Her only regret afterward, as she stood panting among
the ruins of the solar, was that the steward hadn't been
there for her to vent her wrath upon. Then at least she'd
have been able to preserve her pretty things.

Much calmer after her outburst, she began to think more clearly. 'Twas preposterous to imagine that overweening maidservant might have gained the upper hand. The world revolved around Philomena's wishes, because she'd always managed to outwit or cajole or intimidate those who stood in her way. She'd beaten, kidnapped, and murdered men to achieve her ends. She wasn't about to be outmaneuvered by the granddaughter of a common thief.

Somehow there was a way to get out of this. Indeed, before long, an idea wormed its way into her brain.

Perchance all was not lost. Perchance there was a way to preserve at least part of her plan and be rid of this bothersome wench once and for all. 'Twould involve expert timing, a profound sacrifice, and a good deal of risk, but in the end she might get what she'd wanted all along.

If the woman had visited George this morn...alone... and left him in the cell...

'Twas time to pay Lord William a final visit.

Less than an hour later, Philomena hummed a tune as she made her way from his chamber with the empty flagon. With the amount of arsenic she'd put in his wine this time, he'd surely be dead by sundown. She almost wished she could stay to play the grieving daughter and watch him in his final, painful throes of dying. 'Twas the least she deserved for having to suffer the indignity of being rebuffed as his heir in favor of his nephew.

But she had other things to tend to.

Snatching up one of the daggers from the kitchen, she donned her cloak and set out on the road toward the old Canterbury gaol at a brisk pace. By the time she arrived at the horrible spot, she was out of breath and drenched with mist and sweat. Wrinkling her nose, she stole into the dark, dank place once again, struck by its similarity to a tomb. 'Twas fitting enough, she supposed, for that was precisely what she intended.

She'd always meant to kill her poor husband eventually, *after* he'd inherited his father's wealth. What troubled her was killing him *before* Lord William was dead, when there was still a slim possibility that the will might be contested. But she was out of options. Her best hope now was to get this over with quickly.

"Gaoler!"

When the gaoler came hobbling around the corner, she longed to shove the dagger into his fat gut, for he'd doubtless been stealing George's food for weeks now. But she needed him as a witness, so she choked back the urge.

"M'lady," he said in surprise.

"I'm here to see him."

"Again?"

"What do you mean, again?"

"Your maidservant came to check on him earlier."

"Maidservant?" she demanded, feigning confusion. "I sent no maidservant."

He shrugged. "She had the key." He narrowed his eyes in displeasure. "And the bloody wench gave him my supper. *My* supper."

Philomena bit the inside of her cheek. She thought her restraint admirable. But she'd gotten what she wanted. The gaoler could avow he *had* seen Desirée here this morn.

Shaking her head, she took his brand, waved him back into his hole, then proceeded to the cell, making sure the gaoler was out of hearing when she unlocked the door.

Once she secured the door behind her again and turned

to face the occupant of the cell, she heard George breathe, "'Mena?"

And then he breathed no more.

She slit his throat quickly, to silence his screams. Then, when he slumped to the floor, she stuck the brand into a holder on the wall, crouched beside his writhing body, and proceeded to stab him under the ribs several times. Surely one of the thrusts would pierce his heart.

She tried not to think about all the blood. 'Twas bad enough she had to kneel in the filth of the cell, her nostrils shrinking from the stench of human waste.

At last his eyes turned filmy, and he stopped twitching.

Shuddering with disgust, she tossed the dagger onto the floor and let out a shrill scream.

The gaoler came at a run. She crawled toward the door just as he burst in. The door shrieked open on its hinges, revealing the gruesome murder.

He gasped. "Jesu!"

Philomena clutched hysterically at the gaoler's braies and sobbed, "He's dead! He's dead! Ah, God, he's dead!"

The gaoler's eyes widened with panic as he stared down at her. "Did ye..."

"It must have been that woman!" she cried. "Who was she? Who came this morn?" She let go of him and buried her face in her bloody hands. "God's wounds! She killed him! She killed my husband!"

Thankfully, the gaoler was dull enough of wit to take her at her word. He winced at the bloody mess before him, murmuring oaths under his breath, then rubbed a thoughtful hand across his jaw. "God's truth, m'lady, I'm not sure who she was."

"Oh, God!" she wailed. "Oh, God!"

He wrinkled his brow in earnest concern. "But she had a key, m'lady. And I know what she looks like."

That was all Philomena needed. After several more obligatory sobs of faux grief, she persuaded the gaoler to come with her to the constable so that he could describe the murderess.

'Twas ridiculously simple. Philomena wept piteously before the constable, bemoaning the fact that after her months-long search for her beloved husband and finally locating him where his kidnappers had locked him up, right under all their noses, she'd arrived at the old gaol only to find him murdered, and all while her father-in-law languished on his deathbed.

The gaoler knew better than to challenge her story. He relished the idea of being the hero of the hour. And as he described what little he recalled of the wench's appearance—her dark hair, her dark cloak, her pretty mouth— Philomena was able to fill in the details in such a way as to irrevocably implicate the shire-reeve's maidservant.

"Desirée Kabayn," she breathed in revelation, resting a hand lightly atop the constable's sleeve. "It could have been her. She was the granddaughter of that man who committed the murder at Torteval." She frowned, as if trying to make sense of everything. Then she gave a gasp and clasped a hand to her throat. "Could she be the one who had my husband kidnapped in the first place?"

The constable scowled. "I doubt that. She's a good-natured lass. I don't think she . . ." He trailed off, and a peculiar expression came over his face, one that drained the color from his cheeks. "God's blood. She was asking me about the old gaol this morn."

Philomena restrained a smile. This was even better than she'd expected. 'Twas as if the stupid wench had looped the noose around her own neck.

She clenched her fist in the constable's sleeve. "Dear God, if she kidnapped and murdered my husband, what's to stop her from killing m—?" She broke off with a sob, clapping a hand to her bosom.

Then she wrapped both fists in the constable's tabard in supplication. "Don't let her, I pray you! You must do something! You must—"

The constable gently extricated her hands. "Don't fret, my lady. I'll take her into custody at once."

That wasn't good enough. She had to be sure the shire-reeve had no opportunity to intervene on the wench's behalf, and she wouldn't rest until she knew Desirée Kabayn was silenced forever.

"Kind sir," she said softly, clasping his hand in her two, "my father is dying even now. Can you do naught to speed retribution? 'Twould do his heart good to see his son's murderer banished to hell ere he departs for heaven."

The constable looked uncomfortable with such hasty arrangements, but he knew the sway the Torteval nobles held in Canterbury. "The shire-reeve's not in town, but I suppose I can round up witnesses, have a trial. If she's found guilty—"

"Can you hang her this eve?"

He recoiled, withdrawing his hand. "This eve? Nay, my lady! 'Tis hardly time to prepare. I'll need to summon the executioner from Rochester."

Curse the law's delay! "On the morrow, then."

His scowl deepened. "The morrow? 'Tis the Sabbath, my lady."

Her chin began to quiver with rage, but she let him believe she was near tears. "I pray you, constable, grant me this one request. The priest will delay services at my bidding. I don't know if my father will live past the Sabbath," she wailed, choking on a sob. "Please let him see justice served so he may die in peace."

The constable was quite ill at ease. "The shire-reeve won't be pleased."

"Grimshaw?" Philomena reined back the fury rising inside her, knowing the constable wouldn't be moved by her rage. The easiest way to manipulate him was to insult his power. "But constable," she asked pointedly, "does the shire-reeve allow you no authority of your own?"

He let out a disgruntled sigh. "Very well. On the morrow."

Philomena managed a grateful smile, though she would have preferred the constable string the maid up at once, ere the shire-reeve arrived home.

On the other hand, it might prove an entertaining spectacle to watch Nicholas Grimshaw forced to send his own mistress to death. 'Twas almost tempting to brave the rabble this once and attend the execution. Almost.

"One more thing," she said. "No doubt the shire-reeve will be...reluctant...to hang his own maidservant. Please make certain he doesn't see the hanging orders until the last possible moment."

As Nicholas had expected, there were only minor chastisements to administer in Chilham, which was a good thing, because he'd discovered, much to his dismay, that the key he'd confiscated from Desirée was missing. That nimble-fingered imp had somehow managed to steal it back from him.

Knowing she'd be unable to resist the temptation, he was certain she'd gone to the old Canterbury gaol to see if the key fit the lock.

How Hubert Kabayn had come by the key he didn't know, but the sunken gaol had been deserted for some time. The area had been fenced off as a hazard, and only a fool would trespass into the crumbling ruin. A fool or a headstrong wench.

'Twas nearly sunset when he reached Canterbury, but the constable had apparently been waiting for him in the town square. The man seemed unusually uneasy as he called Nicholas over. Nicholas noted that one of his eyes was swollen.

"What happened to—"

"'Tis naught." Then he handed Nicholas a scroll. "This is for a hanging. On the morrow."

"The morrow?" Nicholas frowned. "'Tis the Sabbath."

"'Tis a special situation, a matter for expediency," he said tersely. "The crime was committed this morn. The trial was this afternoon." He avoided Nicholas's eyes as he added, "The execution is to take place in the morn before services."

"But—"

"You might want to pay the prisoner a visit. Straight away."

Before Nicholas could reply, the constable turned on his heel and walked briskly off into the falling twilight.

Nicholas watched him go. An execution on the Sabbath? And with such late notice? 'Twas unheard-of. Aye, sometimes he was called upon to administer unusually swift justice to a lad caught beating a hound or a wife found in another man's bed. But a hanging...

"Satan's ballocks," he muttered.

All the way back from Chilham, he'd looked forward to seeing Desirée—that was, if the impetuous lass hadn't entombed herself in the ruins of the old gaol. He meant to give her a sound scolding for pilfering the key from his satchel. Then he'd punish her. He figured the wench deserved a hundred lashes. He'd smiled, thinking of how he intended to deliver those lashes.

But now his plans were thrown awry. What had the constable meant, suggesting he visit the prisoner? Certainly he knew 'twas Nicholas's custom to stay with the condemned the night before an execution. 'Twas a courtesy he always extended to the poor wretches. Never had he led a man to the gallows without granting him some comfort, some peace of mind, and usually a great deal of strong ale. He couldn't forfeit that courtesy now, no matter how strong the temptation was to go home to Desirée.

He sighed, dropping his heavy satchel of tools. Then he unrolled the parchment in the dwindling light. Who was the hapless outlaw the constable was in such a rush to see executed?

When he saw the name upon the page, it struck him as so unlikely, so impossible, that he knew he'd read it wrong. He chuckled, rubbed at his eyes, held the parchment up to the last rays of sunlight, and looked again.

Desirée Kabayn.

His mind couldn't turn itself around what he saw, but his heart began a slow, hard thud as ominous as rising thunder.

Nay, he thought.

'Twas a mistake.

Or a jest.

Aye, that was it. The constable and Desirée had played a jest on him.

But the more he studied the document, the faster his heart raced, and the more he realized 'twas not a jest at all, but a properly signed writ, a writ demanding the execution of Desirée Kabayn for the murder of Lord George Torteval.

Suddenly he couldn't move, couldn't breathe. His heart knifed against his ribs, and a deep shuddering began in his bones. Stunned, he never noticed the parchment falling from his nerveless fingers.

Chapter 28

DESIRÉE CHEWED ON A FINGERNAIL as she paced the familiar cold gaol cell where Hubert Kabayn had lived out his last days. Just like her old partner, she'd been condemned to hang for a murder committed by Lady Philomena.

In a sense, Desirée supposed she *had* committed murder. After all, if she'd freed George while she had the chance, he wouldn't be dead now. She'd underestimated Philomena's capacity for evil, for surely 'twas the Lady of Torteval who had killed her own husband.

The kind constable had seemed reluctant to arrest Desirée, but that hadn't stopped him from doing it, even after she'd blacked his eye and crippled his knee enough to make him hobble as he accompanied his men-at-arms to the gaol.

The trial was a travesty of justice. With the grief-stricken Lady Philomena as her accuser, the gaoler as a witness to her visit, and her abductors from Torteval claiming she'd previously accosted them in the streets of Canterbury, Desirée was convicted and sentenced within an hour.

But unlike Hubert, she didn't intend to go peacefully. He had taught her there were always escapes. Using guile or deception or, as a last resort, bribery, one could squirm one's way out of any trouble.

The sun was sinking now, as she could see by the dimming of the narrow window at the top of her cell. Soon Nicholas would return from Chilham. But that knowledge gave her uncertain comfort.

How many times had he told her 'twas not for him to render judgment, only to carry out sentences? How often had he reminded her that his role was solely to execute the justice handed down by others?

And who was to say he wouldn't believe she'd committed the murder? After all, the evidence was overwhelming. He knew by now she'd taken the key to the old gaol. He'd known she wanted revenge for Hubert's unjust execution. And he believed she was capable of cold-blooded killing. By the saints, she'd tried to slay Nicholas himself that first day.

Nay, she couldn't rely upon Nicholas's mercy, no matter how she cared for him. She had to find some way to escape, bartering with the gaoler or deceiving the guards. But how could she work her wiles on them if they never visited her cell?

Just as the last sliver of light faded, leaving her in utter darkness, she heard a rattling at the door. She whirled around with a hopeful smile, ready to use her charms at a moment's notice.

The flare of a torch blinded her for an instant as the

intruder entered, closing the door behind him. Then she recognized the black cloak.

"Nicholas!"

Abandoning wisdom and judgment and restraint, she hurtled toward him but was brought up short as he blocked her way with the flaming brand. His upraised hand commanded her to stop. Then he held up one finger, bidding her to wait.

Breathless, caught between relief and dread, Desirée froze, and they both listened as the gaoler's footsteps retreated along the passageway.

He reached up then and pulled back his hood, and Desirée thought she'd never seen a more welcome face. Aye, he looked grim and troubled, and his brow was furrowed in concern, but with Nicholas by her side, suddenly it seemed she could take on the world.

He didn't come to her at once. Instead, he planted the torch in a brace on the wall and ran weary fingers through his hair, sighing, "Oh, Desirée, what have you done?"

She chose to ignore his accusatory tone. Rushing toward him, she collided with his chest and wrapped grateful arms about his neck.

For a long moment, he was unresponsive, and her heart pounded anxiously at the possibility that he no longer cared for her. Forsooth, he might despise her.

Then, when she was about to give up, to fall into despair, his arms came around her, clasping her to him with such force she could scarcely breathe.

Unbidden, a tear squeezed out from between her lashes, and she swiftly wiped it away. "I didn't kill anyone."

He gave her no answer. Neither did he let her go.

"I *didn't*," she repeated.

He stroked her hair, but he still didn't reply. And suddenly anger began to rise in her. With a vexed growl, she shoved him away. "You don't believe me!"

She could tell by the furrow in his brow that he *wanted* to believe her.

"Damn you!" she cried. "You *should* believe me. That's what love is all about. Trust."

He narrowed his eyes, and his jaw tensed with uncertainty. "'Tis what deception is all about, as well."

She couldn't argue with him. He was right. Forsooth, she'd given him no reason to trust her at all. Ever.

From the very beginning, she'd kept secrets from him.

She'd never told him about her encounters with Odger or Godfry or the two Johns. She'd not mentioned her confrontation with Lady Philomena. She'd feigned ignorance about the whereabouts of his cat. Sweet Mary, while she was still aglow from his lovemaking, she'd lied about his gaming box, then stolen the key from his satchel to sneak off to the old gaol.

'Twas no wonder he didn't trust her.

She lowered her head and clasped her hands humbly before her. "What will it take?"

"For me to trust you?"

She nodded.

"Look me in the eye, Desirée. Tell me everything."

She did. With a hard swallow and a great deal of reluctance, she confessed to all the mischief she'd made over the last fortnight.

She told him about the small things—knocking the bacon off the shelf, rummaging through his things, feigning illness to avoid church.

Then she revealed the more significant secrets—that

she'd had several altercations with the men from Torteval, that they'd stolen the gaming box and kidnapped her, that Snowflake had been held hostage by Lady Philomena.

She explained how she'd discovered Lord George in the old gaol and how he'd revealed his wife's intentions—to keep him prisoner until she could poison their father in order to collect George's inheritance, and to eliminate anyone who stood in her way, including the lawyer for whom Hubert had hanged. By the time she told him how she'd threatened Philomena with exposing the truth, how it must have been Philomena who, out of desperation, had killed her own husband and pinned the blame on Desirée, Nicholas's jaw was twitching with suppressed rage.

Still she had to ask. "Now do you believe me?"

Nicholas knew from the moment Desirée looked directly at him that she was telling the truth. She might be an expert at deception, but when she met his gaze openly, he saw deep into her beautiful green eyes, down to her very soul. From her very first word, all doubt vanished.

"Aye."

Desirée might be an imp and a meddlesome wench and an only slightly reformed outlaw. But she was no murderer. And if Nicholas had only been at her trial to defend her character, she'd not be hanging on the morrow.

The trouble was, she'd already been tried and convicted. Her death warrant was signed.

"Then you'll help me?" she asked.

God's wounds, the hope in her eyes was too much to bear. He reached for her, clasping her sweet face between his palms, wishing he could lie as easily as she did. "I'm not sure I can," he choked out.

The light in her gaze diminished. "What do you mean?"

He swallowed hard. How could he make her understand?

She tore his hands away and stepped back, incredulous. "What do you mean, Nicholas? You...you helped that lad in Sturry. You saved him from the gallows."

He grimaced. "Aye. I've bent the law. But I've not broken it." He rubbed the back of his neck in frustration. "You've had a trial, Desirée, and you've been sentenced. There's already a death warrant with your name on it. You've been ordered to the gallows on the morrow."

She staggered at the weight of his words, answering with a whisper of disbelief. "On the morrow? You...you're going to hang me?"

"Nay!" he said forcefully as the image of her frail body, twisting at the end of a rope, assailed his thoughts. "Never!"

Yet even as he spoke the vehement denial, he knew 'twas an empty promise. The situation was hopeless. Short of killing the guards, breaking Desirée out of the gaol, and fleeing with her in the night to be branded forever as a fugitive, he could see no way out of their dilemma.

And he had to admit when he looked at the breathtaking woman before him with the dewy eyes and trembling lips, the woman who had been unafraid of the shire-reeve of Kent, the woman who had given him her virginity of her own free will, he was sorely tempted to do just that.

"Then what do you mean to do?" she asked.

He scowled at the flagstones. "I know what I *want* to do," he muttered. "I'd like to throttle the life out of that Torteval witch."

Desirée shuddered, clasping her arms about her, and

he realized 'twas not his hateful threat but the cold that made her shiver. He took off his cloak and wrapped it around her shoulders. It looked enormous, hanging off of her small frame, and it reminded him once again that Desirée was the only woman he knew who didn't shrink from him in fear.

That thought made him catch his breath.

Of course.

He was Nicholas Grimshaw, cold-blooded lawman, the merciless, powerful shire-reeve of Kent. Everyone feared him.

Including Lady Philomena.

Inspired by sudden hope, he smiled grimly down at Desirée. Then he grabbed her by the shoulders and bent to give her a hard kiss on the mouth.

"Wait here. You'll be safe. I'll return before dawn, I promise."

Giving her shoulders a squeeze, he moved to make his exit. But before he could leave, she snagged him by the shirt.

"Wait!" She arched a brow at him. "If you think I'm going to sit here, helpless, simply trusting you'll return..."

"Exactly. I don't. Which is why I'm locking the door."

Her jaw dropped. "What?"

"You're not going to follow me, Desirée. I want you out of harm's way."

She thinned her lips but couldn't argue.

"I give you my word of honor I'll come back," he said. "But this is something I have to do alone."

"At least tell me what you're planning."

Her fists were still coiled in his shirt. 'Twas clear she wasn't going to let him go until he obliged her.

"I'm going to pay a visit to Lady Philomena. By the time I get done with her, she'll be writing a letter of commendation for you."

Desirée gulped. "Do you mean to...torture her?"

"You know me better than that." He let one corner of his lip drift up in an ominous smile. "I won't have to."

Philomena crumpled the missive in her trembling fist. God's eyes! Didn't she have enough to worry about this eve without the damned shire-reeve showing up at the gates? What did he want? If that constable had betrayed her and alerted Grimshaw to his mistress's execution, she'd have the fool's head on a platter.

'Twas all she could do not to scream. Nicholas Grimshaw was the one loose cog in the complex machine she'd created over which she had no control. But she supposed shrieking at the top of her lungs wasn't in keeping with the role of the bereaved daughter and widow.

She wished she could simply order him away, tell him she was too aggrieved to speak with him. But he was a man who was known to be...insistent. If she didn't grant his request, he'd likely barge into the great hall and demand her audience before all these witnesses, witnesses whom she was attempting to convince that she deserved her late husband's inheritance. And that kind of attention she didn't need.

She frowned at the messenger. "Tell him he's not to come in. I'll meet him outside the hall, at the gardener's shed."

Lucifer's claws! What could that Grim Reaper want?

The idea of meeting with the menacing Nicholas Grimshaw alone was nerve-racking, to say the least. The man didn't seem to recognize his place in terms of allegiance to Torteval, nor did he cower before her like a loyal servant. In fact, she decided, as soon as her claim to the property was clear, she'd seek an audience with the king and see the shire-reeve reassigned or removed.

Till then, she had no choice but to hear him out, pray he wouldn't make a spectacle out of himself, and send him away before he ruined her already compromised plans.

'Twasn't fair. She'd dealt with more than her share of trouble today. She'd been forced to kill the gaoler with her bare hands. He'd started to pry too closely into the details of George's murder, and the greedy fool had begun to get the idea that he might be able to extort coin from her for his silence. So after he'd given his testimony at the Kabayn wench's trial, she'd used a rock to beat him to death and hid his body in the woods.

Yet there were still loose ends to tie, including the burial of her husband and her father-in-law. True, the shire-reeve's mistress had been taken care of, but she wasn't yet cold in the ground, and the fact that Nicholas Grimshaw was at her doorstep didn't bode well.

Lord William had cooperated by giving up the ghost in a timely fashion. For the past hour, Philomena had been doing the obligatory grieving for the benefit of the Torteval household. But there was still the matter of settling the will, and her lawyer had yet to arrive.

Lord knew she didn't want Grimshaw here when he did.

Hoping for a brief encounter, she fetched a cloak and

candle, then slipped from the hall to the courtyard and made her way through the dark to the gardener's shed.

He stood sentinel at the door, like some gigantic tree, his arms crossed over his trunk-like chest. Illuminated by the candle, his eyes gleamed at her beneath the hood of his signature black cloak.

"Grimshaw," she said by way of greeting, and the quaver in her voice was only part feigned. There was naught quite so intimidating as having a hulking beast of a lawman loom over one like a giant crow, waiting to pick at one's bones.

"Lady Philomena," he intoned, the name searing her like a brand. "My condolences."

She hesitated, uncertain what to say. Surely he'd come for more than to offer solace.

He added, "I'd like to speak with you."

Misgiving prickled at the base of her neck. How much did Grimshaw know? He couldn't have talked to the Kabayn wench. He'd been gone all day. The constable had said as much. The wench was locked up, and Philomena had given strict instructions to the constable not to deliver the death warrant until the morrow. The shirereeve shouldn't know anything about the person he was to hang.

Why was he here?

Bloody hell, she was wound tighter than a cocked crossbow. Her nerves couldn't take much more. She simply had to get rid of the beast.

"I hope you'll forgive me," she said, adding a sniffle for good measure, "but I'm not of a mind to speak with anyone at the moment. I've just lost my husband and my father." She covered her mouth with the back of her hand as if to stifle a sob.

The shire-reeve was unswayed by her performance. He leaned toward her and whispered, "I'm sure you'll be dancing a carole upon their graves by the morrow."

She stiffened. The knave *did* know something.

She forced her heart to slow. She dared not let him see that she was intimidated. Above all, she had to maintain control.

"'Tis starting to rain," she said as calmly as possible, shielding the candle. "Let's go inside."

Shuddering as she passed through his shadow, she elbowed open the door of the shed. As she set the candle into a holder above the potting table, she realized with startling irony that she'd left her jar of arsenic there.

'Twas no matter. Grimshaw wouldn't recognize it. If he did, she'd make sure he'd not blather to anyone. Dead men could spread no rumors.

Despite her determination to remain poised, the instant Grimshaw closed the door behind him with a thud of finality, her heart flipped, and suddenly she felt like a trapped moth.

He dropped his heavy satchel on the floor, and the resulting clatter of whatever horrid devices it contained gave her a start. She instinctively glanced at the huge bag.

He flexed his gloved hands, and the leather squeaked with menace. "I trust you'll be reasonable, so I won't have to resort to," he said, nodding to the satchel, "harsher methods."

Repressing a shiver, she decided 'twas in her best interests to get straight to the point. "What do you want?"

After a moment, he hunkered down beside the satchel,

wrenching the top open. She clenched her fists as she glimpsed the sharpened points of the sinister tools he kept inside.

But he only pulled out a scroll.

Standing again, he told her, "This is the death warrant for Desirée Kabayn. I want you to withdraw the charges."

She blinked. Withdraw the charges? Was he jesting? She'd incriminate herself.

And why did Grimshaw have the warrant, anyway? She'd given the constable specific instructions to withhold it till morn.

She bit the inside of her cheek. This was why she had to do everything herself. No one could be trusted to follow the simplest command.

Her heart was beating faster than a caged sparrow's as she whirled away from him with false calm and stepped to the back of the shed. "She had a fair trial."

"She didn't kill your husband. And you know it."

Philomena's mind was working at lightning speed now. Desperation always sharpened her wits. Her pulse racing, she turned back to him, surreptitiously running her fingers over the gardener's hand tools hanging behind her on the wall.

"There were witnesses," she argued, wondering if she should set fire to the shed afterward to get rid of the evidence.

"Witnesses no doubt bought with your threats," he countered.

She forced a chuckle. "No one is going to doubt the word of a noblewoman against the whore of a lawm—"

She jumped as he banged a fist on the potting table. The

force knocked her jar of arsenic onto the floor, scattering the incriminating gray powder across the dirt floor.

Jesu, she was going to have to move quickly if she didn't want him to lose his temper and vent his notorious wrath upon her. Clapping one shaky hand to her bosom, she found what she sought with the other. She clasped her fingers around the handle of the planting awl, secreted the long, sharp spine in the folds of her skirts, and waited.

He clucked his tongue. "You give me no choice, then, but to use more persuasive means."

Holding her gaze, he reached down to randomly pluck an instrument from his satchel. What chilled her to the bone was that he didn't seem to care what tool he retrieved or what damage he was about to inflict.

Her heart fluttered in panic against her ribs.

What he pulled from the bag looked like the bastard spawn of a pair of shears and pincers. He advanced on her, snicking the overlapping curved blades as he came.

She couldn't guess what vile disfigurement he intended, but she didn't mean to let him live long enough to find out. The instant he got within reach, she swung the planting awl around under his arm, aiming to slip it betwixt the ribs to pierce his heart.

≈

Chapter 29

NICHOLAS HAD LEARNED NEVER to underestimate the desperation of a cornered animal. Prepared for anything, he saw Philomena's hand swing forward and dodged back in time to avoid her attack. Still, he was shocked to feel something slash the front of his shirt.

She advanced again with a frustrated grunt, slicing backward, and he retreated once more. But now that she'd lost the element of surprise, she was at a disadvantage.

He could have struck her in return. With a single blow of his fist, he could have knocked the woman into the wall. But he was not by nature a violent man. And he needed her conscious to withdraw the writ.

So he stepped back yet again when she came at him. But this time, he caught the slim awl between the blades of his open shears and snapped it off halfway along the spine.

Sheer fury twisted Philomena's red face into an ugly mask. Spittle flew from her mouth as she cursed him with unintelligible oaths. Then, beyond reason, like a demon riding fast and furiously through the gates of hell, she charged forward with the blunted weapon, straight for his heart.

After that, time seemed to slow to a crawl.

Nicholas sidestepped her as she lunged toward him. The broken point grazed the sleeve of his shirt, and he felt the air stir as her momentum carried her reeling past him.

From the corner of his eye, he saw her skid on the powder that had spilled on the floor. Her gaze widened, and her arms wheeled like the sluggish blades of a windmill as she struggled to regain her balance.

For a lingering instant, it seemed she did. But the foot she planted for leverage came down on the jar she'd dropped. It squeezed out behind her heel, rolling away, and her knee slowly collapsed beneath her. With what sounded to his ears like an endless gasp of dread, she began to stumble forward.

His body seemed weighted with lead as Nicholas dropped the shears and shot out his arm reflexively, trying to catch her. His fingertips brushed the long tippet of her sleeve, but already she'd fallen past his reach.

By the time he saw where she was headed, 'twas too late.

With a sickly wet thud, she landed atop his open satchel of tools, impaling herself on the sharp blades.

"Jesu!" he hissed.

Time rushed onward again.

Acting on impulse, Nicholas dove forward, catching her about the waist. Using all of his strength, he lifted her up, carefully pulling her body free of the blades and rolling her gently onto her back.

But she was beyond hope, too damaged to live. Blood dripped from her belly, and by the wheeze of her breath, he knew her lungs had been pierced. She lingered for a few torturous moments, soundlessly moving her mouth, scrabbling at the dirt, and staring up at him with wide, dimming eyes. Then, with a bloody grimace of disbelief, she exhaled a final rasping breath and slumped over against the satchel.

Nicholas collapsed back onto his hindquarters, staring at her in horror.

The sight of blood didn't sicken him. He was used to it.

And try as he might, he could summon no insurmountable guilt over her demise. It had been an accident, and he'd tried to save her. If justice had been served, the woman would have hanged on the gallows, anyway.

His horror came from the fact that now there was no way to exonerate Desirée. Worse, he had enough blood on his hands to warrant his own arrest and hanging.

What in God's name was he going to do?

Despite his early return, Desirée sensed something was wrong the moment Nicholas stepped into her cell, heaving the heavy satchel from his shoulder while the guard secured the door behind him.

"Oh, no," she said under her breath.

Once he threw back his hood, her worst fears were confirmed. His teeth were clenched, and bleak despair filled his eyes.

She swallowed. "She didn't withdraw the warrant?"

He shook his head.

Her hand went impulsively to her throat.

He steeled his jaw. "I'm not going to hang you, Desirée!"

He hauled her into his arms, kissing her hard, and on his lips she tasted both reassurance and desperation. Then, too soon, he released her, holding her at arm's length.

"Listen to me," he said. "Bad things have happened tonight."

"Bad things? What bad things?"

"You have to leave."

"Leave?"

He let her go and began to pace the room, rubbing a hand thoughtfully over his jaw and planning aloud. "I'll have to kill the gaoler. Otherwise, he'll alert the constable. That should give you a good start. I'll give you what coin I have. If you take the north road—"

"Wait!" She blocked his path. "Kill the gaoler? What—"

"I *have*—" he started to yell, then lowered his voice. "I *have* to. There's no other way."

"Nicholas, what are you talking about?"

He spoke in measured syllables, as if to a child. "You have to leave Canterbury. Now. There's no time."

"Me? What about you?"

He started to reach out to touch her hair, then withdrew his hand. "I can't go with you, Desirée. You'll be safer on your own."

"I can't leave you. I *won't* leave you." She looked into his desolate eyes and realized the truth. "If I leave you, I won't ever see you again."

By the tensing of his jaw, she saw she was right. "But you'll live, Desirée," he said, reaching out to cup her cheek. "At least you'll live."

She pushed his hand away. "What good is living if I can't be with the man I love?"

"Bloody hell, Desirée," he ground out, "if you don't leave right now, you'll die. We *both* will."

She frowned. "What do you mean, we *both* will?" There was something he wasn't telling her. "What's happened, Nicholas? Tell me. You owe me that." She crossed her arms over her chest. "Tell me now, or I swear I won't set foot outside of this cell."

With a scowl of frustration that said that he'd prefer to sling her over his shoulder and carry her off forcibly, he quickly told her what had transpired since he left.

When he finished, she blinked in disbelief. "You mean Philomena...she's dead?"

He nodded. "And all the evidence points to me as the murderer."

'Twas an astonishing tale, and Nicholas was right. No one would believe Philomena's death had been an accident, and since Nicholas was the last to see her alive, he'd be presumed the killer. It appeared they were both doomed to die on the gallows.

But if there was one thing she'd learned from Hubert, 'twas that things were not always as they appeared. No matter how tangled the knot, there was usually a way to unravel it. 'Twas only a matter of looking beyond the expected.

"Desirée," Nicholas pleaded, "you have to leave. I can only hold off—"

"Shh," she said, placing fingers over his mouth. "I'm thinking."

He pulled her fingers away. "While you're thinking, they may already be searching for Philomena."

"What?" She glanced up at him, frowning. "What did you say?"

"They're likely wondering what's become of her."

She narrowed her eyes. "What did you do with the body?"

He closed his lips into a thin line, reluctant to answer.

"Nicholas, where's the body?"

He winced in distaste, and his gaze fell to his satchel.

Desirée gasped. "In there? She's…You…But why would you…"

He scowled. "I didn't have time to bury her, and I couldn't just leave her there." He ran a guilty hand across the back of his neck. "After you're gone, I'll take her body to the crossroads and—"

"Wait."

This changed everything. Desirée chewed at her thumbnail as her mind suddenly lit up with possibilities.

"Desirée!" he said, to capture her attention.

She held up a hand. Before long, a devious idea began to wind its way through her brain. She glanced at the satchel. The more she thought about it, the more she was convinced it could work. If it did, 'twould be the most magnificent piece of deception she'd ever perpetrated.

"Shells and peas," she murmured.

"What?"

Desirée bit her lip. Hubert had taught her well. 'Twould take serious distraction and expert sleight of hand, but together they could do it.

Desirée would escape the gallows.

Nicholas would wash the blood from his hands.

And Philomena herself would see that justice was served.

"Nicholas, my love," she said with a hopeful glint in

her eyes, "how would you like to learn the secret of Three Shells and a Pea?"

Desirée swallowed hard as the first gray light of dawn seeped in through the slit at the top of the cell. 'Twas one thing to come up with a brilliant plan, another to carry it out. Sitting here now, in the naked reality of day, she wondered if she'd made the right decision.

She glanced at Nicholas, sitting beside her, his face shadowed as he stared at the floor, lost in thought. Neither of them had slept a wink.

She had to be brave, for his sake. She was the one who'd talked Nicholas into this, after all, convincing him 'twould work. She couldn't let him down.

But in the distance, when the bells began to ring, she flinched at the sound, knowing they were tolling not for Mass, but for her execution.

Nicholas reached his hand over and gave hers a reassuring squeeze. She squeezed back, and for a long while they stayed like that, lending each other strength by that mere touch.

"Are you sure you want to go through with this?" he murmured.

"Aye."

"There's still time for you to run."

She shook her head and gave him a shaky smile. "You won't get rid of me that easily. Besides, where will you find another maid to burn your supper and beat you at draughts and…" She broke off as her throat closed unexpectedly.

"Listen to me." He clasped her hand against his heart and spoke fiercely. "I'll make this work. I promise."

She bit her lip to still its trembling. Curse her wayward tears. She meant to be strong for *him*.

God, she hoped he was right. They must have gone over the plan a hundred times. In the same way she'd learned Three Shells and a Pea, Desirée had stressed to Nicholas the importance of timing and distraction. They'd practiced over and over until it became like a dance.

But there was always the possibility of failure. One overly shrewd observer, one slip of the tongue or hand, and the entire piece of trickery could be exposed.

And this time, unlike her ventures with Hubert, there would be no easy escape, no fleeing to the next town. If they couldn't pull this off...

Sensing her lingering doubt, Nicholas reached out and turned her head toward him, gripping her jaw and piercing her with his determined gaze. "I won't let you down. And I won't let you die."

She nodded.

He gave her a kiss to seal his promise, then murmured, "Are you ready?"

She blew out a steadying breath. She had to focus now. "Aye," she said, letting him help her to her feet. "I'm ready."

She took off her boots and stockings and swirled his massive cloak over her surcoat, covering herself completely from head to toe. They'd already removed Philomena's bloody clothing and slippers, dressed the corpse in Desirée's clean linen shift, and tucked the body back into the empty satchel.

Nicholas donned his cloak and gloves. Then he carefully shouldered the heavy sack. She nodded, confirming it didn't look suspicious.

He raised his fist and banged on the door, calling for the gaoler to let them out.

The instant they stepped outside and he wrapped his black-gloved fist around her upper arm, she sensed the change in him. She suddenly felt as if she walked beside a stranger. Her tender lover was gone. In his place was Nicholas Grimshaw, shire-reeve of Kent. And in a curious way, that restored her confidence. This *was* going to work.

He was magnificent and menacing and larger than life. Forsooth, if Desirée hadn't known 'twas but a role he played, she would have been quailing in her tracks.

The moment they exited the gaol, a wave of jeering onlookers surged toward her, but he handled them expertly.

"Make way!" he bellowed. "Make way for Nicholas Grimshaw, shire-reeve of Kent!"

Her elbow firmly in his grasp, Nicholas strode with confidence along the road to the town square, and the crowd scattered before him like chickens before a cart.

"Make way!"

As he swaggered past, singling out members of the gathering townsfolk with a steely glare, women cringed in fright and young lads shouted insults and challenges.

Soon a chant of "Grimshaw! Grimshaw! Grimshaw!" arose, and peering from the shadows of her hooded cloak, Desirée saw Nicholas raise his hand high, as if to quell their worshipful cries.

She'd never seen so many gathered for an execution. But then, she supposed 'twasn't every day a woman was hanged from the gallows.

She shivered. The road was cold on her bare feet. Thick fog rolled along the lane like dragon's breath, lending a dreamlike quality to the day. But the mist would be their ally, she knew, obscuring perception, blurring reality.

Suddenly something streaked across the path before her like a small white wraith, then disappeared, and Desirée realized 'twas Snowflake.

Before she could wonder what Nicholas's intrepid cat was doing here, the vicious threats began.

"Hang the witch high!" someone yelled.

"Stretch 'er neck!"

"Break her like a twig!"

Desirée's step faltered, but Nicholas never let her stumble, shouting to the crowd, "Patience, buzzards!"

Desirée lowered her head as they drew closer to the center of town, so she wouldn't have to look at the stark black skeleton of the gallows and the ominous hooded executioner waiting for her. But the journey seemed endless, and she found the whispers far worse than the shouts.

"She's a wee thing. She'll strangle for an hour."

"Nay. Grimshaw'll crack her neck. Probably take her head clean off."

At long last, Nicholas brought her to a halt, and Desirée lifted her gaze from beneath the hood just enough to glimpse the bottom rungs of the ladder leaning against the gallows post. As they'd planned, Nicholas dropped the satchel at the foot of the ladder, near the base of the gallows. He gave her elbow one subtle reassuring squeeze and released her. Now they were on their own.

Desirée let out a bracing breath. With a silent prayer to Hubert for a bit of his good luck, she prepared to pull off the most complex deception she'd ever attempted.

Chapter 30

NICHOLAS KNEW HE HAD to do the performance of his life. Everything depended upon it. Spurred to courage by the haunting vision of his beloved Desirée hanging lifeless from the gallows, he squared his shoulders and began the spectacle, circling her with slow menace.

"Good people of Canterbury!" he called out, his voice ringing as he addressed the crowd. "You see before you a rare sight—a murderess in our fair town!"

The onlookers hissed and growled.

"'Tis the second murder in a fortnight!" he said, punctuating his words with an upraised fist.

The crowd booed.

He shook his head. "Canterbury seems to have become overrun with outlaws!"

Several men shouted in agreement.

"So many, in fact," he snarled, "that I'm dragged from my bed on a Sabbath morn just to keep up!"

The villagers joined in, creating a dull thunder of wrath.

He crossed his arms, pacing before them until they quieted again, then shrugged. "Normally, 'tis little matter to me who dangles at the end of the rope, as long as justice is served." He turned to Desirée and placed a hand atop her hooded head. "But this time, I've found an outlaw under my very own roof!"

With a dramatic flourish, he whipped the hood back, exposing Desirée's ghostly pale face to the gasps of the crowd.

For an instant, his heart went out to her, and he had to fight the urge to cover her again, to take her in his arms and give her comfort.

But that would not serve their purposes. So when the villagers drew in their collective breath, he turned on them with even more venom.

"But justice is blind, and no one escapes the justice of Nicholas Grimshaw. No one!" He singled out several individuals in the crowd with an accusing finger. "Not you. Nor you." He swung around to cup Desirée's chin with his gloved hand. "Nor you." Then he uttered the most difficult words he'd ever spoken. "Desirée Kabayn, you are charged with the crime of murder."

The blood drained from her face, and for an instant he wondered if she was indeed only feigning her shock. She swayed on her feet, then her eyes rolled back in her head, and she collapsed in a faint, twisting to fall strategically facedown atop his satchel.

The townsfolk gasped, and Nicholas snorted, turning away from her, preparing to distract the crowd with a lengthy lecture on the evils of disobeying the law.

But in the silent moment, a quailing monk spoke to those around him. "God will surely frown upon a hanging on the Sabbath."

"Aye," someone added, "is it not a sin?"

"'Tis bad luck, at the least."

"All of Canterbury will be cursed."

"The devil will come to live in our town!"

Bloody hell! This was not part of the plan. The hanging had to take place today. It couldn't be delayed. He had to do something, quickly, before the crowd turned on him.

"Is that what you think?" he demanded, forcing a harsh laugh. "That Lucifer will take up residence here? Be assured, good folk, if ever the devil comes to Canterbury, I'll snatch him quick and string him up by his ballocks!"

A few lads cheered raucously, but at the lack of unanimous response, Nicholas knew he had to raise the stakes. He crossed his arms over his chest and shook his head, issuing a sardonic challenge. "If you doubt me, if you doubt the word of Nicholas Grimshaw, if you truly believe I am *not* God's avenging angel, but the right hand of Satan..." He let out a heavy sigh. "Let me put your fears to rest."

With great spectacle, Nicholas strode through the crowd, which parted before him like the Red Sea before Moses, making his way to the monk who'd spoken earlier. The onlookers backed away, making a wide circle around him as he dramatically knelt before the man of God and crossed himself.

While the monk stood in baffled amazement, Nicholas began to pray, loud enough for everyone to hear.

"Heavenly Father," he cried, "I pray for Your divine guidance. Make me, Nicholas Grimshaw, Your humble servant, the instrument of Your will."

The air was so still, one could have heard the twitching of a mouse's whiskers. But Nicholas trusted all eyes were upon him now.

He continued to pray, loud and long. He prayed for clear eyes that would not be deceived, no matter how pleasing a shape the devil assumed. He prayed for a strong hand to administer what judgment God demanded. He prayed for a true heart to follow the dictates of the Lord, however challenging they might be. And he prayed for the soul of the condemned murderer, that she might find mercy in heaven, if not on earth.

Finally, adding a silent prayer that he'd prayed long enough, he genuflected, and the awestruck villagers around him echoed his Amen.

Then he rose. "Satisfied?"

The crowd cheered wildly in response. He had them in the palm of his hand again.

Cracking his neck and flexing his shoulders, he made his way slowly back to the gallows, where, God willing, everything had progressed as planned.

Desirée hadn't anticipated how much her hands would be shaking when it came to opening the satchel. Sweet saints, she was quaking like a winter leaf.

Nicholas had been convincing, almost *too* convincing. When he'd whirled toward her like some all-powerful mercenary of the Grim Reaper himself, his shoulders broad and menacing, his eyes glowing like dark green coals, his voice booming like thunder, she'd felt the blood leave her face. If she hadn't hung on to the sliver of faith that his threats were empty, his brutality only a performance, that faint would have been genuine.

She forced her nerves to calm. She couldn't afford to make a mistake now. This was the most difficult part of the deception, the point where she slipped the pea under the shell.

For a moment, when the monk protested the hanging on the Sabbath, she'd thought they were doomed. But Nicholas knew his audience, knew how to restore their trust in him. When she heard him move into the crowd and begin to pray, there was no doubt in her mind that all gazes were drawn to him.

Using Nicholas's great cloak as a screen, she parted the top of the satchel beneath her, repressing a shudder as she came in close contact with Philomena's cold body. With painstaking patience, she gradually maneuvered out from under the cloak, inch by inch, squeezing into the space beside Philomena. Making as little motion as possible, she then carefully draped the cloak over Philomena instead. Bit by bit, she pulled the edges of the cloth around the woman, eventually enwrapping her completely and concealing her face within the hood.

Now, to any but the most observant eye, 'twould appear Philomena was the maid who had just fainted.

The trouble was, Desirée discovered, there *was* an observant eye.

As she lay in quiet concealment in the folds of the satchel, she felt a curious tickling atop her head. Her first horrid thought was that Philomena wasn't quite dead, after all, that her cold, bony fingers were scrabbling at Desirée's scalp. A panicked squeal stuck in her throat.

But she'd learned to remain calm in the face of fear. So she drew two steadying breaths and lifted one eyelid just enough to see what plagued her.

Snowflake suddenly mewed in her face.

Desirée suppressed a gasp.

Shite!

This was just the sort of unforeseen loose thread that could unravel everything.

"Shoo!" she hissed as loudly as she dared.

The cat only purred.

"Shoo!"

But Snowflake stuck his nose closer.

Then, as if 'tweren't bad enough to have a cat sniffing at her, giving away her location, when she let her focus drift past Snowflake, she clearly saw the constable, staring directly at her with his blackened eye, his brow furrowed.

She snapped her eyes shut again, held her breath, and prayed for a true miracle. But whatever was going to happen would occur in the next moment, for Nicholas was already returning to the gallows.

Nicholas strode purposefully toward his satchel, but he almost missed a step when he saw Azrael. What the devil was his cat doing here?

Jesu!

Azrael seldom left the cottage. Why had he chosen today to come to town? Did the meddling beast mean to betray the very wench who slipped him scraps at the table? Nicholas had to do something.

He would've liked to give the miserable cat a boot. But Desirée would never forgive him. Besides, the stubborn feline would only come sneaking back. Azrael seemed determined to keep his mistress company.

Nicholas frowned at the cat, whose snow white exterior belied the devilish creature beneath. Then inspiration struck him. He reached down and scooped up the animal, holding him high for all to see.

"'Tis a sign!" he cried. "An angel in the guise of a white cat comes to bless this holy vengeance."

The onlookers gasped and began murmuring in wonder among themselves—all but the constable, who stood a short distance away, regarding him with an unnerving scowl.

Nicholas swallowed down the metallic taste of doubt. He couldn't dwell on what might go wrong. He'd told himself at the start, if the very worst happened, he'd snatch up Desirée, throw her over his shoulder, and flee Canterbury on foot.

He lowered Azrael to the ground, giving him a light swat to send him away. Then he hunkered down beside the satchel, where his cloak was draped over what he prayed was Philomena's corpse. A film of sweat formed above his lip. He had to be extremely cautious now.

Blocking the crowd's view with his back, he made certain the cloak was safely tucked around Philomena's body so she was completely covered. Then he lifted her slowly and carefully out of the satchel and into his arms, making certain the hood concealed her face.

"She's asleep!" cried a young lass at the front of the crowd.

A few people booed in disappointment, but before the mob could join in, Nicholas made an announcement. "'Twould seem the Lord has taken mercy upon her soul, after all. She'll meet her Maker ere she wakes."

He nodded to the chaplain, who began reciting the sacrament. While the executioner readied the noose, Nicholas climbed up the ladder with his burden, and the two of them secured the rope about Philomena's neck.

For all the spectacle and ceremony preceding it, the actual hanging was over in a moment. When her body dropped, of course, there were no death throes. The crowd assumed her neck had broken instantly. The rope squeaked in the ensuing hush as she twisted limply at its end, her hooded head lolling in the noose.

"So sins are punished," Nicholas intoned. "A life for a life." He gazed out at the villagers with mixed emotions, realizing 'twould likely be the last speech he'd give to them. "Go now. Go to Mass, and pray for this woman's unfortunate soul."

The crowd began to disperse, but as they did, the glowering constable shoved his way through the onlookers toward Nicholas, who suddenly felt a sick clenching in his gut. The shire-reeve might hold command over the constable, but one word from his underling and Nicholas's deception would be revealed.

"Bloody hell!" the constable hissed between his teeth. He looked anxiously around him, then whispered tightly, "What the devil have you done?"

Nicholas's heart pounded like a death knell. "What do you mean?" he murmured.

The constable cursed again under his breath. "I mean, who is..." He nodded to the corpse. "That?"

Nicholas swallowed hard. There was no point in lying. Sooner or later their perfidy would come to light. If only he could explain everything...

The constable was a reasonable man, after all. He'd taken the trouble last night to alert Nicholas to Desirée's imprisonment. Like Nicholas, he had a strong sense of justice, as well as a penchant for mercy. 'Twas why Nicholas had chosen him as his constable. Surely if he knew the whole story...

But there was no time.

Nicholas clenched the constable's arm, beseeching him with an earnest gaze, "Give us an hour. We've done no wrong. I swear. I'll send you a missive from...wherever we go, revealing everything."

"Damn it! I..." The constable shook off Nicholas's grip, then rubbed his palm over the back of his neck in aggravation. "You're putting me in an awkward position."

"I know. But trust me just this once. Give me an hour."

The constable's mouth worked in indecision as he studied Nicholas's eyes for any sign of trickery, but Nicholas continued to hold his forthright stare. Then he bit out a vile oath. "That body's already as cold as a gravedigger's arse, isn't it?"

Nicholas nodded.

"And when we cut it down, see who 'tis, there'll be some hellish knot to untangle?"

"Possibly."

"Shite." With a final glance at the corpse hanging from the gallows, the constable blew out a weary breath. "One hour."

With a brief sigh of relief and a nod of thanks, Nicholas turned to the executioner and called out, "'Tis *your* vigil this time."

The executioner took up his post before the gallows to watch over the body for the prescribed hour.

Nicholas clapped a grateful hand on the constable's shoulder. "I won't forget you."

The constable shook his head. "To hell with *me*," he muttered pointedly. "Don't forget your damned satchel."

Epilogue

"A CHURCH?" NICHOLAS ASKED WITH A LAUGH.

Snug beneath the covers of their enormous bed, with a purring cat at her feet, Desirée made ticklish circles atop Nicholas's chest with her fingertip. He seized her fingers, making her stop.

She'd expected, after their deception four months ago, they'd never be able to return to Canterbury. But after Nicholas sent his missive of explanation to the constable, the man had painstakingly unraveled Philomena's fabric of lies, revealing the truth about the mischief at Torteval.

Lord William's nephew, a decent man, had subsequently inherited the holding. At the constable's suggestion, the new lord had seen that Desirée's kidnappers were appropriately punished for their crime, and he'd issued writs of pardon for Desirée, Nicholas, and even Hubert. Ultimately, the constable, for all his hard work in Nicholas's absence, was granted the position of shire-reeve of Kent.

Nicholas didn't seem to mind, and Desirée couldn't have been more pleased. They'd survived the last four months by fleeing to Winchester, where Nicholas had taken up his old trade as a butcher. A widowed noblewoman had offered Desirée a sizable sum to teach her three children to read and write.

But Desirée had begun to miss the walled cottage with the lovely garden and the warm hearth and the enormous bed, and so, at the new shire-reeve's invitation, the two of them had returned to Canterbury.

That had been a fortnight ago, and now that they'd swept the cobwebs from the cottage, tended the overgrown garden, and frightened away the bed fleas with hours of impassioned trysting, they needed to find something to occupy their time and earn a living. A *lawful* living.

"Aye, a church at the crossroads," she told him, turning in the bed to drape her leg coyly across his hips, making him grunt. "But not just an ordinary church."

He lifted a brow. "A church built by a lawman and an outlaw."

"*Reformed* outlaw."

He gave her a dubious smirk, but she wasn't discouraged. She knew with the right...distraction...she could talk him into anything.

She coiled a lock of hair at the nape of his neck around her finger. "'Twould be a refuge of sorts."

"A refuge?"

"Aye, for foundlings, wayward orphans, unwanted bastards..."

He chuckled. "Like us?"

"Exactly."

He snorted. "You'd have to build an entire village to house all the unwanted bastards."

"They won't be unwanted for long. We'll reform them."

"Reform them? Us?"

"Aye. You'll deliver sermons to frighten them out of a life of crime."

"I see."

"And I'll teach them survival skills."

"Survival skills. You mean like Fast and Loose, Three Shells and a—"

She yanked hard at his curl, making him grimace. "Nay. I mean cooking, sewing, counting, writing. Things that will make them useful."

He frowned. "Useful to whom?"

She eyed his delectably muscled arm and decided to punctuate her answer with a path of kisses. "The townspeople. The nobles. The craftsmen. Anyone who will hire them for their keep." She nuzzled his shoulder, placing a final kiss there. "Like you did for me, Nicholas."

Her furry accomplice, Snowflake, chose that moment to clamber up the covers and give Nicholas's jaw a coaxing nudge.

He grimaced and pushed the cat back on his haunches, giving him a thorough scratching.

"I spoke with the shire-reeve yesterday," she cooed, walking her fingers up his arm, "and he said he'd be grateful for anything to reduce the crime in Canterbury."

"Is that so? And is he willing to *pay* for this church of

yours?" With Nicholas's store of coins gone to cover the taxes of the poor, they had just enough to live on.

She snuggled against him, combing her fingers through his hair. "I don't think we have to worry about that. Ever since the Miracle of the Gallows—"

"The what?" He stopped petting Snowflake, and the cat jumped off the bed.

"That's what the townsfolk are calling it, you know. Evidently, 'twas unbearable for them to consider they might have been gulled by sleight of hand. They've decided Philomena's death on the Sabbath was some godly miracle of justice."

"Mary, Mother of..."

She traced the shell of his ear with her fingertip, making him shiver. "So considering your newfound status as a miracle worker, I figure the citizens of Canterbury will be most happy to make ongoing...donations to your church."

"You," he said, arching his brow, "are an incorrigible thief." He flinched. "And stop doing that."

"What?" she teased, running her finger lightly over his ear. "This?"

With a growl, he rolled her onto her back, pinning her arms beside her head. She grinned. This was pleasant distraction indeed.

"By the rood, you're a wicked lass."

"On the contrary, miracle worker. Haven't you heard? I'm practically a saint." She arched her hips upward in a most unsaintly way.

He groaned as his loins stirred to life against her. "If you're a saint, Desirée, then you must be the saint of unrequited desire."

"Oh, is it requiting you want?" she teased.

His eyes smoldered with lust. "You know 'tis."

'Twas so difficult to resist him when Nicholas looked at her like that, all smoky and sultry and inviting, with his wry smile and his darkly twinkling eyes and that tempting lock of hair that insisted on falling across his brow. But she hadn't won her battle yet.

"What say you, Nicky?" she asked, coyly dipping her eyes. "Will you build me my church?"

He gave her a lopsided smile and sighed. "I'll think about it." Then his grin faded and his gaze softened. He released one of her wrists to stroke the side of her cheek. "And what say you, my precious saint?" His touch was as gentle as spring rain, and his eyes glowed with affection. "Will you be my wife?"

Her lips quivered, and her eyes welled with joyful tears. His wife? She'd expected to be his maidservant and his mistress, but she'd never asked for more. His *wife*. She could think of naught more perfect.

Still, she refused to surrender so easily, not while he yet owed her a church. She gave him a little shrug. "I'll think about it."

His brows shot up in surprise. Then he nudged her thighs apart with his own. "You think about it very..." He pressed his cock against her. "Hard."

All her restraint dissolved then like mist in the wind. She knew Nicholas wouldn't be able to say her nay, any more than she could resist him now. Happier than she'd ever been in her life, she embraced him with welcoming arms, opening her heart to him and offering him the haven of her body.

In return, he carried her off on a voyage to the very

brink of heaven. As they strove together in selfless devotion, they left their sins far behind, and in the rarefied air of ecstasy, their spirits were reborn. The darkness of the past was forgotten, illuminated by the flames of their love. And all the promises they made in the depths of their passion, they kept, every single one.

꿍

About the Author

Born in Paradise, California, Sarah McKerrigan has embraced her inner Gemini by leading an eclectic life. As a teen, she danced with the Sacramento Ballet, worked in her father's graphic arts studio, and composed music for award-winning science films. She sang arias in college, graduating with a degree in music, then toured with an all-girl rock band on CBS Records. She once played drums for a Tom Jones video and is currently a voiceover actress with credits including *Star Wars* audio adventures, JumpStart educational CDs, Diablo and Starcraft video games, and the MTV animated series *The Maxx*. She now indulges her lifelong love of towering castles, trusty swords, and knights (and damsels) in shining armor by writing historical romances featuring kick-butt heroines. She is married to a rock star, is the proud guardian of two nerdy college kids and an ever-changing array of exotic pets, and lives in a part of Los Angeles where nobody thinks she's weird.

THE DISH

Where authors give you the inside scoop!

♥ ♥ ♥ ♥ ♥ ♥ ♥ ♥ ♥ ♥ ♥ ♥ ♥

From the desk of Elizabeth Hoyt

Gentle Reader,

Lady Emeline Gordon, the heroine of my book TO TASTE TEMPTATION (on sale now), is an acknowledged expert at guiding young ladies safely through the labyrinth of London high society. So when the notorious and notoriously *wealthy* American merchant Mr. Samuel Hartley needs a chaperone for his younger sister, naturally he arranges for an introduction to the lovely, widowed Lady Emeline. Well . . . at least her social expertise is the reason Sam *gives* for asking for an introduction to Lady Emeline. In any case, whilst researching the book, I examined closely Lady Emeline's own handwritten papers. Amongst them I found the following artifact, which I hope will be of interest to you, my Gentle Reader.

Some Rules for a Young Lady wishing to Sail the Turbulent Waters of High Society without Wrecking Her Vessel against the Rocks of Misfortune.

1. A young lady's costume is of the utmost importance. Her gown, hat, gloves, fichu, and shoes—

especially her shoes—should show Good Taste but not Excessive Taste.

2. A lady should *never* talk to a gentleman not introduced to her. Some men—I will *not* call them gentlemen—will attempt to circumvent this rule. A young lady must not let them.

3. The kind of Male Rogue mentioned above is, in fact, best handled by a Lady of Mature Years and Quick Wit.

4. A young lady may never let a gentleman who is not a relative embrace her. *Note:* Naturally this rule does not apply to a Lady of a Certain Age.

5. If a lady of any age lets a gentleman embrace her, the lady should be certain that he is a Very Good Kisser indeed. She may require several sessions to be entirely certain.

6. Beware of country house parties.

7. When at a country house party it is imperative that a young lady *not* become cloistered with a gentleman. People with too much imagination may think she is engaging in an Affaire de Coeur.

8. Affairs should *only* be conducted by a Lady of a Mature and Not Easily Heated Disposition.

9. However, it is desirable that the *gentleman* in the above mentioned Affair become Very Heated indeed.

10. Whatever she does, a lady engaging in an affair must never, *never* fall in love with her paramour. That way lies disaster.

Yours Most Sincerely,

Elizabeth Hoyt

www.elizabethhoyt.com

♥ ♥ ♥ ♥ ♥ ♥ ♥ ♥ ♥ ♥ ♥ ♥ ♥ ♥

From the desk of Sarah McKerrigan

Dear Reader,

If you're as much of a fan of medieval romance as I am, you know the plots often involve Lady So-and-So being forced to wed Lord What's-His-Name for political gain. But what about the rest of the folk—the butcher, the baker, the candlestick-maker—the commoners, who were free to marry for love?

Sometimes, instead of Brad and Angelina, I'd like to hear about the courtship of John the trucker and Mary the kindergarten teacher. That's what inspired me to write DANGER'S KISS (on sale now). I wanted to weave a tale I could relate to, where the hero and heroine don't live in an ivory tower, don't dine on sweetmeats, and don't always play nice.

DANGER'S KISS is sort of a Sheriff of Nottingham meets The Artful Dodger adventure in which Nicholas Grimshaw, upstanding officer of the law, living happily alone in his thatched cottage, makes the mistake of taking mercy upon a beautiful scam artist by the name of Desiree. And, instead of hanging her for her thievery, indentures her as his servant.

Sleight of hand and sleight of heart ensue as the two clash over what's *right* versus what's *just*, and moral lines become blurred as lawman and outlaw fall recklessly in love. Yet in the end, these two simple folk prove more honorable than their superiors as they work together to foil a nefarious noblewoman's treacherous scheme.

To research DANGER'S KISS, I mingled with a great bunch of peasants—medieval reenactors with fascinating "lives," who were delighted to share their stories. In fact, a marvelous magician named Silvermane showed me the clever sleight of hand tricks that Desiree uses in the book!

I hope readers will find DANGER'S KISS an earthy, refreshing glimpse into medieval times, and I'm wagering the romance and adventure will keep you up all night! Let me know if it did at www.sarahmckerrigan.com

Enjoy!

Sarah McKerrigan

Want to know more about romances at Grand Central Publishing and Forever? Get the scoop online!

GRAND CENTRAL PUBLISHING'S ROMANCE HOMEPAGE

Visit us at www.hachettebookgroupusa.com/romance for all the latest news, reviews, and chapter excerpts!

NEW AND UPCOMING TITLES

Each month we feature our new titles and reader favorites.

CONTESTS AND GIVEAWAYS

We give away galleys, autographed copies, and all kinds of fun stuff.

AUTHOR INFO

You'll find bios, articles, and links to personal websites for all your favorite authors—and so much more!

THE BUZZ

Sign up for our monthly romance newsletter, and be the first to read all about it!